STREET FIGHT

The click of the blade swinging open, so quickly and elegantly, drew sounds of fear from the thugs. Carter caught a thick leather belt in midair, as it moved from a teenager toward him, deflecting the blow with his protected left arm. With an almost ballet-like movement, Carter grabbed another attacker and nicked both his shoulder blades with several swift slices of his knife, incapacitating him.

"Behind you Carter!" Linda shouted, as the thug with the chain attempted to fling it downward with the full force of his body, against Carter's back.

But Carter had heard the sound of the chain as it was being raised and quickly stepped aside. Crouching on his knees, knife in hand, he sliced his assailant along both kneecaps, making deep cuts across his lateral ligaments. When the fellow buckled to the ground in agonizing pain, the third attacker, who had been standing on the sidelines, frightened by what he had seen, motioned to the fourth attacker for some help. Despite his shouts of encouragement, none was forthcoming. He yelled something in Swedish, pulled out a gun and pointed it directly at Carter's head. "Throw down the knife..."

ACTIVE MEASURES

Alexander Court

JOVE BOOKS, NEW YORK

If you purchased this book without a cover, you should be aware that this book is stolen property. It was reported as "unsold and destroyed" to the publisher and neither the author nor the publisher has received any payment for this "stripped book."

This is a work of fiction. Names, characters, places and incidents are either the product of the author's imagination or are used fictitiously, and any resemblance to actual persons, living or dead, business establishments, events, or locales is entirely coincidental.

ACTIVE MEASURES

A Jove Book / published by arrangement with
the author

PRINTING HISTORY
Jove edition / February 2001

All rights reserved.
Copyright © 2001 by S&R Literary, Inc.
This book, or parts thereof, may not be reproduced in any form
without permission.
For information address: The Berkley Publishing Group,
a division of Penguin Putnam Inc.,
375 Hudson Street, New York, New York 10014.

The Penguin Putnam Inc. World Wide Web site address is
http://www.penguinputnam.com

ISBN: 0-515-13016-8

A JOVE BOOK®
Jove Books are published by The Berkley Publishing Group,
a division of Penguin Putnam Inc.,
375 Hudson Street, New York, New York 10014.
JOVE and the "J" design
are trademarks belonging to Penguin Putnam Inc.

PRINTED IN THE UNITED STATES OF AMERICA

10 9 8 7 6 5 4 3 2 1

To those of us who have been branded with the indelible scar of physical and emotional displacement and can only seek refuge in the futile attempt to arrest the nightmares of man's inhumanity to man.
—Alexander Court

"Almost *anything* was permitted, as long as it served the Cause. In my case, this meant presiding over a small but *effective* working group that went by the name *Active Measures* . . ."
—Markus Wolf,
Former East German legendary spymaster.

ACKNOWLEDGMENTS

The concept of the "Physician Assassin" was first suggested to me by General Antonio Noriega, former Commander-in-Chief of the Panamanian Defense Force (PDF), and current inmate of a U.S. federal penitentiary.

Having been sent to Panama in May 1988 by the Secretary of State to assist in the negotiations for Noriega's extradition to Spain, Noriega personally accused me on the front page of the newspaper *Critica* of having been responsible for the assassination of several prominent Panamanians while I was in Panama City.

Needless to say I did not find the accusation accurate, enlightening, or amusing. Like any rational person, I immediately contacted my "guardian angel," a Defense Intelligence Officer attached to the American Embassy, and, with the PDF right on my heels, proceeded post haste to the nearest American air base and caught the next C-141 back to San Antonio, Texas.

In one of our many desultory discussions, Noriega and I discussed the concept of the physician who, at one and the same time, could be a healer of the body and mind as well as a contract assassin. The idea of a medical doctor—which I am—being assigned to kill a target with the very instruments he might have used for healing purposes, stayed with me long after I left Panama.

Looking back at my career as a physician and as an international crisis manager for the State Department, I am intrigued with the ethical question of condoning the assassination of one man if it could save the lives of hundreds of thousands. Dr. Radijan Karadzic, a Serbian psychiatrist and self-proclaimed poet, in recent times has been instrumental in planning and executing the atrocities committed by the Serbian Nationalists in the name of "ethnic cleansing." Only fifty years before, the horrors of Dr. Josef Mengele, a Nazi physician conducting inhumane medical experiments on concentration camp inmates during World War II, still resonate through the tendrils of civil society. And in between, medically trained individuals in positions of power have wreaked havoc on civilians in Haiti, Chile and Malaysia as well. These men were both healers and killers.

My intention in this book is not to recount the miscreant acts of physicians who have, in one way or another, violated their Hippocratic oath. It is, however, to have the reader reflect on some of the more sensitive and disturbing issues described, while being both enlightening and entertaining.

For helping me write this book, I would like to acknowledge the assistance, help, and encouragement of an assortment of different people. I want to thank those individuals who gave me access to the recently unclassified data that many of you will find hard to believe, as I did. For reasons which will become obvious as you read this book, these individuals prefer to remain anonymous. I would also like to thank the wonderful people at the Penguin Putnam group, including Phyllis Grann, David Shanks, and my insightful, supportive Senior Editor, Tom Colgan.

I owe a deep debt of gratitude to two lovely, ebullient ladies who slaved endless hours to transcribe the manuscript into readable form—Linda Lubet and Christie Bond—both of whom graciously reminded me through their encouraging responses that no literary genre is particular to one gender.

Most of all, this book belongs to my wife, companion, lover, friend, and first-line editor of three decades. This book belongs as much to her as it does to me. And her name, for all practical purposes, should be on the cover with mine. She labored countless days and nights over the manuscript until she felt that it warranted the respect of my readers. No thought, no character, no action, no literary content escaped her formidable scrutiny. No words can express my gratitude and appreciation for her unselfish actions beyond the bounds of duty or obligation.

In contrast, all inaccuracies, distortions, misrepresentations, and mistakes are solely within my province, for which I ask your understanding and forgiveness. May you proceed with haste and enjoyment into the new world of the Physician Assassin.

1

STINGRAY CITY, GRAND CAYMAN ISLAND

Nature had blessed the Cayman Islands with the most beautiful white sand beaches, magnificent coral reefs, and clear turquoise water filled with a variety of fish, green turtles, sponges, and all sorts of other sealife. Paradoxically, this pristine setting, often referred to by its sixteenth-century Spanish name, *Las Tortugas* (The Turtles), had been the repository of pirates who used the islands as a base from which to pillage the Caribbean waters. Nowadays, theft came in the more fashionable form of unmarked bank accounts and trust funds protected by secrecy laws, which, not surprisingly, were respected by other countries as long as they did not impact adversely on their respective financial or national security interests. When required, the Cayman Islands banking system became appropriately porous, allowing information to spill forth in a gush of political accommodation. The islands seemed to function well through the divine inspiration of the blasphemous Holy Trinity: corruption, collusion, and nepotism. These were the reliable, universal facilitators of exponentially increasing wealth. One deposited illicit money, swam in beautiful waters, and was asked no questions other than about the beauty of the undersea scenery and the endangered coral reefs.

"Stingrays are highly euryhaline," the thirty-one-year-old

attractive British expatriate stated, holding the stingray between the palms of her hands. The group of twelve inquisitive tourists treaded water around her in the translucent blue-green waters. Wearing their obligatory goggles, snorkels, and flippers, they observed the behavior of a school of stingrays swimming alongside the anchored catamaran which had brought them out to the coral reef. Although a bat-like creature with protruding eyeballs and a long, whip-like poisonous tail, the simple fact was that this malevolent-looking creature was generally harmless.

"What is eury . . . hy . . . ?" asked a heavyset, middle-aged man with a heavy Spanish accent. He was wearing a thick, gold chain around his neck and was having a hard time staying upright in the water for the instructor's talk. The notion that he soon would be floating flat on his belly, with his face underwater, was completely antithetical to any ideas he had ever entertained about living and breathing. He was torturing himself in the middle of nowhere in order to "bond" with his two latchkey teenage daughters treading water next to him, both of whom were more frightened of him than they were of the stingray's tail.

"Euryhaline," the guide repeated, petting the three-foot-wide stingray on its white, soft underbelly, and encouraging the rest of the group to do the same. "It's a technical term which means that they are able to adapt to different levels of salt in the water, so that they can penetrate inland waterways."

"That word is enough to scare me," the burly Spanish man laughed, expecting the rest of the group to do the same. But everyone remained silent. There was something about his three-hundred-pound, neckless physique and demeanor that made the remaining snorkelers maintain their respective distance from him.

"Could you tell us a little bit about the poisonous spine on the stingray's tail?" a tall man asked, as he stroked the stingray's underbelly. He was very conscious of the fact that his calm demeanor was in sharp contrast to that of the burly man.

"This genus of stingray, *Dasyatis*," the guide answered enthusiastically, as if responding to a request for a date, "possess a sharp spine sticking out of its tail with which it can inflict incredibly painful wounds from both the sting itself and the powerful poison the stingray injects into its enemy." She paused. "Are you certain you all want to hear more about such a gruesome topic?"

"Of course, don't be silly," two elderly women, obviously traveling together, responded in unison. They were wondering when the guide would stop talking, and they would lower their masks and start snorkeling. "It sounds absolutely fascinating."

"The poison can cause gangrene and tetanus within a very short period of time," the guide continued, "and more often than not, death follows soon after." She was disturbed by the morbid fascination that this particular group had with the stingray's poisonous tail. There were so many more interesting aspects to talk about . . . its method of swimming by flapping its broad, winglike fins . . . the female's ability to bear her young alive. But each group differed in its character and interests, and it was her job to accommodate them as much as possible.

"Can we go underwater now?" the more restless of the two teenagers asked.

"Remember to make sure your mask is tightly sealed around your face, and stick your head down straight into the water," the guide said, repeating her previous instructions. "Bite gently on the rubber mouthpiece of your snorkel, keep both your hands to your sides, propel yourself with your flippers, and breathe calmly through your mouth."

"That's easy for you to say," the burly man responded plaintively, "but every time I try it, I just swallow a ton of water."

"You've got to learn how to relax," the guide responded, trying to hold him afloat.

Within five seconds the man lifted his head and removed his snorkel. "I'm relaxed!" he screamed. "It's the water that won't let me relax. It keeps coming into my mask."

"May I help you?" the tall man asked, swimming closer to the Spaniard.

"Sure!" the burly man responded, frustrated. "You can't do any worse than she's doing. No offense, miss."

The tall man smiled to the guide, indicating that he could take over at this point. The guide, grateful to be able to continue the excursion and take her group closer to the coral reef, smiled back and swam off, with the group following closely behind her.

"First of all, let me tighten your mask," the tall man said, adjusting its rubber straps with a dexterity that belied his earlier pronouncement to the group that this was his first time snorkeling. Then he placed the mask on the head of the man he had been following for three days, the man who was known as "the butcher" in Central America for killing hundreds of peasants in El Salvador, the Honduras, and Panama, wherever the wealthy could hire a hit man to reclaim "legal rights" to lands they never owned in the first place. After several weeks of stalking, deception, and luck, he would not let *el carnicero* get away.

Examining the burly man's thick fingers and large hands, the tall man could readily believe the rumors that the man he was helping had personally killed many men, women, and children with his own hands. But at this very moment, "the butcher" looked like a helpless, fat adolescent who was grateful that someone had taken some interest in him. "Now, place the mask tightly over your face," the tall man explained quietly, "and then place the rubber mouthpiece of your plastic breathing tube in your mouth." He gently placed the man's head under the water, allowing him to become comfortable with the claustrophobic feeling of breathing underwater into a tube.

After a full minute underwater, the burly man raised his head. "I think I'm beginning to get the idea. Thanks . . . what's your name?"

"There's still plenty to learn," the tall man responded, ignoring the inquiry. "Now, stretch your body out so that your head is in the water, your back is arched, and your body is floating." The tall man held his student with both hands and helped him stretch out his body in the water. He had him just where he wanted. Unsuspecting. Helpless. Dependent. Without bodyguards. And no escape route.

"This is great, buddy." The burly man raised his head, finally feeling confident. "I'm going to recommend that you become a guide." He patted the tall man on his shoulder like a politician who had just been promised a vote.

"Now try it on your own!" the tall man said, smiling.

"You think that I'm ready?"

"I'm absolutely positive!"

By this time the two men were alone. The rest of the group was snorkeling behind the guide toward the coral reef to observe the variety of fish who lived in it. They were already quite a distance away from the catamaran. The burly man looked straight into the tall man's hazel eyes. There was something in them that told him that this man knew what he was doing. He put his head slowly into the water, arched his back just as he had been instructed, and gently kicked his flippers. He had learned how to snorkel.

Surrounded by a playful school of stingrays, seeking the food that the guide had used to lure them to the catamaran, the tall man stroked the white underbelly of a four-foot stingray as the burly man watched through his goggles.

Carefully, the tall man positioned the stingray under the "butcher" and jammed its sharp spine into the man's belly. Immediately, the water turned red.

"Aggghhhh!" The "butcher" clutched his stomach with both hands. As he tried to lift his head out of the water, the tall man held it down and yanked the snorkel from his mouth. With his mouth now opening up with every cry of pain, it took only a few minutes of splashing until his lungs were filled with water.

The tall man watched as the last breath of life left the butcher and uttered the ritual words of forgiveness, *"mal y soit que mal y pense!"* Evil comes to those who think of evil. His job successfully completed, Alison Carter, M.D., repositioned his own snorkeling mask and swam quickly to shore.

2

STOCKHOLM, SWEDEN

There is an old saying that an Italian driver will stop his car to admire a beautiful girl. A Stockholm driver will stop to admire a beautiful salmon. But in the case of the three teenage girls strutting down the Kungsgatan, Stockholm's main shopping center, the old axiom did not apply. Whistles of admiration followed them from passing Swedes as they tried to avoid their obvious embarrassment by focusing their attention on the elegant handblown glassware artistically placed in a display window.

"Look at that one, the one with the blue people in the middle of the thick glass," said the dark-haired beauty with a heavy Moroccan accent. "It's awesome how they are able to make this."

"No it's not, Fatimah," responded Dephne, a Turkish immigrant who had fled to Sweden with her brother only three years earlier. "It's just that you've never seen one of these. If you go to the bazaars in Marakesh or Fez, you'll be able to see glass just like this!" She smiled, satisfied with her worldliness.

"You are always such a know-it-all," added Ilya, an Albanian refugee who, unlike her friends, was fair-skinned, tall, and blonde.

"I'm soooo sorry, Ilya," Dephne replied in her usual

sarcastic tone of voice. "I wasn't aware that Albania was the center of glassblowing. Or as a matter of fact of anything else, except refugees."

"I wonder how the blue figures were put in there," Fatimah said, trying to ignore the continual bickering between Ilya and Dephne. *But how can they help it,* she thought, *when they live together in very tight quarters.* The morning's news had lauded how Sweden provided humanitarian care as part of the country's tradition of neutrality, and a transit point for the displaced. The reporter had noted that Sweden had recently absorbed more than two million refugees from Africa, the Middle East, Russia, and Eastern Europe, particularly those areas in which there were current conflicts—Bosnia, Turkey, Albania, and Montenegro. The majority of the new refugees were Moslems from countries which had been the direct target of ethnic cleansing by their historical adversaries.

Fatimah had left Morocco for Sweden with her entire family for what her father had thought would be better economic opportunity. Her father, a successful real estate developer in his own country, had realized that his potential for making a better living for his family was limited in a country where the Moroccan Royal Family owned or controlled the majority of the finest real estate in the land. Despite the well-cultivated benevolent image generated by the late King Hassan and his American publicity machinery, Fatimah's father understood all too well the constraints of working in a system ruled by an autocrat who would brook no dissension from his followers. The king had appointed himself Minister of Defense, Minister of the Interior (in charge of the country's dreaded security apparatus), leader of Parliament, and spiritual Caliph of all of Morocco. In the guise of a democratic monarchy, King Hassan ruled as a secular and religious dictator. For Fatimah's parents, who had lived in the United States during their college years, a restrictive political and economic situation had become unacceptable. So they had migrated voluntarily, without any thought of ever returning.

Dephne had escaped, with her older brother, from the Turkish government's increasing suppression of university students who were suspected of being Islamic Fundamentalists. Her brother was one of the lucky Turkish emigres who had been accepted into the University in Stockholm, although not entirely convinced he was really welcome there.

Ilya had escaped, alone, from the slaughter of her Albanian family by Serbian militia and their Croatian and Montenegro lackeys. Whatever the real identity of the killers, they had come into town and exterminated her entire family in front of her eyes. She had escaped death only by allowing herself to be raped. After being rescued by some neighbors, and receiving some minimal assistance from the U.S. Agency for International Development, she fled her country, determined to find a safe haven. Sweden's generous welfare system, and the country's sense of tranquillity and prosperity, seemed like a land in which she could reconstruct a life for herself.

The three girls lived in the same building, in an area of Stockholm that had come to be known as "refugee heaven." They had formed a bond of camaraderie based on the concerns and values of teenagers throughout the world. They collected the CDs of Meatloaf, Hootie and the Blowfish, and hip-hop music. They reveled in the ludicrous obscenities of the television show *South Park*, and balanced that with reruns of *Beverly Hills, 90210* and *Melrose Place*. They wore the same stylish fashions of Gap and J.Crew—tight blue jeans, halter tops, and high-platformed shoes. They were daily consumers of MTV and longed to grow up with the sensuality exhibited in the Victoria's Secret catalogue. Their emotional bond was founded upon universal values established by American culture—the right of any teenager the world over, irrespective of race, color, religion, or economic status, to wear the same brand names, copy the latest Hollywood hairdo, and replicate the newest makeup style dictated by hot movie stars.

Despite the fact that they lived in relatively crowded living quarters, they somehow managed to possess a large-screen television set on which they watched approximately three hours of programs per night. They had seen the movie *Titanic* at least three times so that they could imprint the Hollywood personae of Leonardo di Caprio, the lead male star. Discussions revolved around the latest boyfriends and how sexually promiscuous they could allow themselves to be with them, given the strict constraints of their respective religious mores.

At the moment, they were headed to a discotheque called "Beverly Hills" located in Gamla Stan, the Old Town, to practice some of the new dance steps they had learned from the resurgence of 1970's disco music.

Their greatest concern this day were how they could evade the scrupulous control of the bouncer at the front door of the club, where the minimum drinking age was eighteen years old. Each girl had brought with her a false driver's license that had been forged by one of their high school classmates.

As they walked past the elegant shops, ignoring the whistles coming in their direction, they argued about which of their fake I.D.s would be most credible. Dephne, the risk-taker of the group, wagered that they would easily get into the nightclub if they flattered the doorman. Fatimah and Ilya were skeptical, but Dephne dismissed that as being part of their cynical nature.

Walking down Västerlånggatan, the main street of Gamla Stan, they looked inside a favorite antique shop, wondering whether if they pooled their money they would have enough to buy three brass friendship rings. But their thoughts strayed as they saw the flashing neon lights of "Beverly Hills."

Just as Dephne had predicted, the bouncer, a crew-cut, brawny, former wrestler, simply smiled and nodded his head in approval as the girls walked past him, quickly flashing their forged I.D.s. He waved them through the heavy wooden doors, into a cavernous space filled with young people jumping, bumping, and shaking their bodies to produce obscene gyrations to the pounding, electronic sounds of music emanating from dozens of speakers surrounding the room. As they descended a broad, circular marble staircase, they entered a ballroom with rotating electronic balls that flashed iridescent colors over the dancers.

Without a moment's hesitation, the girls plunged into the crowd and lost themselves amidst the frenzy of moving bodies. Whatever memories of deprivation, persecution, and abandonment they might have entertained only minutes earlier, were quickly forgotten.

When the discotheque was at its legal capacity of occupants, the bouncer pulled a small cellular phone from his pocket, dialed a number, spoke a few words, and then waited. A few minutes later a dozen young caucasian men unloaded cans of gasoline and diesel fuel from their motorcycles and cars. Upon a signal from the bouncer, they entered the club and poured the combustible fuel down the marble staircase. With a smug demeanor, the bouncer lit a match and threw it into the liquid fuel.

The human screams arising from the burning inferno pierced the calm midnight sky.

3

WASHINGTON, D.C.

"Eleanor, follow my index finger with both eyes," Dr. Alison Carter, Medical Director for the Department of State, instructed the blonde-haired, well-endowed, grade-three Foreign Service Officer (FSO) seated before him. She had come into his office, in the basement of the State Department, with a presenting complaint of dizziness. "Tell me if you see double or the dizziness becomes worse."

Eleanor remained silent as Carter's finger glided before her face. Doctors always made her feel somewhat vulnerable and infantile. Embarrassed. And it didn't help matters that she found Dr. Carter extremely attractive. Informally dressed, in a tweed sport jacket, outrageous tie, and khaki pants, he reminded her of one of her college professors. All he was missing was the suede patches on the elbows of his jacket. It made him seem accessible. And those seductive hazel "bedroom" eyes he possessed . . .

"Now, rapidly turn the palms of both of your hands back and forth. As quickly as possible."

"You mean like this?" Eleanor asked, hoping that Carter wouldn't notice that the polish on two of her fingernails was chipped.

"Precisely," Carter responded, prepared to make a diagnosis. "As far as I can tell from both the neurological exam and from last week's X rays of your skull you have nothing to worry about."

"What about my dizziness?" she asked.

"It's probably viral in origin," Carter replied. "Take one of these anti-vertigo pills every six to eight hours and come back in one week." He handed her a vial of green pills that he felt would halt the dizziness. He could have ordered a CAT scan or an MRI to clinically protect himself against a future malpractice suit, if his diagnosis proved incorrect. But, unlike most of his younger colleagues, who had recently graduated from the most prestigious medical schools around the country, Carter trusted his skills as a basic clinical diagnostician, and relied more on them than on frequently unnecessary and expensive medical procedures.

"Thank you, Dr. Carter," she responded somewhat coquettishly. Her last thought as she walked out the door was whether she could have a mutual friend arrange a dinner party at which they could "meet" as State Department professionals rather than as doctor and patient. But she sensed that he was too ethical to compromise their current relationship.

When Eleanor closed the door behind her, Carter took off the colorful silk tie that he had bought at the Rock 'n Roll Hall of Fame in Cleveland. He hoped his patient had taken notice of it. Besides medicine, his major passion was '50's and '60's rock 'n roll. Hanging on the wall of his office was a poster of a 1955 concert in which both Little Richard and Chuck Berry appeared on the same playbill, the only concert in which these two performers ever appeared together on stage. He couldn't resist buying the poster despite its steep price tag. As a rock 'n roll aficionado, he knew that he had bought a bargain. Despite the fact that he was entering middle age, with one failed childless marriage behind him, Carter was a bopping teenager at heart—ebullient, inquisitive, irreverent, at times moody, and always testing the limits of authority.

Checking his pockets for gum and keys, Carter locked the door to his office, walked down the empty basement corridor, and took the elevator to the garage. His 1980 green Volvo had over 120,000 miles on its odometer, but its total upkeep amounted to no more than three oil changes a year. Why drive a bigger, fancier car? Like much of his life, his car reflected a certain reverse snobbism. In part, he was still acting out his anger for his father having assigned him a name that could easily be mistaken for a girl's. But he also suspected that because of his name he had developed a very strong sense of self.

The State Department garage was a disaster waiting to happen. Each day's retrieval brought the possibility of a new dent, scratch or theft. And the layout of the garage was a haven for any terrorist attempting to blow up the State Department. As he drove toward the exit, his windows fully open, the radio blasting 1950's do-wop music, Carter flashed his I.D. at the guard. After his customary salute, the guard lowered the steel anti-terrorist barrier blocking the exit onto D Street.

It would take only a minor amount of C4 plastique wrapped around the rim of a spare tire in the trunk of his car to create a significant amount of destruction in the building, he thought. But like everything else in the State Department, security had become a ritual without substance. Much like the absurd questions asked of passengers by airline personnel. "Has anyone unknown to you . . . ?" "Have you packed your own luggage?" Et cetera, et cetera, et cetera. Carter smiled to himself as he drove down Independence Avenue, imagining a terrorist responding "yes" to any of the questions in an attempt to get himself caught. What would the airline do then? They would, he concluded, panic! No amount of questioning could realistically deter a terrorist from successfully accomplishing a mission of destruction anywhere, anytime. The only thing that the worldwide terrorism scare of the early 1990's had created was a self-anointed group of effete experts warehoused in Washington, D.C. think tanks who proclaimed self-aggrandizing absurdities and regurgitated the conclusion of studies that had little or no merit. Carter had made a conscious decision years before, when he was the State Department's principal hostage negotiator, that if he ever left State he would refuse to become part of the "expert" opinion dog-and-pony circus. He felt much more comfortable returning to medicine, his first love.

But it was now time to put on his other hat.

By disposition and training, Dr. Alison Carter was a physician. But by avocation, he was an assassin. With the very scalpel he used to excise a cancerous growth in order to cure, he severed an adversary's carotid arteries in order to kill. Two distinct roles, but no inherent contradictions as far as he was concerned.

As a physician, Carter upheld the precepts of the Hippocratic oath—to heal, cure, and above all else do no harm. As a contract assassin, he fulfilled another set of precepts— to eliminate the evil monsters of this world who were responsible for taking innocent human lives. For Carter, that might mean taking one life in order to save hundreds or thousands of others. In this role, he contracted out his skills, on a fee-for-service basis, primarily to "units" within the United States government which circumvented Executive Order of 1976, prohibiting any federal agency from directly involving itself in an assassination. The order did not prevent quasi-official "units," however, from subcontracting out nefarious assignments to a third party.

Both jobs, as Carter viewed them, were equally essential to society. And in both roles he enjoyed a great sense of professional pride. On one occasion he had actually healed a patient only to kill him at a later time. Life's paradoxes were always a source of inspiration to him.

It was easier than one would imagine for Carter to rationalize his assassin's role. Since his days of political activism as an undergraduate at Columbia University, Carter was intellectually and emotionally committed to the basic proposition that evil prevailed everywhere. Whatever good existed was frequently suffocated by the tendrils of fraud, corruption, terror and murder. So the premise that ruled his life was simple: much like a festering wound which had to be debriefed, lest the limb have to be amputated, excise as much evil as possible from the world.

He claimed to be neither a theologian nor a philosopher. Only an agnostic with a strong belief in the strength of the individual. Since childhood, he had held the conviction that the willful deeds of an individual acting alone could make a significant impact on any given situation. Bureaucracies and groups always proved to be inept and inefficient. He sometimes thought of himself as a modern Don Quixote, continuously striking at recalcitrant windmills. But when he was successful, as either physician or assassin, his belief in the individual was substantiated.

When he was in his office in the basement of the State Department, he was responsible for the medical welfare of all personnel located in thirty-three different agencies which were housed in the overseas embassies, including the FBI, the Drug Enforcement Agency, and the Department of Agriculture. Ironically, the only government organization for which he was not responsible was the Central Intelligence Agency (CIA), which he euphemistically called the "Culinary Institute of America." Consistent with its inherently paranoid character, the CIA trusted neither State nor any other organization to provide the necessary care for its own personnel.

Ironically, sick CIA employees would frequently and surreptitiously visit the State Department "Doc" so that nothing detrimental would be found in his or her CIA medical chart. In turn, Carter had a back channel entrée into the deepest secrets of an organization that he knew to be highly overrated.

Carter put four quarters in the parking meter and ran across Independence Avenue, darting across six lanes of oncoming traffic. He headed for an impressive, circular building surrounded by a series of massive sculptures. While his apartment on Dupont Circle was filled with books on painting, architecture and sculpture, and he spent many weekends "museum hopping" in downtown Washington, D.C., he felt completely out of place in the Hirschhorn Museum Sculpture Garden at three o'clock in the afternoon of a workday. Tourists from all over the world milled about, posturing themselves in grotesque positions, trying to make sense out of the tortured twists and swirls of bronze, iron and stone. He glanced at his watch as he walked down the rampway to the rear of the building, the part of the garden that abutted the Mall. Right on time. As usual, he stopped in front of a bronze sculpture of a massive man with outstretched arms, defiantly screaming into the sky above him and holding a sword in his right hand.

"Interesting, isn't it?" a soft-spoken male voice from behind him asked. "Please don't turn around, Dr. Carter. It wouldn't serve anyone's purpose for you to see me. I'm merely an intermediary."

"For whom?" Carter asked, calculating by the nearness and strength of the man's voice that they were about the same height, but the Voice probably had a slight build.

"Does it really matter?" the Voice replied, with a slight wheeze.

"Emphysema?" Carter asked quizzically. "I would say two to three packs of unfiltered cigarettes per day."

"Impressive," the Voice replied. "But we're not here to talk about me."

"What would you like to talk about?"

"The statue in front of you," the Voice continued, "is 'The Great Warrior of Montaubin', a bronze cast by Emile Antoine Bourdelle. A Frenchman who lived from eighteen sixty-one to nineteen twenty-nine."

"I'm overwhelmed that you can read the placard alongside the statue." Carter was tempted to turn around. But the rules of his business were simple—follow the client's wishes until they no longer made sense or were unprofitable. Clearly, the person behind him was cautious, if not paranoid. Typical. At least he knew his trade, and had made certain that they met outdoors, in a crowded area, so that it would be hard to either photograph or record their conversation.

"Of course," the Voice continued, "if you turn slightly to

the right you'll see the famous 'Monument of the Burghers of Calais'."

"August Rodin," Carter inserted, unable to hide his own knowledge.

"I was told that you were a man of culture," the Voice said. "I'm glad to see that it is true."

"Recognition of that famous scene, one of many cast over the centuries, is hardly a mark of culture," Carter replied, "so your flattery is somewhat gratuitous, if not annoying."

"Very good," the Voice continued, keeping his distance behind Carter so that he could disappear at a moment's notice. "I would appreciate it if you could read aloud the sign next to Zuniga's 'Seated Yucatan Woman'."

"I don't like games—let's get to why we're here," Carter demanded. "I'm due back in my office in twenty minutes."

"Certainly, Dr. Carter," the Voice responded, a trifle disappointed and trying to stifle another wheeze. "You're wanted at Bollings Air Force Base. Be there at six-thirty tonight. He will find you," the Voice responded.

"Where will I be met?" Carter asked, disturbed with the Voice's cat-and-mouse approach.

This time there was no Voice. Carter stood facing the sculpture for another five seconds before he turned around. But there was no one behind him, only a low stone wall covered with ivy, and the cold, mute sculptures.

4

WASHINGTON, D.C.

"Welcome to the base, sir," the corporal standing guard at the entrance of Bollings Air Force Base said. "Who are you here to see? And may I see some identification, please."

"I'm here to see General James Atherton," Carter responded, handing the guard his State Department I.D. The corporal looked at the I.D., glanced once again at Carter, and returned the identification card to him. Then he walked into the guard booth and searched his computer.

Carter knew the procedure by now. But he always wondered whether the guard was bored with it, and if there were any recent foul-ups.

"What department is he with?" the guard asked, having difficulty finding Atherton's name in his computer.

"The last name is spelled A-t-h-e-r-t-" Carter responded.

"o-n." said a man suddenly, entering the car on the passenger side. "Thank the good corporal for his help, and back up as quickly as you can."

"What the hell are you doing here?" Carter asked, putting the car in reverse.

"Thank God," the 6'4" Atherton said, "that one of us can drive well. Could you imagine what it would be like if I drove this indestructible jalopy?"

"General," Carter said, looking at the broad-shouldered man in the out-of-fashion plaid sport jacket, "which way?"

"Head toward Anacostia. To our usual place on Martin Luther King Avenue." Atherton spoke with the affectation of a British barrister about to enter Whitehall. Ever since his schooling at Andover Academy, a highly selective private school in a particularly bucolic region of western Massachusetts, years before it became coeducational, Brigadier General James Atherton, Special Assistant for National Security Affairs in the Office of Defense, had acquired the effete mannerism of the English. He made certain that his midwestern roots from Streeter, Illinois, were well hidden by a cultivated Oxford accent, witty sarcasm, a droll sense of the absurd, and a compulsive need to poke fun with his staff.

But, as Carter knew all too well, this fun-loving overgrown adolescent was an American patriot who had fought and recruited more personnel for nonexistent wars than any other military man he knew. The General could be called the CEO and CFO of a nonexistent quasi-private, quasi-governmental unit informally called the "Virtual Assassin Squad" or "VAS." He frequently worked out of the bowels of the Pentagon or Bollings Air Force Base. Even after a decade of working together, Carter was still unclear about Atherton's formal position in the established bureaucracy. But Carter knew very well that he was only one of a number of private citizens, both American and foreign mercenaries, to whom the General outsourced assignments. As a former Chief of Paramilitary Covert Actions for DOD, Atherton knew personally a number of individuals with Top Secret clearances, many of whom who had completed previous successful "wet works" assignments. His current contractees would convert free time into a profitable second job, and were able to retire early from their regular government careers by just completing a few assignments for him.

"This must be a very special occasion for such a rendezvous so late in the afternoon," Carter said as he drove through the littered streets of a run-down neighborhood populated primarily by African Americans loitering about on the stoops of dilapidated row houses. "Did you ever wonder what would happen, General, if a fire started in this neighborhood? It would spread like wildfire, probably killing more than the Dresden bombing."

"Are you suffering from a case of melancholia or the vapors, my good doctor?" Atherton asked, in a sarcastic tone. "You and I know all too well that there is nothing to be done here except burn the entire place down and then rebuild everything from the ground up. What wonders could actually be accomplished here. But unfortunately, Carter, this area and its poverty are beyond our purview. So please proceed with haste before our dinner reservations are canceled."

"Yes, sir," Carter replied laughing, as he drove into the parking area of the McDonald's across the street from St. Elizabeth's Hospital, a mental institution in which Carter had served his internship rotation in psychiatry.

Atherton's mischievous, childish side frequently strained Carter's credulity. This one man, who was responsible for dozens of unofficial U.S. government interventions around the world—and those were only the ones that Carter knew about—was a character that could only have come straight out of a whimsical twentieth-century children's book like *The Wind and the Willows,* where the characters' madness made them incredibly frustrating, yet appealing. Among the men who worked with him, Atherton was known as the "Virtual General" who fought "virtual regional conflicts" and "managed world chaos" at a time when the formal U.S. government institutions like the Department of Defense (DOD), the State Department, the Central Intelligence Agency (CIA), the National Security Agency (NSA), and the Defense Intelligence Agency (DIA) were being downsized and completely eviscerated of their effectiveness.

Unlike Carter, who could be found daily in the basement of the State Department, Atherton couldn't be anywhere at anytime. It was almost impossible to contact him. He found you. He called the shots and Carter was simply there to receive them. And respond.

In the past, calls to Carter from Atherton had come from a phone booth in a run-down striptease joint in Las Vegas, an extremely fashionable hotel dining room in Manhattan, and a gas station out in nowheresville. This was the first time that an unknown intermediary had informed Carter of a potential meeting with the general. But despite what was part cloak-and-dagger and part Atherton's personal mischievous idiosyncrasies, Carter had a great respect for his integrity, his vast warehouse of knowledge, and his willingness to carry through on any assignment, no matter what the personal cost.

"What would you like?" Atherton asked, as they walked into the relatively empty McDonald's. "Our usual, Big Mac with french fries and Diet Coke?" The Diet Coke was Atherton's token to the nutritional notion that he was saving a few calories in this vast orgy of cholesterol and calories.

"I'll have whatever you have," Carter answered, more for reasons of accommodation than for culinary pleasure.

They sat at a far corner of the restaurant where no one would overhear their discussion, engaging in meaningless chitchat while they ate. By the time the last bite was taken, Carter was eager to learn what it was that had brought him across the city.

"Who was that man at the Hirschhorn?" Carter asked, glancing around the restaurant at the scattered customers.

"Who he is—and what he is, by the way—is less relevant than your assignment," Atherton replied. "All you really need to know is that he represents serious interests in Sweden. But since you are curious, his name is Mack Londsdale. He works on behalf of the Swedish Prime Minister, Johannes Strindberg. And, by the way, Strindberg is a distant relative of the famous playwright. A bit too misogynistic for my taste."

"Who?" Carter asked, smiling. "Londsdale or Strindberg?"

"Is your sadism in the interest of pleasure," Atherton asked rhetorically, "or is it a way of testing me out?" He leaned across the table, beckoning Carter closer. "Your assignment is to terminate a fellow medical colleague, of all people, by the name of Dr. Derek Eriksson. Born and trained as a doctor in Sweden, he came to America for his psychiatric residency, and now is an American trained psychiatrist 'practicing' torture and ethnic cleansing all over Sweden. He works out of a small resort town called Vadstena, about two hours north of Stockholm."

"Who is my client?"

"Right now," Atherton responded, "I'm not cleared to tell you. But it is a consortium of both business and government interests. They want him out. And you've got one week." Atherton paused for a moment, giving Carter a chance to voice any objections to either the undertaking or the timing. "Bring no weapons. Too conspicuous. Get close in. Co-opt him. Then do whatever you have to."

"Terms?" Carter asked, not wanting to sound greedy, but definitely needing to assess the financial seriousness of the offer.

"Same as usual," Atherton replied. "Half up front. Half upon completion of the assignment."

"Amount?"

"The standard five million now, to be wired to your Cayman account," Atherton replied, "and the balance of five million upon completion."

"Charities?"

"I will, as usual, two months later, distribute all of the monies, except one hundred thousand dollars for your own expenses, to the usual thirty charities," Atherton responded with clear frustration in his voice. "Christ, man! Do you have to be such a goddamn saint? You make me feel like Uncle Scrooge sitting opposite Mother Theresa."

"The money doesn't belong to me," Carter said, perfunctorily, "it belongs to these who are in need of food, medicine, a home, a school, and a country."

"No hearts and flowers, please. You know how I feel about your senseless . . ."

"But, General," Carter added, his voice dripping with sarcasm, "you are the one who makes it all possible. I'm just one of your many conduits. I feel so fortunate that I can work with someone like you. That's my payoff."

"If you keep this up," Atherton said, "I'm going to force you to eat another Big Mac! Now let's get out of here."

"Same working rules?" Carter asked, as they walked out of the restaurant.

"Use your vacation days at State," Atherton nodded. "If I have to reach you, I'll call your home phone number and leave a message on the answering machine. Same code as last time. I don't have to tell you that this is a completely 'off-line,' 'wet operation.' Unless absolutely necessary, there will be no calls, letters, messages, or traces of you, until you finish the assignment. I expect to meet you one week from today in front of the Holocaust Museum, at precisely the same time we met this evening."

"That's it?" Carter asked.

"Your briefing documents are already waiting for you in a manila envelope at the reception desk of your apartment building. I think you will find the profile of Eriksson fascinating." Atherton got into Carter's car and buckled up. "No questions asked about your methods. No special papers needed. No written agreements. No fake passports. As someone on vacation, you are completely on your own."

Carter smiled as he looked across the front seat at the general. He wanted to tell him how much he respected and trusted him.

By the time Carter returned Atherton to Bollings AFB, he felt his usual new assignment nervousness coming on. He had a lot to learn about Sweden, Eriksson, and some little hole-in-the-wall town before he could develop a working plan. And then there was always the lingering question . . . what if the plan didn't work?

5

EN ROUTE TO SWEDEN

Carter had a comfortable ride on the nonstop SAS originating from Newark, New Jersey, straight to Stockholm. For most of the flight he listened to his ABBA tapes which, even though they were recorded in English, allowed him to begin to submerge himself in Swedish culture. The Swedish group had been so successful that at one time they were the most profitable corporation on the Stockholm Stock Exchange. What had made them so unusual was their wholesome image, textured musical background, unusual harmony, and catchy lyrics. They were the first Swedish singing group to make it to the top of the pop charts in both the U.S. and around the world. In the 1970's, sales of 100 million records worldwide was an incredible feat. Ironically, it was their massive financial success that, according to group members, led to the death and kidnapping threats that prompted their eventual disbanding in 1982. Their distinctive, upbeat harmony in the songs that had made it onto the Top Ten Singles of the 1970's, "Waterloo," "Dancing Queen," and "Take a Chance on Me," brought Carter immediately back to daydreaming about a past that was decidedly less complicated for him than was his current life.

For Carter, the musical culture of a country was a major clue to its political culture. Whether ABBA was singing "Fernando," a song about a disillusioned soldier in the Spanish Civil War, or "Money, Money, Money," and the importance of it, Carter tried to find the sociopolitical meaning behind the words. It was not an accident that Nelson Mandela's favorite rock 'n roll group during his twenty-five year political incarceration in South Africa was ABBA. Or that current African American entertainers who stretch the musical envelope with profane, provocative rap lyrics, mirror the pains of growing up in the black ghettos of America. Values, norms, mores and social problems of a country were all available to the listener. And Carter listened closely.

In their personal lives ABBA's members reflected the liberal Swedish values of their time, as well as their underlying hypocrisy. Composed of two women and two men, each of whom had been married during their teenage years, the singers went on to have random sexual affairs with each other. Interestingly, when they left the music industry they returned to the norms of the stolid, unrelenting, unforgiving Swedish middle class.

Carter devoured biographies, from singers to military leaders to political figures, always trying to correlate the individual's history with his or her eventual successes and failures. But, ultimately, he liked ABBA for the same reason that tens of millions of people around the world did—they gave him great listening pleasure.

Funny, Carter mused, about life's pathways. For all his academic and professional degrees and awards, he knew that he was just an overgrown kid whose greatest fantasy and disappointment lay in the fact that he never had the talent, audacity, or perseverance to enter the rock 'n roll scene as a player—and not just some voyeur. Growing up on Manhattan's East Side, in a middle-class family of businessmen, his primary concern in life was supposed to have been to obtain and maintain a modicum of wealth and live a life of the status quo. Country clubs in Riverdale, New York. A prep school in Lakeville, Connecticut. Resume-building extracurricular activities after school and on weekends. Every aspect of his life was governed by doing something that was either popular, appropriate for his age group, or allowed him to develop the background needed for his anticipated future. But while he was forced to take piano lessons at the Juilliard School, Carter frequently escaped to the Brooklyn Paramount Theatre to attend Alan Freed's rock 'n roll shows, when Little Richard, Buddy Holly, Chuck Berry, or Jackie Wilson came to New York. He did not have to work hard to be known affectionately by his classmates as "the Black Man's White Man." In rock 'n roll, Carter found, as an only child, the perfect emotional solace that was missing in his everyday life. So the radio was always tuned to Wolfman Jack, Murray the K, Jocko, and Alan Freed, the father of rock 'n roll, in order to cover the unrelenting boredom and emotional barrenness of his family's life. He became a loner by choice.

A multitude of events had transpired over the past twenty-four hours and none of them made any sense to Carter. He was on his way to Sweden on an assignment to neutralize a man who stood behind the torture, mutilation, and killing of refugees who were flocking to Sweden from all over the world. Eriksson, according to Carter's briefing document, was a "Swedish Mengele," the counterpart to the Nazi's most infamous physician who had conducted inhumane experiments on innocent victims at the Auschwitz concentration camp who did not fit the fictitious mold of an idealized Aryan—Jews, gypsies, homosexuals, Catholic priests, Slavs... But now, what should have been an obvious question when Carter agreed to take the assignment, stood out in bold relief: If Eriksson was such an evil man, then why wasn't the Swedish government arresting him and putting him on trial?

This was a question that Carter asked himself, sooner or later, on every assignment, whether it involved the neutralization of a narco-trafficker, the leader of a rogue state, or an aspiring military colonel in a third-world country whose ambition was to overthrow an inchoate democracy. The simplest answer was usually the most true. No one gave enough of a damn. Neither the opposition parties nor the United States government, nor the international community.

The pattern of response to the atrocities with which the "political," rather than "medical" Carter had to deal with was always the same. Genocide of some sort would occur. The international community would express its moral outrage. Television stations would be replete with talking heads reiterating platitudes and forecasting inanities. Newspaper op-ed pieces would request some form of action. Editorials would fill newspapers with "balanced views" of the atrocity. The UN would convene, led by an American statement of moral indignation with an acute sensitivity to the thirty-second sound bite. After an unconscionable delay, a UN committee would form which would try to visit the site of the atrocity. The members would return, express their collective outrage, and after several months of "research," make their report public, after having spent an indecent amount of money to reiterate the two propositions that the world was already aware of: the atrocity could have been prevented and there was a need to convene the two warring groups to negotiate differences. In the meantime, hordes of non-governmental organizations (NGOs) usually possessing some form of salvation in their organization's title, would request millions of dollars from the State Department's Agency for International Development (a frequent inconvenient cover for covert operatives working overseas), in order to study the atrocity and it's aftermath.

Cynical, perhaps, but true. The formal institutional structures of the world would proceed on automatic pilot, heading into a state of entropy. Those who were responsible for the atrocities would generally escape persecution and, ironically, become more powerful and wealthy, like a metastasizing cancer spreading throughout the body, destroying every organ in it's path.

A perfect example was Iraq's Saddam Hussein, who became more powerful after close to two hundred thousand air strikes were launched against him in the first Iraq war and thousands of cruise missiles during a pathetic four day reprise. He outlasted three presidents of the United States, while, at the same time, increasing his personal wealth by billions of dollars.

And so it was in this interstice of institutional entropy and general malaise among world leaders not to interfere in the internal mechanisms of a country that Carter had found a needed role, perhaps more needed than his role as physician. Why him, versus mercenaries from any one of a number of countries who were willing, for a price, to take out someone? Was it his fascination with history, a disdain for repeating its mistakes? Or a family history which included several Jewish relatives who had been killed in extermination camps during the second World War? Or his love of medicine, and a respect for the Hippocratic oath about healing man that he had taken when he graduated medical school? Most likely all of these contributed to his view of himself as someone who was obsessed with taking responsibility for excising the cancer of genocidal malevolence.

He charged a hefty price for his services, knowing that in a world of moral hypocrisy, apathy, and decadence no one would take him seriously unless a significant price had to be paid. The analogy was not too different from the world of medicine, where the patient who felt that the doctor who charged more than others was better than one who gave away his medical skill for little or no money. That was the nature of man as Carter had experienced it; and, so he acted accordingly. He was not there to change the nature of man or the course of history. But, as he saw his mission in life, it was to correct, to the degree it was possible, the small and large injustices of life. A moral "fixer" or "adjuster."

The profile of Dr. Derek Eriksson that had been delivered to his apartment building the day before was more revealing to him than was his life-long study of ABBA. In some ways, Eriksson's early life had mirrored that of the infamous Dr. D., a Waffen SS physician who had been interviewed by a series of American psychiatrists at the behest of the U.S. military, as part of a larger study of Nazi physicians involved in the development and maintenance of the infamous Nazi death camps. According to unclassified Army archives, the most persistent theme in Dr. D.'s early life was his quest for human connection. This need for connection meant a life-long personal search for acceptance, recognition, belongingness, and intimacy. His father, a man whom he truly adored, had brought him up to believe that one must always maintain one's integrity by holding on to one's life project and to one's sense of self, whatever the pressure to yield or dissemble.

Dr. D.'s family shared much of the German nation's experience of having been defeated in the first World War. The psychological consequences of that defeat had never been fully appreciated by the conquering nations. Like most German families, Dr. D.'s felt abject humiliation, isolation, and, above all else, loss. As a result of this sense of loss, Dr. D.'s family, and the German people were able to embark on a series of regenerative causes which embraced the inherent paradoxes of defiance and submission, romanticism and science, idealization and pragmatism. Dr. D., along with his countrymen, ventured through Christianity, traditional utopian movements, nationalistic movements, and finally into Nazism.

As Carter understood from reviewing Eriksson's profile, he grew up with similar emotional needs. His father, a Nazi sympathizer who tried to hide his predilections in light of Sweden's claimed neutrality, influenced his son nevertheless.

In his youth, Dr. Eriksson had been obsessed by differences among races. He had also performed countless scientific experiments, including ablations of specific parts of the brain in order to see their corresponding effect on the body. An electrical shock to the thalamus, for example, would often set off a series of major *grand mal* seizures accompanied by auditory, visual, and olfactory hallucinatory sensations. Eriksson was also fascinated by how one could manipulate the brain through the use of drugs, ideas, and a spectrum of stimuli.

In the nineteenth century, the ersatz science of phrenology used the shape of the skull and its curvatures, bumps, and anatomical variations to explain differences among people. Although subsequently discredited by the international scientific community as nothing more than chicanery, the Nazis had used phrenology to justify their perverted ideology of Aryan supremacy.

Eriksson, no fool or charlatan, understood that beneath all of these pseudo-sciences lay assumptions which, if culled out selectively, could provide him with an invaluable tool for his principal obsession—eugenics and euthanasia. His primary professional quest was to develop a method by which he could create pure races from the increasing variety of Africans, Arabs, Gypsies and Eastern Europeans, who seemed to be repopulating Europe and Scandinavia—Sweden, in particular. World War II might be over, but not the quest for Nordic purity.

As a physician, he knew that on a basic molecular level there were no differences between one person or another. But above the level of molecules, atoms and genetic composition, there were sociocultural determinants that, in fact, made one person very different from another. Or one race very different from another. And those differences accounted for the differential status of individuals or groups in the hierarchy of evolution. In other words, Eriksson could easily argue why Jamaican blacks were superior in intelligence to blacks in the southern states of America. As far as he was concerned, the Jamaican blacks had the advantage of being colonized by a superior British culture, and as a result received all of the positive effects of that colonization, particularly a formidable education and a *zeitgeist* for life. In contrast, he would argue that for over two centuries, American blacks were deprived of the chance to obtain a good education, let alone a superior one. At the same time, the slaves had been forced to relinquish their own identities to a system that was inherently demeaning and depressing.

Eriksson ultimately concluded that since the physician could do nothing to improve the status of inferior individuals it was best to rid society of them and retain only the genetic/cultural pool which would contribute to society's advancement. He would be the first to testify that he had neither personal grievances nor hatred toward any of these inferior groups, but that the biological imperative resulting from a confluence of evolution and increasing technological sophistication made it imperative to rid the world of as much "human waste" as possible, lest dire malthusian predictions come true and the globe became too small to accommodate the exponential growth of mankind.

Eriksson felt he had an obligation as a Swede to make certain that his country would not become a permanent haven for the wretched, the homeless, the refugees, and all those pathetic individuals who, for one reason or another, were currently seeking asylum in his country. In short, Dr. Derek Eriksson envisioned himself a guardian of national security, against those who might destroy his country's way of life.

The Nazis were clever enough to have created a cadre of special physicians who were given the latitude to express their own sense of "integrity" and "creativity" within the protective setting of being a member of an elite collective of specially selected warriors who were fighting for a greater cause themselves—the restoration of pride in their homeland. The Waffen SS provided Dr. D. with the psychological venue in which he could dissociate one part of himself and share in the Auschwitz killing experience without experiencing guilt. In his work-setting in Auschwitz, Dr. D.'s actions were reinforced by camaraderie, professional acceptance, and material comforts. At the same time, he could feel self-righteous and emotionally alive by serving a greater cosmic purpose, the creation of the Third Reich, than that of simply being a physician. Yet he was also able to maintain a humane self-image, nourished by his idealized father, and reinforced through his frequent contacts with his wife and children, and random acts of kindness toward prisoners. In this part of his life, Dr. D. saw himself as a physician-healer.

As much as he could interpret from Eriksson's profile, and current social problems in Sweden, Eriksson and Dr. D. were able to function by dividing their respective selves into two quite functional entities, an act called "doubling" by the famous American psychiatrist, Robert Jay Lifton.

Carter's head spun. Eriksson was as complicated and venal a target as he could ever have taken on for an assignment. Carter's assignment in the Cayman Islands, six month earlier, was going to look like child's play compared to what he might find in Sweden, where politics was as much of the problem as individuals. He closed his eyes to avoid an oncoming tension in his temples, and blocked out everything and everyone from his mind except the comforting strains of ABBA.

6

VADSTENA, SWEDEN

If Heaven had graced the earth with a place of tranquillity and beauty, it would have been the charming, medieval town of Vadstena. Like most quaint Scandinavian towns, Vadstena was made up of narrow cobblestone streets and old wood frame buildings painted in bright colors and bedecked with window boxes filled with brightly colored flowers. The town was located along the eastern shore of Lake Vättern, a clear body of water where fish and children could swim without fear of toxins and predatory creatures.

Shop after shop along Stora Gatan, the town's main street, was a testimony to the patience and craft of the citizens of Vadstena who spent most of their working day producing intricate, filigree patterns of lace. Unlike Stockholm, 159 miles to the northeast, Vadstena was a relaxing, unpretentious stop for tourists on the way to somewhere else.

Unlike many towns, which have innumerable attractions reconstructed or fabricated for the specific purpose of garnering their share of tourist dollars, Vadstena relied primarily on only two basic attractions for the paying visitor. The first was the Klosterkyran (Abbey Church) on Lasarettsgatan Street, a Gothic church, built between the mid-fourteenth and fifteenth century according to the specifications outlined by its founder, Saint Birgitta of Sweden. Of special note was the far side of the church, in which a large multicolored glass pane window was set, above which was the Hebrew word "Adonai" (God). The rest of the church was cold and stark, with nuns scurrying about in their black habits, silently attending to their respective chores.

Next to the Abbey sat the imposing Vadstena Castle founded in 1545 by Gustavus Vasa, king of Sweden. The castle, surrounded by a dry moat, contained the provincial archives, and rented its large rooms frequently for public and private receptions.

Alongside both buildings was a hotel which had been converted from a former convent. The nuns' refectory was adapted for use as a conference room and the nuns' dormitory, with its fifty-nine cells, was modernized into simple lodging accommodations.

A few hundred feet from the castle sat a run-down, two-story building which had been transformed from a flour mill into a small psychiatric clinic and museum. Displayed inside was an extensive exhibit of therapeutic modalities that had been used from the middle ages into the early nineteenth century. On display was a chair which spun around quickly in order to exhaust the agitated psychotic patient. A bathtub was exhibited in which the frenetic patient was immersed, surrounded by ice, until his mental disturbances "cooled down." A collection of leather and cloth straitjackets hung from hooks on several walls. The explanation for all of these devices, both in Swedish and fractured English, implied that as man's understanding of mental health became more scientific, treatment methods became less brutal.

As one might expect in any exhibit on the progress of psychiatry, there was a section on the use of electricity or, more specifically, electroshock therapy (ECT). Its history, as a therapy which passed an electric current through the brain, usually elicited repugnance from the visitor as something inherently cruel. The fact that clinical trials throughout the twentieth century had shown ECT to be extremely beneficial in the treatment of several types of depression received no attention. And so the continuing myth of ECT as barbaric and an unusually cruel treatment persisted.

However, that which is not mentioned does not necessarily mean that it is not appreciated. One of those who understood the value of the use of electricity in healing both the mind and body was Dr. Derek Eriksson, a distinguished mental health scholar who had trained over half a century before at a division of the Harvard Medical College that no longer existed, called Massachusetts Mental Health Center. In its time, the center was considered one of the foremost psychiatric teaching facilities in the world. During the time that he trained there, Dr. Eriksson had been taught to prescribe an assortment of therapies to treat the mentally ill—including insulin shock therapy, hydrotherapy (using a concentrated high-pressured stream of water emitted from a fire hose), ECT, high doses of chloral hydrate, and an assortment of physical restraints, including the use of leather-bound hand and foot braces tied to the bed or the floor, whichever was most convenient.

Eriksson, a lean man of 6'2", opened the door of his meticulously neat office and invited the four youths into it. Strains of the beatific voices of monks singing Gregorian chants followed them inside from the Klosterkyrkan down the street. Eriksson could not imagine a more perfect setting for what he euphemistically called the "postmortem clinical pathological rounds" that he would conduct on a weekly basis with young Swedish men and women who felt as he did, that Sweden had to remain homogeneous. There were no banners, salutes, uniforms, or rituals that marked Eriksson's personal nationalist movement. Quite the contrary. Eriksson wanted to create the completely opposite image of the classical fascist movement. The nondescript group of adolescents who joined him today wore the basic uniform of countless teenagers around the world: sneakers, blue jeans, and an assortment of chains, earrings, and rings. In fact, Eriksson insisted that they be indistinguishable from their peers in every way, except for the fact that ideologically they shared a common purpose for which they were willing to kill and die: Sweden for the Swedish.

Using his psychiatric skills and a battery of psychological tests, he had culled out individuals with specific personality traits that were important to him—compliance, obedience, passive dependence, non-alcoholic, drug-free and with no sexual perversions or sadomasochistic tendencies—based on the lessons of the psychological profiles developed by the elite Nazi unit, the Waffen SS. This unit had consisted of the most loyal soldiers in the German army, and was directly responsible to Hitler through Heinrich Himmler. Contrary to popular misconception, most of the elite SS units were specifically chosen for their normalcy and not their pathology. An SS commander in charge of a concentration camp who was ordered to methodically execute Jews, Gypsies, Slavs, and, in general, all non-Aryans, was not selected for any pathological trait such as sadism. For the most part, the Waffen SS soldiers and the concentration camp commanders were quite "normal." It was the genius of the Nazi socialization process to convert these normal German citizens into monstrous, indifferent killing machines.

It was that socialization process that Eriksson had tried to imitate, adapt and perfect over the prior five years. His training techniques were now so well developed that he could take a normal Swedish youth and create a killer. Contrary to the statements of the famous Jewish philosopher Hannah Arendt, the unremorseful mistress of a high-ranking Nazi collaborator and academic apologist, Martin Heidegger, evil was not banal. It was real. It could be lethal. And Eriksson, like many other manipulators of the soul, understood it well. Like any art form, methodical killing required a specific type of education. In most civilized countries, that education was frequently called basic military training, when a country took its youth, irrespective of background, sifted out any physical or mental pathologies, and in an intensive six-month period, created potential murderers.

Certainly, Eriksson was selective. He was always looking for individuals who felt that their future and livelihood were being jeopardized by the hordes of refugees who were swarming over the borders into Sweden. Everyone knew that refugees were more than willing to work at wages which the ordinary citizen of the host country found unconscionably low. Even in the so-called great democracy of America, Eriksson realized, Mexicans were swarming all over California in order to find work at hourly wages that were a fraction of what the American worker would accept. The American response to this illegal refugee influx was to build a two-thousand-mile steel fence and increase what was euphemistically called a border patrol; in non-democratic countries such an effort would be viewed as part of a nefarious internal security apparatus.

Yet all of these efforts at the physical containment of refugees were futile, Eriksson knew. "They" would always find a means to enter the country. So, the only effective technique to contain the problem was to get rid of them permanently.

Eriksson smiled and nodded to the young man who was the bouncer at the "Beverly Hills" discotheque. He liked successful outcomes. And he wanted his protégés to realize that the world noticed their actions as well. His "post-mortem" technique relied heavily on reviewing what was said in the foreign press. Using this method, Eriksson did not have to rely on the veracity of his young followers, whom he would expect to exaggerate their own accomplishments. And by assessing the media coverage, he could also learn where his own techniques were lacking, which would help him refine his approach in order to attain the proper media coverage the next time.

Jan Andersson, the hero of the moment, began the session by reading from an American newspaper, *The Herald Tribune* International Edition: " 'Fire Destroys Discotheque in Sweden: Popular Dance Center for Immigrant Populace. About one hundred and sixty young people died, and more than forty were seriously injured, late Wednesday night when fire and smoke engulfed an overcrowded makeshift discotheque in Gamla Stan. The makeshift dance hall had only one unlocked door. Most of the deaths were of teenagers whose parents had brought them to Sweden from homes torn by war or terror—Bosnia, Morocco, Serbia, Eritrea, Somalia, Macedonia, and many other places.' "

Unable to conceal his pride, Andersson raised his voice, almost to the level of braggadacio: " 'The fire was the deadliest this country has seen in decades, and it was all the more painful because it highlighted the profound divide between Swedes and the rainbow of immigrants who have found refuge here over the years.' "

"I think that's enough," Eriksson reprimanded Andersson. "There is no need in taking sadistic pleasure from a successful surgical procedure." Eriksson smiled faintly, enjoying his own use of medical metaphors, knowing it would enhance the self-respect of his protégés and allow them to feel a part of a noble profession. But, more importantly, Eriksson, like those who trained the SS soldiers, did not want his followers to view their deeds in terms of emotional joy or sadness, but simply as an aseptic procedure.

Eriksson nodded his head toward Ingrid Andersson, Jan's younger and smarter sister. She grabbed the newspaper from her brother and began to read in a monotone, having quickly discerned Eriksson's disappointment with her brother. " 'Almost all of the victims who had packed the famous dance hall were between seventeen and twenty-five years of age.' " She deliberately slowed her reading pace so that the group could appreciate their success. " 'Most of the victims died from smoke inhalation as they trampled each other in a panicked attempt to escape. Several were burned beyond recognition.' " She paused, with the image in her mind of scores of teenagers her age turning bright red and then charcoal black. She really wanted to stop reading at this point, but knew that if she showed any signs of repulsiveness or disgust, her commitment to the group might be questioned. And belonging to this group was the most important thing in her life.

Eriksson, perturbed by Ingrid's apparent empathy with the dead victims, now nodded toward a short, muscular young man, Art Joachim. He still had a long way to go with Ingrid, before she was able to depersonalize acts of necessary violence. Admittedly, she was the youngest member of the group. She would learn, in time.

Art continued to read the article in a deep, almost melodic voice, determined to avoid the mistakes the Anderssons had made. " 'Firefighters and the police said they had not yet determined the cause of the fire. Its explosive nature has led investigators to suspect arson.' " He read ahead silently. When he resumed reading aloud, his tone of voice mimicked one of the female victims. " ' "We were dancing and then suddenly people were screaming and running and pushing," said Deborah Afeworki, seventeen-years-old, who came to Sweden from Eritrea seven years ago. "There were two exits, but the one in the back was locked. The only way out was the small door at the front where we had entered, and everyone there was trying to get out at the same time." ' " Once again, he paused—this time to assume a more respectful tone of voice. " 'At candlelight memorials held outside of the discotheque and at local hospitals, Kurds found themselves clinging in grief to classmates from Romania, Uganda, and many other countries. Survivors described watching their friends jump from windows on the building's second floor. Others found themselves choking and clawing their way toward fresh air. "It's the most frightening thing I have ever been through," said a sixteen-year-old Iranian survivor from his bed in the Intensive Trauma Unit at Salgranska Hospital.

" 'Many of the dancers said that they saw a lamp explode just before the panic began. Others said they had seen a speaker fall over and appear to malfunction. "Young people were holding on to dead and dying friends," said Sten Schaaf, chief of police. "In such situations, you just can't tear them apart. The discotheque was totally burned out. On the floor were shoes and boots filled with unrecognizable youth." ' " Art, satisfied with his performance, handed the newspaper back to Dr. Eriksson.

Eriksson looked around at the young people before him,

who were trying to act as if what had been read to them had made no emotional impact. There was still a lot of work to be done, he concluded. They will have to learn to separate their emotions from their missions of mercy. But it was a good beginning.

7

VADSTENA, SWEDEN

It was an unusually halcyon day. The Gregorian chant "Ave Mundi Spes Maria," glorifying the virtues of the Virgin Mary, wafted from the monastery as the monks went about tending their flower and herb gardens.

Floating through the open windows of a sixteenth-century castle came the bell tones of an alto soprano rehearsing an aria for her role in Saints-Saen's *Samson and Delilah*. Tourists rowed their boats on the placid waters of the Gota Canal. Mothers scurried about the shores of the canal attempting to keep herd over the children playing happily at the water's edge. Sightseers paraded the cobblestone streets of the old town square, walking in and out of the shops named after the craftsmen who occupied them centuries earlier—Knivsmedsgatan (Cutler Street), Stockmakaregatan (Stockmaker Street), and Hovslagaretan (Furrier Street). It was the type of day that could transform misanthropes, cynics, and workaholics into happy, restful individuals. It was Sunday, God's intended day of rest, a day for charity, benedictions, and good deeds.

An attractive middle-aged woman with her beautiful, seventeen-year-old daughter walked quickly through the town, having come from Karuna, the most northern tip of Sweden, on their way to see Dr. Eriksson.

"Stop chewing on your fingernails," said Mrs. Larsson, a stern, God-fearing woman who had come to Vadstena on the recommendation of the new young priest in her parish who thought that Dr. Eriksson could help her daughter with her problem of promiscuity. According to the mother, Britt, borne out of wedlock from a liaison between the mother and a Turkish sailor, was on the verge of sexual depravity.

"Mother," Britt responded, "please don't talk to me about my nails. You're only interested in controlling my feelings for Murat."

"We've had this conversation before," Mrs. Larsson responded. "Dr. Hoffer just thought that it may be nothing more than normal hormonal changes. But if something is seriously wrong, Dr. Eriksson might be able to help."

"But, is it really necessary?" Britt protested. She paused to pick up a pebble and skim it along the smooth surface of the lake, watching the ripple effect. "There are a lot of girls in my class who feel the same way. Some of them even sleep with their boyfriends."

Mrs. Larsson quickly crossed herself as they passed by the Abbey of St. Birgitta, as if to ward off any evil consequences that might arise from her daughter's blasphemous statement. "You also haven't been doing well in school. Dr. Hoffer just felt Dr. Eriksson could best evaluate you."

I told you that I couldn't do the work on the blackboard because I need new glasses," Britt insisted.

"A beautiful girl like you shouldn't have to wear glasses," Mrs. Larsson responded, trying to ignore her ultimate fear that her daughter's sexual, psychological, and school problems were all caused by the fact that she had impure blood. Because of her own adolescent mistake, thought Mrs. Larsson, her daughter could never be a true Swede, like the Larsson family ancestors. Britt was doomed to be a hybrid of mixed blood, half of which derived from the Turkish/Mongol race. *God help her,* Mrs. Larsson sighed inwardly. *Whatever Britt has, I can't allow it to be passed on to future generations.*

Mrs. Larsson had wanted an abortion when she had found

out she was pregnant, but her parents, who were devout Lutherans, objected to their daughter's tampering with God's creation, no matter how poorly it might turn out. In retrospect, Mrs. Larsson felt that her parents had made a mistake. But this was her chance to rectify it. Her village doctor, like thousands of others in Sweden, held the same philosophy: if there was a genetic abnormality in the purity of the Nordic, it should not be passed on to subsequent generations. Mrs. Larsson was only following what doctors had been telling their patients since the early 1920's. Who was she, a simple person who had sinned, to contradict the recommendations of her doctor and experts he quoted who had done the scientific research to support their recommendations. In years to come, Britt would understand why they were in Vadstena; when she was a little older and more mature. For the moment, Mrs. Larsson consoled herself with the doctor's statement that the procedure for a "genetic correction," as he had called it, was painless and quick. This was the least that she, Mrs. Larsson, could do to assuage her own guilt.

"Mother," Britt protested loudly, "you're so old fashioned. Nowadays everyone wears contact lenses and sleeps with their boyfriends. We are not in the Victorian age."

"Shhh," Mrs. Larsson said, shaking her daughter by the shoulders. "Don't start one of your tantrums here, in front of the Abbey. God will never forgive you of your transgressions."

"Damn your God," Britt replied, "if he or she doesn't understand what it means to be a teenager with a mother like you and a father who ran away when I was born." Before the words were out of her mouth, Britt was ashamed of them. She loved her mother very deeply and knew that being a single parent had robbed her mother of a life of her own. Britt vowed silently to take more care with how she spoke to her mother. She could see that her mother was on the verge of tears.

The two women spotted the small dilapidated building

alongside the convent and knocked on the door. It was Dr. Eriksson himself who greeted them.

"You must be Mrs. Larsson," Eriksson said, in a mellifluous tone that could have charmed all the hidden vermin in the sewers of Stockholm, "and this beautiful girl, I presume must be your daughter, Britt, about whom your physician spoke so highly." He extended his hand to each of them and invited them into the entry room. "Please come in, but don't let some of the ancient artifacts that you see in the next room disturb you. Unfortunately, we are so limited in space, the only way we can operate this clinic is to incorporate a museum of medicine into it."

"It's so kind of you to see us," Mrs. Larsson replied, awed by the imposing figure—this nationally famous physician. Whatever doubts she may have had beforehand completely disappeared in his presence.

"The pleasure is all mine," Eriksson said, staring at the beautiful teenager before him, whose features and skin tones made it clear that she was not truly Swedish. While he couldn't change the fact that she was a hybrid, he knew he could save the future generation from the same mistake that her mother had made. The only question was how to make the girl feel comfortable, whom he was sure had not been told the real reason she was there.

Britt was also taken by Dr. Eriksson's handsome face and his tall, imposing bearing. Any fears she had walked in with began to attenuate.

"Britt, your doctor has informed me of some of your most recent physical problems. And those at home, at school, with boys . . . But those will soon be things of the past. The procedure I will do," Eriksson said in his most reassuring voice, "will be painless and quick, as long as you help me out."

Eriksson led them to his sparsely furnished office, containing little more than an examining table and instrument stand, an operating tray, and several wooden chairs he had borrowed from the museum and planned to return the next day. Eriksson had made certain that the room was bereft of any sights or smells that might indicate that this was, in fact, a small, well-equipped, surgical unit.

"We both appreciate the time you have taken from your busy schedule to see us," Mrs. Larsson said, trying to lessen any vestige of guilt she still harbored.

"Your general practitioner informed me that you are experiencing irregular menstrual cycles, and terrible pains throughout the week of your menses. Is that correct?" Dr. Eriksson tried to sound empathic.

"My gynecologist at home doesn't understand my complaints," Britt stated, "that's why my other doctor sent me to you."

"You may stay in the room with your daughter," Eriksson said to Mrs. Larsson, but focused his attention on the procedure to come that would continue a noble Swedish tradition and insure his immortality in Swedish history. The sterilization of Britt Larsson.

"If you don't mind," Mrs. Larsson responded, "I will give you both your privacy and leave my daughter in your more than competent hands."

"That's very kind of you," Eriksson responded, showing her out of his office and pointing the way to his waiting room. In his experience, when presented with the opportunity to be present during the procedure, 95 percent of the mothers chose to leave. They didn't want to be part of what he was about to do.

Eriksson shut the office door and instructed Britt to undress and put on the blue cotton surgical gown he handed to her. When she was seated on the examining table he raised a pair of stirrups from its underside. "Please place your feet in these metal stirrups and slide down to the front of the table so that I may examine you."

Britt was momentarily confused, wondering why this type of examination was necessary when she had thought her problems were likely to be hormonal. "Is this going to be like my gynecological exam?" she asked, comforted somewhat by the fact that her gynecologist, a woman of great empathy and understanding had performed a similar procedure.

"Precisely so," Eriksson responded, placing latex gloves on both of his hands, and sprinkling them profusely with talcum powder. "You're not afraid, are you?"

"No," Britt replied honestly. "Not at all."

"Good. I will inform you of everything I do. First, I will insert my fingers into your vagina and examine it for any abnormalities. Then I will push them in a little further and examine your ovaries to establish that they are normal as well. That's the entire examination."

"OK," Britt responded, already counting the minutes until the examination was over.

Eriksson separated her labia and gently inserted his middle three fingers into her vagina. As his fingers explored her vagina, he made sure that he rubbed the talcum powder into every crease of her cervix, uterus, and ovaries. The powder would soon create such an inflammation that secondary scar tissue would be produced and . . . voila! . . . neither her cervix, uterus or ovaries could ever receive a live sperm again. In short, he was destroying her reproductive system with nature's own healing process—inflammation and scarring. The technique hardly ever failed. But just to make certain that her ovaries would never function properly, he inserted a long silver metal probe and gently rubbed it against the fallopian tubes, smashing both her ovaries. Then he took the metal probe and inserted it into the hole of the cervix, twisting it enough times to cause an inflammation later on, and possibly an infection. Secondary fiber tissue would soon grow and close off the uterus so that she could never bear children.

"It hurts!" Britt shouted.

"I'm so sorry," Eriksson was almost finished. He withdrew his gloved hand and added more talcum powder. One more insertion throughout her reproductive system, he thought, and the process of inflammation and fibrosis would definitely occur.

Eriksson took pride every time he sterilized an impure

Swedish woman, feeling part of the well-established, highly applauded program of sterilization that Sweden had initiated back in 1922. Sweden's two most famous sociologists, Gunnar and Alva Myrdal, both of whom had written pioneering books about race in the United States, were the Swedish government's official advocates of female sterilization as a way of lightening the economic and political burden of the welfare state. Between 1934 and 1974 over 64,000 Swedish women had been sterilized for such reasons as poor eyesight, possible mental retardation, and incorrigible behavior. Many of the women were sterilized at the hands of the state, often against their will. This state-sponsored sterilization of Swedish women, Eriksson remembered with pride, was part of a national program grounded in the science of racial biology and carried out by officials who believed they were helping to build a more progressive, enlightened welfare state.

What made the national sterilization program even more compelling was the fact that there was nothing secret about it. It was carried out with full publicity at a time when Swedes believed that they were creating a society that would be the envy of the world.

The sterilization program had had its roots in the study of eugenics, whose advocates believed in the potential of human engineering to create a superior race. Sweden, rather than Germany, was the first country to establish an institute on racial biology in 1922, and enacted its first law authorizing sterilization for the mentally ill in 1934. By then, Germany, Denmark, and Norway had similar laws. Even the sanctimonious United States, Eriksson remembered, had sterilized its poor blacks and whites, as well as patients in its mental institutions. But Sweden was different, Eriksson thought, because it was seen by the world as a country with enlightened attitudes toward its weakest citizens.

In 1941, the law in Sweden was broadened to include sterilization not only for reasons of mental incompetence, but for what was considered antisocial behavior. The new law dramatically increased the number of sterilizations from

235 in 1935 to 2000 per year through the late 1950s. It was unfortunate, Eriksson thought, that the law was abolished in 1974 as a result of the growing women's rights movements.

Although the idea behind it was racial, its implementation was based more on economics and social behavior. Even as late as 1963, people of mixed race were subjected to sterilization. Eriksson knew all too well that it was still being practiced for the same reasons that the politicians argued for it twenty years before. It was a way of holding down the costs of an enlarging welfare state, especially in families with antisocial behavior. For the most part, the women were forced into it if they came from a reform school or mental institution, encouraged to sign a document authorizing the procedure if they wanted early release. In one recent court case, a couple judged to be "inferior" parents were sterilized, as were their children when they became teenagers. In another case, a young girl who had not mastered her confirmation studies well enough was ordered sterilized by her priest. And then there was the sterilization case of the girl who was mentally retarded but, years later, turned out to be merely in need of glasses.

Perhaps it was timely, thought Eriksson, that poor economic conditions in the country were forcing the true patriots of Sweden to return to the well-tested procedures of previous years in order to decrease the economic burden of the welfare state and to preserve its inherently Swedish integrity.

"Are we finished yet?" Britt asked, realizing that Eriksson had long ago stopped probing her insides.

"Of course, my dear," Eriksson replied, "you can get dressed now. You can tell your mother that everything will be fine."

8

STOCKHOLM, SWEDEN

A great Swedish pundit once described Stockholm as a noncity. "It is ridiculous of it to think of itself as a city. It is simply a rather large village, set in the middle of some forests and some lakes. You wonder what it thinks it is doing there, looking so important."

Although Carter had been in over sixty countries around the world, he had never been to Sweden, Denmark, or Norway. Despite the fact that a sizable percentage of any group of Foreign Service Officers (FSOs) might be of Scandinavian origin, Scandinavia was never the topic of any medical, economic, or political discussion. It was as if the Scandinavian countries had disappeared from the intellectual radar of U.S. foreign policy experts. Other than for occasional joint military maneuvers and a continued surveillance for Russian submarines around Bergen, Norway, the Scandinavian countries had no major significance in American foreign policy. Even their large domestic constituency in the Midwest was unable to give those countries saliency in America.

Carter took out his Frommer's guidebook on the way to the Grand Hotel from Stockholm's Arlanda Airport. He laughed to himself, wondering whether any Americans knew that many of the travel guide writers of the 1940's, 50's, and 60's used their positions as a cover for intelligence gathering for the Central Intelligence Agency. Researching a travel guide offered the Directorate of Operations (DO), the chief of covert operations, an opportunity to place his operatives in a country with a legitimate cover. During the Cold War, individuals in only a few professions were granted visas to restricted areas in the Soviet Union and the eastern bloc countries. One of those professions was writer for a guidebook or travel magazine.

It wasn't that the host country wasn't aware of this possibility when granted a visa. It simply made it a lot easier for everyone involved in the spy business to know who they were following and what access he might be allowed. Occasionally the host country would arrest a travel writer for possessing pictures that comprised national security—of a disguised ammunition factory, an unmarked airstrip, a cluster of military barracks. Eventually, there would be an informal negotiation between the publishers of the travel guide or magazine and the intelligence service of the host country. And, of course, like anything else, the bottom line was always the same. How much money would be required to release the agent? Which photographs would he be allowed to take with him?

But those days were gone. The Cold War, spies, counterintelligence, sensitive information, were all atavistic memorabilia from the past. Like the KGB service medals awarded at their fiftieth, sixtieth, and seventieth anniversary celebrations that Carter was able to buy at a small store in Greenwich Village, everyone would soon be trading the medals, certificates, and classified papers garnered from the United States government warehouses.

But sometimes a guidebook is just a guidebook. And the beauty of the countryside surrounding Stockholm was not lost on Carter. By nature, Carter was not cognizant of natural beauty. When he skied at Jackson Hole, Wyoming, the Grand Tetons were little more than what the French words denoted, "grand breasts." He barely noticed the rugged whitecapped peaks. When someone at the Rockefeller Lodge spotted a moose, Carter couldn't be less interested in the fuss being made over the siting. In Juneau, the capital of Alaska, he had a hard time appreciating the charms of the nineteenth-century wood-framed buildings, earmarked as historical landmarks. The Red Dog Saloon, supposedly Alaska's most famous bar, was nothing more than a glorified tourist trap as far as Carter was concerned. Nor was he impressed by the nondescript Alaska State Capitol, made from pillars of southeastern Alaska marble, or the five-story totem pole standing alongside the House of Wickersham. Only the grandeur of the peaks and valleys of the Denali National Park and Preserve, comprising more than six million acres of wildlife awed him. By disposition or choice, he was still unable to enjoy the wonders of the Dall sheep winding their way along the dizzying slopes, or grizzly bears "fishing" in streams. In short, it would be safe to say that he was not a nature lover.

Yet he found the city of Stockholm an unusual blend of natural beauty and unique architecture. The city's fourteen islands, marking the beginning of an archipelago of twenty-four thousand islands, skerries, and islets that stretched all the way to the Baltic Sea, sparkled in the sunlight across waterways as far as the eye could see. The land areas contained bridges, towers, steeples, cobblestone squares, Renaissance mansions, steel-and-glass skyscrapers, and broad boulevards like the Champs-Elysées in Paris. One could even fish from one of the downtown bridges, thanks to an edict by Queen Christina.

Before proceeding to Vadstena, where Dr. Eriksson had his home and office, Carter hoped to play sightseer and absorb a sense of the Swedish heritage. The guidebook suggested walking through Gamla Stan, the Old Town, an area of historic buildings and winding alleyways dating from 1252. Two museums were suggested, the Royal Palace, containing the Swedish crown jewels and the Royal Armory, and Drottningholm Palace, home of the royal family. *Perhaps,* thought Carter, *I could actually be a tourist for a day.*

The taxi stopped in front of the Grand Hotel and Carter

tipped the driver generously. Since the doorman was watching, as was the Bell Captain, word would soon spread throughout the hotel that Carter was someone who would pay handsomely for service. Having lived in hotels for long periods, Carter understood the culture exceedingly well. And the size of the tips he spread around spoke far more loudly than the age of his jeans and the wrinkles in his T-shirts.

The first-class tags on his luggage would always be noticed by those seeking to serve the customer. But he only hinted at what the hotel's employees might imagine him to be, never revealing what he did for a living or why he was staying at the hotel. Mystery, combined with discrete tipping, were the lubricants that made Carter's stay in any hotel a singular experience.

The Grand Hotel was grand in both name and execution. The lobby reeked with a clear message that this was a bastion of old money. Rich mahogany woods. Ornate plaster friezes. Persian carpets. Antique furniture from all over the world. The hotel's ballroom was not original, but a copy of Louis XIV's Hall of Mirrors at Versailles. Since 1874, the Wallenberg family, one of the wealthiest families in Sweden, had maintained the hotel's place in Europe's tradition of grand, historic hotels.

After a magnificent set of public rooms, Carter's bedroom was disappointing. While it was elegantly appointed in the old tradition, it lacked air-conditioning and the modern bathroom conveniences that were commonplace in the U.S. So much for facades.

He tipped the bellman and decided to unpack later on. He was hungry and it was time to try the hotel's Swedish Smörgåsbord, for which the country was famous.

Carter entered the Grand Veranda, the lobby dining room which overlooked a harbor peopled with tourists waiting for ferries to the other islands, and was seated at a table for two toward the back of the room.

"Good evening, sir," the waiter said, "would you like to start the meal with something to drink?"

"Aquavit, please," Carter responded, having heard so

much about Sweden's national drink. He noticed the dark good looks of the waiter. Probably from somewhere in the Middle East, he thought.

"Yes, sir," the waiter responded.

As Carter read the menu he broke out into a raucous laugh.

"I like a man who knows how to amuse himself," commented a brown-haired woman standing beside his table.

Mid-thirties, he thought, looking up at her. Dressed in an understated way, with a pale blue sweater under a suede jacket. Angular with very intelligent, deep-set brown eyes. Not what Carter would consider typically Swedish. Neither blonde-haired, blue-eyed, or svelte. But there was something about her alabaster skin and slightly protruding chin that made her look as if she were chiseled from polished granite. She was also an iota short of seeming brazen.

"My name is Linda Watson," she said in perfect English. She held out her hand to shake his. "And I'm afraid that this chair opposite you is the only spot available for a single diner for the next hour. Would it inconvenience you if I shared your table?"

"Not at all," Carter lied. He stood up and shook her hand, clearly taken aback by her sudden presence. By temperament, Carter was distrustful of serendipitous meetings. But he was willing to see where this one would lead him. Whatever Linda was about, it certainly didn't appear to be about sex. She was straightforward to a fault. If he didn't know any better, he would swear that this woman was an American from the midwest with Swedish ancestry.

"Please sit down," Carter motioned her to sit opposite him. "My name is Alison Carter."

"That's a lovely name," Linda said, making herself comfortable. She turned toward the waiter, "May I also have an aquavit."

"Thank you," Carter replied, flushing at the unusual compliment. "No one generally compliments me on my name."

"What's in a name?" Linda asked laughingly. "I gather that, like myself, you are an American."

"Yes," Carter said, "I'm from Washington D.C." As she took off her jacket, Carter quickly assessed her physique. She appeared to be in good shape, probably working out the obligatory three times a week to keep her cardiovascular system going strong.

"I'm from Ann Arbor, Michigan," she responded, "the home of the famous Wolverines."

"Go Blue!" Carter responded, with the only football jargon he knew.

"Don't tell me!" Linda reached over, excitedly, "you're also a University of Michigan graduate?"

"No," Carter replied, "I'm afraid I didn't have that honor. Even if I had gotten in, I am certain that I would have frozen to death after the first semester."

"Oh come on now," Linda said, "I'm sure you're made of sterner stuff than that. When I lived with my aunt in the northern part of Michigan, right around Alpina, we considered Ann Arbor the Miami Beach of Michigan, because it was always thirty degrees warmer down there."

"Do you work there?" he asked, in an effort to steer the conversation away from himself. No matter how sweet or innocent a person looked, Carter was always leery of strangers who asked questions. A professional hazard.

"I'm in the automobile industry," she replied, matter-of-factly.

"You are the president of General Motors?" Carter asked sarcastically, "Ford? Chrysler?"

"Not quite at that level," she responded, not appreciating his sarcasm, "but not too far from that level."

He was impressed. She had deflected his comment well and responded with a sharp but modest retort.

"Then, you must be . . . ?"

". . . the Executive Vice President of the Automobile Manufacturers Association. We have offices all over the world, including Washington D.C."

"A lobbying group?"

"Something like that," she replied. "We advise our members on how to achieve a competitive advantage in the international markets, despite the heavy subsidies going into their own industries by foreign governments."

"So you must be on the road constantly." He was beginning to feel his sugar level drop and glanced over to the Smörgåsbord table.

"I'll tell you what," she said with a broad smile that made her look like a commercial for wholesomeness, "I'm going to stop talking so that both you and I can start eating."

They walked over to a table that looked as if a cornucopia of Swedish delights had just been spilled in front of them.

"May I be so bold as to ask you whether you have ever had a Smörgåsbord—in Sweden?"

"You may be as bold as you like," Carter responded, "This is my first time in Sweden, and I am open to all suggestions. Especially from a Wolverine."

"Listen carefully," Linda said, handing him a plate, "the key to a successful dinner is to sample broadly but eat selectively. If you fill up on any one item, I guarantee that you'll miss the true uniqueness of this dining experience."

"Okay, coach," Carter said with enthusiasm. "I'm all yours." There was something infectious about the way she took charge of the situation and yet was considerate of his needs.

"In my previous incarnation." Linda continued, "I was a junior high school teacher. So if I sound a little pedantic, please don't take offense. It's just an old habit that annoys some people."

"I'm all ears," Carter said, "and stomach."

"The best way to enjoy a Smörgåsbord is to follow seven simple rules."

"Seven?" Carter asked incredulously.

"It sounds worse than it really is," Linda replied, laughing. "Rule number one: Think of the Swedish Smörgåsbord as a four-to-six course meal." She paused to make sure he was paying attention. "Rule number two: Don't overload your plate each time you return to the food table. Rule number three: Begin with the herring dishes, traditionally accompanied by hot potatoes. Then try a slice of sharp Swedish cheese on crisp bread, and a shot of aquavit chased with cold Scandinavian beer."

"So far so good. I'm there with you."

"Rule four: Sample the fish dishes and try the Swedish specialty—gravlax, or marinated salmon. Don't forget the mustard sauce with dill. Try the smoked eel and salmon with a squeeze of lemon."

"Sounds delicious to me."

"Rule five: For the next course, sample a variety of salads, egg dishes, and cold cuts of meat and fowl. Rule six: Then take your pick of the hot dishes—and remember to take some lingonberries with your meatballs."

"Are you sure that a normal human being can eat all of this?"

"Trust me," Linda replied, "this is the only way to really appreciate what Sweden is all about. But I haven't finished. We have the final course, the dessert. Rule seven: If you want something light, eat fruit salad. And then complete the meal with a strong hot coffee with that chilled traditional Swedish digestive, punsch."

"All right, let's start, coach," Carter said, impressed by her knowledge. Clearly, she had spent a lot of time in Sweden.

With herring and potatoes on their plates, Carter and Linda returned to their table.

"Before we begin the meal," Linda raised her glass of aquavit. "We must toast each other in Swedish. *Skäl!*"

"*Skäl!*" Carter raised his glass toward Linda. As he did, he glanced out of the restaurant window at the setting sun and was startled by a familiar face walking by quickly. Mack Londsdale.

9

STOCKHOLM, SWEDEN

The city was aglow in a Van Gogh palette of a swirling orange-red sky, yellow headlights racing through the blackening summer's night, and darkening brown tree trunks sinking quietly into Lake Mälaren. Carter was overwhelmed by the picturesque beauty of Stockholm as he and Linda walked over Centralbron Bridge. He now wondered why visiting this city had never seemed high on his list. The grandeur of the eighteenth- and nineteenth-century architecture, set around a series of romantic harbors, was more exhilarating than San Francisco, New York City, or Washington, D.C. And what made the city even more impressive was the fact that everything Carter had seen of Stockholm in this short period of time seemed to contradict the classical stereotype of the aloof and sedate Swedish national character. The hotel staff, admittedly service-oriented, were pleasant, outgoing, and seemed genuinely hospitable.

"Is the city always this beautiful?" Carter asked, stopping for a moment to allow his eyes to wander across the varied rooftops.

"You're here at just the right time," Linda replied, turning up the collar of her jacket. "June, July, and August are the best months to be in Sweden. The days are finally warm and the sun doesn't go down till after ten pm."

"And winter?"

"Forget about it!" Linda responded. "The sun rises at about five A.M. and starts to go down about eleven A.M. By mid-afternoon this entire city is pitch-black."

"Sounds depressing."

"Don't let this natural beauty fool you," Linda said in an almost ominous tone of voice.

"What do you mean?"

"Sweden has one of the highest alcoholic and suicide rates in the world," Linda replied matter-of-factly. "Apparently, the early darkness effects the psyche. Boredom, depression . . ."

"You mean 'cabin fever' sets in and the way they handle it is with drinking and suicide," Carter added.

"The days are short and the nights are long."

"So what do you do with yourself?" Carter asked coyly.

"Well, I wouldn't know, Mr. Carter," Linda answered, "since I'm not Swedish."

"I have a feeling that you know a lot more about Sweden than you let on," Carter responded. He sensed a well-honed *savoir-faire* and a self-containment that bespoke a personal maturity far beyond her age. If he had to guess her real occupation, he would place her as some sort of intel operative—CIA, DIA, ONI, or NSA. The expansiveness of the knowledge she exhibited at dinner, and the breadth of her travels, was far beyond what was called for in whatever she claimed to be doing for the Automobile Manufacturers Association.

"Perhaps," she responded, "but I wouldn't say that at this point in our relationship either one of us can make much of a balanced judgment about the other."

"Touché," Carter replied.

"Speaking of verbosity," she added, "wouldn't you say that you rank pretty low? I hardly know anything about you."

"Guilty as charged," Carter pleaded.

They strolled down the cobblestone streets of Gamla Stan, surrounded by cluttered antique stores selling fine furniture, bookstores selling first editions, and restaurants extending into narrow streets and alleys with tables and chairs crowded with diners. The sidewalks were filled with young couples strolling hand-in-hand, amusing each other as only young lovers can do.

"What would you like to know?" Carter responded, with a matter-of-fact tone. "My name is Alison Carter. I'm a physician who works in Washington, D.C. and I am here on holiday."

"That was very good, Alison Carter," Linda said, clapping her hand, as if she were a approving schoolteacher.

"That bad, huh?"

"C-"

"Okay," Carter continued with a mocking voice, "I was born and grew up in New York City and went to Columbia University for both undergraduate and medical school."

"Now we're getting somewhere," Linda retorted, "But you don't act like a typical New Yorker."

"What does a typical New Yorker act like?"

"Oh, there is this sense of entitlement, arrogance, brashness..." Linda stopped, "You're embarrassing me."

"Why?"

"I sound like one of those Midwest hicks with all their prejudices about a big city."

"If it makes you feel any better," Carter said, smiling, "I graduated from medical school in my mid-twenties and left New York at the invitation of my kind uncle. So, I had a good twenty-five years to eliminate what vestiges there were of my 'big city ways.'"

"You went to live with your uncle?"

"Yes," Carter tried to maintain a straight face. "Uncle Sam was kind enough to invite me overseas for a couple of years so that I could experience the world. He was extremely generous. He paid for everything..."

"Very funny," Linda interrupted, "I bet he even paid for your education."

"And my captain's uniform," Carter added, "as well as any medical supplies I might need to treat several thousand young boys who had their legs, arms, and parts of their skulls blown away."

"It was that bad?"

"I detest war and violence," Carter paused. He hoped she would believe him. Those awful years were probably some of his most formative ones, despite what Dr. Spock said. They directed him to his "second" profession. "That's why I went into medicine."

So you practice medicine in order to cure and heal," Linda mused. "Do you work for yourself or for some managed care outfit?"

"You could say that I work for a form of managed care," Carter responded. He sensed that if he divulged too much, she would try to press him for more details than he was willing to share. While she was very attractive to him, he still didn't trust her.

"Let's look over here." Linda pulled him toward a storefront with a sign that announced "Antique and Rare Books." "There's a first edition of a hardback book that's out of print."

"Which one?" he asked.

"It's that one in the corner," she said, trying to point under and over the piles of objects and books.

"You mean Tom Clancy's *Hunt for Red October?*"

"Yes," Linda said. "I read it in paperback and loved it. But my father, who was a submarine commander, has always wanted the original hardback. I've tried to buy it for him as a birthday present, but it's hard to find."

"Perhaps you're in luck," Alison responded. "If it's in this store, it's probably The Naval Institute Press edition. It's been almost twenty years since that first came out."

"But if I'm reading the right sign," Linda said, "the book costs eight hundred fifty dollars. Ugh."

"Still want to buy it?"

"I think I'll come around tomorrow when the store opens and see if I can't negotiate the price down," Linda responded. "And I'll read it for the third time before I turn it over to my father."

"Isn't it a little too hi-tech for you?"

"Don't tell me you still believe that old male stereotype," Linda responded. "I love all of Clancy's works. Don't you think it's possible for a woman to understand all that technical stuff, as well as appreciate a well-written story?"

"Touché again, Linda," he responded. She was obviously her own person. But she didn't fit the stereotype of the female lobbyist. She seemed straightforward in what she said—none of the doublespeak he had to deal with in his failed marriage. With the women he currently dated, frequently lawyers, a predominat species in Washington, D.C., he always felt that he needed an interpreter. While he wasn't naive or inexperienced, talking with women was a game for which he was still not well suited.

"You're staring at me, Alison," Linda said smiling. "Is there something that I should know. Is my proverbial slip showing?"

"No," Carter said, his face turning red.

"How charming," Linda said, lightly touching his face, "A man who still blushes. And I believe that's the second time tonight."

"I was just thinking how easy it is to talk to you," Carter responded, as if he believed what he was saying. "There don't seem to be any hidden agendas with you." He wondered whether she would believe him.

"My dear Dr. Carter," she said, "never tell a woman who is trying to flirt with a handsome man that she doesn't have a hidden agenda. It reveals either your naivete or, if I had a more colorful imagination, a Machiavellian-like approach to seducing me with disingenuous flattery."

Carter laughed, enjoying the bantering. She was well-read, observant, and definitely a woman who could catch him off guard.

"And talking about a good storyteller," Linda continued, "no one is a better storyteller and language manipulator than an experienced woman who is on the hunt . . . although she might seem completely genuine."

"I don't believe this!" Carter smirked incredulous.

"What don't you believe, Doctor?"

"That you . . ." he was unable to complete the sentence. He felt a little like a teenager at his most awkward moment.

"Okay," Linda said, stopping in an alleyway between two restaurants, "allow me the indulgence of resuming my previous schoolteacher role and giving you a lesson on the basics of communicating with any woman, no matter how sweet and innocent she might appear."

"I'm all ears."

"Lesson One. When a woman says 'yes' she means 'no.'"

"Why?"

"Forget the 'why's,'" Linda answered, "and just memorize the basics. Later, we'll get into epistemology. Are we in agreement?"

"All the way, teach!

"Good," Linda continued. "Lesson Two is the converse. 'No' means 'yes.' Understood?"

Carter nodded.

"'Maybe' frequently means 'no.' Subtle, but important."

"Got it!"

"'I'm sorry' means 'you'll be sorry.' 'We need' equals 'I want.' Very important. Most women have a very hard time expressing their personal desires no matter how sophisticated they may appear."

"I have a feeling that doesn't apply to you," Carter interjected.

"Don't be so certain," Linda responded. "Let's continue. I've lost track of which lesson we're on. But 'its your decision' means 'the correct decision should be obvious by now.' And here's the *pièce de résistance,* 'Do what you want' means 'you'll pay for this later.'" Linda stopped, wondering whether it was time to change the subject.

Carter stood, waiting for her to go on.

"This one is a doozy: 'go ahead' means, 'I don't want you to.' And how about this: 'I'm not upset' means 'of course I'm upset, you moron.'"

"And I thought that the National Security Agency encryption code was complicated," Carter laughed.

Linda smiled affectionately and locked her arms around his neck.

Carter stood looking at her, not knowing whether to respond to her unexpected tenderness.

"Since I've got you captive," Linda added, "I'll give you a few of the male's cryptic communications patterns."

"I'm all ears," he laughed, pleased with her forthrightness.

"When a man says 'I'm hungry,'" she asked, "what does he mean?"

"As far as I know," Carter replied, "there is nothing subtle about men or the way they converse."

"Don't be so smart," Linda responded. "What does it mean?"

"As far as I know," Carter answered, when a man says 'I'm hungry' it means, precisely that, 'I'm hungry.'"

"'I'm sleepy'?" she asked.

"'I'm sleepy!'"

"Good!" she said, "you're a fast learner. 'I'm tired'?"

"'I'm tired!'"

"'Do you want to go to the movie?'"

"'I'd eventually like to have sex with you!'"

"Excellent!" she declared.

"I'd like to go back to the hotel," Carter said matter-of-factly.

"Are you telling me that you would like to have sex with me at the hotel?" she asked coyly, pulling him closer.

"That depends on whether you are the man or woman talking."

"Shut up!" she said, whispering in his ear. "You talk too much!"

10

STOCKHOLM, SWEDEN

Linda and Carter walked down Stora Nygatan mulling over the proposition that they had jokingly made about returning to the hotel. When Linda's arm fell to Carter's waist she felt a bulge on the side of his hip.

"What is that?" she asked playfully. "A cell phone?"

"Not quite," Carter responded, "but it is an apparatus for communicating one's feelings."

"My God," Linda said, "Now aren't we waxing philosophical. I bet it's one of those miniature Ericssons."

Carter removed her hand from around his waist.

"Touchy, touchy," she added.

"Why do you always have to create problems that don't exist?"

"Because I like to play on the edge," Linda replied, "and I like my men that way too."

As they walked in an awkward silence back toward Centralbron bridge, they saw a crowd milling in front of them.

"I think someone is hurt," Linda said, rushing forward.

"Just take it easy, Florence Nightingale," Carter responded, trying to restrain her. The last thing he wanted to do was get involved in someone else's fight. And he was convinced that a fight had just broken out. The group in front of them consisted of predominantly young males and the whole scene was more ominous than Linda imagined. Exactly the type of situation that Carter had to avoid.

"Look at what those thugs are doing," Linda said frantically.

Three blond-haired youths wearing black leather jackets with the blue and yellow flag of Sweden pasted on their backs, and wielding thick metal chains, were lacing into four dark-skinned, dark-haired teenagers. The victims were bloodied and cowering against a brick wall for whatever protection it afforded. Each time they were hit their hands reached out too late to protect various parts of their body. Fighting back was impossible. Blood was running down the street. The scene reminded Carter of a slaughterhouse he had once toured where carcasses were being stripped of their flesh.

The blond youths continued, encouraged by their feverishly screaming cohorts, yelling at the top of their lungs in both Swedish and English, " 'Foreigners are no longer welcome in Sweden!' 'Go back home!' 'You're not wanted here.' "

"Alison," Linda said, pushing her way through the gathering crowd, "we've got to do something to stop this."

In the distance, Carter noticed three policemen dressed in dark blue uniforms with striped epaulettes on their shoulders, simply looking on the scene as if they were uninterested bystanders.

"Let's call the police," Carter responded, leaving Linda and walking toward them. "Officers, I think we need your help over there. Several teenagers are being brutally beaten by that gang of thugs." The officers had an arrogance about them, as if they knew precisely what Carter wanted from them but couldn't care less.

"I'm sorry, would you please repeat what you just said," the captain said smilingly, "you see, we don't speak English too well."

"Several Swedish teenagers are beating the hell out of four other kids." Carter said slowly, quickly making the assessment that, for whatever reason, the police were not going to interfere. "I think it would be extremely helpful if you were to break up the fight and arrest those hooligans."

"Hooligans?" the lieutenant, a short man with a crew cut repeated the word. "What is 'hooligans'?"

"Bullies, guys who think they are tough," Carter responded impatiently. It was very clear that they were stringing him along. "So you guys just stand around and watch a bunch of punks kick the crap out of some poor helpless kids? Is this an example of what is referred to as the famous 'Swedish neutrality'?" He paused and added for emphasis, "You just sit around while the others do the fighting?"

"I would be careful with my choice of words," the captain replied, brusquely. "You could find yourself in jail for obstructing police in their line of duty."

"Now, isn't it amazing how quickly you learned to speak such beautiful English, Captain..." Carter said, leaning closer to see his identification badge. "... Carl Hansson." The other two officers simply stared at him, without a smile. "So, what you're telling me by not helping out is that you don't really give a shit, do you?"

"There are rules in the officer's manual which prohibit an individual from using profane language in public, especially in the presence of an officer of the law," Captain Hansson replied.

"If you're not going to stop the fight," Carter interjected with hostility, "then maybe it wouldn't be too much to ask you to call for an ambulance. Because you are going to have several seriously hurt kids who are going to need immediate medical attention."

"Again, we appreciate your concern," Captain Hansson said, trying not to be provoked, "but we've already summoned an ambulance. It should be here in a few minutes. In Stockholm, ambulances are very scarce at this time of the evening."

"That's not the only thing that's scarce in Stockholm," Carter said sarcastically as he walked away. "So are compassion and caring."

"Good night, sir, and have a pleasant stay in Sweden," Captain Hansson cried out after him.

Carter pushed his way through the screaming crowd and saw that the helpless teenagers were completely prostrate and one of the thugs was using his thick belt to extract more bruises, blood, and screams. Linda was in the thick of it, pummeling the attacker with her fists. She already had several lacerations around her face.

"Get out of there, Linda!" Carter ordered, taking off his jacket and wrapping it around his left arm. From the carrying case on the side of his belt he produced the knife which Linda had thought was a cell phone, a souvenir he had gotten at Fort Pendleton, California, while on an official visit to the Marine base. It was a specially designed knife with a razor-sharp serrated blade used by police officers to cut seat belts in a traffic emergency, to release the trapped victim from the car. Among professional assassins, it was the weapon of choice for close combat because when properly used, one could completely disable an opponent with only the slightest effort. Carter was extremely proficient but always reluctant to use this knife unless it was absolutely necessary.

The click of the blade swinging open, so quickly and elegantly, drew sounds of fear from the thugs. Carter caught a thick leather belt in midair, as it moved from a teenager toward him, deflecting the blow with his protected left arm. With an almost ballet-like movement, Carter grabbed another attacker and nicked both his shoulder blades with several swift slices of his knife, incapacitating him. Had Carter wanted to be lethal, he would have applied just a bit more pressure, a little closer to the young man's throat, and severed both of the boy's carotid arteries.

"Behind you, Carter!" Linda shouted, as the thug with the chain attempted to fling it downward with the full force of his body, against Carter's back.

But Carter had heard the sound of the chain as it was being raised and quickly stepped aside. Crouching on his knees, knife in hand, he sliced his assailant along both kneecaps, making deep cuts across his lateral ligaments. When the fellow buckled to the ground in agonizing pain, the third attacker, who had been standing on the sidelines, frightened by what he had seen, motioned to the fourth attacker for some help. Despite his shouts of encouragement none was forthcoming. He yelled something in Swedish, pulled out a gun, and pointed it directly at Carter's head. "Throw down the knife!" he demanded.

This was a situation Carter had rehearsed any number of times in his head. Be it the nurturance of life, or the execution of death, a professional had to perfect a methodology of thinking and reacting so that all of his responses had an internal logic, consistency, and effectiveness. In this case, the methodology of survival required that he first evaluate his opponent. What was his mental status? Was he intent on killing Carter or just threatening him? Was he driven by fear? Carter made the quick determination that his attacker was both enraged and frightened, and could kill him because of the frustration and shame he felt. That actually gave Carter an advantage in being able to distract him with quick, unexpected moves.

Then Carter had to evaluate his own situation. Was he capable of overpowering the assailant? No, not in this case, he concluded. Could Carter's actions endanger the people gathered around him? Carter decided that he had very little room to maneuver and that the probability of collateral damage was very great. Was time on his side? Looking at the agitated state of his attacker, he realized that he could string him out for only a few more minutes. There was no possibility of negotiating him out of firing his revolver.

OK. So what type of gun was he holding and what were the most effective ways of disabling it? Optimum Standard Operating Procedure required an assessment of how much training the gunman had and what type of gun he was preparing to use. Was the revolver a double action auto, single action shot or SMG? Was the weapon cocked? Was the weapon in a state of good repair? All of these flashed through Carter's mind in a nanosecond and all had some bearing on his

ACTIVE MEASURES

chances of coming out of the situation alive. As best as Carter could tell, his attacker was using a cheap .38 Smith & Wesson with a revolving magazine.

From his twenty years of experience, Carter knew that a gunman can be disarmed before he can pull the trigger, providing the distance from his intended victim is short and the defensive move made is quick. When initiating a disarming move, Carter could have an advantage of .2-.5 of a second over his adversary.

Instantaneously, Carter shifted his body away from the line of fire and deflected his assailant's gun hand upward as the gun went off. Carter twisted the assailant's other hand and broke his wrist. A swift kick in his left kidney forced him to the ground, writhing in pain and screaming for help. Carter grabbed the man's gun and emptied out the barrels.

"Call the hospital," Carter yelled to one of the assailant's buddies, "and tell them to X-ray his metatarsal and metacarpal bones for any potential fracture. And make certain that they do a urine analysis to see if his kidney has been damaged enough that he is spilling blood."

"Yes, sir!" one of the blond men with several rings through his nose and ears responded, as if he had been given and accepted a military command.

"And make certain that the ambulance takes the four guys you beat up," Carter added.

"Yes, sir!" the fellow responded with alacrity and fear.

"Otherwise, I will find you all..." Carter pointed his index finger at the youth, in an imaginary position of a gun. A little dramatic, thought Carter, but nevertheless, an effective message.

The blond assailant bent over his friend, trying to comfort him. "Everything will be done just as you ordered."

"Carter," Linda rushed up to him, "are you all right?"

"I'm fine," Carter responded nonchalantly, "now where were we?"

"Please put your hands up!" Captain Carl Hansson strode toward Carter, parting the already thinning crowd with his officers. "You are under arrest for possession of a lethal weapon and for having caused a major disturbance."

"I'm glad to see that you do perform your policeman's function, albeit with the wrong man," Carter responded facetiously, offering no resistance.

"Officer," Linda interjected, "there must be some mistake. We are simply tourists who happened to be passing by and witnessed this terrible fight. It was my friend, here, who was able to stop it."

"I admire you Americans," Captain Hansson replied, mockingly, "you never leave your buddies to die alone on the battlefield."

"At least we Americans, as you say, know who our buddies are," Carter responded, "unlike you Swedes, who seem to want to make friends with everyone—the good guys, the bad guys—making certain to profit from both of your friendships." Carter was immediately sorry for his outburst. The background information he had been provided with before coming to Sweden had already soured his feelings for the police.

"Thank you very much, Dr. Alison Carter, of the United States State Department," Captain Hansson replied, clamping handcuffs onto Carter's wrists, "but we Swedes do not like being preached to by so-called tourists. It creates a most uncomfortable situation—for all of us."

11

VADSTENA, SWEDEN

Early evening brought an unusual amount of traffic along the narrow cobblestone streets of Vadstena. It seemed as if most of the vehicles were converging on Mårten Skinnare's house, one of the oldest brick houses in town (circa 1520). Mårten, a rich merchant who had received commissions from the king, had fallen from grace before the former mental institution standing next to it had been built. The inside of his house was deceptively large. But what made its design of particular interest was a stairway leading to the cellar, and an extremely large vaulted room that led to a tunnel that, in turn, led directly into the museum and clinic housed in the former mental hospital.

People parked wherever they could and used either the house or museum entrance to enter the museum. There was an urgency in their steps, because no one wanted to miss the start of Dr. Eriksson's lecture. A few uniformed police were dispersed around the two properties to keep order. But there was little potential for disorder—Swedes were among the most law-abiding citizens in the world. They followed civil and military orders to the "t." Just like their presumed nemesis, the Germans.

Everything about the day had been perfect. The flowers were in bloom. The sky had been bright blue and clear. And the citizens of Vadstena had gone about their normal activities, ignoring the arrival of these strangers, as if this was just another day in their placid lives. But nothing could be further from the truth.

Following this spectacular day was an evening that Dr. Eriksson hoped would change the course of Swedish history, returning the country to its previous economic and political power. He, like most of his contemporaries, knew that Swedish neutrality during World War II was at best a myth, and at worst, a mockery of historical proportion. The collective national lie of "neutrality" was equivalent to that of the equally hypocritical Switzerland, which claimed that it had nothing to do with the Nazi war machinery. The Swiss had cleverly propagated the myth that Switzerland was too mountainous to be invaded by Hitler and that the Swiss army could easily defend itself against such an invasion and create insufferable losses for Hitler's forces. None of which was true, of course. Switzerland, as it was eventually discovered, had been a major conduit for the ill-gotten gains of the Germans and had even manufactured major artillery for the Nazi war machine. At the same time, it returned to the Nazis any Jewish refugees who sought asylum in the country on the pretext that it didn't want to alienate the German government and revoke its neutral status.

But that was not Eriksson's concern. He was interested in today's Sweden, and that foreigners and refugees who were swarming into the country legally and illegally were overburdening the welfare system and adding to the criminal population. Eriksson wanted Sweden to return to concerns that were *a priori* Swedish in nature, and not whether the country had enough money to support Kurdish, Afghan, African, and Balkan refugees. This evening he would explain his battle plan to rid the nation of all these "sub-human creatures." His arsenal would be intimidation, extortion, arson and torture. And the outcome, almost within sight, would be returning Sweden to the Swedes.

He looked at his audience, several hundred members of what he informally called his "silent shield," crowded in among ancient instruments of psychiatry—senior officials of the Swedish government, national and internal security organizations, as well as generally apolitical citizens. He hadn't decided where he would start his speech. With an account of the duplicity and betrayal Sweden had been involved in during World War II through a clever propaganda campaign? Or with the myth of Swedish "neutrality" and "humanitarianism"? All thanks to the efforts of small men like his father, and prosperous industrialist families like the Wallenbergs—a family considered by the international community to be "Righteous Gentiles." What a joke that was, Eriksson chuckled to himself. No family was more venal, duplicitous, and treasonous to the whole concept of "neutrality." Raoul Wallenberg was sanctified by the Israelis as a man who single-handedly saved thousands of Jewish refugees by defying the Nazi High Commander General August Schmidhuber and issuing passports to Jews fleeing the Holocaust. But the idea that Raoul Wallenberg was something of a superman who could single-handedly intimidate the Nazis in order to save the Jews was as close to fiction as one could get.

Thank goodness for the perversity of history and its malleable quality. It was nothing more than convenient for Sweden to declare it's "neutrality" during World War II, profiting handsomely from the declaration, certainly as much as Switzerland did. Very early on in the war, the Swedish government and King Gustav VI Adolf made a treacherous decision of historical proportions that completely violated its stated 1939 oath of neutrality. Even Eriksson's father thought it would haunt the country for decades to come. Eriksson recalled the day his father told him the "deep secret" that Sweden had allowed over four hundred thousand Nazi soldiers to cross its borders with impunity in order to attack Norway. As a result of this decision, thousands of Norwegians died and many cities, towns, and villages were completely decimated. Had it not been for intensive British and American pressure placed on the King and his senior government officials, and most importantly on the industrial oligarchy in 1943 and 1944, Sweden would have been officially declared a "Nazi ally," against whom the allies would have declared war.

The Wallenberg family were knee-deep into the war on the side of the Germans. One was financing the Nazi war machinery directly, as well as collecting Nazi funds that were "relocated" years later to South America. Another Wallenberg family member was manufacturing heavy artillery and ammunition for the Nazis. So, his father told Eriksson, it was no accident that Raoul Wallenberg was sent under the auspices of the International Red Cross, as well as the American intelligence service, the OSS, to "do something that would make the Wallenberg name appear humanitarian and heroic." Well, Raoul did what he was instructed to do, not as a point of conscience, Eriksson's father had said, but as a matter of maintaining the "integrity" of the family name.

Warned that its actions would lead to being considered a Nazi ally, and to compensate for its ignominious behavior during World War II, Sweden decided to allow in Jewish refugees from Denmark and several Slavic countries. Ironically, one of the major leaders of the newly founded United Nations was Dag Hammarskjold, Secretary General in 1953, who became a martyr and symbol for world peace after dying in an airplane crash on a routine UN trip.

Eriksson smiled inwardly. Swedish morality was all contrived myth and internal hypocrisy. Even Alfred Nobel, creator of the Nobel Peace Prize, invented and manufactured dynamite.

Eriksson noted that his audience was getting restless, but he was enjoying his own self-absorption in the paradoxes of Swedish history. If nothing else, these paradoxes allowed him to flourish. Since the seventeenth century, when Sweden was a warfaring nation, invading Russia, conquering Britain, and dominating Normandy, it had never really changed. Even under the guise of "neutrality" in World War II, it played off the Nazis, Soviets, British, Norwegians, and Americans, one against the other. Wasn't it conventional wisdom that France represented the embodiment of manipulation? What a joke, thought Eriksson. The Swedes were inherently aggressive, hypocritical, and extremely sanctimonious. The only difference between them and the rest of mankind was their incredible ability to portray themselves as a peaceful, bucolic, almost soporific country that was only concerned with their own internal affairs. And the portrayal had succeeded beyond anyone's wildest expectations.

Eriksson decided it was time to begin his talk. Like Hitler, he knew he was charismatic in front of an audience. Soon, he would reveal his master plan. With significant representation on Götaland, the southern part of Sweden, Svealand, the central region, and Norrland, the northern part, he would be able to execute his plan within the coming months. But first he had to rid himself of an intruding American who had already created some problems for himself in Stockholm.

12

STOCKHOLM, SWEDEN

The United States embassy in Stockholm was designed with a minimal amount of attention paid to security. The reason was obvious. Stockholm was not considered a dangerous city and Sweden was not one of the group of countries designated as a strategic American ally. Other than a large Scandinavian constituency living in the American Midwest, for all practical purposes, Sweden was not even on the radar screen of the American foreign policy apparatus. It was one of those countries the State Department took for granted.

As a matter of fact, Sweden was considered an assignment usually given to political appointments who had donated generously in the previous presidential campaign. The ambassadorship to Sweden was rarely given to the professional Foreign Service Officer (FSO), but was usually held out as a plum assignment to the well-heeled American businessman (rarely businesswoman). For him, it could be an exotic experience, a time to recharge. Whether he be a real estate developer, publishing magnate, or toy manufacturer, to be identified as the Honorable Ambassador so-and-so for life was difficult to resist. It could also be worth a small fortune after leaving the post. The title of Ambassador was one of those frivolous accoutrements of the very wealthy that money could literally buy, and by doing so, erase a countless number of sins of doing business.

Carter vehemently opposed the long-standing tradition that the President of the United States could directly appoint approximately thirty percent of the ambassadors as a payoff for contributions to his political party or, even more venal, for monies given directly to the presidential campaign. The entire appointment practice reeked of cronyism, corruption, and was extremely demoralizing to the professional Foreign Service, who were selected strictly on the basis of both an extremely difficult exam and an equally difficult oral examination by a Board of Senior FSOs.

Only a very few FSOs would, in their twenty- to thirty-year career of serving their country, ever reach the pinnacle of the FSO hierarchy—Ambassador, Deputy Assistant Secretary of State, Undersecretary of State, or Secretary of State. Most FSOs would leave the service after two or three decades, dependent upon some elaborate civil service retirement formula based on a percentage of their three highest years of pay. No matter how good they were, and because they never could reach their full potential in the Foreign Service, many of the best FSOs would retire early, drink their way into oblivion, or self-destruct after a couple of marriages, punishing themselves for having been a career failure.

The ostensible rationale for the direct presidential assignment of an ambassador to an overseas post was the fact that he or she was personally close to the White House, and, in effect, expressed the president's wishes directly. Senior representatives of the host country saw the political appointee as a personal extension of the president himself. But, Carter knew, as did most State Department professionals, that this wasn't the case. In fact, the ambassador's role had become increasingly less significant as the professionalism of the appointees decreased.

Like the majority of FSOs, Carter treated politically appointed ambassadors as nothing more than glorified travel agents. They spent a great deal of their personal and embassy staff time preparing for Congressional Delegations (CoDels). Yet most CoDels had no information or policy planning purpose, and were really junkets for congressmen and senators who wanted to travel around the world to places they had never been before, and to "political" events completely unrelated to their primary constituent functions. All this, of course, was an incredible waste of taxpayers' money. But since the media and the public seemed to be completely indifferent to this costly problem, nothing was done to change it. However, the Foreign Service Officers were completely demoralized by it and felt that their service had been abused. On several occasions, Carter had insisted to some Foreign Service friends that they appeal to Congress en masse and protest this situation. But the FSOs were completely unable to organize themselves to protect their personal and professional interests. It was not hard for any politically appointed Secretary of State to keep the FSOs divided, despite public statements to the contrary.

Captain Carl Hansson, Carter, and Linda sat in the antechamber of Ambassador Carl LaGreca's office. The Marine guard posted outside of the ambassador's door stood at attention, avoiding glares from all three civilians who had been waiting for the ambassador for the past two hours.

"The ambassador better have a good excuse for keeping us waiting like this," Carter said to the Marine, who did not answer. "Otherwise . . ."

"Otherwise what, Dr. Carter?" the ambassador interjected, opening the door to his office. "I don't believe that you are in any position to make threats to anyone, let alone an American Ambassador." He paused and looked at Linda. "Nice to see you again, Ms. Watson. I didn't realize that you were mixed up in this shameful situation." He had just spent the last hour reviewing official reports of the fight, and getting some background information on Carter from friends in the States. He didn't appreciate having to leave a dinner party to return to the embassy to handle this matter.

"It's good to see you again, Ambassador," Linda said, shaking his hand. "You've come a long way from South

Boston. I'm very impressed." Whenever they met, she always found LaGreca attractive and charming.

Six-feet tall, swarthy-complexioned, with deep set penetrating intelligent brown eyes and salt-and-pepper wavy hair, Carl LaGreca was an honest, hardworking accountant who had become a congressional representative from Massachusetts, and had chaired the House Finance Budget Committee until the President asked him to resign his position to work in the White House. From there he went to head up the Office of Management and Budget (OMB). In that position, he was tasked to reorganize the entire budgeting procedure for the Executive Branch. He had done such an admirable job that the President wanted to reward him with something that would allow him to relax and spend some quality time with his attractive young wife and precocious daughter. So, he assigned LaGreca to Sweden as the American Ambassador. This exalted position was a far cry from LaGreca's poverty-ridden South Boston childhood where he was affectionately known as "The Stud," a "ladykiller," who was a virtual magnet to every attractive female. But he always remained faithful to his wife and his friends.

"Please come on in and make yourself comfortable," LaGreca said, motioning to them to follow him into his office.

The ambassador's office looked to Carter as if it had been stamped out of a cookie cutter. A framed picture of the President of the United States hung on the wall behind his desk. Next to it stood the flag of the United States of America. The ambassador worked at the standard mahogany desk with a secured red STU-3 telephone sitting on top of it. The room held several upholstered club chairs, a nondescript coffee table, and a worn leather couch. A large, faded red, blue and yellow Bukhara rug tried to give a small impression of opulence.

"Well," LaGreca said, in his distinctive Boston accent, "this is quite a strange amalgam of people. One Swedish policeman, one Medical Director of the State Department, and one lovely automobile manufacturer's representative."

Looking from one to the next with a glint in his eyes, he asked, "Now what do all of you have in common?"

"Nothing," Carter answered, "and it is now time to end Captain Hansson's little farce. So if you would tell this kind policeman to release me, I would be very appreciative."

"And how precisely would you show me your appreciation?" LaGreca asked.

Carter was surprised by the ambassador's mocking tone. "By sending a letter to the Sec State suggesting a commendation for your professional handling of this uncalled for arrest." Carter responded, with a hint of disdain.

"And what would you consider to be a professional response, Doctor," LaGreca asked, staring at this man, who seemed inappropriately self-assured and arrogant.

"I think the solution is quite simple, Mr. Ambassador," Carter replied. "Please explain to the officer that I am under diplomatic immunity and, therefore, cannot be touched by any foreign governments for whatever alleged misdemeanors or felonies committed by me or, as a matter of fact, anyone else in the foreign service."

"I must admit," LaGreca said, "that you have presented me with an interesting dilemma. And what do you think, Captain?"

"Captain Carl Hansson," he replied. "Mr. Ambassador, I took it upon myself to bring the doctor here instead of to headquarters, so that we could discuss the issue of immunity. Also, I did not want this ... situation ... to appear in our newspapers, and become a *cause célèbre* which could strain American-Swedish relations. So I thought it best to bring it to your direct attention."

"May I say that both my country and I appreciate the consideration," LaGreca responded.

"Thank you, sir," Captain Hansson replied.

"And what about you, Linda?" LaGreca asked.

"Well," Linda replied, slightly flushed, "As you know, I'm not a diplomat, far from it," she laughed, "but I'm not sure why we are here at all. Dr. Carter broke up a fight in which four possible refugees were being severely beaten by a handful of Swedish bullies, twice their size, using iron chains and large leather belts. It was ugly. And despite the fact that Captain Hansson and two of his officers were there, as far as I or Carter could tell, they were doing absolutely nothing about the situation. There is no doubt in my mind that, had Carter not intervened, the four kids would have been killed by those thugs."

"Is that what happened?" LaGreca asked Hansson. "I've been reviewing your department's report and it varies considerably from Ms. Watson's account."

"Not at all," Captain Hansson responded. "The so-called 'Swedish bullies,' as she has called them, had been walking on the street undisturbed, when four ruffians came up to them and asked them for money. When the so-called bullies told them that they didn't have any money, a fight broke out. In fact, the 'Swedish bullies' were attempting to stop the so-called 'possible refugees' from robbing them. By the time Ms. Watson and Dr. Carter arrived, it was the beginning of the end."

"Thank you, Captain Hansson," LaGreca said. "I will take it from this point. And thank you for your discretion." He shook the policeman's hand and escorted him to the door. "Please give my secretary all the particulars about your job— the name of your supervisor, the name and address of your Chief of Police. If you don't mind, I would like to commend you for evidencing a high degree of professionalism."

"I'm honored, sir," Hansson saluted the ambassador, bowed to Linda, ignored Carter and departed.

"Very impressive, Ambassador," Carter said facetiously, resenting the fact that he seemed to believe the officer's story.

"Don't I get my day in court? If you would just place a call to the Sec State..."

"Dr. Carter, there's really no need." LaGreca sat back in his chair and visibly relaxed for the first time that evening. "I thought the State Department was known for the diplomacy of its employees. Did you really expect me to sit here and call the captain a liar to his face?"

LaGreca's question took Carter by surprise. Of course he didn't, Carter thought. LaGreca had handled the situation perfectly, by the book. The Sec State would be pleased to know that his ambassador was worth his pay. No one really needed to stir up an international incident over this matter. Particularly now...

"Sorry, sir," Carter said, knowing when to eat crow. "You're right, of course."

"We both know that you have no diplomatic immunity. You're here on vacation, under a regular passport. The way I see it, Dr. Carter, you owe Captain Hansson a major debt, seeing that he brought you here, to the embassy, and not to a Swedish police station. And if anyone believed his version of the incident, as false as it may be, you would have been processed and sent to prison with a ten- to twenty-year sentence for assault and battery with a lethal weapon."

"Carl," Linda interjected, "that's not fair. I was there. The police did nothing. Dr. Carter specifically went up to Captain Hansson for help, was insulted by him and was told that the fight was none of his business. What in God's name was Alison supposed to do? Just stand there and watch four youths assaulted, maybe even killed?"

"Unfortunately," LaGreca responded, in a sympathetic tone of voice, "Captain Hansson was right in several respects. As much as you don't like what you may see, this is still his country and not ours! That is reality, like it or not. And as a guest in their country—no, a tourist, as Dr. Carter is—we are all at the mercy of their rules, regulations, and laws. Whatever happens domestically in Sweden is strictly Swedish business."

"That's not right!" Linda responded.

"Being right has nothing to do with anything!" LaGreca corrected her. "I thought you knew better than that." He turned to Carter. "I don't mean to sound so hard-nosed, Carter, but put yourself in my shoes. You mutilated three Swedish citizens—thugs, to both of you, but Swedes, nevertheless. You claim diplomatic immunity when you know damn well that it's not possible." He paused to make sure that his next words would be fully understood. "If I were you, Dr. Carter, I would watch my step while you are in Sweden. Enjoy the museums, buy some glassware, take a few ferry rides. Because if you get into trouble again, I may not be able to be of any help."

Ambassador LaGreca looked at his watch. It had been a long working day. "If you don't mind, I'll go home and join my family. I'll see you both out."

13

STOCKHOLM, SWEDEN

Linda and Carter took a cab from the embassy back to Gamla Stan, where they boarded a ferry from the dock at Skeppsbron. Fifteen kroners took them across the Saltsjön waterway, around the Kastell-Holmen promontory, to their final destination, Djurgården. They needed something to take their mind off the previous events.

The trip was made largely in silence. Carter needed the calm of the sea to clear his mind. Linda sensed that he needed some form a contemplative catharsis, which she should not be a part of, and was satisfied to stand silently by his side, on call, as needed.

"That was unbelievably unfair," Linda tried to sound both upbeat and morally outraged. "Captain Hansson was lying through his teeth. And what was that nonsense about the 'poor refugees' having held up those Swedish bullies? Carl was acting unusually aggressive and inappropriate to a fellow diplomat."

"If I were a hint more paranoid," Carter chuckled, "and slightly inebriated, I might say that I had been 'set up.'"

"But by whom?" Linda asked quizzically, "and for what reason? You're only here on a short visit. And now I know you work for the State Department."

"I have a suspicion," Carter responded, nonplused.

"Why do I have this sense," Linda smiled, "that you're not going to share that suspicion with me?"

"Because you have an acute sense of psychological dynamics and you're frequently right," Carter responded, tongue-in-cheek.

"I hardly know what that means," Linda responded, sensing that Carter was toying with her.

"Oh, I think you do!" Carter said, more abruptly than he had wanted.

"Hey!" Linda declared indignantly, "Have I done anything harmful to you that I don't know about?"

"Maybe you have," Carter replied, turning around toward her with a hardening facial expression. "And maybe you haven't." He paused to monitor her reaction. "You tell me!"

"I don't know what the hell you are talking about!" she responded angrily. "Have I hurt your feelings in any way that I'm not aware of?"

"No," Carter replied calmly, "none of which I'm aware of." He smiled, "As a matter of fact, you have been so incredibly supportive for someone who I met less than six hours ago that I feel as if you've given me an infusion of diabetic sweetness."

"Christ, almighty!" She recoiled, pulling away from him and wanting to smack him across the face. "Are you one of those cryptomisogynists who can't have a woman be supportive without fear of falling into an intractable dependency relationship?"

"That sure is a mouthful of psycho-jargon from someone who claims not to know what the words mean," Carter replied quietly. "I tend to be a lot simpler than all that."

"Right!"

"Can you blame me for wondering about why and how I met you?" he watched as her face flushed. She was clearly angry. But he wanted to find out precisely what she was angry about. Was it his hurtful conversation, or something that the conversation might reveal about her.

"I don't think we should proceed any further," Linda affirmed.

"Why?" he asked disingenuously. "If anyone should be indignant, shouldn't it be me?"

"You've had a few too many glasses of aquavit," she responded, ready to walk away from him.

"Don't you find it a little bit strange," Carter asked, "that out of nowhere I meet this attractive American lobbyist..."

"I'm not a lobbyist," she interjected.

"Whatever..." he replied.

"Whatever?" she reiterated indignantly. "You really are a piece of work!"

"So," Carter continued, "I encounter this midwestern woman who tells me she works for the automobile industry..."

"Now," she interjected, infuriated, "you're going to blame American cars for what just happened to you!"

"And then before I realize it," Carter continued, ignoring her protestations, "I'm breaking up a fight into which the police refuse to intervene."

"Oh come on!" she shouted. "Now you're beginning to sound really scary."

"And then before I know what's happening," Carter continued, "I'm reprimanded by a political hack Ambassador who you conveniently know from some previous incarnation."

"So what?" she asked, shaking her head. "Are you telling me that you never bumped into old acquaintances from the past? And by the way, before he was appointed Ambassador, LaGreca was on a Presidential Task Force that encouraged increased U.S. exports of American automobiles."

"I'm impressed," Carter responded facetiously. "But I think you're beginning to get the drift of what I'm thinking," he responded firmly. "There have been too many coincidences in our brief, entertaining relationship."

"So you believe that this was all cleverly contrived by me?"

"No, not necessarily" he replied calmly. "But in my field of work, one coincidence may be one coincidence too many."

"And which line of work is that, Dr. Carter?" she asked. "You've got enough narcissism, gall, arrogance, impudence, gall . . ."

"You're beginning to repeat yourself," he interjected.

"God!" she declared, "Are you intolerable!"

"That might be the truest thing you've said all day today," Carter responded, contemplatively. "As a matter of fact, it's the nicest thing anyone has said to me since I've arrived in Stockholm."

Carter checked his watch, and a moment of reality entered his thoughts. According to his assignment, he had exactly seven days to complete the terms of his contract. Otherwise, he would have to refund the five million dollars. He had already wasted one day. If he kept stumbling into these desultory episodes he was bound to fail in his task. And the word failure had no place in his lexicon. No matter how gruesome or complicated the assignment, if it fit into his sense of morality, he completed it. Although he didn't know who his ultimate employer was, he had a suspicion. That was why Linda was becoming of increasingly greater interest to him. If his suspicions were correct, she would become indispensable to the completion of his assignment. So it was now going to be a waiting game to find out whether he was correct.

"I see you lovebirds are already fighting," a man in an overcoat said, emerging from the shadows. "And you've known each other less than twenty-four hours. My, my, my . . ."

"Welcome on board," Carter said, not surprised by the intrusion. "I've been waiting for you. I thought you might show up sooner, but what's a few hours when you're having fun." He turned to Linda. "Oh, how rude of me! Mack Londsdale, meet Linda Watson."

14

STOCKHOLM, SWEDEN

This was the first time that Carter realized that Londsdale had flaxen fair and a slight Swedish accent. If Carter had not known any better, Londsdale looked like the image of what the Nazis had portrayed during the Third Reich as the "perfect Aryan," tall, thin, sinewy, handsome, with chiseled facial features. Only his brown eyes, surrounded by long, dark eyelashes, altered his Nordic look.

"But I almost forgot," Carter continued, "that you two already know each other." Londsdale and Linda exchanged glances. Then everyone laughed.

"Alison, how did you know that Mack and I knew each other?" It was a disingenuous question because she thought she knew precisely the moment Carter figured out that she was in some way tied in with Londsdale.

"Perhaps," Carter responded, "you would prefer to answer that question yourself. I think it's time to stop pretending to be so innocent and naive and see if we can't build a little bit of trust among the three of us. I suspect we will be working very closely together."

"The moment I walked up to you in the restaurant at the Grand Hotel," she answered without any apology or rationalization, "you caught a quick glimpse through the window of Londsdale walking past the restaurant. And since you are

ACTIVE MEASURES

not a professional who, by nature, believes in coincidences, you quickly surmised that I was affiliated in some way with Londsdale."

"Jackpot," Carter responded. "You're just as smart as I expected, especially for someone recruited by or reporting to some intelligence organization."

"Very impressive, Dr. Carter," Linda complimented. "Then exactly what is my relationship with Mack Londsdale?"

"Please excuse me, Mack," Carter said, ignoring Linda's question. He opened Londsdale's Burberry overcoat and sport jacket to reveal a shoulder holster. "May I?"

"Of course," Londsdale replied without a moment's hesitation, which told Carter that Londsdale trusted him.

Carter took out the gun, making certain the safety was on and keeping the barrel raised. "From the way Mack carries his Sig-Sauer P226, I would say that he is some sort of Swedish law enforcement agent. But the fact that he was sent overseas to recruit me told me that he is part of an elite unit. That means he probably is at a senior level, not the chief, because they would never send the chief overseas alone. Mack may be working for the Pöni, the Ordninspolisens Nationella Insatsstyrka, translated into English as the National Rescue Unit of the Stockholm Police Department. A very interesting police force, by the way. Correct me if I'm wrong. Your unit has about fifty members divided into five groups—two assault/hostage rescue groups, two dive groups, one demolition group, one sniper support group, and, most importantly for us, one command/intelligence group. I would guess that is the one with which our dear friend Mack Londsdale is affiliated. And, by the way, so that we all understand how important this seemingly modest, handsome man is, I am also convinced that he works directly for some VIP in Parliament."

"Very impressive, Dr. Carter," Londsdale, said, clapping his hands as if he had just attended a concert of a violin virtuoso.

"Why is that so impressive?" Linda asked, clearly peeved.

"Jealous?" Carter asked. "Don't they teach you deductive reasoning and human patterns of non-verbal communication anymore at the Farm?"

"You simply could have looked up his file at the State Department's Bureau of Intelligence and Research."

"Linda," Londsdale interjected, his voice clearly irritated, "he couldn't have looked me up in any intelligence bureau or classified reference manual . . ."

"Why? she asked, clearly annoyed by something more than the fact that Carter had guessed who Londsdale was. She needed to understand how Carter thought. He was a far more dangerous man than she had been led to believe by her employers.

"Because I don't exist," Londsdale replied bluntly. "Like any good undercover operative," he explained, directing his words toward her, "my entire history, background, and name is fictitious. So there was no way for him to know who I was—even by sight. I have had enough changes made to my face that no two pictures are alike. And Carter knows that."

"So I assume that now it remains for you to figure out what I do and who I really am?" she asked, defiantly.

"Speaking of doctors," Carter said, completely ignoring Linda's question, "what has happened to our good friend Dr. Eriksson?"

"As far as we can tell," Londsdale replied, "he's still working at the medical clinic, or museum, whatever you want to call it, at Vadstena."

"Don't you want to know who I am," Linda asked, irritated that she was being purposely ignored. She was losing her highly honed self-control.

"Mack," Carter said, continuing to ignore Linda, "I don't understand why your employer doesn't simply send in your Pöni unit to take Eriksson out?"

"It's a very good question," Londsdale responded, "but unfortunately I don't have a good answer."

"Try one." Carter said.

"First, Eriksson has a large number of well-trained paramilitary soldiers protecting him at Vadstena and wherever he goes."

"But that wouldn't stop an elite assault unit like yours," Carter said, clearly unconvinced, "And given the fact that he has violated every conceivable law in Sweden, couldn't he be arrested without any problems."

"Not exactly..." Londsdale responded with some chagrin in his voice.

"Political sensitivity?" Carter asked.

"It's a little more serious than that," Londsdale replied.

"You mean to tell me that if you attempt to arrest him," Carter queried, "or even attempt an abduction, you would create political turmoil in Parliament?"

"As strange as it might seem to someone from the outside," Londsdale replied, "Eriksson has an extremely large political following in the Swedish population, particularly in the regions around Vadstena—Skara, Gothenburg, Uppsala, Sigtuna, Karlstad. The truth is that he is capable of bringing down the entire Swedish government if the Prime Minster were to arrest him."

"But if a stranger or an alien happened to assassinate him," Carter continued Londsdale's thought, "that would be less of a problem for Sweden. This way Eriksson would not be viewed as a martyr, merely killed by a 'deranged person' of 'unknown origin.'"

"You get the idea," Londsdale responded. "We don't really know how many men and which men in the military support Eriksson. We've received information which indicates that the Swedish military might even fight the Prime Minister's interior forces to prevent anyone from taking Eriksson out of Vadstena."

"So what you and your compatriots are asking me to do," Carter summarized, "is to somehow make my way into Eriksson's clinic, past a formidable array of guards, kill the good doctor, and try to escape without getting killed myself. All in the next six days." He looked at Linda, who was not at all shocked by what he had revealed. Just as he had guessed.

"That's why I was sent to you personally, on behalf of..."

Londsdale hesitated. He was divulging more information than he was instructed to.

"... of whom?" Carter added, looking at Linda, who had her hands folded and stood in front of them, pouting.

Londsdale started again. "There are several clients ... besides the Swedish Prime Minister, and other concerns."

"I understand," Carter said, deciding to give Linda the attention she had been silently demanding, "including those of our American automotive industry. Capitalism and patriotism, what more can one want. A stable Swedish government means a stable economic buyer. Isn't that right, Linda?"

"I don't know," she responded curtly. "You seem to have all the answers."

"Stop this nonsense, Linda!" Londsdale ordered her. "There is too much at stake for you to act like a petulant teenager. Tell Carter the truth or I will tell him."

She glared at Londsdale, knowing that she would tell Carter exactly what she wanted to, and when she wanted to. She didn't need this harassment.

"Let's talk straight," Londsdale offered. "for the ..."

The sound of something striking flesh caused Londsdale to stop short. Blood seeped onto the wooden deck.

15

VADSTENA, SWEDEN

The majestic sounds of Wagner's *Lohengrin* permeated the small room in the clinic. Eriksson stood tall and straight, inspired by the crescendo of the German music, and nodded his head to the blond-haired guard with the pierced earring to increase the volume.

"Has this patient been deprived of sleep for the past week" Eriksson asked, "as I requested?"

"Yes, Doctor!" responded Jan, one of the teenage thugs who had been in the street fight with Carter. He patted the wet, filthy burlap bag that covered the prisoner's head, partly so that Eriksson wouldn't realize that he, Eriksson's protégé, was still squeamish watching him torture his hapless victims.

"*Shabeh* is a most effective form of torture," Eriksson said matter-of-factly. "I must admit that as much as I detest those Israelis, they are, nevertheless, masters when interrogating a Palestinian prisoner. They have perfected the art of *Shabeh*."

"Aaahhh!" shouted the prisoner, his hooded head bent forward, his arms and legs shackled to the small chair in which he sat, angled to slant forward so that it was impossible to feel in a stable position.

"Remember, the key to the effectiveness of *Shabeh* is

sleep deprivation." Eriksson said, indicating that his protégé use his bamboo stick to slap the prisoner across his bent back so that he would remain awake. "The Israelis are no fools! They taught me that *Shabeh* is a combination of methods, used over a prolonged period of time, utilizing sensory isolation, sleep deprivation, and the infliction of pain. The Israeli General Security Service often uses variations of *Shabeh* to elicit the information they want."

"The 'Refrigerator' exposes the prisoner to an air-conditioner shooting cold air directly at him. After a while, believe it or not, this can be quite painful," Eriksson added, pleased to pass time educating his assistant.

Jan hit the hooded prisoner with the bamboo stick. This person was taking longer to talk than expected.

"Aaahhh!" the prisoner screamed, his hooded head falling ever more forward, straining his back and arm muscles.

"Then, of course, there is the 'Standing *Shabeh*' where the prisoner is forced to stand, his arms tied behind him affixed to a pipe attached to the wall." Eriksson clearly enjoyed talking about torture in the same way that a photographer enjoyed telling a stranger about how he set up an important shot. He enjoyed the discussion of torture almost as much as he enjoyed the act itself. "Then there is the modified *Shabeh*," Eriksson continued, "where the prisoner's arms are drawn back and upward so that the upper body is forced forward and down.

"The Greeks and Romans thought nothing of torturing slaves and foreigners," Eriksson announced, as if addressing a university class.

Jan relaxed his hold on the prisoner, knowing what was coming, and actually glad for the short reprieve he would have from this messy part of working with Eriksson.

"However, like most political systems, the immunity of the Roman citizens eroded in the empire's later years and they, too, were eventually tortured on a regular basis.

"Torture possessed its own inherent paradoxes. At any given point, roles could reverse. Christians were tortured for treason, until Christianity became the imperial religion.

Thereafter, torture fell into relative disuse, although trial by ordeal was common. But with the growing belief in confession as the highest form of proof, torture was revived under the Inquisition in the twelth century. It became so acceptable that Pope Innocent IV," no pun intended, Eriksson thought to himself, "formally authorized torture as an aid to the interrogation of suspects. Eventually it became part of secular law. The ecclesiastical purpose of torture was to exhume heresy from the graveyard of religiosity. Torture was used to elicit accusations against fellow heretics as well as confessions. However, torture had the contrary effect of spreading heresy, or the suspicion of it, rather than eliminating it."

Eriksson could enumerate reflexively a variety of techniques that had been developed during the Inquisition, from stretching limbs, to hanging the body upside down, to infliction of massive rope burns, to branding irons, and to the infamous rack where the body was placed over a wheel and continuously stretched until the victim passed out from the excruciating pain. But he decided to stay with history, rather than methods. That would wait for another time.

"During the sixteenth century, Hippolytus of Marseilles added a uniquely distinctly French Cartesian-like concept to the notion of torture. He felt that if the victim were prevented from sleeping it was far more humane than the other tortures." In all fairness to the French, Eriksson thought, there was a short respite during the Enlightenment in which Cesare Beccaria and Voltaire, as well as other intellectuals, demanded the complete elimination of the use of torture.

"Throughout history it was extremely easy to recruit and train torturers. That led, of course, to the metaphysical, yet extremely practical question, if society were morally and socially 'correct' would that, in and of itself, eliminate the readiness to inflict pain. Or was there a moral fault for which the individual was responsible." Eriksson knew that he was now speaking above Jan's ability to comprehend. But for Eriksson, torture was as much a part of man as was his need to eat, sleep, and fornicate, and the higher level questions must be asked, even if there were no clear answers.

"Torture is now approaching epidemic proportions. It is not confined to any one area of the world. What I find encouraging is that the methods of torture have become more sophisticated as technology has progressed and as man has become complacent with his own sense of morality. The absolutes of 'bad' and 'good,' to the extent they exist, have dissolved into a sophomoric deconstructionist debate as to what constitutes 'modern torture.'" Eriksson stopped, realizing he had totally lost his audience. It was time to continue the practice of torture.

The young man hit the prisoner several more times, until the screaming became intolerable, even to Eriksson.

"Please tell me, if you would," Eriksson asked the prisoner very politely, "when your fellow refugees will hold their illegal rally to embarrass Stockholm before the world?" Even as he spoke, Eriksson found the situation ludicrous. Usually he could find out the information from a bribed infiltrator or from the Swedish police, who, by law, had the power to grant demonstrators a permit to protest. But this time around, the refugee groups had not taken out any permit because they, correctly, no longer trusted the police. They knew that before they could organize themselves for the march, the police would have broken up the groups and dispersed them.

Eriksson had to know the precise date and time of the upcoming demonstration. His intelligence network had uncovered the fact that a massive demonstration would be mounted, soon, probably in Stockholm, but he was still unable to find out exactly when and where it would occur. An illegal gathering would give Eriksson and his organization the moral high ground for the first time in a very long time. If his followers took the offensive, national television would do the rest—it would show how ineffective the Swedish politicians were, and how effective his group was. They alone could be trusted to maintain a pure Sweden of law and order. "Law and order" were the key words that guaranteed the politically passive citizens of Sweden a continuation of their hard-earned life of civility and safety.

The details of the precise date, time, and meeting place of the demonstrators had to be forced from the man in the chair, so Eriksson could mobilize his own "troops" with military precision. Eriksson was convinced that this prisoner, an insignificant leader of a group of refugee Kurds, possessed this knowledge.

Jan grabbed the prisoner's hooded head and pushed it further forward.

"Please!" the prisoner screamed. "No more!" His arms were about to pop out of their shoulder sockets. Every nerve, muscle, and tissue fiber was being stretched to its limit. If his head was to bend one inch more, he felt that he would literally fall apart, like Humpty Dumpty.

"When is the rally?" Eriksson asked politely.

"I don't know!" the prisoner replied.

Eriksson nodded his head. Jan pushed the prisoner's head down further.

"Ugggghhh!"

Even Jan, a proud student of the famous Dr. Eriksson, had to swallow several times in order to prevent himself from gagging. He turned up the volume on the Wagner tape so that he could drown out the screaming.

"Untie his arms and legs, Jan. We're going to try the *Qas' at a-Tawleh* technique. Also developed by our good friends the Israelis."

"Sir?" Although he had heard the Arabic term before, Jan was uncertain what it meant. And with a teacher like Eriksson, there was no room for misunderstandings or mistakes.

"It refers to painful stretching, using a table and direct pressure," Eriksson replied.

"Of course," Jan responded, "now I know what you are referring to."

"Good!" Eriksson responded with a sense of pride, knowing that he had once again chosen the right youth for the job.

Jan freed the prisoner from the chair only to force him

to kneel in front of a wooden table. He bound the prisoner's arms behind him and stretched them over the tabletop. Jan sat on the table with his feet on the prisoner's shoulders and pushed the prisoner's body forward, stretching his arms even more than in the previous torture. When it seemed as if his sockets were about to snap, Jan stretched the prisoner's bound legs while Eriksson held down his arms. Both interrogators were amazed at the torture the Kurd was willing to sustain without speaking—or fainting.

"The date, time, and place?" Eriksson asked, his voice more irritable.

"Nooooo! I'll tell you!" the prisoner finally screamed.

This was the moment that Eriksson was waiting for. Just as the prisoner was willing to reveal the information, it was then that more pressure and pain had to be applied, not lessened. This way the prisoner would understand that this truly was his last chance. If he were to lie, that would be his last lie.

"The date, time, place?" Eriksson shouted. He was impatient. These Goddamn Kurds!

"Six days from now, Gamla Stan, six P.M."

"Thank you," Eriksson responded. Nodding his head toward Jan, he instructed him what to do next.

Jan forcibly twisted the prisoner's hooded head. The sound of cracking vertebrae reverberated through the stifling air.

16

E-3 AUTO-ROUTE WEST, SWEDEN

Speeding west along Route E3 at ninety kilometers per hour, Carter pressed his foot on the accelerator of the rented Volvo and pushed it as far down as it would go. He figured that the ride to Vadstena should take about four hours at that speed. The auto-route was largely empty. Only one pair of headlights trailed his car at a far distance.

Linda tried to erase the image of the horror she had just witnessed, yet all she could see when she closed her eyes was Mack Londsdale, splattered with blood, sprawled out on the deck of the ferry. After the "accident," she and Carter had lost themselves in the throng of people rushing to leave the docking boat. There was nothing that they could do for Londsdale. But both of them realized that whoever killed Londsdale may have wanted to kill them as well, and they had run as far from the body as they could get after they realized he was dead. She stared out the window, hoping that dawn, if she ever saw it again, would rekindle the confidence with which she had originally taken on her assignment.

"Remember what Mack said to you before he was killed?" Carter asked.

"He told me to stop acting like a petulant little girl!"

"Since we are all professionals," Carter continued, glancing at the rearview mirror, "and your life is as much at risk as mine right now, I would strongly suggest that you start telling me the truth." For a moment he thought that the headlights were catching up to them, but decided he was wrong. They seemed attached to an old Mercedes, but the darkness could be playing tricks on his eyes.

"Or else what?" Linda asked defiantly.

"Or else I let you out right here, and we part company now," he stated matter-of-factly.

"Is that meant to intimidate me?" she asked.

"No," he responded. "I was simply trying to show you what the alternative was if you did not feel like collaborating with me."

"Definitely intimidation!" she responded, her hands folded on her lap and her lips pursed. "What's next on your list of techniques? Extortion? Torture?"

"If need be," Carter responded coldly. "I would have no qualms. I think you know that."

"I think you would do anything to get what you wanted. You're not any better than those thugs that got us into this whole stupid mess. But at least they're out in the open in their methods. Nothing subtle about them."

"Well," Carter laughed, "that's the first time that anyone has accused me of being subtle. Subtlety is not a virtue I ever thought I possessed. Nor intend to develop expressly for you." His voice turned ice cold. That alone, he knew, would put some fear into her sarcasm.

They drove for a few minutes in silence, before Linda announced, "My automotive clients have a relationship with Dr. Eriksson. Finish. End of story." Where she felt that someone was taking advantage of her, less was always more.

"That much I figured out on my own," Carter responded. "You know that you are not telling me anything new."

"By the way," she asked, changing the subject, "why are we going to Vadstena when Londsdale told you that it was impossible to get into the clinic?"

"Please, don't avoid my question," Carter responded brusquely.

"I'm not in therapy, Dr. Carter," Linda replied. "Nor am I under a court subpoena."

Carter turned the wheel and swerved onto the grassy edge of the highway. He reached over her and opened her door for her to get out.

"Hey, wait a minute," Linda argued. "You can't leave me out here in the middle of nowhere!"

"Out!" Carter ordered. "I have a strong feeling that the Mercedes following us would be very interested in what you know and what they think you may have told me. So you lose either way, Linda. It's either me, or it's them! Whoever 'them' might be."

"Do you always play this hard?" she asked, closing the door and motioning him to proceed onward.

"I have six days to fulfill my assignment," Carter replied, "and I don't have any time to play with someone whose entire professional life has been spent twisting words and images around in order to create or conceal truth."

"That's my job!" she replied, self-righteously. "And if you weren't aware of it, let me notify you that I have the same privileges of confidentiality with my employers that you, as a doctor, have with a patient. God only knows what privileges you might have as an assassin! I certainly wouldn't want to find out."

"That's the first truthful comment you've made all night," Carter said. "Please, if you would, return to the first question I asked you." He checked the rearview mirror and saw that the Mercedes was closer than before.

"I can only tell you what I know," she responded, more out of a sense of frustration that if she did not tell him something about her clients, he would torture her mentally until he finally got out of her what she suspected he knew already. He certainly had perseverance, she thought. For Carter, impediments transformed into challenges and the impossible became a continuum of more or less likely probabilities. But his obstinate nature was an exasperating annoyance that negated any features that had made him initially attractive to her.

"Do you always think so long before you divulge information?" Carter asked. Concerned by the car behind him, he accelerated. But the Mercedes kept pace. Carter knew that his Volvo would be no match for the Mercedes if it was, in fact, following them. He might have to take evasive procedures if he wanted to lose it.

"You really are beginning to get on my nerves," Linda responded. "Is there also a specific form of presentation you would like?"

"Linda, please!" Carter insisted. "This is not some mind game we're playing. As you saw, all too well, people get killed around here. So before either of us wind up like Londsdale, I would like to know where you fit into all of this, and whatever you know that will help me make more sense out of our situation."

"Fair enough," Linda responded, also becoming concerned about the Mercedes. "About three years after the Swiss banks became the principal target of the international Jewish organizations over their illicit financial practices with the senior officials of Nazi Germany..." Linda continued with caution, wanting to help Carter, but only to the extent that it would not damage her clients. In truth, she realized that the only thing she had was the word of her clients which, by definition, was self-serving at best, and a complete fabrication at worst.

As Linda hesitated for a moment, deciding how to frame her next remark, she felt the Mercedes ram the back of the Volvo. Her body lurched forward as the safety belt tightened against her chest and shoulders, effectively restraining her forward motion.

Carter reacted instantaneously. He swung the steering wheel 180 degrees, slammed on the parking brake completely turning the Volvo around, released the brake, and sped off in the opposite direction. By the time the Mercedes was able to stop and turn to pursue the Volvo, Carter and Linda had disappeared. Carter silently thanked the old trick his grandfather had taught him in the back roads of North Carolina. The bootleg turn! An evasive maneuver used to outrun the police cars chasing the backwoods men making moonshine. What a paradox, Carter thought, that the time-tested techniques used to evade American laws would, on this occasion, save his and Linda's life.

17

LAKE VÄNERN, SWEDEN

Some pundit once said, "Sweden seems to be the most comfortable country in Europe—and the least cozy." But for Swedish Prime Minister Johannes Strindberg, a traceable ancestor of August Strindberg, the brilliant playwright who wrote such world-renowned plays as *Father, Miss Julie,* and *Easter,* the true soul and tenderness of Sweden resided within two southern provinces: Dalarna and Värmland. Of course, as a seafaring man who spent most of his after-office hours on his latest state-of-the-art yacht, the *Conquest 51,* he loved these two particular regions because they contained some of the most beautiful lakes in Sweden. Lake Siljan in Dalarna and Lake Vänern in Värmland, were considered the majesty of inland waters, the latter attaining the distinction of being the third largest inland sea in Europe.

Johannes, a tall, thin, middle-aged man with a weatherbeaten, rugged complexion and thinning flaxen hair, felt like the uncle who had to choose between his two favorite nieces when, in fact, he loved them both. The province of Dalarna appealed to the more conservative part of him, replete with all the traditional Swedish customs of his forefathers—maypole dancing, fiddlers' music, folk costumes, and handicrafts, including the famous Dala horse. In English, which—like most Swedes—he knew exceedingly well, Dalarna was transformed to Dalecarlia, which meant "valleys." In the coming week, the citizens of Dalarna would celebrate the custom of maypole dancing, an event in which they would run through the woods garnering birch bows and wildflowers to cover the maypole. Then the pole would be raised and they would dance around it until dawn. A remnant of an old respectable pagan custom.

In contrast, Värmland was a land of mountains, rolling hills, islands, and rivers. It was a province of merriment, a Swedish version of Disneyland. Throughout the year there were different types of festivals, from concerts to poetry readings, to a variety of handicraft exhibits. The forests that covered a large part of Värmland were brilliantly described by the Nobel Prize winner Selma Lagerlöf in her lyrical *The Saga of Gösta Berling* in which she portrayed life in this region as it was in the early nineteenth century. As far as Johannes was concerned, nothing had changed, and he wanted to make certain that the area stayed that way.

Johannes's greatest enjoyment came from cruising the 170-mile-long Klaralven River which carried logs to the industrial areas around Lake Vänern. He stood on the deck of his fifty-one-foot fiberglass yacht, the wind slapping across his face as if to remind him that life was more than just political ambitions and social accomplishments. Life was also the reaffirmation of the basic sense of self, pitted against the greater forces of nature.

The occasion for this midweek afternoon excursion was purely hedonistic and self-congratulatory. Phase one of his plan to rid Swedish politics of what had become a potentially destructive force had been accomplished. Within the week, the nefarious Dr. Eriksson would be dead, without making the doctor a martyr to the right wing extremists, and without exposing the government's prior involvement with Eriksson. This would then open the way to economic stabilization under his own party's banner.

Just like the relationship between King Henry VIII and Thomas Becket, Johannes had had to struggle with the question of how to rid himself of "this mettlesome priest." What better way than to hire an assassin who had no relationship to Sweden or its principals, and whose only loyalty was to the successful outcome of the deed? And, of course, monetary payoff. This way, the murder of Dr. Eriksson could be blamed on a deranged foreigner who was not affiliated with any political or social causes in Sweden, and was working on his own. Although somewhat ashamed of the path he was about to take, Johannes felt a little like Winston Churchill when he realized that, more often than not, a nation had to hide behind a "bodyguard of lies" in order to maintain its viability and moral integrity. Hypocrisy was frequently the price a world leader had to pay in order to continue to play in the game of international politics.

He had convened his associates for a very psychological reason: to compliment them—the Swedish industrialist Nils Olsson, U.S. Ambassador Carl LaGreca, and Police Captain Carl Hansson—for developing a strategy that would ultimately strengthen Sweden and its increasingly powerful economic role in the international community.

Nils Olsson, the pudgy, beady-eyed, nervous industrialist had been the prime minister's childhood friend. Their wealthy families had been close for three generations, and at an early age the two of them had been unofficially anointed the "Crown Princes" who would one day determine the future of Sweden.

Each son had been programmed to pursue a career that would maintain his family's power in the country. Like all fine Swedish families, each son was sent to England to attend college, either at Oxford or Cambridge University. However, if a son, rarely a daughter, was somewhat more daring, and the family wanted to exhibit a streak of acceptable societal defiance, the son would attend Harvard, Princeton or Yale University, in the northeast coast of the United States. More recently, if they were truly foresighted, a son would be sent to Stanford University in Palo Alto, California, in order to learn the latest computer technology, connect with the hi-tech rulers of the future, and return to Sweden to bolster Sweden's position in a global communications pecking order.

Johannes was the "Crown Prince" chosen to pursue politics and political power, eventually to become Prime Minister. Olsson, the more self-centered of the two, had created a life and career based upon the acquisition of greater wealth and increased political influence, which he considered a legacy passed on by his family. He was the "Crown Prince" who now represented the interests of a handful of exceedingly wealthy and powerful Swedish families. The early, unwritten understanding was that both Johannes and Olsson would work together on Sweden's behalf.

Olsson was simply carrying out the tradition of a small oligarchy which, for many generations, had determined the fate of Sweden. The credo of both men was to continue tradition. Sweden was never to be allied with any country at war, but always positioned to profit from conflict.

As Olsson understood all too well, reality could not accommodate the Swedish traditions and myths passed on from one generation to another. Sweden could no longer maintain its long-fabricated myth of neutrality, so carefully shaped by his ancestors. It was now up to him and Johannes to maintain the delicate balance between public image and the financial interests which were in serious jeopardy. Without being overly dramatic, Olsson had recently pointed out to Johannes that Sweden was balanced precariously on the vortex of history. Without sounding megalomaniacal, as Sweden would go, so would the rest of the world. Its financial and political tentacles were intertwined so carefully and deliberately in the fibers of the ruling superpowers that they, too, would be in jeopardy of collapsing, both economically and, inevitably, politically. Otherwise, the complicity of the American ambassador would not be so important.

As far as Olsson was concerned, America was in as much danger as was Sweden. If the frontiers of illegal immigrants could not be stopped now, in a small country like Sweden, then imagine, Olsson thought as he stared at the ambassador, the time when America could no longer contain the sanctity of its borders against the onslaught of illegal immigrants from Mexico and Latin America, as well as all those other areas of the world where people were trying to run away from impoverished homelands. The Swedish problem was just the start of a potential world crisis, Olsson had concluded.

On the surface, Captain Carl Hansson seemed an unlikely member of the group. But the importance of the captain's strategic post, and the length of his pedigree, made Hansson's credentials impeccable. While the Strindbergs and Olssons were still *parvenus* in the eighteen century, the Hanssons were a distinguished family descended from Swedish nobility and, as far as he could determine, their pedigree went all the way back to the Vikings. The Hanssons had not only helped to create Sweden, but more importantly, they helped settle and found America.

In 1771, John Hanson, his name already Americanized, was the last man to ratify the Articles of Confederation when Maryland became the last of the original thirteen colonies. Soon after, the Continental Congress unanimously elected John Hanson the first President of the United States in a Congress assembled for a twelve-month term—eight years before George Washington was elected. During his one-year term (1781–82), he established the Department of State, the Department of War, the Department of the Navy, and the Department of Treasury. He helped set up a national judiciary, a national bank, and a post office. But, like most silent American heroes and statesmen, he was virtually ignored by history. Occasionally, thought Hansson, someone must remember his family in Maryland, on April 14, John Hanson Day.

Hansson was a medium-sized, tightly compact man who had been sent to America by the Swedish government to receive training at Fort Bragg, specializing in Special Operations, a euphemism for covert and irregular off-line assaults. He was an officer's officer, completely dedicated to the mission at hand. But like any good Special Ops soldier, he also knew how to ask the right questions. In his seemingly unimportant role as captain, his task was frequently to clean up the mess that others made.

But like all ambitious military men, he knew that the path to promotion and success in any military system was through politics. And that was where his family's money was an additional asset to his already strategic police position.

Ambassador LaGreca was on the surface, odd-man-out. He was clearly of non-Swedish origin. He had only been appointed to his post two years earlier. And he worked in the service of another government. But in some ways, these potential "negatives" were what gave additional strength to Johannes's plans.

As a conservative who was pro-business, LaGreca could empathize with Sweden's oncoming economic crisis and its immediate cause. As a representative of a powerful nation which had a national interest in keeping Sweden politically and economically stable, he was in a position to lend his good offices to the job of helping Sweden, a diplomatic act which would not be forgotten when Swedish industry expanded its manufacturing plants to foreign soils. Over the last few years, LaGreca had shown his friendship and shared his power with Johannes in ways small and large, acts which had resulted in an immense amount of both personal and professional trust.

In retrospect, Johannes felt that his decision to include LaGreca on his "team" was a good one. Each man on board the *Conquest 51* had his own particular reason for wanting to eliminate Dr. Eriksson. To Olsson, who represented a conglomerate of Swedish industrialists, including Volvo, Saab, Ericsson Electronics, and Upjohn-Pharmacia, the integrity and economic viability of Sweden could be destroyed by Eriksson, whose initially interesting theories had become detrimental to the country. But for Olsson, the elimination of Eriksson had to be done without any possibility that it could be traced back to a Swedish citizen. He didn't want the Swedish press to probe labor issues and start to ask a lot of embarrassing questions.

For Captain Hansson, a man whose ancestors were historically important in the development of the country, Eriksson could be the rallying point around which millions of pseudo-nationalists would try to topple the democratic parliament and, very possibly, precipitate a major civil war within Sweden.

For LaGreca, the debt owed America by the Swedish government would be its own reward for the service rendered. The U.S. had the machinery in place to handle Johannes's request for help in eliminating Eriksson. Economic favors in the future remained an unstated assumption.

For Johannes, it was nothing less than the ability to maintain his position as Prime Minister—his life's accomplishment.

18

VADSTENA, SWEDEN

Carter and Linda arrived at Vadstena exhausted and irritable. Each looked at the other with suspicion and distrust. While Carter always worked alone, his instincts told him that Linda was very much enmeshed in the entire Eriksson affair, and to abandon her here in Vadstena, would not serve his purposes. What she knew, he would learn sooner or later. Although she might be serving several masters, she was also risking her own life by staying with him.

Carter parked the Volvo in the former convent's parking lot and sat silently in the car, thinking. Was genocide a real possibility—in Sweden? Ask the average adult in America about the land of tall, beautiful blonde bombshells and the country would be described as peace loving, and a potential model for the rest of the world. Yet here he sat, comparing Germany with Sweden in terms of a potential genocide scale.

There was no question that Germany had been indicted twice within the twentieth century by the international community for committing genocide. And that didn't even account for the information lying buried within history books about the German Military High Command's intimate involvement with the Turkish military. It isn't every day that two countries conspire to exterminate two million Armenians by outright killing, starvation, and an inexorable forced march of several thousand miles over mountain and desert terrain from Mount Arat in Armenia to Aleppo in Syria. Most history books seemed to have forgotten this first act of genocide in the century. A group of second-rate academicians, with third-rate minds and first-rate pretensions, had become apologists for the Turks.

Carter was fearful that a forgotten moment of history might repeat itself in Vadstena. How could he not attempt to take Eriksson's life? He would be little more than a co-conspirator if he knew that genocide, or any other form of systematic killing was going to take place, and he did nothing. The world might be able to rationalize, forget, or ignore the occurrence but whatever the reason, he could not. And to paraphrase a famous British statesman, "One man with courage could inflict more damage than all the bureaucrats of 10 Downing Street."

Carter still wasn't sure what he was going to do with Linda . . .

"Hey Sterling Moss," Linda's voice lifted him from his reverie, "where are you going?"

Carter had left the car and was walking toward the entrance of the hotel that the convent had become. His eyes roamed the grounds, looking for its security system. "Keep your voice down!" Carter responded.

"I'll keep it down," she replied, following him, "as long as you don't play Shakespeare with me." She quickly caught up to him.

"What has Shakespeare got to do with this?" He generally enjoyed her wit, but right now, repartees in the middle of the night—in Eriksson's backyard—seemed particularly inappropriate.

"Remember the line 'send her to a nunnery'?" she said.

"And Sterling Moss?"

"About several decades ago," she responded, "when you were in your pubescent period, Moss was racing high performance cars all over the world."

"Did he win any races?" Carter asked, totally uninterested in continuing this conversation.

"The majority of them," she answered, trying to return to the spirit of the relationship they had while walking in Gamla Stan.

"So I assume that I can take that statement as a compliment?"

"I would say that racing *afficionados* would certainly embrace you and *fête* you as one of the greatest sports car drivers of all time." She paused, realizing that he couldn't care less about her line of chatter. She decided to try another tact. "Is this some kind of ritual that you have to go through?"

"What are you talking about?" he asked, taking mental measurement of the height and length of the building, and its proximity to the adjacent clinic. "Why are you suddenly deciding to attack me?"

"Did you ever hear of something called 'fear'?" she asked.

"Of me?" he asked, watching for any shadows darting across the immaculate grounds.

"Is having a swollen head a professional hazard?" she asked, following two paces behind him.

"If it's not me," he responded, laughingly, "then whom would you be afraid of?"

"If you hear hoofbeats, don't think of zebras," she replied.

"Another aphorism?"

"No," she answered, "but considering the mission we are about to undertake, wouldn't you think that exhibiting some fear would be more than appropriate?"

"Ah, now I see the problem we've been having in our intimate *tête à têtes*," Carter declared.

"And pray tell," she asked, "what might that be?"

"A slight change in pronoun from 'me' to 'we,'" he responded.

"I think I've earned the right to that change," she stated adamantly.

"I don't know what gave you that idea."

"Oh something stupid like having been shot at," she answered, "then arrested along with you, taken with much embarrassment to the American Embassy, and, the *pièce de résistance,* being almost killed by a Mercedes."

"Perhaps it's a little late to remind you," Carter interjected, "but I don't recall inviting you to accompany me. If anything, I tried on several occasions to discourage you." Carter was much less interested in Linda's fears or entitlement. He was trying to figure out the best way to gain entry into Eriksson's clinic. He decided that the front door might be the most effective way.

"You really are a cold-blooded animal," she said.

"Thank you," he responded. "In my profession that's considered quite a compliment."

"Trust me," she answered, "I'm not complimenting you."

"Shhh," he said, tired of the sound of her voice in the stillness of the night. "You're going to notify everyone in the entire region that we've arrived. I still don't know what your agenda is," Carter continued, "and I probably won't know for quite a long time. I'm not sure who you really work for and what you really want from me. But my paranoid suspicions tell me that you're here with me for reasons which I can't begin to fathom. And maybe, shouldn't want to."

"Isn't it a little late for truth or consequences?" Linda stopped in place and stared at him with contempt.

"Look, do you intend to accompany me inside?" Carter asked, annoyed with her games. "If not, it was nice knowing you."

"Single or double beds?" she asked coyly.

"Sex certainly has an interesting way of raising its voracious head," Carter responded. "I'm simply suggesting that if you stay with me you may find yourself in a situation which will continue to be dangerous."

"Well, at least we have something in common," she responded, "besides our mutual mistrust."

"And what is that?" he asked.

"Our common passion for action and danger," she answered, confronting him with her own assessment of their situation.

"You're telling me that you're addicted to the adrenaline rush?" he asked.

"Bravo!" she clapped. "You finally caught on to my agenda. It wasn't all that difficult, was it?"

"Linda, I don't know about you, but I'm exhausted," Carter said. "Could we just check in and continue this discussion tomorrow morning?"

"Whatever the good doctor desires," Linda answered. "Just remember, we want two rooms."

Although it was too dark to fully appreciate the architecture of the former convent, Carter couldn't have been happier that it had been renovated ten years before into a charming hotel. The barren nuns' rooms were now intimate guest rooms. The long corridors that were once stark and ascetic, now were adorned with paintings by local artists. One of the chapels had been converted into a hospitable breakfast area. What had remained intact, thankfully, in addition to the exterior stone walls, was the original air of calm and restfulness. Both Carter and Linda were in rooms that faced the lake.

The view of the moonlight rippling off the water relaxed Carter as much as anything could at that point. In some ways he was dreading tomorrow, and the start of his search for Eriksson. He would have to figure out what to do with Linda; maybe he'd pick a fight with her and make sure she left before she became a liability to him. He certainly didn't want her to be with him when he found Eriksson.

It was the thought of killing Eriksson that kept him from sleeping. Carter lay in bed, his eyes closed, hoping that he could get some rest. But his mind was preoccupied by one thought. How would he get to Eriksson with the least amount of exposure to himself, execute him without a weapon, and leave the scene undetected?

It was one of the mysteries of his profession that every assignment had a definite ebb and flow, a tidal wave of distinctive emotions and practical concerns. He would always feel euphoric when asked to undertake an assignment that was clearly stated, time delineated, handsomely compensated—and worthy. After a cursory check of the *bona fides* of the assignor, in this case Atherton did not require one, he would enter a period of latent activity and planning, appearing as if nothing was happening. Indeed, nothing focused was really happening. But by not focusing directly on the assignment he was allowing the different elements of the task to unconsciously brew in his mind until he could discern a central point of focus around which to develop a strategy.

Contrary to movie stereotypes, a "freelancer" like himself, with years of experience, did not spend most of his waking hours planning out the details of a mission. If truth be known, he belonged to the group that were proud to identify themselves as procrastinators, much as he was in completing his homework in college or his autopsies in medical school. He waited until the last minute, the point at which he felt the guilt of inactivity. Then, and only then, all the intellectual and emotional juices would rush through his body, urging him to concentrate on the details of the assignment before him.

He repeated to himself the mantra of his overall strategy—surprise, mystify, and deceive. These were principals that he had culled from his own experience as well as from the writings of the brilliant military strategists Sun Tzu and Baron von Clausewitz, both of whom believed that physical assault or battle was simply an extension of policy.

As for surprise, he suspected that if Captain Hansson and the American ambassador knew why he was really in Sweden, there was a serious degradation in the element of surprise. And that meant that Eriksson might even know of his presence. So the element of surprise had to be stricken from his strategic approach.

This left the elements of mystification and deception. It was the paradoxical nature of strategy from which Carter liked to work. Logically, common sense might dictate that he assume a disguise and approach Eriksson as someone other than himself. But Carter decided to meet him directly, as a fellow physician, who had heard of his experiences, and was interested in setting up comparable clinics in the

United States, especially California, where there was an uncontainable flood of illegal immigrants.

This approach would obviate his more typical *modus operandi* of observing his target's pattern of behavior, evaluating his target's security apparatus, acquiring necessary blueprints of grounds and buildings, and deciding on the most effective secret means of attack.

Since Atherton had made it explicitly clear that the use of a weapon was forbidden, Carter would have to rely on both his psychological guile and physical prowess. That's why, he guessed, the mission was assigned to him. Atherton knew that Carter rarely worked with any weapons, other than his serrated knife. Carter was well aware of Atherton's sensitivity to the collateral damage that could be caused if weapons were discovered upon boarding a plane, when entering a country, or on a routine customs search. Atherton did not want an international incident before Carter had even entered Sweden. And once inside any country, the likelihood of being discovered with an unauthorized weapon would significantly increase Carter's chances of being apprehended for more than illegal possession of a lethal weapon. Neither Atherton nor Carter could afford to take that chance.

So what would be his method of execution? Eriksson, according to the profile Carter had been given, was a smart, wily, paranoid fox. Even if he believed Carter's story, and allowed him inside the clinic, Eriksson would be continuously monitoring Carter's activities, paying special attention to his non-verbal behavior.

So the crucial strategic element once inside the clinic was to impress Eriksson by being cooperative, sympathetic to his work, and then at the proper time, strike. And the window of opportunity for that strike was going to be small.

But when it occurred, what would be the best way of killing Eriksson? Carter wondered. A quick thrust with a fist straight into his vocal cords would affect instantaneous death? Or use the heel of his palm and ram Eriksson's nose straight into the cribiform plate protecting his brain. That would transform a broken nose into a lethal weapon, creating significant damage in the frontal lobe and sepsis in the spinal fluid. Or, if he could approach Eriksson from the back, Carter could apply an inordinate amount of pressure on the carotid artery, cutting off circulation to the brain, leading to syncope and eventual death. He decided to go with whatever seemed appropriate at the time. Even the use of his serrated knife.

Once the assignment was accomplished, Carter had to worry about his exit strategy. But he was very drowsy, and, more often than not, the escape strategy could not be planned in advance. In this case, the movies paralleled reality; an escape was far more spontaneous than one could imagine. The solution generally didn't appear until Carter was executing the target.

As a sliver of daylight pierced through the wooden shutters, Carter finally fell asleep.

Linda slipped out of her room the moment she decided that Carter was in bed and went downstairs to a pay telephone. For all of the convent's modernization, it had not installed telephones in each room. She disliked talking about sensitive matters on an open public telephone; there were too many variables that she could not control. But this was probably better than having someone trace a call from her hotel room.

She knew beforehand that this would be an uncomfortable conversation. But she had to keep her client informed about the status of the assignment. And yet, be vague on the telephone.

"No," she said, almost surprised to have found him, "he has not yet found them . . ."

"What is the problem?" the scrambled, deep male voice on the other side of the telephone asked.

"The good doctor has yet to accomplish his original mission," she answered defensively.

"How long will that take?"

"I can't tell you," she explained, "because there have been too many intervening variables."

"Please be specific!"

"It's hard on the telephone," she responded defensively, "but it involves officials here who seem to know exactly what his mission is. Secrecy has been breached . . . somewhere."

"Whom do you suspect?" the voice asked, in such an electronically garbled manner that she wasn't certain that she had heard every word. But the gist was quite clear.

Linda already had a clear suspicion of who was leaking information on Carter. But she did not know why. And she certainly couldn't tell the voice on the telephone. It was a hazard of her profession as a Washington "information gatherer" to often find out things that she did not want to know.

"I'm not certain, sir!" she said curtly, sounding like the intelligence operative she had been for five years, before she had decided to leave and dedicate the subsequent twenty years of her life to making money. The contacts she had made in the Washington political establishment, throughout DOD, on "the Hill," and in the various industries for which she gathered information—automotive, telecommunications, and aerospace, corporations that needed intelligence about what was going on in Washington relative to their operation—had been invaluable to her. And life as a capitalist was so much easier than she had ever imagined. Primarily, she attended Congressional hearings that were relevant to a particular client. She usually would collect intelligence on the status of a specific piece of legislation in committee, how much money would be appropriated if the legislation passed, or which regulatory agency would be involved.

But this particular client and assignment was different. It harkened back to her years in the intelligence community, and involved entrapment, surveillance, co-optation, betrayal, duplicity, and most likely, extreme danger. All of the essential elements required of a seasoned field operative. That was why she had been chosen. And that was why she was willing to take on the assignment. It was a welcome break from her everyday "research" job, which frequently was routine and boring. More importantly, she would acquire a new major client, one even larger than her current biggest, the automotive industry.

Success in this assignment was very specifically spelled out from the beginning. When she had accepted the assignment, she felt that she was capable of accomplishing everything that she was asked to do. But she was becoming increasingly uncertain of her own abilities. And her feelings for Carter were getting in the way. He was attractive, sensitive, amusing, almost boyishly so—and lethal. If she had known from the start precisely how lethal, she would have asked for a larger retainer and fee. But her client had been very clever. He had only hinted at the fact that while Carter was a physician, he was not always a man "predisposed to healing." That was a hell of an understatement, she thought. But she certainly couldn't reveal that to her client. The "can-do" attitude was what he expected—and would get.

"That's not an acceptable excuse, Linda!" The words were still garbled, but the anger came through quite clearly.

"There's nothing more I can say over this line," Linda repeated, trying to deflect the wrath of her client.

"Have you made contact with our mutual friend yet?"

"What do you think?" she asked facetiously. She knew that this response would annoy him.

"You know what I expect," he responded curtly.

"As you know all too well," Linda said, "our personal and professional relationship goes back a long way."

"Let's get it over with," the voice ordered. "No excuses!"

"Yes, sir!" she responded, hanging up the receiver. She walked back to her room and lay down on the bed to rest and blot out the image of Londsdale's death that wouldn't leave her. There was no doubt that she was wading in dangerous waters. Now she had to figure out how not to drown accidentally—or by someone else's design.

Neither Carter nor Linda slept well. They arrived at breakfast minutes before the kitchen closed, but they never made it through the arched doorway. A young blond-haired man with a ring through his ear interrupted them. "Dr. Alison

Carter? Ms. Linda Watson? Would you both please follow me," he asked politely.

"Haven't we met before?" Carter asked, focusing on the earring.

"This way, please!" Jan stuck a gun into Carter's ribs and motioned him toward the entrance of the convent. He was still stinging from the knife wounds Carter had inflicted on his back and shoulders when they had fought in Gamla Stan. "Watch your step," he said to Linda. "We wouldn't want you to fall accidentally on church grounds. It would be sacrilegious, if you know what I mean."

19

VADSTENA, SWEDEN

"I welcome both of you to Vadstena," Dr. Derek Eriksson said with a warm, cheerful disposition. "Dr. Alison Carter..." Eriksson nodded in respect, "and charming companion, Ms. Linda Watson." He was elegantly atavistic, dressed in a dark blue velvet smoking jacket and a striped silk ascot, both of which had been extremely fashionable in the mid-1940's.

"Thank you very much for inviting us," Carter replied, looking around the room filled with antiquated psychiatric equipment. "It's very hospitable of you and your friend..."

"His name is Jan," Eriksson interrupted. "You seem a little bit upset, Ms. Watson. Are you all right?"

"I'm fine," she responded coldly, pressing her body more closely against Carter's in an attempt to draw from his quiet strength. On the other hand, Eriksson came off as steel hands in velvet gloves. Smooth, egregiously polite, but lethal. While she was definitely used to sharks in the male-dominated world of automotive manufacturing, he was of a different species. She could sense that in his hardened blue eyes, the stakes he played for were lives, and not corporate advancement.

"Is there anything I can offer you to drink?" Eriksson asked casually, as if they were about to chatter over cocktails before the meal would be served.

"Nothing for me," Carter replied.

"Anything for you?" he asked Linda.

"No, I'm just fine," she answered, her voice wavering slightly.

"I assume that there was a special reason for you to be in Vadstena today," Eriksson said, continuing to maintain calm.

"I would presume that if we told you that we came here to visit the abbey," Carter answered, "it would not be too convincing."

"Correct," Eriksson replied, smiling. "You might want to try out some other reasons, however, just to test out my credibility level," he laughed and turned toward Linda, "or at least we would have some idle chitchat just to keep you that much longer in a state of fear."

Sadistic son-of-a-bitch, she thought. But he was right. The longer they maintained their desultory conversation, the more psychologically painful it became.

"What about this one, Dr. Eriksson?" Carter continued. "As a fellow physician, I've heard through the medical and political grapevine that you have been engaged in some very interesting, if not unusual, research."

"On that point, Dr. Carter," Eriksson replied, "I certainly can agree with you. If, however, something untoward were to happen to me, would you be willing to undertake the completion of my projects?"

"It would depend on precisely what projects you were working on," Carter responded, wondering how long Eriksson was planning to maintain this ridiculous charade.

"Let me see," Eriksson responded, "there are several projects which could use someone like yourself to be, perhaps, a Project Manager?"

"Is that a job offer?" Carter laughed.

Linda looked at both of them with disbelief and disdain. Jan, who was standing near Eriksson chuckling, seemed a total fool.

"Perhaps you'd like to see what you'd be getting yourself into," Eriksson replied, leading them down a long hallway to a room replete with all types of instruments of torture that Carter recognized immediately.

"I see you are interested in the endurance of pain," Carter said, noticing the falagas and bamboo canes. He felt Linda squeeze his right hand.

"Don't be afraid, Ms. Watson," Eriksson said, noticing her movement. "That's a very natural reaction when people are shown into this room. But since Dr. Carter and I share the same medical background where, shall I say, we are used to these tools of our trade, I would be extremely surprised if Carter were to show any signs of fear or concern. Isn't that right, Dr. Carter?"

"I would say, Dr. Eriksson, that your analysis is right on the mark," Carter answered facetiously, almost beginning to enjoy the verbal jousting.

"As for your previous question, Dr. Carter, regarding your participation in one of my major clinical studies, I may have one that would be of interest to you. It deals with the concept and application of torture. Shall I continue, Dr. Carter?"

"Of course," Carter responded, his mouth feeling very dry when he saw Jan place two heavy telephone books on a table near Eriksson. Carter knew that it was time to prepare himself mentally for what was about to come.

"In this experiment," Eriksson pointed to the telephone books, "I am trying to perfect methods of torture designed over centuries to promote the well-known three D's—debility, dependency, and dread. I have worked with sensory deprivation—you know, isolation, hooding, constant noise, darkness. Also, the restriction of physiological needs, like food, water, sleep, and use of the toilet. Social isolation frequently serves the same purpose. Not to forget such humiliations as overcrowding, living in filth, sexual abuse, threats, or the use of drugs to distort reality. And I trust you are familiar with the use of psychological interrogation techniques that reinforce helplessness, such as abusing victims regardless of their responses to the interrogation." Eriksson smiled a self-satisfied smile.

"Most fascinating," Carter responded, as if Eriksson's little speech had no bearing on what was to follow.

"From an expert like yourself," Eriksson responded, with almost a hint of pride, "I would say that was quite a compliment."

Still smiling, Eriksson smacked the two telephone books together with his large, powerful hands. The sound it made achieved what he hoped for, a noticeable increase in fear in Linda. "The real problem for this evening, I am afraid to say without offending Ms. Watson in any way, concerns me and Dr. Carter. Because the real purpose of your visit to Sweden," he turned to Carter, "is my extermination. Is that not right, Doctor?"

"I think you can say that with close to 100 percent accuracy."

"How, when, and where he plans to do it," Eriksson retorted, with an even more affable smile, "is strictly up to Dr. Carter's professional assessment. Not very different from if he were scheduling a major surgical procedure."

"Perhaps for the sake of time, we could proceed directly to the experiment you want to show me," Carter added, tiring of Eriksson's preening.

"Good," Eriksson declared, with a certain childish glee in his voice.

Eriksson motioned to Carter to sit down on a wooden chair alongside the examining table. "This technique is one of the more basic ones that could be used with an assortment of different objects. For this occasion, I have decided to use these two telephone directories," Eriksson added solicitously. "Does this in any way disturb your sense of aesthetics?"

"Not at all." Carter seated himself, knowing what was to come. Linda withdrew to one corner of the room, visibly shaken.

Again, Eriksson balanced each telephone book in the palm of each of his hands, but this time he swung them simultaneously against Carter's ears.

"Agggghhhh!" Linda screamed.

Carter said and did nothing, except close his eyes.

"This is the Telefano Project," Eriksson reported. "I use telephone books to study levels of bodily damage."

"Stop it!" Linda yelled. "This is sheer madness."

Carter shook his head. Both ears were ringing in the aftermath of the blow.

"Stop this craziness!" Linda screamed out, feeling totally helpless.

Eriksson raised the two telephone books and again slammed them against Carter's ears with the force of Moses cracking the tablets at Mt. Sinai.

20

VADSTENA, SWEDEN

The scream that Carter let out as the two telephone books slammed against his ears was as much to convince himself that he was still alive, as it was to express his pain. He didn't have to touch his neck to know that the warm sensation he felt was blood flowing down his face.

He heard nothing. Everything around him grew surreal. His mind dissociated itself from his body. It was as if he was observing himself being tortured without the immediate sense of the pain. His eardrums had to be injured, but he could not tell whether he was now in pain.

There was something diabolically comical as he watched Linda's mouth contort into an image that recalled Edward Munch's *Scream*. No sounds emanated from her mouth that Carter could hear, but the image of his favorite painting stayed with him.

Carter watched Eriksson's lips move, but nothing was comprehensible. He could make out a few words here and there, but nothing that constituted a coherent sentence or thought. Without attempting to resist, Carter watched as Eriksson slowly raised the two telephone books high into the air again, and brought them crashing down against his ears a third time. This time Carter felt as if his head was being crushed by a vise. His mouth changed into an expression that he inferred was screaming out in pain.

He felt increasingly more dissociated. The pain was no longer part of him, but belonged to the carcass of a man on a chair whom everyone called Alison Carter. Watching blood drip from his face onto the back of his hand, Carter had to admit that he was probably not a pretty sight. But at least he still had a modicum of hearing.

The dissociated Carter was feeling extremely drowsy. But he knew better than to ask for any respite. The purpose of torture was to debilitate your victim, lowering his physical and psychological resistance. And Carter was determined not to give Eriksson a modicum of satisfaction that he was accomplishing his goals. There would be no pleas. No resistance. No obdurate attitude. Carter even imagined himself being released by Eriksson because he was such a good victim. A good student. And a good teacher should appreciate that fact.

Suddenly, something was happening that his mind could not process effectively. His shoes and socks were being taken off. Jan, the sorcerer's apprentice, was holding his two bare feet in the air. Eriksson now took a long bamboo cane with frayed edges from a highly polished chrome tray filled with several gleaming metal implements. How professional Eriksson seemed, approaching the entire torture process as if it were simply another mundane medical procedure. Managed care might have given it inpatient status allowing the torturee one day of recuperation, and then insisting that he return home.

Carter tried to force his mind to concentrate on the here and now as he watched Eriksson place rubber gloves on his hands and rub the bamboo stick down with a clear fluid he assumed was alcohol. He wondered whether managed care in the United States would give torture a diagnostic reimbursable category. Was there a fixed fee schedule based on a clinical differential of types of torture? No sooner had that thought crossed his mind than Carter began to realize that he was beginning to confuse the absurd and the irrational with the real world.

Eriksson raised the bamboo stick and smacked the sole of Carter's right foot.

"Jesus Christ!" screamed Carter, suddenly thrust from his throbbing world. His mental state of dissociation had been disrupted. Real pain had been substituted for observed pain. Excruciating pain, thought Carter, was really the only appropriate term to describe what he felt.

"Fuck you!" Carter screamed at Eriksson.

Eriksson simply smiled back, clearly taking great pleasure from the fact that he was hurting Carter.

Linda blanched at the sight of his suffering, but felt entirely helpless, a position she had not been in in years.

"What the hell do you want from me?" Carter screamed.

"I'm so pleased that you are back with us, Dr. Carter!" Eriksson responded, smacking Carter several more times, leaving deep red lines on both feet. "As you and I know so well," Eriksson continued, "we can always count on the falanga to bring someone back from his protective state of mental dissociation."

"Nothing is as effective . . . and as cheap. Every little dictator, sadist, and murderer can have his own falanga at a minimal cost," Carter answered, as the bamboo welts radiated intense pain throughout his body. He tried to laugh, just to piss Eriksson off. "I think it might be worthy of a television infomercial."

"Please don't mock me, Dr. Carter!" Eriksson responded, clearly irritated. "I have, to the best of my ability, treated you with the respect due one professional to another." He swung the stick hard against Carter's left foot.

"Ohhhhhhhhh!" Carter screamed. He tried desperately to dissociate his mind from his pain but it wasn't working. The pain of "telephono" was more adaptive than the pain of "falanga." And to think that the National Institutes of Health had declined to fund a study he had proposed years before on various torture modes and their lasting effects.

"I see that it doesn't take very much to get your attention," Eriksson said. "Hold his feet higher!" he instructed Jan. "Who bought your services?"

"I don't know what you are talking about," Carter responded, wondering just how much Eriksson did know.

"Don't play coy with me," Eriksson smacked his left sole again with the bamboo stick.

"Nooooooo!" Carter screamed. The pain was becoming unbearable. Soon he would pass out. But he wouldn't give Eriksson the benefit of an answer. Marx was right, he thought. The dialectic between the slave and the master was really determined by the slave. As it was with torture. The torturer was weaker than his victim precisely because he had to use force to elicit information. As Sun Tzu said in *The Art of War*, "He who must use force has already lost!"

"I know you are in Sweden to kill me," Eriksson said. "Who gave you the orders?"

"Mark Londsdale!" Carter revealed. He was going to use the smaller fish to try to deflect the larger one.

"He is just a go-between!" Eriksson shook his head with annoyance.

"If you don't mind my correcting you," Carter grimaced as he spoke, "Londsdale no longer is. The proper verb in English concerning his status is 'was.'"

"What?" Eriksson asked, completely surprised. "He's dead?"

"As if you didn't know that already," Carter responded. "Now, would you mind asking your assistant to lower my legs? It would make it much easier for me to talk to you."

"But, of course," Eriksson said, confused by Carter's statement. "Jan, lower the good doctor's feet and bathe them so that he doesn't become infected."

"Thank you," Carter said, wincing as the young torturer washed the blood from the soles of his feet with what he guessed was pure ethanol. "This is certainly very considerate of you . . ."

"So, Londsdale is dead!" Eriksson repeated.

"That's right," Carter said, still in pain but grateful that his head was no longer feeling numb and his ears had stopped bleeding.

"How did it happen?"

"He was killed on board a ferry Linda and I were taking in Stockholm. Are you telling me that you didn't..."

"And you did not catch a glimpse of the murderer?" Eriksson ignored Carter's supposition.

"No!" Carter responded, determined to play along with Eriksson's charade.

"That son-of-a-bitch!"

"Who?"

"The man who hired you!" Eriksson spit the words out in disgust.

"And who was that?" Carter asked. "I thought you didn't know." Perhaps, if he waited long enough, he would learn more from Eriksson than Eriksson would learn from him. Very frequently, in Carter's profession, the person you are to neutralize knows more about what is actually going on than you do. Perhaps he, Carter, was finally on his way to learning whether his assignment was a cover for deceit, mistake, or betrayal.

"Prime Minister Johannes Strindberg, of course!"

"What?" Carter was somewhat incredulous.

"Yes, my dear colleague," Eriksson responded, motioning Jan to end his ministrations. "And several others."

"Which others?" Carter asked, wondering what effect the knowledge of Londsdale's death would have on Eriksson. Who knows, thought Carter. It would not be the first time that someone shifted allegiances in the middle of the hunt.

"Your own ambassador," Eriksson spit out with contempt, "Carl LaGreca!"

21

VADSTENA, SWEDEN

Carter lay on the examining table in silence while Eriksson applied ointment to the soles of his feet. Eriksson appeared absorbed in thought, his erect, elegant body transformed into one of a hunchback mendicant. Linda stood at the other end of the table, washing the blood from Carter's face and neck. She had regained her composure, grateful that neither she nor Carter had been killed, but worried about their future. There appeared to be some kind of detente between Carter and Eriksson, but she was confused about the reason.

"You're extremely good at your profession, Dr. Eriksson," Carter said grudgingly.

"Thank you," Eriksson responded, aware that it was a backhanded compliment. In the beginning, he had intended to destroy Carter. But before he did, he had wanted to validate his information that the prime minister was behind the plot to assassinate him. After it became clear that Carter really didn't know who he was working for, the torture became purposeless. Carter had obviously not had any contact with anyone other than Londsdale. And worse yet, Carter had been convinced that it was he, Eriksson, who had killed Londsdale. Nothing could have been further from the truth. Perhaps there was greater utility in having Carter as an ally than as an adversary.

Jan handed Eriksson a portable cassette and pushed the *power* button. Music filled the room. "... dancing queen ... you can dance ... you can die ... having the time of your life ... see that girl ... dancing queen ... you are the dancing queen ..."

"ABBA," Carter stated without surprise. "I imagine your file on me is as thick as my file on you."

"Of course," Eriksson smiled, trying to be conciliatory.

"Maybe it would be more appropriate if you played their song, 'Knowing me, Knowing you,' " Carter said, singing in his distinctive atonal voice: "... knowing me, knowing you ... is the best I can do ..."

The irony of Carter's words were not lost on Eriksson. Perhaps Carter did appreciate his overture of reconciliation after all. "Knowing me, knowing you"! How adolescent, he thought, that now they were communicating through music.

Eriksson wondered whether Carter could understand a man like himself, a man who understood the paradoxes of good and evil. What often appeared evil was, more often than not, something else. True, he was ruthless, even sadistic in his methods. But he had a cause. And that wouldn't change. What right did the Swedish government have to continue accepting immigrants from all over the world when, in fact, Sweden was going bankrupt? His country had become a welfare state unable to provide for its own people, let alone the immigrants. The quality of the education offered in the schools had deteriorated. Socialized medicine as the Swedes knew it for decades was constantly excluding treatments from its register. Chronic medical care had succeeded the concept of curing illness, since patients waited an incredibly long time for basic diagnostic tests. A patient with cancer of the lung could be assured of waiting for a chest X ray so long that it came just about the time one would expect a metastasis of a lung tumor, already too late for remedial therapy. That was the new system of medical care that Sweden provided to its residents. And on top of controllable diseases becoming incurable due to lack of treatment, negligent feeding and regular medical care of current patients resulted in severe malnourishment, tuberculosis, cholera, and typhus. A situation of malignant malpractice. And it was Prime Minister Johannes Strindberg, that sanctimonious S.O.B., and his minion of political fools, who were responsible for the evils that permeated Swedish society.

The influx of immigrants had also brought men who would work at a fraction of the pay that Swedes were requesting. So Swedish youth, with all of its optimism, education, and political promise, were bereft of everything—a job, an honest wage and, worst of all, a future. That was criminal, thought Eriksson. An irrevocable injustice to the people of Sweden. If properly explained, he was certain that Carter would understand.

Eriksson's intelligence sources had informed him that Carter, not unlike himself, distrusted his own federal government and international organizations. But how did he justify working for the State Department while he was also performing "freelance" work? Perhaps, Carter was addicted to the very same thing that he, Eriksson, was.

"You know," Eriksson said, "I have been such a poor host. I completely forgot to ask you two what you might want to drink or eat."

"Nothing, thank you," Linda retorted. "I'm just very tired. If we are free to go, I'd like to return to the hotel and go to bed."

"Oh, no, please!" Eriksson begged. "I implore you not to take away what little sense of dignity I have left after my behavior today. I would feel better if I could offer you some appropriate hospitality."

"I must say I'm quite flattered to have been elevated from ignoble assassin to guest, all within a span of an hour," Carter responded, leery of Eriksson's mental state. It was too labile. His emotional thermostat went from hot to cold too quickly.

Jan brought in a tray of sandwiches, sodas, and a brown sealed envelope. Linda looked at the goodies before her and remembered that she needed some food or she would pass out.

"You win, Dr. Eriksson," Carter said, humoring his captor and careful not to offend him by omitting his professional title. "Linda and I would love to join you for lunch. As you know," Carter nodded toward Jan, "we missed our breakfast."

Eriksson was oblivious to Carter's words as he read the message contained in the envelope.

"We have to get out of the building now!" he shouted, and motioned to Jan to take some papers from the desk. Eriksson ran to the door, pulling Linda with him by the arm, followed by Carter, who was limping as fast as he could behind them. They raced down the hallway and out of the building. Jan, papers in hand, brought up the rear. They didn't stop until they were well behind a row of trees approximately one hundred feet from the building. No one else exited the building; it was closed to tourists that day.

"Either get down on the ground, or press your bodies tightly against a tree. It will protect you!" Eriksson ordered.

"From what?" Carter asked, out of breath.

The answer came in the form of an explosion. The building that had been their prison a few seconds ago exploded into a massive yellow-white flame. The sound of the explosion could only have been reduplicated by the roar of the canons in Tchaikovsky's "1812 Overture."

22

VADSTENA, SWEDEN

"What in God's name happened?" Carter asked, totally confused about who was the real enemy. "How did you know that we should evacuate the building?

"When you receive a note telling you that the building you are standing in will blow up 'shortly,'" Eriksson replied, brushing the debris from his clothing, "I don't think that it should be second-guessed."

Crowds of onlookers began to gather around the fiery building.

"Who did this, Eriksson?" Carter asked, disturbed that it made no sense to him. "And why?"

I don't know," Eriksson answered, "but I certainly have very definite ideas."

"Like whom?" Carter asked.

"Someone who knew that both Ms. Watson and you were my guests," Eriksson answered, as if life were too simple to keep explaining, "and didn't want you to be killed. Make no mistake. The explosion was intended to warn or possibly kill me. Not you. Or Ms. Watson."

"Then why didn't they blow up the building during the night, when we weren't there?" Carter asked.

"That's a good question," Eriksson replied. "I can only surmise it was because they knew I wasn't there either.

Someone was monitoring our entire . . . meeting, and at the appropriate moment, decided to deliver the note." He paused and turned toward Jan. "Did you see the messenger?"

"No, Doctor," Jan replied, nervously.

"Was he wearing a mask?" Carter asked.

"Yes!" Jan answered. "He was at the front door on one of those small Japanese motorbikes when I went for food. He said 'For Eriksson' and threw the envelope at me."

"Clearly, they were trying to frighten us," Linda interjected.

"Who, Ms. Watson, is 'us'?" Eriksson asked.

"That's a good point, Linda," Carter complimented her and reaffirmed Eriksson's point. "If 'they' had wanted to kill Eriksson, it could have been done without our having been in the clinic. So, clearly, the message of threat was sent to all of 'us,' Eriksson, you, and me."

"What about me?" Jan interjected, feeling unimportant.

"I'm certain the bomb was intended for you as well," Carter replied, sarcastically. "When it comes to murder and mayhem, you're certainly part of the team."

"So now we are a team?" Eriksson chuckled. "First, you come to Sweden on an assignment to kill me. Then, I use my . . . skills . . . in partial retaliation, but also to elicit information from you. This is quite a team."

"At least it shows that we are flexible," Carter smiled. He looked at Linda who seemed completely bewildered by the flippant, friendly attitude of these two recent adversaries.

"Whoever tried to assassinate us . . ." Eriksson said.

"I'm not so sure they tried," Carter interrupted. "If they had wanted to kill any or all of us, they had plenty of opportunities. They could have conveniently disposed of me when I was arrested. They could have taken out Linda when they shot Londsdale. She was standing right next to him. And, as we already said, they could have terminated both you and Jan and, quite frankly, your entire operation, despite its supposed tight security, here in Vadstena. But, for whatever reason, they didn't want to."

"Then what are you saying, my dear colleague?" Eriksson asked, smiling at the realization that they had become co-conspirators by dint of being fellow targets.

"Tell me if this scenario makes any sense," Carter replied, summing up what was obvious to him. "You have had some type of formal or informal relationship with the ruling government. Otherwise, your operation could not have existed and your own safety could not have been assured, as it has been up until now. But as soon as I appeared in Sweden, whatever understandings you may have had disappeared, for reasons still to be determined. As a result, both you and I were placed 'on notice', you could say, that we are in danger of losing our lives." Carter was also smiling; he had been addressed as "dear colleague" by a professional adversary who, at any given moment, could turn on him.

"I'll be quite frank with you," Eriksson said conspiratorially to Carter, "I know that you consider me repugnant for all I have done in the name of Swedish nationalism."

"Don't tell me we're about to hear a *mea culpa*," Linda interjected.

"No," Eriksson responded seriously. "I make no apologies for what I believe in—a Sweden for Swedes. It's that simple. You forget, Ms. Watson, that we Nordics are a homogenous group. And many, if not most, of us would like to keep it that way."

"Maybe," she added, "it's time to dilute your genes, so you don't become achondroplastic dwarfs with contorted, truncated bodies, like Toulouse-Lautrec, whose parents were first cousins."

"Heterogeneity may be useful in the United States," Eriksson responded, "where you have so many different ethnic and religious groups. And I might add, where you also have a very healthy economy. Need I remind you that Sweden does not have the economic, social, or political advantages of your formidable country? We have completely bled out our economic resources and political will. Our major industrial firms are all relocating offshore. The industrial part of our tax base, which provides the necessary revenue for maintaining our world-renowned welfare safety net, is fast disappearing. Why do you think I was able to continue to pursue what you call 'atrocities'?"

Carter was surprised that Eriksson was willing to reveal so much, so quickly, and was hesitant to say a word, lest it stop his monologue. He needed either a confessor or an ally or both. Because of his age and grandiosity, Carter suspected that Eriksson was determined not to die without someone knowing his side of the story.

Carter thought about his own hurting feet and splitting headache. If he had not been subjected to Eriksson's torture, this perverse relationship that was forming between both men would never have occurred. Was it doctor-to-doctor? Or assassin-to-assassin? Whatever it was, it seemed to be facilitating a special emotional bond on Eriksson's part.

"Rest assured, my dear doctor, I could not have accomplished what I have if the chief of police, several prime ministers, and the Swedish High Court of Industry and Finance hadn't all tacitly, if not overtly, agreed with me."

"Not unlike the officially sanctioned sterilizations of sixty thousand women in Sweden?" Carter added.

"No, that can't be possible," Linda responded, horrified. "Why is it that I have never heard about it before?"

"Because," Eriksson responded, "that was kept as much of a secret as our current attempt at ethnic cleansing. But the reasons and the pattern of implementation were the same. A theory of welfare reform was postulated by one of our more famous social scientists that, in turn, was passed on to the prime minister and members of the Cabinet. They detailed a plan for implementing these—what you would consider barbaric—ideas, couched most elegantly in social science theories that had no basic validity, other than the fact that the authors were famous personages and they could contrive numbers that could justify their half-baked ideas."

"You are saying that they are like most of our American social scientists," Carter confirmed. "Frustrated human engineers who attempt to design a universe irrespective of the human cost. The Vietnam War's body count was very much along those lines. The more Viet Cong 'kills' we posted publicly, the more we expected to convince the American public that we were winning the war. Even when our senior officials at DOD, the White House, and the State Department knew differently."

"I can't tell you, Dr. Carter, how pleased I am to achieve this mutual understanding," Eriksson reached out to shake Carter's hand, having recognized a fellow cynic—or realist. A hesitant Carter responded.

Ironic, thought Carter, how mere hands could inflict so much damage and pain. He never ceased to be impressed by man's incredible desire to torture another human being. He wondered if animals tortured one another.

"Pardon me if I'm presumptuous," Carter said, as he watched the afternoon sunlight shimmer across the lake, "but what exactly do you intend to do next?"

"I think it's time for you and I to form an alliance," Eriksson responded.

"And what would be the purpose of this alliance?" Carter asked.

"Very simple," Eriksson replied. "I know that your assignment is to kill me. Right?"

"Correct," Carter said, knowing that game-playing was a thing of the past.

"I advise you to skip that step," Eriksson responded, clearly excited, "and try to uncover my former co-conspirators, those who are hidden so deep in the forest of anonymity that few know them."

"And then what?" Carter asked, realizing that the answer to this question would determine whether they could or would work together.

"It's quite simple, Dr. Carter," Eriksson responded with a devilish smile. "We document their collective treachery and, since I know that you Americans are foolishly enamored with 'the rule of law,' bring them in front of the Swedish public. Let the people decide what to do with them."

"And what if it destabilizes your country?" Carter asked,

still unclear whether it was wise to link up with this potential madman.

"And what if it destabilizes yours?" Eriksson asked, cryptically.

23

LAKE VÄNERN, SWEDEN

"I'm pleased that your clinic visit was successful," the prime minister said, responding to the voice on the other end of the secured telephone. His long legs were stretched across the carpeted galley of *Conquest 51*, which lay anchored near shore.

The galley looked like the aftermath of what American fraternity boys refer to in college as a "pig party." But in Sweden, when four men get together and allow their testosterone and libidos free rein, fueled on by Carlsburg beer, there was usually only one outcome: a quasi-adolescent free-for-all. All in the name of good fellowship, of course.

Only Johannes had kept completely focused on why they were really there. Reveling with old friends was a wonderful break in a tedious schedule, but only so far as political prudence permitted. In politics, friendships shifted as quickly as a teenage girl in love. More important than drinking to the point of inebriation, Johannes was receiving shore-to-ship telephone calls from intelligence agents and other operatives who were continuously updating the prime minister on the status of specific tasks that had been assigned to them weeks earlier. By dawn, he had to know whether those tasks had been fully accomplished.

If truth be known, Johannes was hoping that none of his

people would be successful. But that was the private Johannes, the one who could not reveal himself to his "friends." The political Johannes had made his decision a long time ago to cast his lot with the three men in his galley—Captain Hansson, Ambassador LaGreca, and Nils Olsson. The die was cast. Johannes and his friends were acting to preserve the political and financial viability of Sweden, and perhaps all the Scandinavian countries.

The stakes couldn't be higher. If Sweden fell, like Russia had, on a financial default of non-repayment of private international banking loans, loans extended by the International Monetary Fund and the World Bank, then the world capital markets could collapse and the least likely nation in the world, Sweden, would have precipitated a major world depression. It was hard for even him to believe that the outcome of Sweden's predicament was tied into the fate of two physicians—Dr. Derek Eriksson and Dr. Alison Carter.

As Prime Minister he was also committed to preventing the genocide of hundreds, if not thousands, of immigrants who had sought political sanctuary in Sweden. He had learned through informers that Eriksson was planning a major confrontation with the refugees that was to take place within the week, that could destabilize the government. But where would it take place? In which out-of-the-way town? In Stockholm itself? By God, he thought, the potential places were endless. The former Cambodian leader of the Khmer Rouge, Pol Pot, had killed close to two million of his countrymen without the world knowing anything about it for close to five years. And it still wouldn't have been known if not for the astute observations of a United States career FSO, Kenneth Quinn, who was doing his doctoral dissertation in Vietnam on fleeing Cambodian refugees. Who would have believed that Chancellor Adolf Hitler could have killed millions of Jews, gypsies, homosexuals, priests, and political dissidents before being stopped?

The history of twentieth-century genocide was one characterized by a collective desire to prevent mass violence, and the world's complete inability to do so. In 1999, the

Serbs killed and displaced approximately one million ethnic Albanians who wanted more independence for their province in Yugoslavia.

As recently as 1998, hooded men armed with axes descended on an isolated farm village near Algiers, Algeria, and slit the throats of sleeping residents, decapitating women and children, and gouging out the eyes of old men. Then, as if to complete the task, one village was burned to the ground so that one thousand more people could die from direct burns and smoke inhalation. In this particular case, the authorities blamed the Armed Islamic Group, a violent and militant Islamic organization. But Johannes knew enough about statecraft to suspect that it could be equally plausible that the authorities, who had remained in power for decades through illegal means, could have dressed up as Islamic militants and committed the horror so that the militants could be blamed.

And what about the incomprehensible massacre in 1994 of close to one million Tutsis by Rwandan Hutus? Contrary to what most people thought, more than a historic tribal conflict was being played out. Ninety percent of those massacred by non-Christians were proselytized Christians. Yet, this was a tragedy that could have been prevented. The United States of America had a month's warning that this massacre was going to happen, precipitated by France and Belgium; but neither the United Nations, nor the Organization of African Unity (OAU), nor the coalition of Christian churches and charities did anything to prevent it.

But the greatest indictment, Johannes thought, belonged to the grossly ineffectual United Nations. He recalled receiving copies of a cable sent by a Canadian, General Romeo Dallaire, who was the leader of several thousand UN peacekeeping forces in Rwanda. The general, sent there to prevent renewed outbreaks of violence between the Hutus and Tutsis, transmitted the cable to the Department of Peacekeeping Operations at UN headquarters in New York, informing senior officials that another genocide was being planned. He even went so far as to delineate precisely how the genocide would occur. That same day, the general received a reply that he had no mandate to intervene or do anything except observe. Within a period of less than a month, after the genocide had occurred, UN officials responded to a query into their negligence by a formal investigating committee, that "Dalliere's cable was just one piece on an ongoing daily communication. We get hyperbole in many reports." Johannes knew bureaucratic mumbo-jumbo when he heard it—anything that would obfuscate the fact that, like most senior bureaucrats around the world, these officials were numbed, blinded, deafened, and completely indifferent.

"Ask him about the bumper car ride!" Olsson begged Johannes, trying to pull him away from the telephone.

"Gentlemen," Johannes's tone was serious amidst his friends' increasingly loud banter, "the problem at the clinic seems to have been handled quite effectively."

"And what does that mean, Mr. Prime Minister?" Captain Hansson asked, half-inebriated.

"Hey, Hansson," LaGreca interjected jocularly, "I'd watch my tone of voice if I were you. Johannes is still the prime minister and you're just a measly captain in the police department."

LaGreca knew he was provoking Hansson. But there was much he still had to find out. Something did not make sense. Why would a captain of the police be included in this elite group? Of course, LaGreca appreciated Hansson's tactical and operational utility to everyone on board. But there was something more to it than that. And, as usual, the CIA Station Chief and Defense Attache could not, or would not, provide him with requested information because, contrary to all of their bureaucratic mumbo-jumbo about "need to know" and "compartmentalized intelligence" to which the ambassador was not privy, the basic answer was quite simple. No one knew. Not the ambassador. Not the CIA. And, as befits all good bureaucrats, no one could admit their deficiencies.

"The American ambassador is correct," Hansson said, slurring his words, "as usual, of course. So, if you don't mind, Mr. Prime Minister, would you please explain to us simple folks what it means when you said that 'the problem at the clinic seems to have been handled quite effectively'? Remember, I'm just a humble servant of the state and I only eat simple foods without any fancy sauces."

"Hansson," Johannes angrily responded, "you might try that simple 'humble pie'—as the Americans call it—routine on someone else. But, please don't insult our intelligence. Everyone here knows the Hanssons have a pedigree far more distinguished than anyone else in this galley. So don't play your theatrics to an audience that isn't there."

"You still haven't answered my question," Hansson responded, laughing out loud. He loved to banter with Johannes because the prime minister always took himself so seriously.

"The answer is quite simple!" Johannes replied curtly. He was tired, and becoming irritable. And he had mixed emotions about the plan that was being executed. "Dr. Eriksson's clinic was blown up!"

"Was anyone killed?" LaGreca asked, concerned.

"No, fortunately!" Johannes replied.

"Then," Olsson interjected peremptorily, "what was the point of just blowing up some bricks and mortar?"

"Good question," Hansson mused.

"If I must remind you gentlemen," Johannes stood up, stretching out his arms, indicating that he was ready to retire, "the plan called for merely eliminating the facility in which Eriksson was torturing his victims."

"And equally important," Olsson added, in support of Johannes, whom he could see was becoming annoyed with Hansson, "the explosion was executed, so to speak, in order to place Eriksson on notice."

"Why didn't we just kill him?" LaGreca asked, hoping to see where the fissures would arise in this ersatz coalition of interests.

"We've been through this before," Johannes replied, only slightly less irritable with the American ambassador. Above all else, he couldn't afford to lose the Americans as an ally.

"First, we don't want to create a martyr out of his death. Second, the entire right wing of the populace and Swedish Parliament, if I might remind you, consists of close to 29 percent—"

"Almost the same majority," Hansson interjected, "that Chancellor Hitler had when he took over power in the Reichstag."

"If I may continue," Johannes said, "the right wing would immediately suspect me and my political coalition and, if they acted civilly, would demand my immediate resignation, and turn the country completely over to the Fascists, led by none other than one of Eriksson's successors. And if they didn't act civilly..."

"And by allowing him to remain alive?" LaGreca asked, "What advantages do we gain?"

"The ability to monitor his activities, unobtrusively dismantle his work camps, slowly expose his followers, and eventually arrest them for treason," Johannes responded.

"But why do we need the American, Dr. Carter?" Olsson asked.

"That's a good question," LaGreca added. "You stand to place my country in an awkward position. Despite his present guise, he does work for the State Department."

Johannes did not answer. He had his reasons. And his reasons alone. He would share them with no one. Not his best friend. And not the dispensable American ambassador.

As far as he was concerned, genocide defined the twentieth century and was about to become the prologue for the millennium. The rest was commentary.

Johannes maneuvered his cruiser into its berth at the dock at Kasdan at the same time that Mack Londsdale's dead body was being rushed to Karolinska Sjukhuset Hospital.

24

VÄXJÖ, SWEDEN

History is replete with contradictions, distortions, and fiction. But it is at times bereft of poetic paradoxes. Nothing could be more ironic than the fact that the very region of Sweden which had absorbed the greatest numbers of recent refugees was also the very same place from which 1.5 million Swedes, one hundred years earlier, had emigrated to America. The reasons for both mass movements of people were the same. Those leaving Sweden were forced from their country because of poverty and starvation. Those legal and illegal refugees entering Sweden now were also forced from their respective homelands because of poverty and starvation. Perhaps that is why the only true chroniclers of history are those who can capture a sense of history's sadistic teasing, and by definition, are not formally trained academicians. More often than not, it is the novelist, the weaver of a fictional tale, who can best capture the paradoxes and ironies of life.

It was in this ironic vein that Eriksson, Carter, and Linda arrived in a countryside region often referred to as Småland. Ostensibly, Eriksson wanted to give his companions a sense of the verdant opulence. Stockholm wasn't Sweden. But Carter was waiting, wondering when Eriksson's real purpose would be revealed.

Eriksson drove at a leisurely pace, stopping to show his companions the collected archives Svenska Emigrantinstitutet—House of Emigrants—housed in Växjö, the principal city in this southern region. The group traveled over the same gravel roads of Småland that the famous author Vilhelm Moberg had described. While both Carter and Linda breathed a sigh of relief for having lost their hostage label, Eriksson was taking his time, as if they were vacationers, showing them highlights of the countryside of Växjö. There was the farmer's cottage in Korpameon where Moberg's fictional Oscar and Kristina toiled in the field. Here was a gold miner's cabin in Längasjö parish that became an emigration museum in miniature. There were memorials at every road-crossing where the wooden emigrant carts met, traveling away from a Småland filled with stony fields, immense stone fences and magic forest tarns.

The primary occupation of the residents in the area, however, was glass-blowing. This was "The Kingdom of Crystal," a several-hundred-mile radius of world-famous glass-blowing factories, which included those of Kosta-Boda, Orrefors, Sandvik, Lindshammar and many others.

Each glass-blowing "house" was similar, composed of four to ten independent designers. Each designer had a great deal of freedom in developing his or her artistry in glass. To watch skilled hands create prism-like vases from simple grains of pulverized glass was an unusual moment of aesthetic pleasure. But the pain and agony of creating that sparkling crystal was unique. Ibsen, the famous Norwegian playwright, once said that the man working alone was the strongest man in the world. Although the glassblowers worked in teams, each man was, in effect, working alone and had to confront his own moment of truth.

Eriksson took particular delight in showing Carter and Linda the Kosta Boda glassmaking facility, one of the most prestigious houses, founded in 1742. They walked into a large, red log cabin "house," containing a brick furnace in the center which produced a brilliant light of fire. A disheveled, dark-haired man in his late fifties, wearing a stained apron and plastic eye goggles, was seated on a wooden stool, holding a long metal rod which was attached to a ball of hot molten glass. He sat and twirled the molten glass around one end of the rod as if it were a piece of chewing gum, winding it tighter and tighter with each rotation.

It was an unusual day at Kosta Boda. Since there were no tourists clustered around him to entertain, the glassblower was making a beer mug for himself rather than an expensive vase. As he looked up, his craggy face, etched by the lines of age and repetition, half-heartedly greeted the three tourists. But he was particularly pleased to see an attractive woman. *Not Scandinavian,* he thought. *Probably American or British.* Either nationality was fine with him. It was only for the blacks from America or Africa that he had little, if any, patience. Ironically, the color black was his favorite. But having a human being colored black was different. He could not explain the contradiction, but it was there, as it was for all those who considered themselves true Swedes.

The glassblower took a more studied look at the three visitors. He visibly shuddered when he realized that he had seen one of his visitors on several different occasions, but did not acknowledge him in any way. He was one of those visitors about whom the glassblower never wanted to know more than he had to. All he cared about was making the finest glassware that he could from prosaic particles of sand, to be pridefully sold under the Kosta Boda trademark. As Kosta Boda advertised, "strong individual creativity is combined with collective power and authority to create that distinctive Kosta Boda feeling. Distinctive colors and shapes, dynamic imagination and bold innovation—these are the elements that mark Kosta Boda's unique visual appeal."

Like countless glassmakers before him, he talked to the three guests in an almost automaton voice, explaining what he was doing. But, in effect, he was trying to demonstrate that glassmaking was far more sophisticated and complicated than anyone would have imagined.

"We use a number of different glassmaking techniques at Kosta Boda." The glassblower, whose name was Frederick, addressed his small audience as if there were multitudes in front of him. "The most common technique is called mould blowing, although free-hand blowing is also used a lot. There are other methods of manufacturing glass such as casting, pressing, and centrifuging." He paused to let his visitors process these words. "Kosta Boda is renowned for the excellence of its crystal clear and colored glass. After the glass has been annealed, it can be decorated by cutting, engraving, etching, sandblasting, or painting."

"Why don't you tell these people," Eriksson interjected, "what you use in the manufacture of your glass." He nodded toward Carter and Linda.

"As one might expect," Frederick continued, "when you are making the finest crystal and colored glass, it is essential that only the finest of raw materials be used, which we obtain locally."

"Specifically, what raw materials?" Eriksson asked, pressing the glassmaker to be more specific.

"We use Swedish sand," Frederick answered hesitantly, "which contains iron oxide, which colors glass green. But there are also other elements, all of which are extremely toxic. They include silica sand, borax, red lead, barium, antimony, potash, salpetre, and the deadliest agent of all, arsenic." Perhaps his visitors were chemists or geologists, he thought. Most of his visitors would not have wanted this level of specificity.

"Would it be fair to say that everyone working around these toxic materials could be in danger of their lives?" Carter asked, recognizing the direction Eriksson was leading them.

"In order to minimize the health risk to everyone," Frederick answered, "we mix the raw ingredients of glass thoroughly into what is called a batch. The batch, in turn, is mixed by a sealed process in order to minimize health hazards—in a pelletizing plant, where it is moistened, then pelletized and dried. These pellets, which are easier and safer to handle than if the batch were in powder form, are then melted at high temperatures and become molten glass."

"And then what happens," Linda asked.

"We place the melted batch in the crucibles, or pots, located in the furnace," Frederick answered. "Melting begins in the afternoon or evening at the end of the working day and goes on until midnight. By the time the blowers arrive at 5:30 A.M., the glass in the pot is ready for production. At least as long as the heat can be maintained at 1430 degrees centigrade. When the furnace temperature sinks to 1130 degrees, the glass has acquired the consistency of thick syrup. To ensure clarity and luster in the finished ware, the molten glass must 'shine,' that is, be clean and free from bubbles."

"Then what happens?" Eriksson asked, waiting patiently for this part of the tour to end.

"We take the molten glass and dip a one-meter iron pipe into it. With the proper amount of molten glass on its end we shape it by rolling it on a smooth iron table, known as a marver, or we sharpen it with a simple wooden scoop. Then we blow gently down the pipe. At this point in the process, the soft mass of molten glass is known as the gather or post. Then, we begin free-hand blowing, in which we use a variety of ingeniously designed, yet simple tools, such as shears, smoothing boards and callipers. With a solid iron known as a pontil or 'ponty,' one of the craftsmen gathers a post of molten glass and attaches it to the bottom of the blowing pipe. The blowing pipe is now cracked off and the rough edge where it was attached is heated so that the glass becomes soft and malleable again. The edge is then cut smooth with a pair of shears and the opening at the top is widened with an instrument known as a pucellas. Wet newspapers may even be used to shape the glass. The edges of the handsheared glass are finished before annealing, so there is no chance of adjusting the shape or height of the glass once it has cooled."

When he finished his description of the process, Frederick waited a few seconds for questions, and when there were none, went back to the mug he was working on when his visitors arrived.

"On behalf of myself and my two American colleagues,"

Eriksson said, "I want to thank you for that most informative talk. Now I want to show them the areas surrounding this factory, and show them how beautiful it is."

Frederick looked directly at Eriksson for the first time, with anger in his face. I prefer you don't ... subject these people to ..."

"It's none of your business!" Eriksson responded sharply.

"Subject us to what?" Carter asked, clearly seeing what he had only suspected before—the power that Eriksson held over the glassblower.

"Nothing!" Frederick declared, with a scowl on his face.

"What are you afraid of?" Carter asked, noticing the glassblower's face blanche.

The glassblower did not answer. He turned his back to Carter and walked over to the mug he had been working on.

Eriksson made a slight bow to the glassblower, opened the door for Carter and Linda, and led them toward the main building where the finished Kosta Boda glassware was being sold.

25

KOSTA, SWEDEN

As they exited the glassblower's workshop Eriksson insisted that they walk to the main retail shop where the glassware produced in the factory was either shipped out to domestic and overseas markets or placed on sale directly to the tourist market.

The showroom was sufficiently large to hold several hundred people, most of whom came from other regions of Sweden. The foreign buyers were largely from Germany, France, and England, if language spoken was used as identification. Everyone in the showroom seemed to have one idea in common—to leave with the most impressive-looking item at the cheapest cost.

Eriksson said nothing. He simply watched Carter and Linda take in the buying scene of shoppers grabbing vases, bowls, and glasses as if pressured to buy on a time limit, and examining the pieces in the glare of the halcyon lights. There was no question in Carter's mind that Eriksson had some form of surprise for them that had nothing to do with buying Kosta Boda glassware.

Carter had begun to understand Eriksson. And the briefing papers he had been given by Atherton were definitely on the mark. Eriksson was a physician who was proud of what he did. And that was the irony of his very being. He was both a healer and a killer (or physician warrior, as a romantic might say).

Carter felt a chill climb up his back as he watched Eriksson's show of courtliness: bowing, kissing, and congratulating sales personnel whom Carter could see had frightened expressions on their faces as Eriksson approached them.

Linda was speaking in English to an attractive dark-complexioned saleswoman who was examining a multicolored wineglass which had come out of a "seconds" bin for flaws. As they spoke, the woman started to cough uncontrollably and dropped the glass, which shattered on everything around her. She reached inside her pocket and brought out several discolored handkerchiefs. Using one handkerchief after another, she tried to contain the mixture of phlegm and blood that stained the cloth each time she coughed.

While Eriksson watched, Carter ran over to the woman and sat her on the floor, but he could do nothing to stop the coughing or the bleeding. Most of the shoppers, not wanting to witness the scene, scattered throughout the room. A few remained, pretending to be unaware of the human drama unfolding around them.

"Let's get her to a hospital!" Carter said, cradling the coughing woman in his arms.

"Trust me," Eriksson replied, "there is nothing left to do. It's too late. She, like hundreds of other saleswomen, know that once the cough starts, and the blood flows, she might die, within minutes, of pulmonary hemorrhage."

"If we get her to an ER," Carter insisted, "there might be time to clamp off her arteries."

"You don't understand, my dear Dr. Carter," Eriksson responded in a calm, almost patronizing voice, "this woman is doomed to die a horrible death. That's why she was given this job. As a way to pay her back."

Linda wanted to scream "Let's take her to the hospital!" but something told her that Eriksson was right, that there was nothing to be done.

When the saleswoman's coughing finally stopped, her life was over as well.

"She, like the rest of the immigrant saleswomen here, suffer from intractable silicosis of the lung. It's not the pulmonary arteries that are the basic problem. It's the fact that after having worked in the sand pits and mixing areas of the glassblowing factories for several years, she has ingested enormous amounts of silicone dust from the air. No doubt, she was moved to this shop as a reward for service when it became apparent that she was ill and no longer able to work in those areas. She has probably worked as a saleswoman for six months. But her end was never in question. She would die drowning in her own blood."

26

LINDSHAMMER, SWEDEN

Eriksson drove Carter and Linda into the hills ten miles outside of Kosta, having left the dead woman in the hands of the store manager. Without having to say very much, he believed he had made his point—the Swedes weren't all they appeared to be. If Carter was disturbed by the idea that Sweden could be killing its citizens by giving health and safety standards a low priority in its capitalistic enterprises, he would be appalled at what he was about to see next.

From their bird's nest vantage point they viewed a ribbon of men, women and children marching in single file from a small town to what seemed to be a campsite in the middle of a plain. Because of their dark skin, a spectator might assume that some transient migratory laborers were shifting from one glass manufacturing town to another, going to where work was being offered.

Nothing, however, would have been further from the truth. For the last six months, the Swedish Nationalists, an ersatz title taken by a group of Swedes who opposed the influx of immigrants into their villages, were engaged in the serious business of evicting refugees who lived and worked in their towns. If Nazi Germany had become the model for genocide in the 1940's, and the Serbian drive to rid Kosovo of its ethnic Albanians the model for ethnic cleansing fifty years later, the Swedish Nationalists were definitely imposing a new model of indentured servitude in their own country.

Weekly, a ramshackle group of men, without anything in particular to designate them as an organized, cohesive group would storm through a village and evict whomever they identified as a Muslim or African immigrant worker. But unlike the German experience, they weren't exterminated. And unlike the Kosovan experience, they weren't pushed over the country's borders. Instead, they were relocated.

Barbed wire was strung around a seventy-acre parcel of land. Swedes armed with rifles patrolled the perimeter. It didn't take any leap of faith to recognize the scene below as a makeshift "concentration camp."

"What you see at this work camp is based on a concept the Nazis during World War II would have called *'Lebensunwertes Leben'*—a life unworthy of life," Eriksson said, speaking to an ashen-faced Linda and Carter. "But in Sweden, we refer to it as a 'new town.'"

Endless rows of makeshift canvas tents and cardboard huts splayed out before them, where hundreds of men, women, and children appeared to live in unsanitary conditions. The look of the area was similar to countless numbers of refugee camps that had become part of the daily menu of images the world had learned to consume—and be innured to. In this particular camp, however, the men weren't standing around chatting idly; the women weren't cooking food over open pits; the children weren't playing in puddles of dirty water. In this camp the entire population was moving boulders, chipping rocks, digging ditches, and constructing a watchtower which would eventually be used to encapsulate the camp even further. Within the "new town" rose a massive factory-like structure.

What Eriksson had taken Carter and Linda to view was one of a dozen such towns in the area, a well-organized system of exploitative labor where refugees were paid a subsistence wage by the Swedish owners of glass factories throughout the region. However, once the costs of their unsanitary living space, meager food ration, work clothing, blankets, and medical care were deducted from their minimal wage, they were indebted to their employers. In short, no matter how many hours they worked, and how much they earned, they always remained in debt. The refugees were caught in a vicious cycle of indenture, which they could escape only by physical and mental atrophy, and death.

As a physician, Carter was aware of the illnesses which had to be rampant from the simple lack of appropriate sanitation and from working in the glassblowing industry. Typhoid, measles, tuberculosis, and silicosis were probably common. The camp itself smelled like a cesspool. Under these conditions, thought Carter, it would not be unusual for workers to faint for lack of adequate nutrition. Or cough up blood from the particles of glass that they ingested while they worked which became lodged in their lungs. Or to defecate, urinate, and expectorate in open spaces.

"At first, we established these camps as transit points in the refugees' flight to other countries, or to other regions in our own country. But between small quotas in other countries, and Sweden's generous welfare policy, most of the refugees applied to remain here. So our small towns were flooded with cheap labor and people who didn't know our language, customs, or traditions. And didn't really care to learn." Eriksson stopped for a moment to assess the interest level of his guests. He found that his audience of two wanted him to continue.

"As you might have guessed already, our rural Swedes did not appreciate the influx of these foreigners. Schools were swamped. Local health care systems applied for an increase in national funds. Swedish jobs were lost to lower-paid immigrants. Fights broke out between the Swedes and their new neighbors. What started as a humanitarian effort on the part of the Swedish people backfired.

"As a result of the disruptive force the immigrants became in our towns, the transit camps were turned into immigrant towns, as a means of providing the refugees with a safe haven. For their own safety, we restricted the refugees' movement within the country. And once there was a concentrated group of laborers—no, they weren't meant to be concentration camps—some of our larger employers convinced the government to allow them to use the population as day laborers which, of course, meant to 'abuse' them as laborers. The woman who died in your arms today was a resident of this town."

If Eriksson had tried to shock Linda and Carter, he couldn't have done it any better. It took Carter a few minutes of his own internal dialogue before he was ready to question Eriksson.

"Are you saying that these camps transformed themselves four times from transit camps, to living camps, to work camps, to death camps?" Carter asked, finding it difficult to believe that Sweden, of all countries, could be operating death camps.

"Not exactly. There is no planned killing—at least in the way you are thinking about it," Eriksson answered. "There is death through 'attrition,' and death arranged through medical channels by doctors' decisions. The deaths are supervised by a cadre of physicians who believe in our cause."

Carter was clearly disturbed by what Eriksson was telling him. Nothing was darker or more menacing to him or, quite frankly, harder to accept than the participation of physicians in murder. What he did in his black box assignments was always to prevent mass murder. But in his trained profession he was a healer, a person whom most cultures revered— and depended upon. Knowing that doctors had joined the ranks of commercial exploiters of human misery added another grotesque dimension to what he was viewing.

"What you see here," Eriksson said, "is a biocracy. It's killing taken to the level of theocracy, where the new priests are the physicians, transformed into 'healer-killers' under the basic principle of 'life unworthy of life.' As we stand here talking, sick refugee children are being sterilized for no medical reason in modern Swedish Hospitals."

"But you need the collusion of the population-at-large," Linda stated.

"Not necessarily," Eriksson responded. "More often than

not, the layperson does not know what is going on behind the ascetic fortresses of the medical establishment."

"Because they are not physicians," Carter stated.

"Correct!" Eriksson responded, certain it was now time to tell them why he had brought them there. "As a physician, Carter, I assume you see the easy jump to 'therapeutic euthanasia'—the purposeful killing of 'impaired' adults? And after nine months in one of these camps, anyone would be impaired."

Eriksson, Carter and Linda watched emaciated stick figures walk about the camp, performing their tasks as if they were playing the part of a zombie in a grade B horror film. For Carter, the silent, hollow eyes indicated people already condemned to die for sins they had never committed and for diseases they should never have contracted. They were the unfortunate objects of opportunity in an organized death machine, in which physicians played a major role. Politics aside. Economics aside. These were doctors who were willing accomplices to death.

"Remember what we're dealing with here," Eriksson pointed out, "one group of peasants, who happen to possess blond hair—let us be kind and say—'confining' another group of peasants, who happen to possess black hair. But who also are using a disproportionate amount of the country's resources." Looking at Carter and Linda's reaction to the scene in front of them, he felt their disgust and condemnation. And for the first time he felt ashamed. Ashamed of what he was witnessing and ashamed to have instigated it years before.

Word had recently reached him that his activities were also proving to be an embarrassment to the leaders of his country. And Eriksson was no one's fool. His time was limited. That was exactly why Carter was in Sweden—to stop Eriksson and his movement before it embarrassed the country in the eyes of the world and destabilized the Swedish government. Even if Carter, himself, didn't know it. Well, if he was forced to, as the Americans liked to say, "change horses in midstream," Eriksson would bring down his "employers" and the others who so cleverly tried to distance themselves from him.

He wondered whether Carter had given any thought to who was financing the movement to expel and eliminate the immigrants from Sweden. He, Eriksson, was simply the tool, the movement's scalpel, so to speak, to make a clean and bloodless incision so that the welfare state could continue without an economic drag factor.

"How is this happening in Sweden of all countries?" Carter asked rhetorically.

"Welcome to the new world order," Eriksson responded. "As you see, it's marked by the same characteristics as the old world order manifested during the Holocaust—indifference, platitudes, fear of engagement, lack of moral courage, and above all else, hypocrisy."

Carter remained silent and pensive. He stared at the refugees, living like cattle in pens. Dying by default, if not by design. The step from concentration camp to extermination camp was surprisingly small. What he was witnessing once again affirmed his basic distrust and dislike of mankind.

The modern age had made it easier to look without seeing. When useless knowledge was accumulating at an exponential rate, it became increasingly harder to assess what was relevant intelligence and what was garbage. People were learning how not to see. For, if they did, it would force them to take action.

Carter doubted that Eriksson had changed in any way from the man he had been sent to kill. But the clinic bombing, and Carter's employment as Eriksson's assassin, may have unnerved him enough to realize he needed to make new alliances. And Carter was in no position to turn away potential co-conspirators.

27

LINDSHAMMER, SWEDEN

"If the march in Stockholm goes off according to plan, not only will the marchers be met by force," Eriksson continued, "but the poor bastards in the camp below us will be attacked, as will those in other camps around the area."

"What march?" Carter and Linda asked, almost in unison.

"The march that our good prime minister is trying to find out about," Eriksson answered. "The march that he wants to be prepared for; to look wise, and strong for in the eyes of the world," Eriksson said sarcastically. "With just a little bit of advance planning, he can assure that the marchers are beaten by the harassing crowds, after which, of course, our national troops ride in to save the day. The prime minister looks like a hero, the cause of the immigrants receives the kind of attention that forces international social agencies to find better homes for our friends down below and international economic agencies to cough up—pardon the pun—more aid for Sweden." Eriksson spit in disgust. "And if he's lucky, our prime minister can do a fast dance around the issue of how he let it all happen in the first place. The bastard might even become a hero in the eyes of your average Swedish citizen."

"Isn't there any way you can stop this insanity?" Linda

implored. She was both surprised and angry that Carter had said so little. And why hadn't he tried to kill Eriksson? He certainly had had several opportunities. What, in God's name, was he waiting for?

"Linda," Carter spoke sternly, purposefully trying to distance himself from her so that Eriksson could sense that a bond was developing between them. "This is no time for hysterics or self-righteous moral outrage."

"Self-righteous moral outrage?" Linda screamed. "Have you fallen on your head?" She paused trying to compose herself. "Don't you see what is going on all around you? And what will happen in only a few days if these madmen aren't controlled?"

"Linda," Carter responded coolly, "I'm sure that Dr. Eriksson's plans have been well thought through."

"What the hell are you talking about?" she asked, becoming emotional. "I haven't heard any plan, have you? You were sent here to stop this insanity and instead you seem to condone it," Linda screamed.

"Enough!" Carter responded, slapping her across the face. Above all else, he thought, now was not the time to show self-righteous indignation, moral outrage, or emotional histrionics. Eriksson was probably testing him. To react now, as Linda wanted, would be precipitous and foolish. Even if he did kill Eriksson, someone would replace him immediately. For the present, Carter needed Eriksson as much as Eriksson seemed to need him. Furthermore, he still didn't trust Linda. What she knew, and why she was there with him, was still unclear.

"My dear Ms. Watson," Eriksson said in his most calming, mellifluous tone of voice, "I know how you must feel, with all this potential death surrounding you like a disease—ugly, monstrous, bestial. Yet, there is something about it that is also surreal."

"Please don't continue," Linda said, nauseated by the pictures she was conjuring in her mind; pictures of unarmed people being slaughtered in the streets, and possibly in the camps. All she knew was that she wanted no part of any of this. But as she contemplated her situation, Linda realized that she really had no choice but to seem agreeable. She also had an assignment to complete.

"Perhaps Ms. Watson would feel better if she realized that there are very real advantages in helping each other," Eriksson offered. "The best way to handle an ambiguous situation is to deal with it directly."

"I think that we both agree that our best chance for mutual survival is to help one another," Carter responded, reminded of the old adage "Pick your enemy well, lest you become like him."

"I don't believe what I'm hearing," Linda interjected. "I'm watching the evolution of a mutual admiration society between two physician-killers." She added, unable to restrain herself once again, "This is nuts!"

"Since we are being very frank with one another," Eriksson responded, "I will tell you both that I need Dr. Carter more than I would need you, Ms. Watson. Please take no offense."

"None taken!" she replied. "Just think of me as an invisible tree against which you can both piss."

"Linda! Enough!" Carter said, annoyed.

"I think that we are all, as you Americans like to say, a little bit on edge," Eriksson continued.

"That's true," Carter added, "so let's stop talking around issues and get to the heart of them." He was annoyed with the time he was wasting on Linda. He was far more interested in finding out what Eriksson had to say. If he were just a bit more paranoid, he would think that Linda was trying to prevent Eriksson from telling Carter anything.

"As I was saying," Eriksson continued, "I want to make certain that Carter knows as much as he needs to, just in case . . ."

". . . we're captured," Carter finished Eriksson's sentence and looked at Linda, who still appeared skeptical.

"I have an intuitive sense that as long as I remain with Carter, the better my chances are to survive," Eriksson stated.

"You mean that I am your insurance policy against anything happening to you," Carter concluded.

"Precisely," Eriksson replied.

"So what do you want from me?" Carter asked.

"I want to continue this discussion," Eriksson replied, "so that you will understand my role in our current situation, my co-conspirators and our overall plan. You are the equivalent, if I may say, to the letter that one sends to a special friend or to the newspaper, in order to insure your own safety. You know, in case of death and all the secrets come out."

I've been called many things, in my time," Carter laughed, "but this is the first time that I have been called a letter. But tell me, who are you afraid of, that forces you to choose me as a confidante?" Carter asked, sensing that Eriksson was ready to talk.

"On the very top of the pyramid," Eriksson answered, "I would place the prime minister."

"And below him?" Carter asked.

"A series of political handmaidens. But they have neither real power nor influence. These rest with an unholy trinity: the prime minister's powerful friend, Nils Olsson; the man who controls our police, Carl Hansson; and, your own American Ambassador, Carl LaGreca."

"Tell me about the prime minister?" Carter asked, much more interested in hearing about LaGreca, but knowing he would have to take third billing.

"Believe it or not," Eriksson answered, "the prime minister is basically a decent man who has extremely well-honed political instincts. But at this point in his career he is in a very precarious political situation, holding only 29 percent of Parliament and falling daily in popular support."

"That's not much support," Carter interjected.

"No," Eriksson responded, "not even enough to consider him legitimate. That's why he had to build an alliance with my ultranationalist party, Olsson's conservative industrialists and Hansson's security forces. Without this unholy alliance, he has no power base, the government topples, and extreme elements of my party take over."

ACTIVE MEASURES 167

"What prevents them from taking over now?" Linda asked, overcoming any hurt pride.

"Believe it or not," Eriksson replied smiling, "my moderating influence. Of course, I am sure that you understand that 'moderating' is all very relative."

"Of course," Linda lied.

"Our party fears Captain Hansson and the security apparatus that is personally loyal to him and the prime minister. Hansson's men would have no qualms about destroying me, you, the immigrants, or anyone else if the prime minister gave the orders."

"And from whom," Carter asked, "does the prime minister take orders?"

"Nils Olsson," Eriksson replied, "or more precisely the industrial complex he represents. Above all else, they are interested in only one thing..."

"Let me guess," Carter interrupted. "Money?"

"Political stability first," Eriksson responded, "so that they can continue to make money. They need the continued stewardship of Johannes, and his hold over our well-equipped and trained security apparatus. In a very real sense, the immigrants on the bottom of the pyramid have more power than they know. And more power than they know how to use. What happens during and after the demonstration in Gamla Stan will really determine the fate of the current power elite."

"So that's why Hansson, Olsson and his business cohorts are afraid of you," Carter said.

"I don't know if I would call it fear," Eriksson responded, "but I would definitely say that in the past they have cleverly played their political cards by supporting our nationalist party when it served their interests. Certainly as an insurance policy if we ever get into power. But now..."

"It's not unlike our Fortune 500 companies," Carter added, "who always give approximately an equal amount of money to both the Democrats and Republicans."

"A good analogy," Eriksson said. He paused and looked down the hill. It was filled with security police climbing up, toward them.

28

STOCKHOLM, SWEDEN

"You know," Hansson said, "I think we should approach this situation with a little creativity and panache in tribute, of course, to your preeminence in the field."

"So Johannes has left his dirty work to his lowly Captain Hansson," Eriksson replied, particularly calm for a man whose arms and legs were fastened by leather straps to a wooden chair. The last impression he wanted to leave with Hansson was that he was frightened.

"As usual, your arrogance is sublime," Hansson responded, standing next to a wooden table covered with all types of instruments of torture—a rubber hose, blackjack, electric prods and other "toys."

The room was located in a small building on a side street near the City Hall in Kungsholmen. No bigger than a maid's closet, with the proverbial naked lightbulb hanging from the ceiling, the room had no ventilation or windows. Screams of men and women raced through the long corridor Eriksson had walked, what must have been one hour earlier. But he wasn't certain whether they were really prisoners being tortured or a form of intimidation that his captors were using to set the stage for his own session with Hansson. Where Carter and Ms. Watson were remained a mystery. The three of them had been split up and placed in separate cars after they had been arrested by officers guarding the work camp.

"Was it Johannes?" Eriksson asked imperiously, "or Nils? I think Nils must be behind this betrayal. Johannes could never have the cunning... or mettle."

"Although you haven't asked," Hansson ignored Eriksson's musings, "I thought you would want to know that your two 'colleagues' are also my guests."

"So it was Nils who gave you the primary order!" Eriksson blurted out, totally unconcerned about the Americans. They deserved anything Hansson meted out, he thought. "Well, Captain, what little 'game' do you have in store for me? And if I may be so direct, what exactly do you want from me?"

"In due time," Hansson responded, annoyed by Eriksson's defiance. "I thought it might be useful for us to be innovative, considering your importance and your own skills. I certainly wouldn't want to bore you with some old prosaic technique that you, yourself, might have used on countless occasions.

"Let us work backward," Hansson said gleefully, anticipating his joy in torturing the master torturer. "Instead of my telling you the instrument of torture, why don't you tell me which type of physical consequence of torture you would prefer to carry with you for the rest of your life." Hansson was less concerned about the outcome of this session than he was about being able to brag to his unit that he, alone, was the only one ever to torture Savanarola himself.

"My God," Eriksson feigned a laugh, "I'm overwhelmed by your Christian charity." He noticed that Hansson was completely unmoved by his sarcasm. "Okay, let's play the game your way! As if I really had any other choice."

"Would you prefer to suffer total body pain?" Hansson asked.

"So you're telling me that the torture there would involve beating me," Eriksson responded, "with a club, fists, kicking, stickbeating, or using a rubber hose over my entire body. I'm afraid, it's a little too crass for my own taste. If I must be in pain, let it be for something for which I can be proud. A torture with a certain distinction to it."

"In this particular category," Hansson continued, wary of Eriksson even as he was bound and impotent, "would you prefer to suffer psychosomatic and neurologic symptoms?"

"That torture would involve suspending my limbs as well as abducting my legs." Eriksson thought for a moment. "Too prosaic. I'll pass on that one. Thank you, though, for offering me one of the 'tried and true.'"

"Electricity and various methods of burning—cigarettes, chemicals—may leave characteristic skin changes."

"I'll pass on that also," Eriksson responded, "we all know how carcinogenic cigarettes are."

"You wouldn't be smoking it, as you know. The lit cigarette would be applied against your entire body."

"I wasn't concerned about me," Eriksson laughed. "I was concerned about your developing emphysema or lung cancer because of your secondary exposure to cigarette smoke."

"Very cute!" Hansson responded, clearly not amused.

"Levity, my friend, is an integral part of the game. Without it, what pleasure is there really?" Eriksson asked sardonically. "Torture would simply become an extension of sadism. And that is so primitive."

"How would you entertain the possibility of having some form of Organic Brain Syndrome?" Hansson asked.

"I'm afraid that if you beat my head with a rubber club it really wouldn't do much more harm than Mother Nature has already done to me," Eriksson responded. "I'm already suffering from several OBS symptoms—memory loss, disorientation, irritability, perspiration. I'm afraid that you really would be wasting your time. And, on a purely selfish note, you would be wasting my time."

"Well, that leaves me with sexual dysfunction," Hansson replied, reaching for a long rubber catheter attached to a clear plastic rubber bag hanging from one end.

Eriksson said nothing. He realized that he had outwitted himself.

"If you don't mind, Dr. Eriksson," Hansson said, approaching him with the catheter, "I must pull your pants and underpants down. I apologize in advance for any embarrassment I might create for you."

"I'm afraid that I can't assist you in your undertaking," Eriksson responded calmly, "but you can see that my hands and arms are tied down."

Hansson pulled Eriksson's pants and underpants down around his ankles without any problems. Quite the contrary. Hansson was counting on the fact that Eriksson would be cooperative because, more than anything else, he wanted to appear dignified throughout whatever humiliation he might have to endure.

With the subtlety of a vengeful whore, Hansson pulled on Eriksson's penis, stretching it to its full length. And with the surgical precision of a plumber, he began to insert the rubber catheter into Eriksson's urethra.

There were no screams.

Normally, catherization was done in a hospital or a doctor's office with the patient receiving a hefty dose of pain medication.

"I admire your stoicism, Dr. Eriksson," Hansson said, slowly but firmly inserting the hard rubber catheter into the shaft of the penis. "It would be helpful if you told me precisely what you told Dr. Carter about our organization and our plans."

"Go fuck yourself..." Eriksson could barely finish his sentence before he felt a rod of rubber scraping its way up toward his bladder. The pain was unbearable. He broke into a cold sweat and began to feel faint. But he couldn't let Hansson know. Being restrained in the chair made the pain that much more concentrated and piercing.

"Dr. Eriksson, it's extremely important that you cooperate with me," Hansson said, studying Eriksson's every facial gesture. The pleasantries were over, but he knew from experience that it would be extremely hard for him to extract any information from Eriksson. If pride and arrogance prevented Eriksson from talking, pain would only accentuate his stubbornness.

"You clumsy fool!" Eriksson screamed. "A doctor would never be so—"

Hansson jabbed the rubber catheter upward and sideways creating additional major abrasions and pain inside Eriksson's penis.

"Chhhrrist!" Eriksson shouted. The room was starting to spin around. He could feel his stomach contract involuntarily and punch out its contents of acid and masticated food through his mouth.

"You son-of-a-bitch!" Hansson yelled, as Eriksson vomited on him. "I'll teach you to mind your manners, Doctor." He jammed the catheter all the way up through the shaft of the penis. "What do they know about Nils Olsson? About Ambassador LaGreca? About me?"

Eriksson couldn't utter a word, even if he had wanted to. His only consolation was knowing that Hansson and company would never know how much had been revealed—and how much they had been compromised.

"What do they know about the government's plan for the protest march?"

"Aggggghhhhh!!!"

Blood poured through and around the rubber catheter. The plastic bag filled completely with a bright red liquid. Eriksson was hemorrhaging internally.

He closed his eyes. Now, he, like the Nazi doctors in Auschwitz, could embrace death as a cure.

29

STOCKHOLM, SWEDEN

"Welcome, Dr. Carter," Hansson greeted the prisoner being escorted into the room by a trustworthy sergeant. Satisfied that he and his nine millimeter Beretta were in control of the situation, he dismissed his subordinate.

"I see that you managed to screw up," Carter said, looking at the ashen-faced Eriksson, his head hanging on his chest as if his neck had been broken. "Basic Torture 101 says 'don't kill your victim.' Otherwise you are not able to get any information from him. Dead people don't talk."

"He told me pretty much what I wanted to know," Hansson lied.

"If he had," Carter walked toward Eriksson, surveying the blood-filled plastic bag, and the blood and urine sprayed all over the floor, "you wouldn't have had such sloppy results. You messed up, Hansson. If I were any of the boys upstairs, I would be pissed off with you, no pun intended." Carter could barely stifle his disgust. The urine stench was unbearable. Carter surmised from the amount of blood in the bag and on the floor that Hansson must have ripped Eriksson's urethra. It reminded him of the smell he would have to endure whenever he went to visit a patient in a nursing home. Everything—the patient, the bed, the food, even the washbasin—would reek of urea.

"Well, let me tell you that your disappointment doesn't really upset me," Hansson responded, trying to avoid being defensive. "I had you brought in here so that you could see what will happen to you if I don't get when I want."

"Oh, give me a break," Carter responded derisively. "Trying to intimidate one prisoner by showing him a brutally tortured fellow prisoner is really beneath you. The Red Brigade in Italy tried it with me. General Noriega in Panama tried to force me to talk after showing me his best friend's decapitated head. Nice try, but it's not going to work." Carter glanced at the heap of flesh slumped in the chair. "Do you mind if I examine the former Dr. Eriksson?"

Hansson stepped back from the body in silent assent and began to circle the chair. Carter felt as if he were one of two buzzards ready to descend on a cadaver.

"You may examine him," Hansson replied, "with the proviso that you don't attempt anything foolish." He pointed his Beretta at Carter's head. "I can assure you that I'm quite a good marksman."

"At this close a range," Carter replied, "anyone with a single digit IQ and the ability to squeeze a trigger could blow me away. So I wouldn't flatter myself, if I were you."

Carter placed three fingers of his right hand on Eriksson's carotid artery to feel for a pulse. "By the way, how is the other prisoner of Zenda?"

"Your female companion is in a cell two doors from here," Hansson replied, "waiting for her moment of recognition."

"A true gentleman to the very end," Carter added mockingly. He couldn't feel any pulse from the carotid artery. He opened Eriksson's drooping eyelids and examined his pupils. They were both dilated, which meant that he may have been dead for several hours. If Carter had use of an ophthalmascope, he would have seen the retinal arteries in the back of the eye, niched at small intervals. They were described in medical textbooks as "boxcars," and the final test of death was to see if the "boxcar" niches of the retinal arteries surrounding the retinal papulla were there. Barring the absence of that test, it was still not difficult to surmise from the absence of a heartbeat, lack of mental consciousness, and the fact that rigor mortis was setting in, that Eriksson was dead.

"Is it your medical opinion that he is dead?" Hansson asked, letting his gun hand drop to a more relaxed position at his side.

"What do you think, Einstein?" Carter replied. "No one deserved to die this way, not even Eriksson. Now you really have your job cut out for you: how to hide the news of Eriksson's death at the hands of the same fascist police who will be patrolling the refugee protest march only two days away." Carter stopped to assess Hansson's reaction to his knowledge of the march. From the way Hansson's brows arched, it was clear that Eriksson had not talked. What a pity. It certainly wasn't worth dying for. "Should I assume that it will be your job to keep your police force from overreacting at the march and precipitating a massive racial riot on a level that would shame your government? And what about those 'concentration camps' I saw—how are you all going to explain them away?" Carter smirked. "Do you realize that you're going to be the fall guy?"

Hansson had difficulty restraining his anger, but he had to honor the group's wishes to keep Carter alive.

"I think you got to like Eriksson, even after what he did to you," Hansson responded, ignoring Carter's provocation. "And don't forget, the man you were contracted to kill is now dead, thanks to my 'clumsiness,' as you just said. As far as I am concerned, I am entitled to your fee. Now what is it this time? One million? Three million? Five million?"

"I'm so glad that you are interested in my finances," Carter said facetiously. "But, of course, we still don't know who will be paying it, or do we?"

"Don't worry," Hansson interjected, "I can look into that matter. If you will just give me your Swiss bank account numbers..."

"What a piece of work you are, you venal, disgusting..." Carter spit out. "At a time when you should be concerned about the potential loss of lives coming in only a few days, the only thing that you can think of is money, money, money. And I'm sure how to screw your partners out of any."

"I think you'd best stop where you are!" Hansson ordered, becoming nervous hearing Carter's recriminations. He lifted up his gun hand again, as Carter examined Eriksson for bruises and edema.

"Since you botched up this job," Carter added, noticing the slight tremor in the hand holding the gun, "why don't you just shoot me right here and now? At least you can kill two birds with one stone, so to speak."

"And how would that benefit me?" Hansson asked. "You are worth more alive to me than dead."

"Then let Ms. Watson go," Carter replied. "She's of no use to me or you."

"Then why is she with you?" Hansson asked.

"I don't have the faintest idea," Carter responded. "I thought she was working with your people."

"Well, that certainly would be news to me!" Hansson retorted.

"It looks to me like a lot of people in this game might have more than one agenda," Carter said, watching Hansson's eyes dart nervously back and forth. "Are you certain you've done this kind of work before?" Carter asked, purposely questioning his competence. Torture came in all forms, and nothing was more disconcerting than having someone manipulate your self-esteem, powers of observation, or belief system. The technical jargon for what Carter was trying to do was called Psychological Operations (PsyOps). But Carter preferred to call it "mind-fucking."

Hansson glared at Carter, choosing not to reply.

"I bet no one gave you the instructions to kill this poor bastard," Carter continued, as he continued to examine Eriksson. "Am I right?"

"It's none of your business!" Hansson replied defensively.

"It certainly is my business," Carter replied. "That's why I was sent to Sweden." As he retracted the catheter, blood flowed out of Eriksson's limp penis. "But you knew that from the very moment I came into this country, didn't you?"

Carter withdrew the entire tubing and held it up in the air. "See the tip of the catheter? It's filled with blood and tissue, probably from the urethra."

"So what?"

"So what? You dumb fuck!" Carter shook his head, disgusted.

"Don't provoke me!" Hansson moved in front of Carter and prodded his Beretta into his stomach. "A nine millimeter bullet can create quite a large hole in the abdomen."

"Shoot me!" Carter screamed. "Kill me the same way you shouldn't have killed Eriksson! See what your bosses will do to you!" He watched beads of sweat form on Hansson's forehead. "You've already created one martyr for your right-wing nationalists. And I am certain that you were instructed simply to extract information from him."

"Stop!" Hansson shouted, backing away from Carter.

"Or what?" Carter approached Hansson, shaking the bloody catheter at him. "The minute you pull that trigger, your fucking destiny is sealed. You will have taken a national incident and made it into an international one."

"You . . ." Hansson tightened his grip on the Beretta. The bullet was in the chamber. All he had to do now was pull the trigger. He could always say it was an accident or that Carter tried to attack him. But no matter how much he wanted to kill Carter, he knew that Carter was right. Even though Carter's assignment and presence was off-line, he was still an American. And an American whose full-time job was at the State Department. Dammit! Hansson felt trapped. If he killed Carter, there would be an investigation. His "group" would lose the support of the American ambassador and the interests he represented. But he couldn't let Carter go, or Olsson and Johannes would know that he had killed Eriksson, after being specifically warned to keep him alive. What was he going to do?

"Maybe you were right," Carter responded, in a calming tone of voice. "Both of us have to cool down. Otherwise, no good will come out of this for either of us." Carter realized that he was still in a danger zone.

"Yes, yes," Hansson responded, conflicted. He turned the barrel of his gun away from Carter.

"Now, you're catching on, Hansson," Carter said, holding one end of the rubber catheter in each of his hands. "Let's make this a win-win situation. Because no one wins if the other one loses. We either both lose—I don't get the information that I need and you don't get the outcome you need—or we both win."

"What do you want to know?" Hansson asked. "I know what you came to Sweden to accomplish. Well, the deed is done. Will you be leaving the country now?"

"Of course. I only do what I'm paid to do," Carter responded, trying to lull Hansson into a false state of security. "But I would like to know who gave you the instructions to . . . scare . . . Eriksson and me."

"Don't ask me that," Hansson said, slowly shaking his head. "It's dangerous for me to tell you and dangerous for you to know. Believe me, I am trying to protect you. The less you know, the more likely it is that you will be let out of the country alive."

Carter sensed the timing was right. He moved forward quickly and wrapped the catheter around Hansson's neck. He pulled as hard as he could in opposite directions until Hansson's face turned red and then blue. Carter looked Hansson straight in the eyes, his disgust and anger no longer contained. "Who is giving the orders?"

Only a wheeze came from Hansson as he struggled to free himself from Carter's strangling grip.

"Who blew up the clinic?"

"I don't . . ." Hansson's eyes began to bulge, like a Popeye cartoon.

"Who ordered the 'concentration camps' built?"

"Plea . . ."

"You are turning blue," Carter said matter-of-factly. "You have exactly three seconds from this moment to save yourself." His arms pulled harder. The catheter was now cutting into Hansson's neck.

"Let . . . me . . . breathe."

ACTIVE MEASURES 179

"I'm going to loosen up," Carter said, "but that will be the last chance for you to save yourself."

"Nils Olsson," Hansson blurted out, his face returning from blue to red. "He's the industrialist who supports the prime minister." He felt relieved that his life was once more his own.

"What does Ambassador Carl LaGreca have to do with all of this?"

"I don't know," Hansson said, feeling the catheter loosen around his neck.

"Why did you take me to him?" Carter asked, his hands still gripping the catheter.

"Because you were never supposed to be part of that harmless street fight in Gamla Stan. And because I didn't want to embarrass the U.S. government." Hansson saw Carter's facial muscles relax. That was good, he thought.

"Exactly when and where is the attack on the refugees supposed to take place?" Carter asked, wanting to check Eriksson's information against Hansson's.

"In two days," Hansson replied, aware that the catheter was still around his throat. "The nationalists, along with police disguised as civilians, will attack the refugees in Gamla Stan."

"Who devised the plan?"

"I just told you," Hansson said, "Nils Olsson."

"How is Linda Watson involved in all of this?"

"I don't know!" Hansson replied, beads of sweat dropping over his brow. "I swear, I don't know."

"I'm going to ask you one more time..." Carter said, tightening the catheter.

"I already told..." Hansson was having a hard time breathing.

"Who devised the plan?" Carter tightened some more.

"I..." Hansson's face was turning blue.

"Who paid me the five million dollars?"

"Nils." Hansson's eyes were bulging out of their sockets.

"Who besides Nils?" Carter was convinced Nils wasn't

the person in charge. There had to be an additional accomplice who had tracked his movements ever since he entered Sweden. He had finally realized that he, Carter, was to be the fall guy. Not Hansson. Not Eriksson.

"Aaaggh."

"Who?"

Carter could barely hear the name. But now it all made sense. He gave one strong tug and Hansson expelled his final breath.

30

STOCKHOLM, SWEDEN

Carter stared at the two dead bodies. Eriksson sat slumped in a bloodstained chair. Hansson lay on the floor in a fetal position. Two security cameras peered down on the threesome from opposite corners of the room and Carter had no doubts that everything that had transpired in the room was on tape. At some future time, that tape would be viewed by the security officers monitoring the room. The room couldn't have been monitored live, or security guards would have rushed into the room to prevent Hansson's death.

But, why had he, Carter, been brought into Eriksson's room by Hansson? Was it really an attempt to intimidate him? Or was there another purpose? With Hansson now dead, Carter might never learn the answers to his questions.

Seeing and smelling death all around him, Carter felt like he was once again in the Munch Museum in Oslo, Norway, standing in the center of an endless series of black-and-white paintings, each a stark and terrifying image of modern alienation and despair. So fearsome and disturbing were Munch's pictures, and so threatening in their symbolism, that when his paintings were exhibited at a major Berlin art show in 1892, shocked authorities ordered the show closed. At this precise moment, Carter could identify with Munch's anomie, anger and displacement.

Nothing about this assignment was making any sense. In Cambodia, neutralizing a key member of the Khmer Rouge was clear and definitive. Even the task of assessing the mindset of the notorious physician-assassin of Serbia, Dr. Karadzic, was exactly what it was supposed to be. Only the present assignment to neutralize Eriksson had taken on a very indefinite quality. He wondered, for example, why he, Carter, had been tortured by Eriksson, instead of "disappearing." And why a bomb had destroyed Eriksson's clinic, but not Eriksson. And, looking at Eriksson in his current state of rigor mortus, why hadn't he been killed long before Carter was tasked that assignment?

An anxious chill traveled up his spine, as if it were a current of electricity shocking his senses to a state of full alertness. So far, he was following a scenario that someone else had scripted, without any clues as to who was really in charge, what were the rules of the game, or how he could possibly win. Like the physician he was trained to be, he abhorred the uncertainty, indecisiveness, and convolution of events that surrounded him since the day he landed in Sweden.

"Are you all right?" Linda asked, brought into the cell by two guards. She ran across the room to Carter and threw her arms around his neck. She whispered, "Each guard is carrying a gun, a can of mace and a set of keys."

She looked around the room and gasped when she saw Eriksson and Hansson.

"The locked door at the end of the hall is controlled electronically by a guard," she continued. "And there are no other guards in the hallway between here and that door."

"You've been quite observant," Carter whispered back to her, watching the guards as they noticed Eriksson and Hansson.

As the reality of the situation registered with them, they drew their guns and ran over to the bodies.

"It's now or never, I guess," Carter whispered to Linda, and with that he lunged at one of the guards, knocking him over and taking his gun from him. Linda, with almost reflexive precision, jumped on the back of the second guard. She grabbed the container of mace that was in a black leather case attached to the guard's belt, and sprayed it directly in his face. When they both fell to the floor, the guard shrieking in pain, rubbing his eyes with both hands, Linda took both his gun and mace.

Carter had knocked "his" guard unconscious, and sat on the floor watching Linda subdue "her" guard. From her well-defined body and self-assured, balanced movements, he realized that she was not a novitiate to the world of violence.

Carter grabbed the temporarily blinded guard and pulled him along with them down the long, dark hallway.

A guard sat in front of a console at the far end of the hallway controlling anyone coming in or out of the cell block.

"Motion your friend to open the door, if you want to stay alive," Carter ordered the guard.

Confused, the guard at the desk stood up in order to unstrap his gun from its holster. Linda, as if on cue, sprayed him with the mace and pushed the button herself.

When the door opened, Linda and Carter rushed through, leaving the two guards behind. At the end of this second hallway was a large oak door containing a plaque in Swedish, which Carter surmised meant that the area from which they had just come was highly restricted. Carter pushed it open and realized that they were now in the main foyer of City Hall. Under a large cupola hung paintings representing Lady Justice, Truth, Honesty, and several other virtues that Carter could hardly remember.

"Maybe some of the boys downstairs should visit these ladies," Carter said, pointing to the painting. "It would make this world a kinder, gentler place to live in." He paused for a moment and smiled. "Don't you think so, Linda?" He still did not know what to make of her. But he certainly wasn't going to let it effect their escape.

"Sarcasm won't help you very much," Linda warned, as they walked out of the building onto Norr Mälarstrand Street.

"You're right," Carter laughed, stretching out his arms toward the sky and staring straight into the sun. "Oh sunlight! Oh, blessed sunlight! How I missed you!"

"Be careful. That sun is pretty powerful," Linda said. "It's much brighter than you think." She walked quickly in the direction of the Grand Hotel making certain they were a safe distance away from the prison. "You need a few days of rest and recuperation before you head back to the States."

"Why don't I just head state-side now?" Carter replied, retrieving several kroners after having slammed an automatic soda machine a few times. "As far as I'm concerned, my job is finished." The only thing left for him to do was collect the rest of the money. Screw Sweden, and its problems. He couldn't take them all on his shoulders.

"Look at that!" Carter said, ignoring her statement, and walking over to a woman making sandwiches on an aluminum folding table. "May I have a *sotare*?"

The woman, dressed in a thick quilt jacket, despite the temperature in the mid-70's, gave him a small cardboard box in which she placed a grilled Baltic herring and a boiled potato. Carter ate it voraciously. It seemed as if he hadn't eaten for days. And now he was going to make up for it.

"Take it easy!" Linda cautioned him. "This is not your last supper!"

"I wouldn't be so certain of that," Carter said with a forced smile. "Bad things happen to me when I'm around you."

"You're not blaming me for your troubles, are you? Why you ungrateful . . ." she trailed off, frustrated.

"It's amazing how good a little nothing of a fish can taste," Carter said with his mouth full. He went over to another vendor and bought two Carlsburg beers and handed her one can. "Nothing like good beer and some basic staples. Like most things in life, mankind tends to overcomplicate his problems. Putting all kinds of kinks, twists, and turns that no one really needs."

"What in God's name are you talking about?" she asked, clearly peeved.

"Oh come on, Linda!" Carter responded, swirling down

the last drops of his beer. "The cutesy, innocent professional ingenue from the Midwest isn't holding up too well."

"You don't have to be insulting," Linda responded with righteous indignation, but not contradiction.

"I'm sorry," Carter replied, "but you tend to get a little bit cranky when you're in the hole or being tortured for too long. Know what I mean?"

"No!" she said. "I can understand that you underwent quite an ordeal. But that doesn't allow you to become a nasty..."

"I'm not nasty," Carter laughed. "I thought I was very civil with the street vendor, considering the ordeal you just put me through."

"What are you implying?" she asked. "That I ordered your arrest and torture?"

"We can either discuss this unpleasant matter now," Carter responded, his mouth still full of food, "or we can..."

"What?" she asked defiantly.

"Or..." He walked over to a taxicab. "We can find out what's happening—my way!"

"No! If you feel that way," she said defiantly, "I'm not going with you anywhere! You're either nuts, drunk, or you have post traumatic stress syndrome."

"Thank you, Doctor," he responded, throwing her onto the back seat of the taxicab. "Driver, the Grand Hotel, please!"

31

WASHINGTON, D.C.

The black Lincoln sedan stopped in front of the metal gates of Fort McNair.

"Identification, please," the corporal said curtly to the driver. The man pulled out his plastic I.D. card and presented it to the guard. "You may go through, sir," he said, deferentially.

"How do I find the National Defense University?" the driver asked.

"Go straight down this main street," the corporal responded, "which is an extension of Fourth Street. At the stop sign, make a left turn and go all the way down to Fifth Street, make a right, and then proceed about a quarter of a mile. You will see a modern-looking building. Park anywhere you want to on the right-hand side of the building."

"Thank you." The driver drove past the guard and onto the base. The corporal saluted as the sedan went by.

The driver had been on the base several times before in the last few years, the last time to give a lecture on foreign policy to military officers. He smiled as he passed a huge manicured lawn dominated by a white flagpole flying the American flag, recalling the Sundays he brought his youngest of two daughters to this field to play soccer.

The area looked more like a college campus in the heart

of Washington, D.C. than it did a military base. Yet this was the place which had spawned some of the America's greatest generals—George Marshall, George Patton, Omar Bradley, David Eisenhower. It was a fort where young military officers, for the most part army personnel, were trained in the strategies and tactics of war by more experienced military and civilian personnel. Everything from logistical supplies to warfare simulation was offered in courses taught at the three different universities co-inhabiting Fort McNair, the most important of which was the National Defense University.

NDU was housed in a semi-circular building, which attempted to imitate the German Art Deco movement of the 1920's. Once again the visitor showed his I.D. to the military security guard stationed at the front door, who indicated the floor to which the visitor should be going. When asked whether he wanted the intended host to know that he was arriving, the visitor politely declined, indicating that this was a "surprise visit" for his fiftieth birthday. The security guard nodded his head and smiled, allowing the visitor to think that he had been co-opted by the response. Once the visitor was out of sight, he immediately picked up the telephone.

"Good to see you again, Carl," General James Atherton greeted his visitor at the door. They shook hands like men who were very familiar with each other. Atherton stood in a completely empty office, except for a huge map of Sweden hanging on a wall. Red and blue markers were positioned all over the country.

"How long has it been?" Ambassador Carl LaGreca asked. "A couple of months since we last worked together?" He was still jet-lagged from his overnight flight from Stockholm to Dulles Airport.

"The drug trafficker in the Cayman Island," Atherton responded with a twinkle in his eyes and a perverse sense of joy in his voice. "That was a nice piece of work. Fast. Elegant. Organically whole, wouldn't you say?"

"General," LaGreca interrupted, "let's not wax poetic on what was a simple assassination, ordered by you, executed by Alison Carter, and covered up by me, when I was the government's czar for narcotic's."

"All in all," Atherton added, annoyed by LaGreca's peremptory tone, "I would say that it was a well-executed operation."

"For the record, you and I both know," LaGreca said curtly, "that an execution never occurred and was never ordered by anyone in this or any other government. And the less we talk about it, the better off we are."

"If I remember correctly," Atherton responded, walking to the map, "there was an unofficial sizable bounty, offered by an unknown party, allegedly called the 'Association for a Drug-Free Country,' for the elimination of a drug problem allegedly created by the unfortunate creature who died on Stingray Island."

"I see you have the map of Sweden," LaGreca said, determined not to get sucked into a self-congratulatory discussion of an event that never officially took place.

"Yes," Atherton responded smiling, "I was thinking of taking a trip to Scandinavia and visiting the region where they blow that famous glass..."

"Kosta Boda, perhaps?" LaGreca interrupted.

"Yes," Atherton answered disingenuously, "and, of course, to visit my favorite ambassador." He paused. "Are you receiving old friends in your new position? I forget."

"You know damn well," LaGreca responded angrily, "I was given that post to keep me away from any media attention that might be focused my way as a result of the Stingray affair."

"And I thought that you were placed there because you were so good at understanding the periodic need for assassinations," Atherton responded, "at a time when the Presidential Executive Order of 1976 has made everyone in this government afraid of 'taking people out.'" He paused again to assess LaGreca's response, but he made none. "But then again, I might be mistaken. For whoever really knows how that chocolate fudge factory called the State Department really works. I certainly can't make claims to know how those chaps on the seventh floor make their ambassadorial assignments. It's always been a mystery to me; and, I would suspect to them as well."

"Let's stop all this game playing. I want you to order Carter out of Sweden. Immediately," LaGreca blurted out, impatient with Atherton's patronizing manner. "He's putting himself, as well as a lot of other people, in harm's way. I can't afford to have him there. He's causing too much trouble for everyone. And he's on the way to completely destroying the excellent relations the United States enjoys with Sweden."

"Foreign policy is not my field of expertise, as you well know," Atherton responded, realizing where the discussion was headed. "Why don't you go to your boss, the Secretary of State? That's his province. They can recall him anytime that they want. You know that."

"Oh, God!" LaGreca blurted out, "I'm a saint! Listening to all this horseshit from you as if there was any truth behind it!"

"I have nothing to do with him," Atherton added brusquely. "I don't even know why you came to see me."

"Carter works for you!" LaGreca screamed. "It's your goddamn organization of nonexistent assassins working for a nonexistent agency in a nonexistent government for one real entity—money!"

"You're tired and jet-lagged from the long trip," Atherton responded solicitously. "I think you should go back to Sweden, where you have a job to do and take a rest at one of those quaint seaside resort towns. Like Vadstena."

"General," LaGreca lowered his voice, trying to contain his anger, "you are known as a man of integrity and fairness. Carter is technically on vacation. You know quite well that he does not work for the Secretary of State when he is on leave. He is in Sweden . . . working . . . for a general in the U.S. government, who works with all of our principal Cabinet officers, and reports directly to POTUS, the goddamned President of the United States. In an unofficial capacity, of course. But I can't guarantee Carter's safety in

Sweden any longer—even if I am the ambassador. And I won't hold myself accountable for an ... accident ... that might befall Carter ... and others."

"I sincerely wish that I could help you out, if only for the good ol' times," Atherton replied, mockingly sympathetic, "but I'm afraid that what you are describing to me is above my jurisdiction and authority. All I do is to think up different scenarios for war and then play with them on the computer downstairs with a bunch of colonels." He placed his arm around LaGreca's shoulder, "I am sorry. I can understand your frustration. Bureaucracies have gotten so big that no one person is accountable anymore. If we go to war and innocent citizens are killed by accident, you can't point the finger at anyone at DOD and call them 'murderer.'" He pointed to the map of Sweden. "And if atrocities are systematically organized in different parts of the world in the name of religion, ideology, ethnicity, or whatever, who is there to stop it? The United States government? No. We no longer want to see our boys return in body bags to Dover Air Force Base. The UN? No. They're just an overblown organization of welfare states and a decrepit repository of spies from around the world who have nowhere else to go. NATO? Try to coordinate nineteen nations on anything. So, I really do empathize with your problem. I believe that Carter is a physician at the State Department. If there is nothing that the Secretary of State can do, then go one step higher."

"And to whom might that be?" LaGreca asked, realizing he had just wasted twenty-four hours trying to prevent what he knew would become a human rights catastrophe in Sweden as a result of Carter's presence there.

"POTUS!" Atherton responded with alacrity.

"I already spoke with him, you prick!" LaGreca said, with contempt. "It was the president who authorized me to talk directly to you about this matter and ask for your help."

"Just what did he say?"

"That he had no knowledge of any ... mission ... in Sweden," LaGreca stated, "And, if he did, he would have no authority over it because it was completely illegal. But he suggested that General James Atherton had studied the issue of assassination at the war college and he might be of some help..."

"Well," Atherton said, leading LaGreca to the door, "I'm glad to see you again. But I am genuinely sorry that I cannot do anything to help you... or Carter."

It had begun to rain when LaGreca stepped out of the building and into his car. *One down and one to go,* he thought, as he headed for the White House... again.

32

STOCKHOLM, SWEDEN

The taxicab ride from City Hall to the Grand Hotel along the busy boulevard of Norr Mälarstrand was a testimony to the professionalism of the cabdriver. With Linda screaming for help, and Carter trying to restrain and silence her, the driver heard nothing, saw nothing and, certainly, did nothing but drive at an appropriate speed to avoid any accidents.

"I'm going to report you to the police if you don't let me out of here," she threatened.

"I'm quite certain that Captain Hansson can't help you," Carter responded with a sadistic tone that sent chills up his own back. It was not his usual habit to gloat. First, it was indiscreet. Second, he took no real pleasure in neutralizing an opponent. And third, in some ways, he had screwed up. He had violated one of the major edicts of warfare espoused by Sun Tze: Always be sufficiently prepared so that you never have to fight a war. The real battle was in the complete psychological preparation of oneself, so that the need for war would be unnecessary.

The most important thing he had to do right now was to get Linda to the hotel and find out what was going on. Was the prime minister behind his Eriksson assignment? And now that Eriksson was dead, what would be the real consequences? Knowing Linda's role in all of this was key.

"You think that by your killing Hansson, and Hansson's killing Eriksson—which was really your job—you've resolved your problems?" she asked, settling into her side of the backseat.

"Why don't you tell me?"

"Let me assure you," she replied, with an air of superiority, "your problems haven't even begun."

The doorman standing in front of the Grand Hotel, dressed in a long green coat with golden brocaded epaulettes, opened the back door of the taxi for Linda and Carter. His "Welcome to the Grand Hotel, Mrs. Carter" was unctuous and obligatory. Like all professional doormen, he derived a sense of pride and satisfaction from the fact that he knew all of the hotel's guests by name. In this case, of course, he was wrong. Linda was gracious enough not to correct him.

"Linda!" Carter yelled to her just as she was stepping out of the cab. "I don't have any Kroners to pay this gentleman."

The cabdriver, who had been hoping to be tipped handsomely for his discreteness, had now decided that he would be lucky to receive the basic fare.

Linda smirked and reached into her pocketbook.

They walked through the main glass doors, up the marble stairs, and toward the elevators, nodding their heads in tandem to the concierge.

"So where is our interrogation session going to occur?" she asked. "My room or yours?"

"Yours. And thanks for bailing me out with the taxi driver," he said. "My jailers emptied my pockets."

"A feeble excuse," she responded, "you should always have your American Express card with you. Remember," she said facetiously, "it's there for you for any and all occasions, especially when you've lost your every other possession."

"Very funny," Carter said, as the elevator climbed to the second floor. He glanced at Linda, standing next to him so composed, mysterious and pretty, and felt that he wanted to kiss her. Bizarre, he thought. He could just as readily kill her. Well, perhaps not kill her. But do whatever needed to be done to find out what the hell was going on, that might end up killing him. But his anger had transformed into lust—that he would have to control.

They walked down the regally carpeted hallway toward her room. Like all women who have had to live off their intuition in order to advance their careers in a male-dominated world of glass ceilings, she had survived by being able to read nonverbal cues. And she had no doubt that Carter was attracted to her. And despite his wane, disheveled look, he was somewhat attractive to her. As the elevator had ascended, so had their body temperatures. This change of events would complicate matters, she thought. But the time for accountability was approaching inevitably. She was prepared. She had been for some time now.

As Linda slid her card key into the slot, Carter realized that for all the time they had spent together, he knew very little about her. He was getting sloppy. Or, worse yet, he thought, he just didn't care anymore. Could it be possible that he was burning out? Maybe he should just remain a doctor and leave the hocus pocus to others. Or maybe he was only suffering from post-traumatic stress syndrome. The symptoms were obvious, yet disguised, for they included fatigue, anxiety, nightmares, uncertainty, and depression, among other mechanisms of unconsciously working out the trauma over a protracted period of time. The syndrome's symptoms were a call for help.

"Welcome to my home away from home," Linda said, as they entered a small room containing a queen-sized bed and two wing-back armchairs that had seen better days. Contrary to the name of the hotel, its rooms were not as "grand" as their prices. And they had no air-conditioning. The room's only four-star feature was a set of French doors that led onto a small balcony that overlooked a magnificent harbor panorama. "Would you like something to drink?"

"No, thank you," Carter, looking longingly at the bed, where he would give anything to be able to just lie down and fall asleep. "Wait a minute," he said. "I think I'll have a shot of aquavit." He needed something to keep him awake.

"What about half of that?" she asked, kicking off her shoes and taking off her jacket.

"You mean just plain aqua—water?" He wondered why he hadn't noticed her sense of humor before. Something was definitely happening to him which he couldn't explain. He felt exhausted from his ordeal, yet, at the same time, felt exhilarated by her presence. Christ, he thought, he'd better straighten himself out quickly.

He watched as she inserted a key into the mini bar lock. The very act suddenly had all kinds of sexual connotations for him. He shook his head rapidly, as if he could snap it out of its current state. *Absurd,* he thought. *Maybe I'm just horny. Or starved for the emotional affection of a woman.* At this point, he decided, both were true.

"Here's a bottle of Römulus," she said, handing him his favorite Swedish sparkling water.

"Thank you," he said, covering her hand with his, not allowing her to disengage. "I'm very thirsty."

"So am I," she responded. "How about sharing the drink? That was the only one left."

"But I'm supposed to be interrogating you," he added as a complete non sequitor.

"Let's share this drink first," she responded, drawing him closer to her, "and then you can do whatever you want with me."

33

STOCKHOLM, SWEDEN

The night of love swept through the ether of meaningless promises, sensuous teases, tender caresses, passionate thrusts, and childish mutterings, which they both knew would be forgotten by the next morning. But there is nothing more wonderfully self-deluding than a passionate affair. Every wishful thought becomes a stanchion of truth around which more lies are constructed, eventually leading to the greatest lie of all, when both parties utter falsehoods of fealty, love, and everlasting devotion. Unfortunately, embarrassment frequently sets in when passions die down, and the evening becomes nothing more than a neuro-hormonal trace of emotional imprints embedded into the cortex of the brain, to be retrieved in a moment of nostalgia, longing, or desire.

Neither Linda nor Carter were typical lovers. They had already been branded by the mark of time and experience, having been herded through the stockyards of disappointment, betrayal, deceit, pain, and loneliness. Each was wary of the other's intentions, be they physical or emotional, but willing to park their respective souls in each other's arms for the evening. Perhaps it was the highly charged state of excitement and tension that made them confide in each other with words that could have been truths or could have been lies. Neither one really cared how their words and actions would be interpreted by the other because nothing really counted for either one except to get through the night as emotionally intact as possible.

"You're quite good," Carter said, lying on his back, his head leaning against the goose feather pillows.

"Well, thank you," Linda replied, raising herself with her right arm so that she could look at him. "You're not so bad, yourself."

"It sounds to me as if we were in some kind of daycare center, learning to work and play with one another."

Linda smiled.

"I'm glad you smiled."

"Why?" she asked coyly, playing with the strands of his hair, seeing if she couldn't tie them into a braid.

"Since we met a couple of days ago," he responded, "I have rarely seen you smile."

"There was very little to smile about," she responded. "You were focused on your assignment. And now that you have completed it, you should probably return home soon."

"That sounds more like a warning," Carter said, "rather than a point of fact. Should I be going home soon?"

Carter examined her naked body with his eyes. It certainly was less than perfect. Her muscles had no definition; she clearly was not one of those women who worked out in a gymnasium several times a week. Her breasts were small, something along the proverbial pear-shape. Her long neck led into shoulders that were somewhat rounded, probably genetic in origin, and given enough time she would develop into a slightly humpbacked older woman. Her hips and buttocks were larger than one might have expected from the way she looked in clothes. Clearly, clothing was something she understood well and was selected to hide some deficiencies and maximize those aspect of her body that were more attractive. What made her most physically interesting to Carter, however, was her face. Dark blue eyes, somewhat slanted, but not quite Oriental. High cheekbones overlaying tight, thin lips. A broad face with a well-sculpted chin and perfect Greek nose.

But more important than her actual physical features was the kindness and gentleness that radiated in her lovemaking. Beneath that hardened professional exterior, Carter thought, was a tenderness she probably rarely revealed. But a tenderness well worth waiting for.

"I think there is very little I could tell you that will influence a decision I think you have already made," she answered. Her eyes narrowed with a hint of sadness and tension. "You know what you will do."

"And so do you!" he said, playing with her hair. "It's ironic. Several hours ago, I had to restrain you from biting, kicking, and screaming at me. This evening I rather enjoyed the biting, kicking, and screaming."

"It's all a matter of context, my dear Doctor Carter," she said, outlining his thin shoulders with her index finger. "We could either excite each others' passions or fuel our manifold differences. For a while, I thought it was going to be the latter."

"Were you aware of this from the beginning?" he asked, warily.

"Do you mean, was I sent over to be the sparrow in a honey trap?"

"Something like that," he responded, "to set me up in a love trap so that you could elicit information from me and manipulate me."

"On the contrary," she said, "I was simply sent here to monitor what you learned and did."

"How did you learn about my arrival?"

"It wasn't hard," she replied, smiling sardonically at him as if he already knew the answer.

"Why do I have this feeling that I'm not quite up to par here?"

"Think of the obvious," she replied. "What is the business of foreign affairs?"

"Business!"

"That's why I'm here," she said with the assuredness of someone who feels that she had made herself extremely clear.

"I understand that you represent United States automotive interests here in Sweden," Carter responded somewhat irked. While she was leading him toward the answers that would unravel a lot of questions, he still felt as if he were very far away from solving the puzzle.

"The people I represent," she said, looking at him sternly now, with that midwest no-nonsense attitude of hers, "are major car manufacturers. Major! Do you understand me?"

"You make it sound as if I needed eight air bags before I asked you the next question," he said. "So your clients are from Detroit. I got that point. So what? Why are they interested in Eriksson? In my assignment? In illegal refugees used for slave labor in timber, glassblowing..."

"... in the manufacture of cars," she added.

"Do you mean that the refugees who are streaming over the Swedish border are being used as slave labor to make so-called United States manufactured cars?"

"To put it crassly," she answered, "as well as you did in bed with me this evening, I would say that you're pretty close to scoring another—of many—home runs."

"But that's not all, is it?"

Linda pointed to the brass chandelier hanging from the center of the ceiling, indicating that the room could be bugged.

"So certain U.S. car industrialists and certain Swedish car..." Carter whispered.

"And other financial interests besides cars," she whispered back.

"... are in collusion," Carter continued. "They jointly exploit the illegal refugees. But somehow these companies, U.S. and Swedish, are also involved in the systematic elimination of these refugees by so-called loyal Swedish patriots—like the late Dr. Eriksson and Captain Hansson. It still doesn't make sense."

"You forgot Mack Londsdale," she added, leaving the bed to dress. All of a sudden she was feeling uncomfortable with the conversation and the pressure Carter would start to put on her for more information. Carter dressed as well.

"So your clients sent you over here to monitor my activities and what I would find out," he continued, "about the refugees and about the joint U.S. and Swedish industrialist complex."

"You forgot one minor character," she added. "A man who is central to this entire elaborate scheme."

"Who is that?"

"The name that Eriksson whispered in your ear before he died," she replied, "and the name you finally elicited from Captain Hansson, literally from his last breath."

"You mean . . ." Carter sighed deeply, knowing that it was an important moment of truth for the both of them. ". . . Ambassador Carl LaGreca?" Saying the ambassador's name aloud finally made it real. "But what about—?"

Before she could answer him, they both saw the doorknob on the room door turn slowly.

"Let's get out of here!" Linda said, motioning toward the French doors and the balcony.

The door to the room opened suddenly and two men in Pöni uniforms, holding uzzi machine guns, started to spray the bedroom with bullets.

34

STOCKHOLM, SWEDEN

Bullets whizzed all over the room as if a formation of killer bees were on a vicious foraging rampage. Intricately designed plaster mouldings, wood paneling, beveled mirrors, and even an antique porcelain sink became fragments, free-floating in a state physicists call Brownian Motion.

Together, Carter and Linda dropped from the ledge of the balcony onto the hotel awning, and then slid down to the street on its posts. For the second time in four days, a sense of the surreal hit Carter. He felt as if he were executing an escape he had seen dozens of times in the movies—and it had worked!

They ran quickly down the street, out of sight of the Pönis who were firing selectively from their second-floor vantage point. At the end of the block, a taxi was dislodging a customer. The closer the taxi loomed in front of them, the greater their collective sigh of relief. But they couldn't outrun the distinctive white and blue striped police cars, red lights flashing and sirens blasting, that surrounded them. Seven police cars filled with two policemen each drew their guns.

"Stop where you are!" the police captain shouted in English through a megaphone. "You are both under arrest for the murders of both Dr. Derek Eriksson and Captain Carl Hansson."

"Looks like your 'friends' have turned against you as well as me," Carter said, realizing they were surrounded. The only benefit of their worsening situation was the fact that the gunfire from the hotel had ceased.

"Oh shit!" Linda blurted out. "I should have known better than to share a lovely evening in a bugged room."

Carter realized that if they didn't find a way out of this situation, they wouldn't even make it alive to the police station—or the embassy—this time.

"LaGreca must have ordered this," Linda blurted out, deciding that it was time for Carter to know everything. Unless it was already too late. "With an OK from Johannes and Olsson."

"Why would LaGreca order our assassinations?" Carter asked, shocked.

"It's exactly the preposterous scenario he would concoct," Linda answered, seething with anger for having been betrayed by her own colleague. Who would ever suspect that an ambassador of the United States would order the death of two American citizens in a foreign country in which he had nothing to do but act as a glorified travel agent for congressional delegations?

"Please give yourselves up," the police shouted through the megaphone. "Otherwise, we will be forced to shoot and someone might get hurt." He paused, "I will give you exactly ten seconds to put your hands in the air and surrender."

"You were set up, sent here to be a foil for a combined Swedish/American effort to mask what Eriksson was doing to those immigrants," Linda talked quickly. "If anyone actually investigated all the recent fires, tortures, and murders, as the prime minister's government was being forced to do, they could blame them on the fanatic Dr. Eriksson, who had been killed by an unknown, foreign-paid assassin. Who, in fact, paid the assassin would remain a mystery, much like the unknown aspects of the Aldo Moro killing in Italy. This way, the Swedish government would not be seen as the bad guys. From their point of view, this explanation would prevent the right-wing nationalists from rising up and causing demonstrations to demand the overthrow of Johannes's government, and at the same time make Eriksson a martyr, polarizing the nation." She suddenly realized that her confession had come too late. They were both about to be killed. And if by any chance they were able to escape this situation, they might have even more to fear. A fast death might be a welcome respite.

"Nine ... eight ... seven ..." shouted the police captain.

"Why me?" Carter asked, still trying to make the incomprehensible clear.

"Six ... five ..." the captain continued, he and his men walking toward them.

Carter felt as if he were a fish, caught in a net that was closing tightly around him.

"Your profile fit! It was that simple. LaGreca learned about you from an ex-CIA buddy," Linda responded. "A physician who worked in the State Department and killed bad guys on assignment. If need be, Eriksson's assassination, as well as the destruction of his ethnic cleansing machinery, was to be blamed on a typical CIA screwup. Like the one in Belgrade, where they used old maps and had NATO bomb the Chinese Embassy instead of a munitions storage facility. You would be sitting there, with the CIA's money, so to speak, holding the proverbial bag of shit."

"Four ... three ..."

"And what about tomorrow's march?" Carter asked, mindful that they had only seconds left.

"It's the perfect time for the government to round up significant numbers of illegal aliens—hundreds of thousands—and to deport them without very much effort. It's like cooping up the squawking hens and waiting for the fox to call. Except the hens are the refugees and the fox is the government. Very efficient, is it not?"

"Very clever," Carter realized.

"Two . . ." Then there was a prolonged pause.

"The march is a way of killing two birds with one stone," Linda said. "It gets rid of both sides of the problem—Eriksson's right-wingers and the source of their anger—the illegal aliens. Both groups will be at the march in full force. This way the men in power can sustain the fiction created by the famous Swedish sociologist Gynnar Myrdal. By eliminating people on both sides of the equation, the number of people you have to provide for drops dramatically. Expediency gets covered by layers of regret, remorse, and sanctimonious testimony."

"It's amazing that none of this has come out in the newspapers or come through diplomatic channels," Carter said, realizing that time had run out.

"One . . ."

"That's the advantage of having an ambassador working for you," she replied.

"Is our government behind this crazy plan?" Carter asked.

"Not officially," Linda replied. "It's like everything else they've done throughout our history of screwups—plausible deniability. Unofficially, they support Sweden's need to 'clear the decks,' so to speak. But publicly they have to denounce the entire situation of human rights violations."

"Would both of you please face the police car and place your hands on the roof," the police captain ordered, as his officers surrounded Carter and Linda. Once in that position, they were handcuffed with their arms in front of them.

"Furthermore," Linda added, "neither the CIA nor any other military, security, or intelligence organization wanted to be involved in this situation. That's why an independent like you was chosen. You're their 'true believer.' Quite frankly, they couldn't have made a better choice."

"Would you two please proceed to that van," the police captain ordered. "You will have the right to call your ambassador as well as a lawyer of your choice once you are in official custody at police headquarters."

"Captain," Carter asked with an inappropriate smile, "what is the maximum penalty for our alleged crime?"

"Don't worry," the captain responded, "you will never reach the judge's bench to be tried, Dr. Carter."

35

STOCKHOLM, SWEDEN

Johannes and Olsson stood at the entrance to the Royal Flagship Vasa Museum in Djurgarden. It was after the museum's normal hours of operation, but someone had called from the office of the prime minister and requested that the museum remain open for an off-hours visit by an "important" government official.

Bewildered by the request, the museum curator, Carla Milles, a fastidious woman in her early fifties who tended to overreact to anything out of the ordinary, initially had refused the request, citing a lack of staff. In reality, Carla despised the immense amount of administrative work she would be required to submit to the Minister of Culture just so that some self-important, pompous dignitary could impress another self-important dignitary with a piece of Swedish history and the power he had in being able to change the daily routine of a state-owned attraction.

"Thank you so much for allowing us to come in after hours," Johannes said, glancing around his favorite museum.

"Of course, Mr. Prime Minister," Carla responded, impressed that the official was the prime minister himself. Now this was a story to tell her neighbors. "We are always pleased when you take the time out of your busy schedule to visit us."

"How do you do?" Olsson extended his hand to Carla in a gesture of gratitude. "My name is Nils Olsson."

"If you are with the prime minister, you are a friend of Sweden, and clearly a friend of the museum," Carla said, pleased with her own sense of hospitality. She led them through the uniquely designed building. "As you know, this museum was specifically constructed to house the *Vasa*, the world's oldest identified and complete ship . . ."

"I wonder if it would not be an imposition on our part," Johannes said in a gentle voice, "if we were left alone to admire the ship ourselves. By this time, I think I know the details of its voyage by heart." Johannes didn't mind interrupting her standard museum lecture, knowing that her main interest, quite legitimately, was to rid herself of them as soon as she could to finish unending administrative tasks.

"Of course," Carla responded with relief, "how inconsiderate of me, not to think that you two would want your privacy."

It wasn't until she walked toward her office that she noticed the prime minister's guards following behind the country's leader and his associate at a discreet distance. Suddenly, she questioned whether these two men were there to learn about the seventeenth-century man-of-war ship resting in the middle of the building.

"You have to admit, Nils," Johannes said, surveying the two-hundred-foot restored gunboat, "that it is quite amazing," he paused, "or should I say 'entertaining', that in 1628, this ship was on its maiden voyage, and in front of thousands of horrified well-wishers, the Royal Flagship *Vasa* capsized and sank, almost instantly, to the bottom of Stockholm harbor. For want of a few architectural modifications, this magnificent boat would have made history as the largest and most lethal warship of its time."

"I imagine it's a story the Polish navy would appreciate," Olsson said sardonically, remembering its destruction of the Swedish fleet in World War II.

"Now, now, Nils," Johannes was almost paternal to his

childhood friend, "you're impatient. And you want to know why I dragged you here at the end of the day."

"You know me well, my friend. Or is my impatience that obvious?" Olsson asked. "But I know you well enough to speculate on the answer as well."

"Speculate away," Johannes responded.

"When history reconstructs what you and I have planned for Sweden," Olsson said, "you hope that it will be as merciful as it was to the reconstruction of this ship. But at the same time, you're trying to tell me that you have some major concerns about what it is we are trying to accomplish by having brought Carter to Sweden... Londsdale killed... And now my intelligence sources in the Swedish security have informed me that both Eriksson and Hansson have been murdered."

"By whom?" Johannes asked, annoyed that he had to learn what was going on from his civilian friend. He realized that the killer could have been any number of people in Parliament, a political enemy, an Islamic fundamentalist, some illegal refugee.

"They were killed in the prison cells beneath City Hall," Olsson replied, disturbed that Johannes did not hold as tight a rein on his national security staff as he should have. "If you ever believed that we could reconstruct a new welfare state without some foul-ups occurring, like the maiden voyage of this ship, then you were sadly mistaken." His admonition was over. Now he tried to look reassuringly at his friend. "We will not sink in the harbor to become the laughingstock of this country."

"So who killed Eriksson?" Johannes asked again, concerned that he would now have a major national problem on his hands. Once the news leaked out to the public, the Nationalist Party would capitalize on the death.

"An overzealous Captain Hansson," Olsson replied.

"Hansson?"

"Yes," Olsson responded. "Hansson's interrogation skills were less than skillful, so we ended up without any information about how much Eriksson revealed to Carter."

"Did you reprimand Hansson?" Johannes asked.

"Let us just say that like the *Vasa*," Nils replied, "he went under very fast. Carter was brought into Eriksson's cell in order to intimidate him into talking after he saw what happened to Eriksson..." Olsson continued.

"And?"

"And... he killed Hansson with the very torture instrument Hansson used on Eriksson."

Johannes was stunned. He had now lost Londsdale, Eriksson, and Hansson. In two days, would he look back and say that it had been worth it? More and more he realized that, with all of his meticulous planning, his plans could turn into another *Vasa*-like incident. But this time, it would not be a man-of-war that sank on its maiden voyage. Instead, it could be the entire Swedish government.

"And where is Carter now?" Johannes asked.

"He's on his way to central headquarters, waiting for the 'final solution.'" Olsson gave Johannes a wry smile.

36

STOCKHOLM, SWEDEN

"On an official level, the United States Government is having a difficult time supporting your government's policy on illegal refugees." LaGreca felt awkward, having to address his friend in this official manner. He sat on a worn leather couch in Johannes's office, surrounded by walls covered with oil portraits of the prime minister's austere-looking predecessors, all of whom were from the same party. If nothing else, Sweden, like Holland and Switzerland, was a nation of non-risk takers. Regularity and habit ruled the day as well as the centuries.

"To what, specifically, does your government object?" Johannes asked, maintaining the charade. He moved around his large mahogany desk, covered with reports, memos, files, charts, and a STU-3 secure telephone. Behind his leather chair was the Swedish flag, with its off-center white cross on a red background. A large colored photograph of the King and Queen hung on a nearby wall. Although the reigning monarchy had no official political affiliation, much like in England, the fact that the country had a Constitutional monarchy made it attractive to the tourists who, if uncertain what there was to see in Sweden, besides the legendary beautiful people, were certain that there would not be riots in the streets or muggings in front of their hotels.

But tourism was not the concern of the day. The problem which had spurred this meeting was America's increasingly strained relationship with Sweden over the treatment of Sweden's illegal immigrants. Several human rights organizations had already accused Sweden of human rights violations.

"As the personal representative of the President of the United States," LaGreca continued, "I can assure you that he finds what you are doing repugnant." LaGreca realized that in the language of diplomacy "repugnant" was a word that might carry serious consequences. It was not a word that, as an ambassador, he would use frequently. But he had to make it very clear to Johannes that the U.S. insisted that the Swedish policy would have to change. Unofficially . . . well, that was different.

"I have a personal and professional admiration for your president," Johannes responded. "Is your Congress taking the same position?"

"The only bureaucracies that have objected to the president's position," LaGreca replied, "have been the Commerce Department and the Department of Defense. However, a congressional fact-finding delegation will be formed, to visit Sweden during Congress, next recess." He relaxed, having said what he had come to say as an official representative of the government.

"Johannes, isn't it ironic that we, Americans, have to reprimand you and your country for—"

"'Alleged' human rights violations," Johannes interrupted.

"You're right," LaGreca smiled, "'alleged' human rights violations. Sweden has always been the world's watchdog in this area. But we've got a lot of pressure mounting from the NGO's and the various immigrant groups in your country whose families live in the U.S. They are putting pressure on our Congress, which in turn is pressing hard on the Executive branch."

"Then why doesn't your country take them in?" Johannes asked, half-seriously. He already knew the answer. They were both playing out the parts they had been previously assigned in this Kabuki called "diplomacy."

"The quotas for Macedonians, Albanians, Russians, and most Eastern European and Middle East countries have been filled," LaGreca responded, with chagrin. He knew what the response would be.

"Then change your quotas, at least for the refugee groups who have a loud voice in your country," Johannes responded. "Let them spill over your borders."

"Changing legislation is almost close to impossible," LaGreca replied. "As you know all too well, it took close to two years and over $20 million in campaign donations for me to obtain preferential trade advantages for Sweden."

"How do you see this impasse resolved? By further restricting the trade advantages Sweden has always enjoyed with the United States?" Johannes asked. "Or by placing Sweden on the list of human rights violators?"

"We're in agreement. Neither of us want this situation to continue," LaGreca said, "or we will end up in a major trade war, where you won't be able to sell your cars, cellular phones, and pharmaceutical products to us, and we won't be able to open up our hamburger franchises in Sweden."

They both laughed, as LaGreca was hoping they would, and the meeting, which had already gone on for fifteen minutes, lost a bit of its chill.

"Carl," Johannes said, "I speak to you in confidence." He shifted his posture, reflecting a greater relaxation. "My term as Prime Minister is in serious jeopardy, as I am sure you know. I'm besieged on my right for having placated the socialists and kept the welfare state going . . . to the point where they accuse me, and perhaps justifiably, of creating governmental bankruptcy."

"And on your left," LaGreca continued, "you're being attacked for having brought too many nationalists into government who want to cut the welfare budget and throw out those lazy, parasitic foreigners who are the source of all your problems."

"I think you call that being caught between a hard rock and a hard rock," Johannes said, mangling the phrase.

"But that's why you were elected Prime Minister," LaGreca responded, "and I remain a lowly representative of the U.S." He paused to reflect on his own role in world politics. And he liked it. "Fortunately, I don't make policy. I simply follow through on whatever foreign policy we may have—"

"—or may not have," Johannes interrupted. As far as he was concerned, U.S. policy since the Reagan administration, some twenty years ago, had been drifting on a reckless course of sanctimonious posturing, self-righteous harangues, and acting the dual role of world's policeman and social worker. For decades, lack of policy crippled the United States from acting proactively. Instead, the country was always reacting to a crisis situation and never anticipating what might be coming around the corner.

"Touché," LaGreca responded. "So you see, you are not the only one who is caught between ... I believe the expression is, 'a rock and a hard place.'"

They both laughed, and each man remembered how fond he was of the other.

"I am restricted in recommending any economic policies that would be beneficial to Sweden without running the risk of being accused of having 'clientitis,' of overidentifying myself with Swedish concerns and not enough with the concerns of the United States. I can't emphasize enough the degree to which the refugee and labor camp issues are a real thorn in our side."

"As you know," Johannes responded sheepishly, "I would be the first one to shut down those abominable labor camps. But, the majority of my supporters are industrialists who need cheap labor, the same way that your government turns the other way when your major businesses use illegal, cheap laborers from Mexico, Central America, and Latin America. In many ways, your situation is no different from ours. But our country is significantly smaller than yours, so everything we do seems magnified. That same degree of magnification turned on one of your largest states, California..."

"Then we seem to be at our usual impasse," LaGreca said, disappointed.

"I'm afraid so, my friend," Johannes responded. "But I have full faith that even if we can not resolve our respective country's impasse, we can maintain our own friendship. Then, who knows? We still might find a reproachment for our countries."

"I hope so," LaGreca said, starting to leave. "Oh, by the way, concerning that mutual problem of ours—Dr. Carter. I've not been successful in getting Carter recalled. Sorry, no one will take responsibility for him."

Johannes's mood changed instantly to one of anger. "Then we'll have to deal with Dr. Carter ourselves."

37

STOCKHOLM, SWEDEN

Carter and Linda sat facing each other on steel benches in the back of the police van. Two police officers guarding them sat near the rear metal doors. In the front of the van sat another two officers, who could barely be seen through a small Plexiglas porthole.

The average Swedish citizen sought solace from the notion that a steel reinforced truck, filled with men trained in law enforcement, was the embodiment of security itself. Unfortunately, nothing could be further from the truth. Any military or paramilitary operative knew that the logistics of close-quarter entrapment was, at best, problematic. So these particular officers couldn't wait until they arrived at their final destination. The sweat on their respective brows gave away that concern.

Linda raised her cuffed wrists from her lap. "I can't thank you enough for such a generous token of your affection," she said, with an ebullient smile. I knew our night was good, but I didn't realize how good it was. Until your present came."

"Tiffany, of course," Carter responded mockingly. "Only the finest jewelry for you." The lighthearted interchange was much needed, but he quickly refocused on how they could escape without getting killed. The weakest link, he decided, was the guard who seemed jumpy.

"You did not, by any chance, happen to buy the sterling silver key that accompanied these handcuffs, did you?" Linda continued. The least she could do was try to keep the guards, who she knew spoke English, as off guard as possible, while Carter figured a way out of this impossible situation.

"No, but as I look at you," he said, staring intently at her disheveled hair, "I wonder if a lock of hair might have been a more perfect gift."

Linda was perplexed for only a few seconds. Then she realized what Carter meant. Hairpins. Did she have any hairpins with which he could try to pick the locks on their handcuffs. She shook her head like a shaggy dog after an unwanted bath. But nothing fell out.

They sat in silence for a few minutes as the van made its way through the streets of Stockholm.

"Dammit!" Carter suddenly yelled at Linda, "can't you do anything right? I blame this all on you. We were in your room. I bet it was a setup all along."

"Don't yell at me!" she screamed back, quickly realizing that Carter had shifted strategy. Since Carter always seemed to remain calm in a crisis, this inappropriate outburst was probably part of a plan he was developing to escape. She hoped she could follow his cues.

The guards motioned to him to keep his voice down.

"What the hell have you been doing this week?" he yelled, ignoring the guards' concerns, "playing footsy with the cops?"

"The hell with you!!"

"The hell with me?" he screamed. "Shove it, Linda!"

"You coward!" she screamed, "sitting there, blaming me for all your failures. What happened to the great physician-assassin? He's sitting opposite me, locked up in a prison van for . . . ineptness. Very impressive! What do you do for an encore?"

"I leave you in this shit hole of a country with your friends!" he screamed even louder.

This time the dark-haired officer got up from his seat and walked toward Carter, just as Carter had hoped. Without saying a word, the officer slapped him across the face. "Shut up!"

"Make me," Carter defied him, blood running down from a cut on his lip, "you stupid Swedish meatball!"

"Swedish meatball?" The officer struck Carter again, this time with his fist, bloodying Carter's nose. Linda wanted to cry out and order the man to stop. But she knew she couldn't.

"This is the only way you could ever dare to touch me without my killing you," Carter said defiantly.

"Very clever!" the officer responded. "But you can't provoke me into taking off your handcuffs."

"You're too Swedish to even get an erection," Carter retorted, literally hitting below the belt to provoke the officer into coming closer again.

"You American son-of-a-bitch!" the officer retorted, stepping into Carter's preconceived zone of attack.

Before the officer realized what was happening, Carter had placed his handcuffed arms around the officer's neck, and smashed the policeman's face against his own forehead. Blood spurted out of the officer's nose and eyes as he slumped unconscious to the floor. Carter reached for the officer's holstered Beretta and opened fire on the other officer before he could drawn his own gun.

"Aggggghhhhhh!"

"Quick, find the key in his pocket before the van stops and the officers up front come back here."

Linda stood up, repulsed by the sight of blood and carnage. But this was no time to become queasy. She riffled through the pocket of the dark-haired officer and removed a belt filled with bullets, a police radio, a nightstick, handcuffs, and mace. "Carter, there's nothing on him!! He doesn't have the key!"

"Then check the other cop's pockets."

Before she could reach the dead officer, the van had stopped.

"Quick, his pockets!"

"There's nothing there either!"

The barrel of a rifle burst through the porthole as a burst of mustard gas permeated the back of the police van. Linda and Carter started to cough uncontrollably.

"Get back here!"

"I can hardly see or breathe!"

"Crawl along the floor to me and position yourself behind this cadaver!"

"Which cadaver?" she asked, since the officer Carter was propping up with his own body was still alive.

"This cadaver!" Carter responded, shooting the officer at the base of his skull with his own Beretta. Blood splattered all over Carter.

"Ugh!" she blurted out, nauseated, as Carter let go and the officer's body slipped to the floor.

"Use him as a body shield," Carter instructed. "Lie down behind him. Here's his gun. Use it when the police open fire, no matter what I may say or do! Do you understand me?"

Crawling over to the other dead officer, he took his Beretta, checked it for its full load of thirteen bullets, grabbed a handful more and placed them in his shirt pocket. "If the guys capture us alive, we're dead meat! Believe me! Sorry, but there is no way you can rationalize your way out of this. Before, I was the marked assassin. Unfortunately, you have joined a dishonorable club of one! Welcome, on behalf of the membership committee!"

"Thanks, pal. I appreciate everything you've done to get me nearly killed. And now into an exclusive club. I can never thank you enough."

"Just keep calm and do as I say."

"Okay!" she said, coughing. "But I don't know how long I can take this gas without wretching."

"Don't worry," he replied. "You'll get plenty of ventilation in here very soon." Dragging the body of the dead officer over to her, Carter propped both dead bodies up in front of them.

ACTIVE MEASURES

Suddenly, bullets started to whiz through the van.

"I told you," Carter said, "you'll get a lot of ventilation. Don't panic! Just aim carefully!"

The back doors of the van were thrown open and bright sunlight shone through the mist of the gas.

"Throw out your guns," a voice from the outside yelled, "otherwise you'll end up looking like Swiss cheese."

"Don't shoot!" Carter responded. "We're holding your men hostage! "

Silence pervaded. The muted whisperings of the officers told Carter that they were not sure what to do next.

"Show them to us!"

"Not until I can see you and your men more clearly. Step forward!"

"Okay!"

As the gas cleared, Carter could see that now there were two police cars, two officers per car, in addition to the two officers from the front of the van. Six against two, or no— one and a half. Not great odds! But the only ones he had.

"I want all police to get out of here, right now! Everyone gets back into the cars, turns them around, and races them out of here."

"That's impossible!"

"Take a look at your man I'm holding up! He'll be dead in ten minutes from internal bleeding unless you do as I say. And the other one is in worse condition. Decide quickly!"

38

STOCKHOLM, SWEDEN

"Let your two hostages out so that we can see them."

"I'm sorry," Carter said, "the hostages will remain in the van as long as I'm not convinced that we have an aseptic zone—no cops, no hardware, and no snipers." He quickly looked around at the warehouse district in which the van had stopped. At the top of one of the buildings he saw the sharp glint of light characteristic of the scope of a sniper. "Get that snake-eater off the roof!"

"Snake-eater?" The officer was confused. He was extremely proficient in English, as were most of the Swedish population, but this was a new term for him.

"Get your snipers off the roof!" Carter shouted. "There is one over to my left. Then you've got two more on buildings to the right. And maybe some others behind me."

"What do I get in return? One hostage would be a gesture of goodwill on your part."

"Nothing!" Carter responded, avoiding the normal sequence of hostage negotiations. This was a situation in which he had to bluff his way out. "That's the way it's going to be! What's your name?"

"Captain Gustaf Andersson," the officer replied, realizing that Carter was trying the oldest trick in the negotiating book; trying to personalize the relationship so that there would be an emotional bond between them, making it less likely that he would want to kill Carter and Linda if they were caught.

"What would you prefer me to call you? Gustaf? Captain Andersson?"

"Whichever you prefer."

"Andersson. You can call me Carter," he suggested, "or whatever else comes to your creative mind."

"We are off the principal subject, Carter," Andersson said, clearly annoyed by the procrastination. "Where are my two officers? I want to see them now!"

"You'll get to see them when all of your officers and snipers are out of here."

"Nonsense!"

"If your men are not out of this entire area in two minutes, I will turn around and kill one of my hostages. The only one I want to remain here is you." Carter knew that he was pushing the negotiation envelope. "Then I'll bring out your men."

"How do I know that my officers are still alive?"

"The snipers! Get them out of here!" Carter repeated forcefully, starting to doubt his ability to get the police to leave.

There was silence for what seemed like a long two minutes before Andersson blew into a bright shiny whistle. Within seconds, a half-dozen policemen scurried about what had become a cordoned-off area.

Carter sighed ever so slightly, uncertain how successful he had been. He was certain that there were a few snipers still around.

That was standard operating procedure. But with the odds shaven off a few points, Carter's risk-reward ratio was improving.

"Now you have everything the way you want it!" the captain said. "I want to see my men."

"Okay," Carter yelled back. He turned around to Linda and asked, "how are the hostages doing?"

"Are you nuts?" she whispered, "they're dead."

"Well," Carter responded, "that does present a minor problem. What do you want to do now?"

"Wait a minute!" she said, in disbelief. "I thought you had a plan!"

"I did," he answered, "and I've been successful!"

"If you've been so successful, why are you asking me to come up with a plan?"

"I thought you might have something up your sleeve that they would be willing to negotiate for," he said, "better than two dead bodies."

"Like what?" she asked, furious.

"There is only one thing that I can think of," he responded, "that would be worth something to the Swedish police. And that's you, my dear."

"What the hell are you talking..." Before she could finish her question, Carter had grabbed her around the throat with his left arm and had a gun pointed straight at her right temple with his right. They walked out of the van together, joined like Siamese twins.

"What makes you think that I'm not worth shooting?" she asked, trying to pull away from him.

"Just plain good old economics," he responded, as they approached Andersson. "It's the moment of truth, Linda. Right now, we are going to find out what you are really worth to your 'friends.'"

"But you already saw that they don't give a damn whether I live or die when they attacked both of us at the hotel."

"No, Linda," Carter responded, "what I saw were a few Pöni trying to assassinate me, who happened to be in your room. They had no idea who you were."

"How do you know?" she asked, resenting having to defend herself before Carter.

"If they had really wanted to kill you," Carter continued, "they would have booby-trapped that door. Presumably, if you walked through it, you would have been blown away. Or they would have assassinated you while you were alone, asleep."

"But even you said," she protested, "that once we had

slept together, my 'friends,' as you call them, could no longer be certain of my loyalties. Like you, I would have become one of their enemies."

"True," Carter replied, "and we are going to test that hypothesis out right now." He looked at her with sadness in his face. "You see, my dear, I still don't know why you came to Sweden in the first place."

"I told you," she responded, hoping to talk herself out of a bad situation, "that I was sent here to keep an eye on you and whether you constituted a potential threat to the interests of my clients."

"Precisely, Linda," he responded, maintaining his grip on her and walking toward Andersson. "But I'm afraid that as long as I'm alive, your assignment is not complete."

"Nonsense!"

"No one hopes that it's nonsense more than I do," Carter replied, scanning the rooftops of the buildings surrounding the van. He stopped in front of a completely bewildered Captain Andersson.

"What in God's name is this? Some type of joke?" Andersson asked.

"What's the matter, Captain," Carter asked, "isn't she good enough for a hostage?"

"I told you," he shouted, his face red with anger, "I wanted to see my police officers!"

"Captain Andersson," Carter replied nonchalantly, "both you and I know very well that both are very dead; otherwise, we wouldn't have been playing this game."

"I don't know what you're talking about!"

"Of course you do, Captain," Carter responded. "Those snipers I told you to get rid of are still there. I don't need a telescope to see the refraction coming off a high-definition viewfinder on a rifle. If I turned around, I'd find one Pöni at one o'clock crouched behind three garbage cans and a pile of debris, another one at six o'clock, behind the doorway of the redbrick building, and a third at nine o'clock."

"Okay," Andersson responded, "you've made your point." He blew his whistle again and all the men whom Carter had identified stood up, their guns cocked and pointed at him. "What do you want?"

"Take both of us to the American Embassy!" Carter responded. "No ambushes, no snipers, no roadblocks. Otherwise, she's dead. And you know all too well, Captain, or whoever you are, that your immediate boss, Prime Minister Johannes, would never accept Ms. Watson's death as 'collateral damage.' I'm truly sorry about killing those two good officers. But I had no other choice. You and I both know that we were headed for a prison from which I would never return."

Captain Andersson did not utter a word. Carter was right in everything he had surmised. They were headed for a one-way trip to the prison where Carter had killed Hansson. Linda would have been released. Johannes had warned Andersson that Linda must be left unharmed, and, if necessary, protected. But Carter . . .

"I agree," Andersson decided. "Put down your gun! And both of you get into my car."

"Thank you, Captain Andersson," Carter responded, with a sigh of relief. "I thought you were a reasonable man. However, for reasons you can well understand, I will have to keep this gun until I am delivered safely inside the grounds of the embassy." Carter opened the front door of the police car. "Captain, if you would take the driver's seat, and Linda, if you would take the front passenger's seat . . ."

Carter sat in the back, his gun pointed at the back of both Andersson and Linda's head. Now he had two hostages with which to bargain. A simple law of supply and demand.

39

STOCKHOLM, SWEDEN

"Do you have an appointment with the ambassador?" the nineteen-year-old Marine guard asked curtly. It was his duty to make certain that only authorized personnel were allowed through the iron gates of the United States Embassy. Everyone else was turned away.

"This is my State Department I.D.," Carter responded with equal brusqueness. "Just inform Ambassador LaGreca that Dr. Alison Carter and Linda Watson are waiting to see him, as well as a Captain Andersson of the Swedish police." Carter handed the guard a multicolored plastic identification card with his name and picture on it. The blue background with a red band running horizontally across the card designated a classification that allowed Carter to accompany any visitor throughout the State Department building in Washington, D.C.

The guard picked up the telephone and dialed the ambassador's extension. While Carter's appearance at the gate without a specific appointment was out of the line of protocol, he was impressed by the State Department identification.

"Ambassador LaGreca will know who is calling on him," Carter added.

After a few words on the telephone, the guard waved the three of them on through the gates.

When they had parked and walked through the tortuous hallways of the embassy, a heavyset secretary motioned them to enter the ambassador's office.

"Why do I get this feeling that I am a truant officer, Dr. Carter?" LaGreca greeted the group sternly and motioned them toward the sofa and club chairs at one end of his office.

"Maybe because I show up with a personal police escort every time I come into your office," Carter responded, turning toward Andersson. "This is Captain Andersson of the Swedish police, and I might add, taking Captain Hansson's place as the new commander of the elite Swedish hostage rescue team."

"It may not surprise you, Carter," LaGreca responded, with disdain, "that I happen to know Captain Andersson."

"Why does that not surprise me?" Carter asked rhetorically.

"Because there are no surprises anymore." LaGreca pulled up a metal chair covered with black leather for himself. "I would presume that by now Linda and you have pretty much shared confidences that are based on both fact and fiction."

"This is not the time to play games, Carl," Linda said. "What was all that gunplay in the hotel about?" She spoke with more than a hint of betrayal in her voice.

"This is the first I've heard about it," LaGreca responded, glancing questioningly at Captain Andersson, who sat on the sofa like a wooden statue.

"Would you mind, Mr. Ambassador," Carter interrupted, "if Captain Andersson left the room so that Linda and I could talk to our ambassador in private? You can sit right outside, Captain, and make certain that we don't escape."

Andersson got up and left the room.

"Always the diplomat, Dr. Carter," LaGreca said.

"Let's cut through the crap, Ambassador," Carter said, slowly walking around the room, like a cheetah stalking its prey.

"Carl," Linda interjected, "I've explained everything to Carter. He knows the real reason he was sent here, Eriksson's role in the misbegotten policy of ethnic cleansing, and the reason you were chosen as Ambassador. And the groups you and I represent."

"Did you leave anything out?" LaGreca asked, trying to fathom Carter's implacable facial expression. He had to admit that Carter's skulking around the room did make him irritable. But there was nothing he could do for the moment.

"Yes, she did. I'm sure of it," Carter responded. "But before you tell me to ask Linda herself, and we keep on going around this insane merry-go-round, tell me about—"

"First of all," LaGreca interrupted, "please remember that you are talking to the personal representative of the President of the United States. I demand that you maintain the appropriate attitude and tone of voice."

"Okay, Mr. Ambassador," Carter whispered into LaGreca's left ear, "what the fuck is she really doing here and who really sent her? And why are you so deeply involved in the internal affairs of this country?"

"One question at a time," LaGreca responded, nonplussed. "Linda was sent here on behalf of the Automobile Manufacturers Association in order to report to them what was happening in the country. Specifically, the country's financial situation in light of its increasingly greater welfare obligations."

"Ambassador," Carter said, staring him straight in his face, "I've killed a lot of men today. Men whom I had no intention of even hurting. Isn't it strange that Eriksson is dead because someone killed him—just as I was sent here to assassinate him? Linda meets me out of the blue, knows everyone here from the valet at the Grand Hotel to the Prime Minister of Sweden... and then some. Perhaps most importantly, she knows you extremely well, ostensibly because you both worked together years ago. And our new friend, Captain Andersson, drives us to the embassy because I'm holding a gun on her, when he really would like to have my head on a silver platter." As he spoke, the absurdity of it all hit him. "From the moment I arrived in Sweden, my life has been hanging on a thin filament of luck, happenstance, and the kindness or malevolence of strangers. What the fuck is going on?"

"The correct question is, what does all of this have to do with me?" LaGreca asked, pulling away from Carter.

"I have this terribly uncomfortable feeling that everything that happens in Sweden has something to do with you!"

"That's crazy!"

"Is it?" Carter asked. "Captain Hansson told me that you were behind the explosion at the clinic and Londsdale's death. Is America also assisting the Swedes in their 'final solution' of the immigrants?"

"Enough!" LaGreca shouted, standing up to face Carter. "The only thing you haven't accused me of is extortion, prostitution, and drug trafficking. The fact that I'm Italian by origin doesn't mean that I'm the kind of thug you are trying to portray."

"Now, that's a new one on me," Carter said, laughing out loud, "an Ambassador of the only superpower in the world has to rationalize and hide his allegations behind his ethnic identity. Maybe that can work in front of Congress or the Anti-Defamation League. But quite frankly, I could give a shit if you were a marsupial platypus sucking up ants all day. But the truth of the matter is that you are holding most, if not all, of the control levers in your hand. So before this turns into a session of name-calling, or one in which you and she are blowing sunshine up my ass, I strongly suggest that you tell me exactly what I want to know."

"Or what?" LaGreca asked. "Are you going to kill me like you did Captain Hansson? Are you going to become the caricature of an Italian mafiosi?" He paused. "Now, that's a headline! 'Paid Assassin with Daytime Job as Doc for State Department Earns Second Income as Hit Man.'" He looked at Carter as if he were taking the measure of the man for the first time. "Get the hell out of this office! And as a matter of fact, the hell out of this country, before you discover that all your potential escape routes have been cut off!"

"Ambassador LaGreca," Carter said, grabbing the ambassador's ears and flinging him against a wall, "what are you hiding from me?"

"Agggghhh!" LaGreca screamed.

"Are you crazy?" Linda asked indignantly. "You could kill him!"

"He ordered my assassination this morning in your bedroom," Carter explained, "without too much concern, I might add, that you might be killed in the process."

"Stop it!"

"Ambassador! Are we going to play more games?" Carter asked.

"Go to hell!" LaGreca mumbled defiantly.

"Wrong answer!" Carter slammed LaGreca's bloody head against the wall again.

"Try again!"

Carter slammed it once more.

"You're crazy!" Linda ran toward Carter and started to hit him with her bare fists in a futile attempt to stop him. "Let him go!" He pushed her off. His only concern was whether the commotion could be heard outside the office.

Linda rushed over to the ambassador's desk, looking for some object that would make Carter stop. She did not want to call the embassy's security staff, knowing that what was happening in this office must remain private and had to be resolved among the three of them.

"Once more with feeling!" Carter raised LaGreca's head, ready to fling it against anything hard.

"Put him down gently," Linda ordered in a firm, cold voice. She gripped Carter with her left hand, her fingers constricting around his throat like a tightening vise.

"I'm holding a pair of sharp scissors against the base of your skull. One sharp thrust into your brain and you are dead!"

40

STOCKHOLM, SWEDEN

"I mean it, Carter!" Linda repeated. "Let the Ambassador go!"

Carter released his grip and LaGreca crawled over to the sofa.

"OK, Mr. Ambassador, we'll play it Linda's way. But I still want answers."

"I don't have to answer any of your questions!" LaGreca replied, wiping blood from his face with tissues Linda had gotten him from his desk. "I could call in the guards right now, have you deported, and make certain that along the way you had an 'unfortunate accident.'"

"Ambassador," Carter said, "you're in no position to do anything to anyone." He turned around and grabbed the scissors away from Linda.

As soon as LaGreca collected himself, he walked slowly to his desk and opened up a small metal safe located in the left bottom drawer.

"I am about to show you some very sensitive documents that will hopefully answer some of the questions for which so many people have died," LaGreca said, not sure whether or not he was doing the right thing.

"Spare me the sentimentality," Carter responded, moving quickly behind the desk in order to make certain that

LaGreca was not reaching for a gun. He grabbed the folder that the ambassador was about to hand him and flung open all of the desk drawers to make certain that there were no hidden weapons.

"Take it easy!" Linda said. "Carl is trying to help us! Believe me, if he had wanted to kill you, he could have ordered it by now."

"Thanks for the Valentine's Day reminder," Carter responded. "I'm certain that LaGreca and Al Capone have a lot in common. But one thing he and I know that he cannot do, and get away with, is kill me. Right, Mr. Ambassador?" Carter leafed through the stack of frayed, yellowing documents, all marked TOP SECRET/SENSITIVE/EYES ONLY/NO DISSEMINATION.

"What do you mean?" Linda asked, wondering whether Carter was once again bluffing.

"Ask your comrade-in-crime!" Carter retorted harshly.

The documents Carter scanned were a confusing assortment of contracts, bills, and correspondence in English, Swedish, and German. There were also faded photographs of faces that Carter could not recognize. References were made to several American automobile companies and specific executives. Carter recognized the Swedish name Wallenberg. Quite frankly, what he was leafing through did not make much sense to him.

"I resent that accusation!" Linda protested.

"What does this all mean, ladies and gentlemen?" Carter asked, raising the thick file in the air. "If this is what I think it is, it's damaging to the United States government, the American automobile industry, and the Swedish government."

"Your suspicions are pretty much on target," LaGreca responded. Linda looked at LaGreca, who nodded sheepishly to her, and decided that it was now her turn to be forthright.

"Those documents are the reason I was sent here," Linda offered.

"What do you mean?" Carter asked.

"I was to make certain," Linda said, helping LaGreca

wipe some dried blood from his face, "that that particular file was to remain away from any and all prying eyes, except those with a need to know."

"And I bet you're going to tell me that the 'need to know' criteria we use in the government applied to you, the Ambassador, the Swedish prime minister, and a few of his specially selected cronies."

"That's precisely right!" Linda replied.

"Why don't we start with a name that I recognize?" Carter asked, "For example, the Wallenberg family."

"The popular myth," LaGreca responded, "is that Raoul Wallenberg saved somewhere between ten thousand to one hundred thousand Hungarian Jews toward the end of World War Two by issuing them Swedish visas so that they could escape to a neutral country."

"Are you telling me that's a lie?"

"Not quite," LaGreca answered. "But there is evidence in these papers that he had been an OSS agent recruited by Wild Bill Donovan and sent into Hungary as a way to rectify the ignominious nature of his family's behavior during the war."

"What do you mean 'ignominious behavior'?"

"His father and uncles were extremely wealthy financiers who had owned banks, companies, and other major Swedish assets before the war."

"What's wrong with that?" Carter asked.

"Raoul Wallenberg's father and uncles were the principal Swedish financiers of the Nazi war machinery." He paused to assess Carter's startled reaction. "Furthermore, they also laundered and diverted Nazi money toward the end of the war to Latin America for safekeeping. Not content simply to make money for and with the Nazis, they also manufactured a significant portion of their heavy artillery."

"And you two are co-conspirators in keeping this information hidden," Carter concluded, still unsure why this information would be something to kill for. "If that story were revealed to the public, what would it do?"

"At best," Linda answered, "it would embarrass the Wallenberg family and Sweden. At worst, it would completely destroy the myth that Sweden was politically neutral during World War Two and a haven for refugees of persecution. In fact, the country was quite pro-Nazi."

"So that's it?" Carter asked, completely unimpressed.

"No. Not content to simply stand by and waste an opportunity to make money, Jacob Wallenberg, one of Raoul's uncles and the principal shareholder of Enshilda Bank, made a secret deal on behalf of the Swedish government and himself with Boris Rybkin, the KGB *rezident* in Stockholm in 1942."

"So Sweden and the Wallenbergs were also playing footsies with the Soviets," Carter said. "Big deal. Remember, they were our allies during World War Two."

"True," Linda inserted, "but once again, the Swedes and the Wallenbergs violated both their own national laws and international laws of neutrality."

"What did they do that was so heinous beyond what you already described?" Carter asked, still feeling that there had to be more to those classified documents to force representatives of two countries to try and kill him in order to maintain a terrible secret.

"They worked out a secret deal in which the Soviets would trade their reserves of platinum for Swedish high-tensile steel. The deal was brokered by Jacob Wallenberg through Enshilda Bank. He made a hefty profit in the deal. But it brought him to the attention of the KGB, who figured that the Wallenbergs could be of further help to the Soviet Union."

"Ambassador, this is still not what I would call 'highly sensitive' material," Carter said. "It may embarrass some Swedish historians, but that's about it. No one gives a damn about Sweden's having broken it's neutrality during World War Two."

"True, Carter," LaGreca responded. "But let us continue so you can see where this road of seemingly disingenuous behavior leads us."

"I'm all yours!"

"Marcus Wallenberg, another uncle, owned major financial interests in Finland."

"So?"

"He secretly approached Rybkin, the KGB agent with an offer. Given his influence in Finland, he would try to work out a peace deal between Moscow and the Finns. With nothing to lose, the Soviets gave him their blessing. In 1944, Marcus played a key role behind-the-scenes in creating a peace treaty between the Soviets and the Finns under which he, of course, made a handsome sum of money while at the same time protecting the Wallenberg assets."

"You get the picture, Carter?" Linda asked.

"As I see it," Carter responded, "the Wallenbergs allied themselves with the Nazis, the Soviets..."

"The British and the Americans," LaGreca responded.

"The KGB discovered that the Swedes had secret negotiations with the British government during World War Two in order to sell them raw materials, again in violation of Swedish neutrality."

"Shameful," Carter said, "but still not earthshaking."

"On top of that," Linda added, "Marcus tried to broker a secret deal between the British government and the anti-Nazis in Germany, like Karl Goerdler, a German Socialist."

"These guys were playing fast and footloose," Carter responded, disgusted, but still unimpressed by the degree of Swedish misbehavior. At least Raoul Wallenberg tried to save the very same Hungarian Jews that Ben Gurion and the Jewish Agency had just refused to trade for one hundred trucks. Who was more morally reprehensible, Carter wondered, the Zionists or the Swedes? Did it really matter? His major concern was why everyone was trying to kill him.

"Now we come to the part that brought us all together," LaGreca said. "The so-called moment of truth."

"Why do I feel as if I'm on a TV quiz show waiting to hear the right answer?"

"Carter," Linda replied, "there is no right answer. There was one more deal that the Wallenbergs might have been involved with."

"Might?"

"Yes," Linda replied, "We have no direct link. But we have strong circumstantial evidence that the Swedish government, along with the Nazi's were collaborating with both General Motors and Ford Motor Company to make Nazi war machinery, specifically cars, trucks, and tanks. While at the same time, GM and Ford were making the very same 'toys' for our boys."

"If I understand you both correctly," Carter said, "America, or at least some of her major companies, was as guilty as Sweden in helping to develop the Nazi war machine?" Now he was shocked. As a lifelong student of history, he had never once come across such an indictment.

"The proof is in the documents you are holding," La-Greca said, carefully observing Carter's sagging facial expression.

"I don't believe it!" Carter responded reflexively.

"Then find the one on individual lawsuits initiated by captured Eastern European women who worked as slave labor for GM and Ford in Cologne, Germany during World War Two."

Carter took the documents over to one of the club chairs and started reading slowly.

"There's more," Linda added, "much more . . ."

41

STOCKHOLM, SWEDEN

"General Motors played a key role in Hitler's invasions of Poland and the Soviet Union," Linda blurted out, as if she had contained a secret she could no longer suppress.

"General Motors was far more important to the Nazi war machine than was Switzerland," LaGreca reaffirmed. "Switzerland and Sweden were repositories for looted funds. But GM was an integral part of the German war machinery itself. The Nazis could have invaded Poland and Russia without Switzerland. But they could not have done so without GM."

"I can't believe that GM has not or would not contest that so-called 'fact,'" Carter said, playing the devil's advocate. Still, if what he was hearing was true, it made sense that Linda was sent to Sweden to make certain that this revelation of the American automotive industry's cooperation was kept a secret, and would not be dug up during his assignment there. Or could it be that someone had wanted him to uncover the self-incriminating documents.

"Both General Motors and Ford insist that they bear little or no responsibility for the operations of their German subsidiaries," Linda responded, "which controlled 70 percent of the German car market at the outbreak of the war in

1939, and rapidly retooled themselves to become suppliers of war material to the German army."

"However, documents discovered in German and American archives show a much more complicated picture," LaGreca added. "In some cases, American managers of both GM and Ford went along with the conversion of their German plants to military production at a time when U.S. government documents show they were still resisting calls by the Roosevelt administration to step up military production in their plants at home."

"Is this the first time that this information has surfaced?" Carter asked.

"Certain of these allegations against GM and Ford surfaced during the 1974 Congressional hearings into the monopolistic practices in the automobile industry," Linda replied. "American corporations had been largely successful in playing down their connection to Nazi Germany. What they are afraid of now is that, like the Switzerland inquiries which have forced the country to pay a $1.25 billion settlement to Holocaust survivors, GM and Ford could be financially, as well as morally, liable to survivors. Their incredible public relations success in projecting a wholesome, patriotic image of their companies could easily be turned against them."

"By someone like me?" Carter asked. "Who inadvertently uncovers a secret collaboration?"

"When you think of Ford," Linda retorted, "you think of baseball and apple pie. You certainly don't think of Hitler having a portrait of Henry Ford on his office wall in Munich."

"I assume that Ford and General Motors have wartime archives," Carter said.

"In anticipation of your question," LaGreca responded, "the answer is 'no.' Neither company has accepted requests for access to their wartime archives."

"And the federal government can't force them?" Carter asked, bewildered that this type of information could be kept secret for so long in a country where the president's slightest eructations are immediately reported over the Internet.

"That's a good question, Alison," Linda responded. "No one has yet compelled the automobile companies to open up their World War Two records, except for a few law firms in Washington, D.C. that are suing both companies on behalf of the women I mentioned, who claim to have worked in German factories as slave labor."

"So you are telling me that the pattern of having used illegal immigrants as slave labor during World War Two is not solely the province of Germany and Sweden?"

"Correct," LaGreca replied.

"What a devilishly gruesome irony," Carter mused, "that American GIs invaded Europe in jeeps, trucks, and tanks manufactured by two of America's largest motor companies in one of the largest militarization strategies ever undertaken, to destroy a mobile war machine created and maintained by the very same manufacturers who made their own vehicles." Carter paused, exhausted by the endless circles of deceit and betrayal practiced not only by other countries, but most disturbingly, by his own. The home of the free and the land of the brave. He felt sick to his stomach, not wanting to believe what they were telling him. But knowing, somehow, that it was true.

"The U.S. Army confronted enemy trucks manufactured by Ford and Opel—a 100 percent GM-owned subsidiary," Linda added, "as well as the Opel-built warplanes."

"What about Chrysler's role in German rearmament?" Carter asked.

"Much less significant than the other two companies," LaGreca replied.

"When the U.S. Army liberated the Ford plants in Cologne and Berlin," Linda added, as if she now had a compulsive need to explain the full extent of the Big Three's participation in the rearmament of Germany, "they found destitute foreign workers confined behind barbed wire, and company documents praising 'Hitler's genius,' according to reports by soldiers at the scene, found right here in this file of documents." She paused to assess Carter's reactions. Slightly depressed by the news, but not totally shocked or disgusted. She felt that he was listening to her as if he were listening to a patient. Deliberate. Focused. "A U.S. Army report by investigator Henry Schneider, dated September 5, 1945, accused the German branch of Ford as serving as 'an arsenal of Nazism, at least for military vehicles' with the 'consent of the parent company in Dearborn, Michigan.'"

"And the response by Ford?" Carter asked.

"A Ford spokesman by the name of Spellich, I think, described the Schneider report as 'mischaracterization' of the activities of the American parent company, and noted that the Dearborn managers had frequently been kept in the dark by their German subordinates over events in Cologne."

"The relationship of GM and Ford to the Nazi regime goes back to the 1920's and 1930's, when the American car companies competed against each other for access to the lucrative German market. Hitler was an admirer of American mass production techniques and an avid reader of the anti-Semitic diatribes written by Henry Ford." LaGreca pointed to a picture of Hitler's office with Henry Ford hanging on the wall, and Ford's tracts on anti-Semitism on his desk. Reading from a faded 1933 Detroit newspaper clipping quoting Hitler, LaGreca added, "'I regard Henry Ford as my inspiration,' in explaining why he kept a life-size portrait of the American car manufacturer next to his desk."

But I recall somewhere in the distant recesses of my memory," Carter said, "that Ford later renounced his anti-Semitic writing."

"True," Linda interrupted, "but, despite that, he remained an admirer of Nazi Germany and sought to keep America out of the coming war. In July 1938, four months after the German annexation of Austria, Ford accepted the highest medal that Nazi Germany could bestow on a foreigner, the Grand Cross of the German Eagle. The following month, a senior executive for General Motors, James Mooney, received a similar medal for his 'distinguished service to the Reich.' In April 1939 German Ford made a personal present to Hitler of thirty-five thousand Reichmarks in honor of his fiftieth birthday."

"It's been my experience that when a so-called senior statesman receives an award," Carter said, "it often implies a much deeper commitment to a particular cause than simply a symbol of gratitude."

"You're exactly right," LaGreca reaffirmed. "The granting of such awards reflected the vital place that the U.S. automakers had in Germany's increasingly militarized economy." He paused and skimmed over another document until he came to the part he was looking for. "In 1935, GM agreed to build a new plant near Berlin to produce the aptly named 'Blitz' truck, which would later be used by the German army for its blitzkreig attacks on Poland, France, and the Soviet Union. German Ford was the second-largest producer of trucks for the German army after GM/Opel, according to U.S. Army reports."

"It sounds like a never-ending spiral downhill," Carter said, becoming disgusted by the degree of collusion that existed between Nazi Germany and U.S. industries. Moral self-righteousness and political pragmatism were the continuous dialectics of American foreign policy, Carter thought. And, he was certain that there were many more examples, involving other countries and other wars where the U.S. was playing both sides. But, without being too self-righteous himself, he suddenly wondered whether he wasn't doing the same thing by being, at one and the same time, a physician and an assassin?

"Again," LaGreca said, "you're more correct than even you realize. The Schneider report stated that American Ford agreed to a complicated barter deal that gave the Reich increased access to large quantities of strategic raw materials, notably rubber. Albert Speer, the principal architect of Hitler's war machine, was once quoted as saying that Hitler would never have considered invading Poland without synthetic fuel technology provided by General Motors."

"But how long could this collaboration continue?" Carter

asked. "The U.S. and Germany did, in fact, go to war against each other."

"There are documents in this folder," Linda interjected, "that show that as war approached, it became increasingly difficult for U.S. corporations like GM and Ford to operate in Germany without cooperating closely with the Nazi rearmament effort. Under immense pressure from Berlin, both companies made their subsidiaries appear as 'German' as possible."

"These documents," LaGreca added, "show that the parent companies followed a conscious strategy of continuing to do business with the Nazi regime, rather than divesting themselves of their German assets. Less than three weeks after the Nazi occupation of Czechoslovakia in March 1939, GM Chairman Alfred P. Sloan defended his company's strategy as sound business practice, given the fact that their German operations were 'highly profitable.' As a matter of fact, Sloan states quite explicitly in one of the documents that 'the internal politics of Nazi Germany should not be considered the business of the management of General Motors.'" LaGreca paused to catch his breath. Every time he looked at the documents in this file, he still felt shocked, angry, frustrated and helpless. "Sloan went on to explain to a concerned shareholder on April 6, 1939 that 'We must conduct ourselves [in Germany] as a German organization . . . We have no right to shut down the plant.'"

"I think I've heard enough," Carter said, totally disgusted. It was frighteningly clear to him that the most important collaborator with the Nazi war machine was not Switzerland or Sweden, but the greedy, amoral automobile industry of the United States of America. And there was no way that the automobile industry could have acted without the knowledge and consent of the U.S. government. He recalled the words of the famous comic strip character who said, "I have seen the enemy, and the enemy is me."

42

STOCKHOLM, SWEDEN

"Before you reach any conclusions," LaGreca suggested, "I think I have earned the right to tell you just a little bit more about how deep America's involvement was and why it has been hidden from our people for over six decades."

Linda laughed. "A few minutes ago you had to bang heads to get information from us and now you have to bang heads to keep our mouths shut."

"That's why I like to treat humans, and not animals," Carter replied, only half joking. "It's far less lucrative, but more entertaining, and filled with many more surprises."

"After the outbreak of war on September 1, 1939," LaGreca continued, "James Mooney, the GM director in charge of overseas operations, had discussions with Hitler in Berlin. That was two weeks after the German invasion of Poland. Typewritten notes by Mooney himself show that he was involved in the partial conversion of the GM automobile plant at Russelsheim to production of engines and other parts of the Junker 'Wunderbomber,' a crucial weapon in the German air force, under a government-brokered contract between Opel and the Junker airplane company. Mooney's notes show that he returned to Germany the following February for further discussions with Luftwaffe commander Hermann Goering and a personal inspection of the Russelsheim plant."

"Couldn't it be possible neither GM nor Ford had any control over their German subsidiaries after the outbreak of the war?" Carter asked, hoping that there was a big mistake being made somewhere. His country couldn't have betrayed its own principles.

"Again," LaGreca continued, "we have evidence in this file from the Reich Commissar for the Treatment of Enemy Property that the American parent company continued to have considerable say in the operations of Opel after 1939. The document further details how wily the U.S. companies were. Apparently, GM issued a general power of attorney to an American manager, Peter Hoglund, in March 1940. Hoglund did not leave Germany until a year later. At that time, the power of attorney was transferred to a prominent Berlin lawyer, Heinrich Richter. The same document goes on to describe how French and Belgian prisoners were abused at the Russelsheim plant, at the same time Hoglund was still looking after GM interests in Germany."

"The Nazis had a clear interest in keeping Opel and German Ford under American ownership, despite growing hostility between Washington and Berlin," Linda interjected, wanting to make certain that Carter did not miss any of the essential details that would corroborate the myth of America having been anti-Nazi, until it's own declaration of war against Hitler. As Sweden and Switzerland had created their respective myths of "neutrality" during WWII, so had the United States. "By the time Pearl Harbor was bombed by the Japanese on December 7, 1941, the American stake in German Ford had declined to 52 percent, but Nazi officials argued against a complete takeover. Again, a memorandum in this file dated November 25, 1941, acknowledged that such a step would deprive the German Ford of the 'excellent sales organization' of the parent company and make it more difficult to bring 'the remaining European Ford companies under German influence.'"

"What would be the motivation for that?" Carter asked.

"To protect their respective investments, of course," LaGreca responded. "An FBI report dated July 23, 1941, quoted

Mooney as saying that he would refuse to take any action that might 'make Hitler mad.' In the fall of 1940, Mooney told FBI agents that he would not return his Nazi medal because such an action might jeopardize GM's $100 million investment in Germany. He basically thought the war would be over very quickly, so why give his wonderful company away?"

"What about the U.S. declaration of war against Germany?" Carter asked.

"First of all," Linda answered, "Henry Ford vetoed a U.S. government-approved plan to produce, under license, Rolls-Royce engines for British fighter planes. Secondly, it was illegal for any U.S. motor companies to have any contact with their subsidiaries on German-controlled territory. So, at GM and Ford plants in Germany, reliance on forced labor increased. Immigrants fleeing the war were immediately secunded to work, against their will, at the plants." She paused. "Sounds familiar? The more things change, the less they change. Many documents contained in this folder are personal testimonies from slave laborers on the conditions that they had to work under. Let me quote from one testimony: 'conditions were terrible. They put us in barracks, on three-tier bunks. It was very cold. They did not pay us at all and scarcely fed us. The only reason we survived was that we were young and fit.'"

"What were the U.S. auto companies' response to that?" Carter asked, certain that it would be evasive or disingenuously contrite.

"American Ford acknowledged that there was slave-labor," LaGreca responded, "which was forced 'to endure a sad and terrible experience' at its Cologne plant but maintains that correcting such 'tragedies' should be a government-to-government concern."

"Did American Ford receive payments from its subsidiaries in Germany?"

"The documents reveal that they received significant amounts of money from 1940 to 1943," Linda responded. "A Robert Schmidt, the Nazi custodian of the Cologne plant, traveled to Portugal for talks with Ford managers there. In addition, there is evidence to indicate that Ford had illegal contacts with its subsidiary in occupied France, which produced German army trucks. And to add insult to injury, Ford was eager to demand compensation from the U.S. government for 'losses' due to bomb damage to its German plants. After the war, GM received $32 million from the U.S. government for damages sustained by its German plants."

"Incredible," Carter said. "Mendacity, hypocrisy, greed, amorality, duplicity, betrayal, criminal behavior. And for all that, both automakers demanded reparations."

The information had been thrown at him too quickly for Carter to comprehend either the magnitude or ignominity of the offenses. There was no question in Carter's mind that the documents were extremely damaging to the automotive industry, even sixty years later. The American people would be incensed to learn that two major auto manufacturers had collaborated with the Nazis in the development of their war machine. Sometimes at the expense of American lives. Carter wasn't naive enough to think that GM and Ford wouldn't contest the allegations, but, in fact, they were extensively documented in the Army archives as well as in the FBI's files. Despite all the pecadillos of which J. Edgar Hoover had been accused, he was still a very effective force in the break-up of the American Bund and the futile attempt of the Nazis to set up an intelligence network in the United States during WWII. The fact that Hoover had to personally insist that the principal officers of both car companies end their relationship with the Nazi war machine would prove exceedingly embarrassing to the entire automotive industry.

At a minimum, the companies involved would be forced to admit to the American public, the men and women who fought in WWII, and the rest of the world, that they collaborated with Germany until practically being blackmailed into stopping. But if it were up to Carter, he would want to see them forced to set a significant amount of money aside, probably in the billions, to compensate those Americans and their descendants who fought against the Nazis at the start of the war, and another fund to repay the Department of Defense for all the monies the companies received in reparation for the destruction of their German subsidiaries during the allied bombing raids. Under either scenario, reparations plus apologies should be made to the civilian refugees who had been used as slave labor in American factories in Cologne and other cities. The media, Carter hoped, would have a heyday. And it would be very interesting to see what an Internal Revenue Service audit of the financial records of GM, Ford, and Chrysler before, during, and immediately after WWII would turn up.

Vox Populis. Vox Dei. The voice of God will be heard through the outcry of the ordinary American citizen, thought Carter. Once they found out about this grotesque distortion of American capitalism, the American public would mete out justice.

The notion that even one American soldier had died because an American GM or American Ford helped make the Nazi weapon that killed him, whether on the beaches of Normandy or in the Battle of the Bulge, made Carter feel sick to his stomach.

43

STOCKHOLM, SWEDEN

"Sorry to bother you and your guests, Ambassador"—LaGreca's secretary walked in unannounced—"but I think we have a problem that can't wait." She was shocked to see the ambassador's white shirt and dark, pin-striped suit stained with blood, and the disheveled look of the room, but she knew enough not to ask any questions to which she did not already know the answers.

"What is it?" LaGreca asked, disturbed by her sudden appearance.

"Captain Andersson wants to see you immediately," she responded.

"Tell him I can see him in a few minutes," he stated, clearly annoyed by her intrusion.

"I'm afraid that won't be possible." She regretted her own breach of protocol, but she had no other choice. This situation was unique. "Sir, would you mind stepping closer to the window for a moment?"

She drew up the venetian blinds so that a full panorama of the embassy grounds, walls, gates, and the street fronting the building was visible at a glance.

LaGreca surveyed the scene before him for a few seconds before asking Carter and Linda to join him at the window.

"Impressive, isn't it?" Captain Andersson asked in a peremptory tone as he barged through the ambassador's doors. "Thank you, Mrs. Rovner," Andersson said to LaGreca's secretary. "We would like to be left alone. Please take a seat at your desk, but do not try to use the telephone. My officers will assist you with anything you need." When Rovner had closed the door behind her, Andersson continued. "Let me assist you all in identifying what you are looking at."

"What in God's name is the meaning of this?" LaGreca demanded.

"On the right and left of your main gate," Andersson continued, ignoring both LaGreca's question and tone of voice, "are two assault groups armed with various HK MP5 models and Sig-Sauer P226 guns. Just behind these two groups, and a little bit to the right, are four sniper support groups armed with PSG 90 7.62mm rifles. I can assure you all that right now the crosshairs of their respective high-powered scopes are aimed at each one of you."

"Again," LaGreca demanded, looking straight into Andersson's placid face, "what is the meaning of all of this?" He picked up the phone, "I'm calling the prime minister. This is unconscionable."

"I would advise you to put down the telephone," Andersson responded calmly, withdrawing his gun from his shoulder holster and pointing it at the group. He spoke with the certainty of someone in full control of the situation.

"What do you mean by this?" LaGreca screamed, releasing the hot-blooded Mediterranean temperament he usually kept under control when playing his ambassadorial role.

"It's quite clear, Mr. Ambassador," Carter said, noting the two recoilless anti-tank rifle/machine gun marksmen and three dog handlers armed with AK5s. "The Swedes intend to take us all out of here, by force, if necessary. This is the way your former associates intend to pay you back for your help. I suspect that you've been so comfortable here that you haven't had the embassy swept for bugs in a long time. Too long, I guess. The information you just divulged has sealed our fate. We've all become traitors to the cause of sustaining myths—Swedish and American."

"I would say that Dr. Carter has an astute comprehension of this situation," Andersson acknowledged. "You might have noticed by now that unlike America, we have managed to keep the press away from our problematic ... issue ... and any story that might potentially arise from an ... untoward event."

"This is totally against any principles of international diplomacy," LaGreca added. "I demand to talk to the prime minister. By being inside this compound you are technically on American soil. And as such, you are violating the national sovereignty of America. I can have your representatives recalled at anytime for this imprudence on your part."

"My government is well aware of that, Mr. Ambassador," Andersson retorted. "We have already taken the necessary precaution to withdraw our ambassador and embassy staff from the United States. They are currently out of your country, attending a conference."

"So," Carter said, "after monitoring the last two hours of our conversation you decided to call off the deal between the U.S. government and Ambassador LaGreca."

"Again, very astute, Dr. Carter," Andersson responded, "except for one or two minor points of difference. Ambassador LaGreca has been officially recalled from Sweden."

"I've never received any instructions to that effect," LaGreca responded angrily.

"You will! Andersson replied, handing documents to LaGreca, Carter and Linda.

"Christ!" LaGreca blurted out. "I've been declared Persona Non Grata here. After all the work and effort that I put into building a strong and trusting relationship."

"I've been requested to leave the country, too," Linda said.

"If misery loves company," Carter added, "you should both know that I've been PNGd as well. Effective immediately."

"That is why you see the impressive array of 'escorts'

outside," Andersson said. "They are here to protect you, and make certain that I am successful in placing all three of you on an American plane heading back to Washington, D.C. within the next two hours."

"Very considerate of you, but what if we decide to stay?" LaGreca asked defiantly.

"That would not be a wise decision," Andersson responded.

"You're not, by any chance, threatening the president's personal representative to your country, are you?" LaGreca asked, his face almost pressed up against Andersson's.

"You've received official orders from Prime Minister Johannes Strindberg, who has the right to expel any foreigner he deems to be a threat to the national security of Sweden," Andersson said. "I'm simply here to do my duty and enforce the law."

"And what about the march today in the Old City?" Carter asked, realizing that they were also being evacuated out of the city so that they couldn't witness the blood bath that was about to begin against the thousands of refugees who had been streaming into the city over the past few days to protest their inhumane treatment at the hands of the Swedish government. Carter had to smile at the cleverness of the plan. The Americans, who had purposely ignored the Swedish "problem" were now being deported just like the other foreigners Sweden wanted to expel.

Carter was still disturbed by one question: Why deport them? They could be found missing or dead in an unfortunate accident to which there were no witnesses. And as a concerned, reasonable response of one ally to another, the Swedish Prime Minister would appoint an official board of jurists, politicians, and industrialists, probably headed by Nils Olsson, to investigate their mysterious deaths. So why bother deporting them?

44

STOCKHOLM, SWEDEN

"I'd like to know exactly why I'm being asked to leave the country," Carter said, trying to buy some time so that he could formulate a plan for their escape without endangering the lives of the remaining embassy personnel in the building.

"I think you all have a clear understanding of why we're doing this," Andersson answered.

"No, I would also like a clarification of why you are deporting us," LaGreca added. "You know, we could just refuse to leave with you and remain in the embassy."

"Mr. Ambassador," Andersson replied, restraining himself from a threat that would lead to a premature confrontation, "the government of Sweden respects the sovereignty of the United States. You, however, as an individual, not as an ambassador, have meddled in the internal affairs of Sweden, and our government feels that it can no longer be tolerated. So it is asking your State Department to recall you, which as you know, we have the right to do."

"And to expedite the recall," LaGreca responded, "you've simply PNGd me. On what pretext?"

"There is no need to become legalistic at this point," Andersson responded, realizing that he was wasting valuable time.

"Am I PNGd because you think I'm a spy in the guise of an ambassador?" LaGreca asked, knowing that the real CIA operatives attached to the embassy would find his question amusing. "Or because I am currently in possession of extremely sensitive information about your country and its current political leadership?" He wanted to make certain that Andersson understood his underlying threat of exposing Johannes, Olsson, and the rest of the "team" to the media. He glanced at Carter for support, but he seemed unaware of LaGreca's remarks, glancing surreptitiously around the room, and occasionally at his watch.

"I'm afraid, Ambassador," Andersson reiterated forcefully, "that it's time to go."

"Would you mind if the ambassador evacuated the entire building before we left?" Carter suddenly interjected. He had to convince Andersson to clear the building as part of a plan he was devising.

"Why?" Andersson asked quizzically.

"Because," Carter answered, "he has an obligation to embassy personnel to evacuate them in case of any potential danger."

"What danger exists for them?" Andersson asked.

"You said it yourself," Carter responded to a confused and mistrustful Andersson. "If anything unusual were to happen in this room, your armada standing guard around the building would open fire. And an untold number of innocent embassy personnel would be hurt in the chaos that would follow. And that would not look good for the Swedish police or the Swedish government. You would be placing at risk well over twenty Swedish nationals who work here."

What was left unstated was the fact that the Swedish nationals, like most indigenous personnel hired to work in American embassies around the world, reported to the local police or intelligence service of their country. It was an old custom that had outlasted its utility, but still existed.

"All right, Dr. Carter," Andersson agreed reluctantly. "But, if this is a trick, you are the one who will be responsible for the death of innocent people."

"I'll take on that responsibility," Carter responded. "Perhaps you should initiate E&E procedures, Ambassador."

A confused ambassador picked up the telephone and dialed his Deputy Chief of Mission. "Initiate E&E procedures for everyone in the building. Get them all out within ten minutes. Please make sure that everyone knows we are merely testing procedures."

"Five minutes," Carter turned toward Andersson. "And make certain that the infirmary is open so that I can get some medical essentials for your diabetes, hypertension, and gout, Ambassador."

"And what if the ambassador doesn't receive his medication?" Andersson asked.

"Why don't you tell him, Mr. Ambassador" Carter suggested, since I don't want to violate the sanctity of our patient-client relationship."

Linda continued to remain silent. She was beginning to realize that Carter had devised a plan for them to escape. She only hoped that she would understand any hints, clues, or nonverbal instructions that he might give her.

"Linda, would you mind getting two two-liter glass bottles of orange juice, or any non-dietetic soda, from the ambassador's bar in the back of the room. If there's none there, then ask his secretary where she stores them."

"I hope you're not playing games with me, Carter," Andersson warned. "With a simple wave of my hand from this window, our snipers . . . and with no questions asked."

"I can assure you as a physician, Captain Andersson, that if the ambassador does not receive his timely dose of insulin and at least one bottle of carbonated sugar water, you will not need your snipers. His 'brittle' diabetes will cause him to faint, develop a cardiac arrthymia, and die." Carter looked at the ambassador, hoping that he understood what Carter was trying to do.

"Captain Andersson," LaGreca responded, "according to the Geneva Convention of War, POWs or their moral equivalent of hostages, which we are, are entitled to proper medical care. As you know through my State Department service,

Dr. Carter is my physician. And quite frankly, if you will not acquiesce to Carter's request, you may as well shoot me now. At least this way you spare me the nuisance of taking medication for the rest of a very short life."

"Not to put too fine a point on the issue," Carter added, looking at his watch. "The prime minister would not be pleased if the ambassador was shot in his own embassy by a Swedish policeman."

"It looks as if everyone is leaving the building," Linda observed from her place at the window.

"Good," Carter responded, "but would you mind getting what I asked?"

"Only if you say 'pretty please,'" she replied, realizing that Andersson was becoming increasingly disturbed by a situation that wasn't going according to plans.

"Pretty please," Carter replied, playing along. "Meet us at the infirmary!"

"The infirmary?" Andersson echoed.

I can't help it if that's where medical supplies are kept," Carter responded.

"And, if I can't get the non-dietetic drinks," she asked, "then what?"

"Just find the ambassador something to drink in the two-liter size bottle," Carter reemphasized.

"What's wrong with drinking from the water fountain outside the Ambassador's office?" Andersson asked.

"The same reason why Swedes spend a fortune producing and drinking Romulös, your famous bottled sparkling water," Carter answered. "The water fountain is fine enough for his immediate thirst needs. But he needs to get both sugar and liquid inside of him before his already two hour-late insulin shot."

I don't trust you, Carter," Andersson declared, but impotent without the medical knowledge to contradict him.

You shouldn't, Carter thought to himself. He walked out of the ambassador's office, toward the infirmary, the file tucked under his arm.

45

STOCKHOLM, SWEDEN

As Carter, LaGreca and Andersson entered the infirmary, Linda met them carrying two bottles of ginger ale, wondering what Carter was going to do with them. All three knew that the ambassador was as healthy as a horse and did not have any of the illnesses Carter had enumerated to Andersson. But like LaGreca, she had no choice but to follow Carter's lead. And it was a lead she admired. As usual he appeared calm, self-assured, almost jocular, and Linda was sure that his plan was going to be nothing less than creative.

Andersson was highly skeptical of Carter's portrayal of LaGreca's medical problems. But what did he have to lose by going along with it—just in case Carter was telling the truth? The entire embassy was surrounded by his men. So why not cover his bets and play out Carter's charade—if it was one. This could be nothing more than the respected bureaucratic game of cover-your-ass for Andersson, but at least all bases would be covered.

The infirmary at the embassy was like most doctors' offices, an ascetic-looking room containing an examining table, highly polished metal cabinets containing syringe's, bandages, endless packages, vials, and small bottles of medications stored alphabetically. There were also portable tanks of oxygen, which Carter had counted on finding there.

"If you would just sit down here on the table, Ambassador," Carter said, "I will be able to administer the proper medication."

Andersson surveyed the room. Nothing unusual, as far as he could see. He had been informed through his cellular phone that the evacuation was proceeding without any problems. The police roster of individuals who worked in the building would be used to assure them that everyone had gotten out. That would take ten or fifteen minutes.

"Linda," Carter asked in his most pleasing manner, "would you mind helping me out?"

"Not at all," she responded. "What would you like me to do?"

"Get me some dry ice from that freezer."

"Dry ice?" she asked quizzically. "What do you need the dry ice for?"

He glared at her harshly. She got the message and headed for the freezer.

"Why are you holding two bottles of ginger ale?" Andersson asked, walking over to them.

"I need fluid that can be absorbed quickly by the human body," Carter stated with his most professional voice. "LaGreca needs liquid with a high sugar content. And the carbon dioxide that produces all the bubbles in the bottle helps to kill any germs in the regular water, like cholera." Carter was trying to stave off Andersson with a lot of medical mumbo-jumbo.

"Cholera?" Andersson repeated the word as if it was fraught with the spirit of death itself. "There is no cholera in Sweden!"

"That's correct, Captain," Carter responded, realizing that he couldn't afford to alarm Andersson.

"Carter, I feel extremely faint!" LaGreca whined from across the room.

"Just lie down while I prepare everything," Carter ordered.

"Why do you need dry ice?" Andersson asked, still not convinced about the carbonated water explanation. But so far, everything looked as it should. The patient was on the examining table. Carter was lining up the items necessary for treating the ambassador. And Linda was trying to be of some help to both of them. She seemed the most confused and Andersson felt more sorry for her than he did for the ambassador. That was probably due to the fact that she was an attractive woman and he was considered a ladies' man by many an attractive woman.

"The dry ice will be broken into little pieces," Carter explained, "to cool the bottle of insulin quickly, to a temperature that will make the insulin enter the ambassador's body fast." Once again, Carter was banking on the fact that Andersson knew nothing about diabetes or its treatment. If anything, the reverse phenomena was true. Carter needed little pieces of dry ice to fit into the two bottles. But time was against him. If he took too long preparing what he needed, Andersson's officers would start allowing embassy personnel to reenter the building.

Linda returned with the announcement that the only dry ice in the freezer was in plastic-covered packs.

Carter inserted a three-inch needle into a small bottle of crystalline insulin. "It's not quite what I want, but it will do. Bring as many packs as you can without freezing your hands." The 50cc syringe filled with a mixture of short and long-acting insulin that could throw an elephant into immediate hypoglycemic shock—and death.

Linda wrapped a towel around her arms and began to pile some ice packs on top of it. "Oh my God!" she said, "it's freezing."

"Here, let me help you," Andersson interjected, wanting to speed up the process. "A pretty woman like you shouldn't have to ruin her beautiful skin for any reason. Even to help a sick man."

Carter worked quickly at a counter near LaGreca to break open the ice packs he had. Linda and Andersson worked together across the room. With a metal hammer used to test neurological reflexes in the knee, Carter smashed the ice into small pieces. The few pieces that landed on his bare skin left singed flesh behind, but Carter couldn't exhibit any pain. That was the price he had to pay to stuff the ice chips into the bottles. The ice contained so much energy that when compressed into a very tight space, like a two-liter glass bottle, the ice would become what most amateur arsonists affectionately call a "dry ice bomb," and explode. The bomb could be quite lethal, creating the explosive sound of an M-100 artillery piece, and enough shards of glass to kill anyone within the room. At the same time, the bomb would precipitate secondary, and tertiary mechanical and electrical explosions within the embassy. In other words, these innocuous materials would create a bomb that would allow them to escape.

"I am extremely thirsty; may I have my ginger ale?" LaGreca asked, catching quickly on to what Carter was doing. From his earliest days in South Boston, he and his friends would make homemade bombs and zip-guns from basic elements, like car antennas, metal pipes and nails.

"Of course," Carter responded, pleased that LaGreca realized that the bottles needed to be emptied before the ice could be pushed in. "Captain, would you mind breaking open packs of dry ice that Linda will bring to you and smashing them up? Make certain not to get any on your fingers or skin. I don't need another patient." Carter was pleased with his last statement. It sounded so genuine.

"Of course, if it will speed things up," Andersson replied. This way he could also spend some private time with Linda.

"Mr. Ambassador," Carter said quietly, "drink as much of the ginger ale as you can and spill out the rest. If you bring them over to me, I'll fill them up with dry ice."

"I understand," LaGreca responded.

"Then start a fight with Andersson over anything," Carter added, "so that he has to call in some troops to help him out."

"I guess you want to take out as many of his men as you can?" LaGreca asked.

"No, I just want fewer men outside, on the grounds, when we get there," Carter corrected him. "When the time is right,

I'm going to give Andersson the insulin injection. Unless I forgot my medicine, he will pass out immediately. When that happens, we run like hell through the exit stairs on this floor down to the garage, and out the back."

"And from there?"

"Let's hope we get outside intact. If we can avoid getting shot, we'll play it as we go," Carter replied.

"How about a twenty-second countdown," LaGreca added, "so that we can synchronize our movements."

"Great idea! Start now."

Twenty . . . nineteen . . . , LaGreca started counting to himself.

LaGreca walked over to Andersson and started yelling at him about being purposefully slow with the dry ice chips so that he, LaGreca, would suffer longer. Meanwhile, Carter started filling up the two glass bottles with the chips that Linda and Andersson had been producing.

"Why are you pushing me?" Andersson yelled back. You're trying to provoke me."

"Don't listen to him, Andersson," Carter yelled from across the room. "He's just highly irritable without the insulin."

"And you, you little tramp," LaGreca said to Linda. "You're conspiring with our enemy."

"Don't talk to a lady like that," Andersson responded, self-righteously.

"I'll talk to my subordinates in any fashion I want, Captain," LaGreca answered back, looking menacingly at him.

Andersson's face turned red. He picked up his cellular phone to call his commander to send men into the building.

"Sixteen . . . fifteen . . ." LaGreca counted out loud by accident.

"What the hell—What's going on here?" Andersson asked.

Thirteen . . . twelve . . . , LaGreca counted in his head. Carter finished stuffing the bottles with the dry ice as Andersson placed his call.

"Is there anything else I can do?" Linda asked Carter, realizing that something was happening, but not knowing what to expect.

Eleven... ten..., LaGreca turned toward Andersson. "I insist you release us immediately."

"We're in the infirmary," Andersson yelled into his telephone.

Nine... eight... seven..., LaGreca lunged for Andersson and the telephone flew out of his hands.

"Linda, take these two bottles and when I yell 'seal it,' do it!" Carter ordered. "But not one second before. Do you understand?"

"Only when you yell 'seal it!'" she repeated his instructions.

"And then follow me and the ambassador and run as fast as your pretty feet can go!"

"Got it!"

"*Six... five...*" LaGreca shouted out loud to Carter, struggling with Andersson for control of his gun.

Carter ran over to them and jabbed the long needle filled with insulin into Andersson. He pushed the plunger all the way in. As Andersson felt the pain of the needle being stuck directly into his shoulder muscle he released his choke hold on LaGreca.

"I've lost count!" LaGreca coughed out.

"That's okay!" Carter said, as he heard the sound of boots running down the tile corridor toward the infirmary. The Swedish security forces had arrived, just as he had anticipated. "Linda," Carter yelled, "seal it!"

Linda took the two two-liter glass bottles, screwed on their tops and placed them on the floor. Captain Andersson lay muttering unintelligibly.

"Let's get the hell out of here now!" Carter yelled, grabbing the incriminating file LaGreca had carried with him.

LaGreca started to run when he felt a hand grip his right ankle, forcing him to the floor.

"Come on, Carl!" Linda shouted.

"We've got to keep running!" Carter screamed at Linda. "We've got to get out of here now!"

"No!" Linda shouted, "we can't . . ."

Before she could complete the sentence, Carter grabbed her and flung her ahead of him, pushing her forward as he ran toward the back door of the embassy.

The soldiers had stopped at the infirmary to assess the situation and receive their orders from Andersson. By the time they realized what was happening, the bottles exploded.

Carter and Linda were running through the underground garage when they heard the first blast. They were outside, in the embassy's expansive backyard, when the second bottle exploded. They lay on the ground, between the bushes and the embassy's seven-foot concrete wall, her body covered with his.

The sound was louder than anything Carter had imagined. A ball of fire and smoke rose from the windows of the infirmary. Glass and debris flew through the air. Embassy employees standing around the building were startled, but safe. Surrounding office buildings shook as if there was an earthquake in progress. The fire moved from room to room and floor to floor.

With the pungent smell of cordite in the air and the suffocating black particles of debris floating to earth, Carter decided they should remain where they were for a while. He could hear the wail of sirens from fire trucks speeding toward the embassy from different points around the city. Soon the whole area would be swarming with firemen, police and soldiers, searching for survivors and for the perpetrators of the explosion. He decided that it would be safest to leave the area during all that commotion.

Carter decided not to think about what had just occurred until he put some distance and time behind him. Premeditated murder in Sweden carried a mandatory death sentence. If he was accused of murder, the Swedish government, out of courtesy to America, would ask if the United States wanted Carter to be extradited back to the States. The answer, unfortunately, might be "no." As far as any official in the United States government was concerned, Carter was not in Sweden on official business. "Plausible deniability" would be the operative term. And Linda? He'd think about her later.

Carter checked his watch. In thirty minutes the march would begin in Gamla Stan. At some point, the crowd that came to jeer would become unruly. Beer bottles would be thrown as readily as curse words. Upon orders, the police would help precipitate a riot, provoking the marchers into some kind of emotional, uncontrolled action. The Pöni would have even more of an excuse to use excessive force to disburse both marchers and hostile onlookers, alike. Some would be slaughtered in the name of containing a potential nationwide state of emergency.

By now, the refugees were being arranged into orderly groups of marchers. If some violence hadn't already begun, however, Carter would have been surprised. The stakes were high. Confronting the prime minister with condoning slave camps in the country by looking the other way. Requesting a change of government and war trials so that the world could bear witness to the inhumane conditions under which refugees lived. And these were only starters. If Sweden's political system was actually destabilized, the flow of legal and illegal immigrants might actually decrease, but where would they go? To another uncaring country to be taken advantage of? Would history repeat itself? Carter wasn't sure what one man could do, but he knew that he had to head toward Gamla Stan. And Linda might even be of help.

"Linda!" he said, realizing that he enjoyed holding her close, "look what would have happened to us if I let you help the ambassador. I know it's a terrible tragedy. But somebody had to make it out alive to tell the tale," he said pointing to the file of documents he held.

"But he's dead!" she said somberly. "It would only have taken just a few seconds more . . ." she paused, knowing that guilt would be her companion for life.

"Are you all right?" Carter asked, caringly.

"Ask me again in ten years." Linda looked at her rumpled clothing and started brushing off the debris. She started to laugh uncontrollably, but wanted to cry as well. She felt

ACTIVE MEASURES

sad, frightened, vulnerable, and grateful. Thanks to this man, she was alive. She pulled Carter closer and wouldn't let go.

He held her tightly as she began to sob, but he knew they had to leave the embassy grounds. It would only be minutes until they were discovered. He heard the bark of German shepherds starting to search for live bodies.

Carter swore to himself that Ambassador Carl LaGreca's name would be placed on a plaque in the impressive entrance of the State Department's wall of individuals who had died courageously in the service of their country.

46

STOCKHOLM, SWEDEN

Carter and Linda arrived in Gamla Stan after the marchers had already gathered. The movement of what Carter estimated to be two thousand marchers—mainly teenagers and young adults—was larger, noisier, and already more unruly than he had expected. One homemade sign read STOP SLAVE LABOR. Others stated SWEDEN—MORE THAN BLONDES WITH BLUE EYES; YOUR ALIENS ARE NOT FROM OUTER SPACE; JUSTICE AND FAIRNESS FOR ALL.

"Hold my hand tightly," Carter instructed Linda. "It's easy to get lost in a crowd like this." He shifted the file so that it was hidden under his shirt.

"I'd like that," she muttered under her breath, surprising herself with the emotions the words conveyed. Watching Carter take control of the crisis at the embassy, she realized that this was the type of man with whom she could settle down. Usually she felt, like many of her unmarried friends, that there were no men available who were capable of providing a sense of safety and security, while not being threatened by a strong, career-oriented woman. Maybe what she and Carter had experienced together was an important reminder of her desire for male companionship. It had been several years since she had had a serious relationship with a man. Those years had been spent as a high-achievement, can-do, no-nonsense, self-directed, independent professional who, like the Soviet Union's Politburo, would design a five-year Gozplan—when she would get married, when she would have children, and when she would return to her high-powered, executive job. But beneath the professional veneer, and like many of her friends, Linda was seeking a significant other who, in time, would turn into a husband. Yes, she was beginning to grow fond of Carter. And that bothered her.

"Stay close," Carter urged, not having heard Linda's remark through the din of the crowd. He was elbowing his way along the narrow, cobblestone streets toward what he thought was the front of the march. His plan was to identify the leaders and inform them of the plans of the Swedish riot police.

That was his plan. But Carter did not deceive himself; the likelihood of successfully executing it was minimal. For one thing, he looked so disheveled and dirty, he wondered if anyone would believe that he worked for the State Department, the official identification he would use. Second, the crowd was unruly. Marchers were shouting curses at each other. The teenagers, in particular, were violent, kicking in the windows of small shops along the marching route, Lilla Nygatan Street, and stealing tourist souvenirs from the shops—cheap sweatshirts, expensive Kosta Boda glassware, even replicas of the Swedish flag. One young man raised the flag only to burn it. The crowd cheered him on with "Down With Sweden!" Hecklers stood at the periphery of the lines of marchers, jeering the workers with ethnic slurs and occasionally splattering them with paint and tomatoes.

Visions of the anti-Vietnam war protests came to mind. At that time, the marchers were snaking their way through the streets of Washington, D.C., heading toward the White House, when they encountered D.C. police with canisters of teargas. Thrown into the crowd, it had made everyone nauseous, including Carter, who had volunteered to provide emergency medical assistance.

It did not take long before Carter saw history repeat itself. As more and more shops were looted, the Swedish police started to assemble in formation, like Roman legionnaires. They were dressed in riot control gear—plastic helmets with transparent plastic shields, billy clubs, and rifles that could shoot off canisters of gas. Groups of thirty to forty police gathered in a V-shaped phalanx, their plastic shields held high enough in front of them to deflect the flying bottles, pieces of cobblestone, and other debris that were being tossed at them. Carter pulled Linda into the doorway of a music store which already had been partially looted. From the relative safety of the store they watched a phalanx of police drive a wedge into the crowd, beating the marchers with hard rubber blackjacks until they could no longer stand up.

Linda recoiled with horror. Nothing was more repulsive than to witness a fully-armored policeman beat a teenager senseless. She tried to run to the youth, but Carter pulled her back. Only five days before he had chosen to interfere in a street fight, and look what had been the result of it all. He didn't need to learn a lesson twice.

Under "ordinary" circumstances, the police would be playing the old strategic game of terror and intimidation, hoping that when the demonstrators saw what happened to their leaders, they would disperse. What the marchers did not realize, however, was that no matter what they did, the Pöni were out to end the march as well as the refugee problem, even if it meant brutalizing and killing their leaders and physically abusing, arresting, and deporting their followers. This was the prime minister's plan. And nothing was going to change it. Not even the capitulation of the leaders. This "day of blood" had been planned from the beginning in the name of Swedish stability and national interests. The right-wing agitators who stood on the periphery of the line of marchers would become victims as well. Johannes was determined to take care of both his right and left wings at one time. What could be more efficient?

Carter pushed open the door to the music store, a high-end retailer of antique musical instruments as well as old sheet music and long-playing records.

"What are you looking for?" Linda asked, perplexed why Carter was exploring the music store while the main action was occurring outside.

"Something..." Carter responded. "I can't tell you what it is right now."

"I didn't know," Linda replied, "that we were in a Top Secret store with a 'need to know' clearance."

"No," Carter said, "it's nothing like that. It's simply that I'll know what I want when I find it."

Linda laughed for the first time in several days. "Sure makes a lot of sense to me. *Alice in Wonderland,* here we come!"

Carter sifted through the debris of what once were guitars. He then went over to the section of the store that contained old records and sheet music.

"Are we getting warmer? Or colder?"

"We're definitely getting warmer," he responded, riffling through the covers of old records as if he were the "Energizer Bunny" on a mission.

"Goddamn it!" Carter cursed. "When tearing this place apart the least they could have done was keep these in alphabetical order."

"I'm sure that the next time they decide to hold a demonstration," Linda said, facetiously, "they will consult you on protocol."

"Wait one minute!" Carter picked up a torn album cover with its long-playing record still inside. "Please God, make this the one."

He rubbed the torn album jacket with the palm of his hand as if it were a lucky charm. "Come on, Lady Luck. Don't fail me now!"

"This sounds like a poor man's production of *Guys and Dolls*," she laughed.

"Yes!" he shouted with childful glee. "Yes!"

"Yes, what?" she asked, perplexed.

"Yes," he shouted, "ABBA!"

"ABBA?" she asked. "The old rock 'n roll group?"

"You got it!" he shouted. He gently removed the intact record from its beat-up cover and replaced it with the file clutched beneath his shirt. The question now became, where would it be inconspicuous? And the answer was to refile it in the record rack with all of the other record albums. Even if Linda wasn't aware of it, they had probably been followed since leaving the embassy. It was just a matter of time until they were apprehended.

"Let's find a stereo and play some music," Carter suggested. "We might as well have some fun while we're waiting to be arrested.

"Are you crazy?"

"Probably! "

"Why don't we just get out of here," Linda asked, "before the police arrive? Now, even the ambassador can't help us."

"ABBA!" Carter repeated, delirious with happiness for the moment. "What a way to go!"

47

STOCKHOLM, SWEDEN

Carter studied the album cover closely. Which of their many message songs was appropriate for this occasion, he wondered. "S.O.S.," "Mamma Mia," "Fernando," "Dancing Queen," "Name of the Game"...

"'Waterloo'! That's the one we'll play!" Carter exclaimed. He set up the stereo on a display cart near an outlet and then had what he thought was a brilliant idea. He rolled the cart over to the store window, attached the most powerful speakers he could find to the stereo, and positioned them toward the street. He knew it would be no more than a minor distraction, but years of experience had taught him that the purposeful use of absurdity sometimes works. Nothing jars violence like irrelevancy.

Carter placed the ABBA record on the turntable and moved the needle onto the record. But what came out of the speakers was not what he had intended. Inadvertently, he had placed the 33-1/3 rpm record on a 45 rpm setting. The song "Mamma Mia" came out sounding as if Donald Duck was high on helium.

Demonstrators and helmeted police were caught off guard. Billy clubs hung momentarily in the air. Tomatoes remained in hands, unthrown. Heads turned to seek out the source of the silly, but somewhat recognizable, sounds.

Carter quickly switched the song and the speed. "Waterloo" came booming through the loudspeakers and a smile actually crept over many faces. Most of the crowd stood dumbfounded, not knowing what to think or expect.

Unfortunately, the moment of respite from the violence was no more than that. One moment. By the time the Pöni's clubs had smashed the record, stereo and cart into pieces, the store itself was being invaded by six Pönis flanking what appeared to be civilian officials. Carter realized that the music that had stopped the mayhem for a short time had also led the police to him more quickly than he had anticipated.

"I think you dropped this document as you ran from the embassy," one of the civilians said, handing Carter a yellowed invoice written in German.

"Thank you, Mr. Prime Minister," Carter replied. "I'm certain that you know how important that paper is to me."

"And to me, Dr. Carter," Prime Minister Johannes Strindberg said, hand outstretched. "So we finally meet."

"I would like to say that the pleasure is all mine," Carter responded, keeping his hands at his sides, "but quite frankly I don't feel all that magnanimous." He watched as the police carefully prodded curious marchers away from the storefront. "I presume this is the illustrious industrialist, Nils Olsson?" Carter's sarcasm was unmistakable.

"It is certainly a pleasure to meet you, too," Olsson responded, ignoring Carter's tone. "I particularly appreciate your taste in music. Did you really think that it would divert attention from . . ."

"A calculated slaughter?" Linda interjected.

"Histrionics has never been a Scandinavian trait," Olsson dismissed Linda's comment brusquely. "It certainly does not become an attractive woman of Swedish descent."

"I'm quite certain that my great grandparents would never have approved of what you and the prime minister have done," she responded angrily. Carter had motioned to her to moderate her anger, but as far as she was concerned this was the time for righteous indignation, not diplomacy.

"I don't think this is either the time or place for unwarranted accusations," Johannes responded quietly. "It is apparent that we currently have a mutuality of interests, and I trust that we will be able to settle our differences in an amicable way, that is satisfactory to all parties concerned."

"And what are you suggesting, Mr. Prime Minister?" Carter decided that he would address Johannes with all the respect due his position if that would ease their negotiations. He was tired of all of the betrayals and deceits of the last week, and was willing to listen to anyone about anything if the outcome was an end to the violence. What he and Linda had uncovered about Sweden's history of pro-Nazi collaboration, and the manner in which they were handling their present refugee problem, could give them some leverage with Johannes and Olsson. But Carter still wasn't sure to what end. The documents he had hidden were enough to fuel major losses in Sweden's domestic politics, international standing and prestige, and its economic interests. But if it came down to exposing the Swedes publicly, Carter also had to indict the United States and one of America's largest industries. Suddenly, his end goal, now that Eriksson had been killed, was unclear.

"Would you mind if we chatted here in the store?" Johannes asked. "I will order my officers to remain outside." Johannes gave commands in Swedish that sent the police into the street.

Carter's mind was racing. LaGreca hadn't lived long enough to tell him how much Johannes and Olsson knew about the documents he had been collecting.

"I hate to point out the obvious," Olsson rudely interrupted, "but our soldiers, police officers, and some of the general population expect our prime minister to find and arrest suspects responsible for the death of Dr. Derek Eriksson."

"Right now, the only thing that your population is concerned about," Linda interjected defiantly, "is to make certain that they are not treated like indentured servants. Naively, they bought the myth that Sweden welcomes all, regardless of race, color or religion. How were they to know that they were, in fact, owned."

"Thank you, Ms. Watson, for reminding us what Sweden represents," Olsson replied, with little patience for what he considered almost childlike behavior. He would have liked to have ordered the police to remove her from the store; then they could proceed with Carter. But it was Johannes's game, so he decided to take his lead and appear more conciliatory. Wasn't it the Americans who had this quaint expression that you could catch more bees with honey than with vinegar? A little sweetness at this point in the conversation would not hurt. "But you do bring out an extremely important point that we should never take for granted—we do consider ourselves a land of equal opportunity."

Johannes looked through the glassless window and realized he had lost a strategic opportunity. "I congratulate you, Dr. Carter. Very clever."

"What do you mean?" Carter asked, disingenuously, knowing full well that his strategy had worked.

"I was wondering why you seemed so comfortable, here in this store," Johannes said. "Why you broadcast music into the street. Now, I know."

"What is he talking about, Carter?" Linda asked frantically, as if she had just missed an important news bulletin.

"Why don't you look outside, Ms. Watson, and tell me what you see," Johannes responded.

"Hundreds of marchers—people—staring at the four of us," she answered, "and three television cameras." A smile crept across her face.

"Is it now apparent what your colleague has accomplished in these last few minutes?"

"An audience!" Linda concluded. "I guess if anything was to happen to us now . . ."

"All we really need is a little time and patience to discuss our differences, . . ." Carter spoke like the chicken who had purposely gotten the fox into the henhouse.

"That's called diplomacy, Ms. Watson," Johannes interjected.

"In America," Linda responded, "we call that common sense."

48

STOCKHOLM, SWEDEN

"You do realize that I could have you arrested for the death of Dr. Eriksson, don't you?" Johannes addressed Carter from his seat on an old piano stool. Carter and Linda sat opposite him on a piano bench which had seen better days in the company of a Steinway piano.

"That, and more, no doubt," Carter responded, nonplussed.

"But that doesn't interest me. Hansson got, as you Americans say, 'just rewards.' I do need to know, however, just how much the late Ambassador LaGreca told you about my government's involvement in . . . No. What I really want are the documents in the file LaGreca showed you. An astute man, such as yourself, would never have let go of such information—"

"We want that file," Olsson interrupted, "I'm not as patient a man as my friend." He had spent the last few minutes pacing nervously around the store.

"Let's just say it's in a safe place, among friends," Carter responded. *I'm not even lying,* he thought. The ABBA album was probably near Aerosmith and The Allman Brothers.

"What do you want for the file?" Olsson demanded.

"Your Swedish version of slave labor camps has to stop immediately," Carter responded, not knowing himself where he wanted to go with this. "And a commission must be established to identify those who were involved in the heinous work camp program. "

"What else?" Johannes asked.

"What else?!" Olsson repeated Johannes's question angrily. "Isn't that already asking for the moon?" He looked quizzically at Johannes. "Carter basically wants to bring down our entire government. "

"I want all refugees who have been legally working in your country to have the right to apply for the appropriate permits that allow them employment wherever they choose, and permanent residence and citizenship if that was promised them." Carter responded with the self-assurance of a political leader who was representing his constituency. "I'm only asking for what they were entitled to all along."

"Next," Olsson pointed an accusatory finger at Carter, "he's going to dictate who is going to be Prime Minister of Sweden. Isn't that right?"

"Nils," Johannes said in a tempered voice, "you're not helping the situation." He looked at his childhood friend and realized how frightened he really was of Carter. Olsson was afraid that by making concessions, his financial and industrial complex would be destroyed. And Johannes knew that if the information LaGreca collected was exposed to daylight, the respect and power of families such as Olsson's would be destroyed as well.

Unlike Olsson, Johannes had faith in his constituency and the ability of his government to navigate the bumpy months ahead. Olsson was right; Carter was asking for major policy changes, but certainly no more than Johannes and his advisors had realized months before had to be made. They just never believed a day would come when the terms of these changes would be dictated to them by a foreigner. But given what might be revealed and blown out of proportion by Johannes's critics in the press and parliament, he knew it would be smart to make some concessions to Carter. Somehow he would have to convince Carter that if he valued stability in Sweden, he would have to sanction the existence of Johannes's government, warts and all. But how could he get Carter to turn the file of documents over to him?

"Now that you have heard what I propose," Carter said, "may I ask you what it is that you want, Mr. Prime Minister?"

"Don't say a word!" Olsson ordered Johannes. "We don't have to sit here and answer his questions!"

"Why don't you try to be helpful," Linda interjected, looking straight into Olsson's steely blue eyes. "You have a chance to undo some awful things..."

"Pollyanna naiveté," he shouted back. "All your accusations will be refuted by our government as nothing but disinformation and lies." He stared at her immobile face; clearly she was not intimidated by him. "Unlike your newspapers, which carry inordinate political weight in your country, our newspapers follow the guidelines of civil reporting set down by the prime minister and Parliament. We have some very rigid standards about what information we can and cannot report."

"You're not being very helpful," Johannes interjected. "Neither Ms. Watson nor Dr. Carter appear to believe what you are saying. So, I ask you as an old friend and a patriot of Sweden, to stop."

"Are you crazy?" Olsson yelled, flinging his hands around in the air. "Don't you see what they are doing? Generations of our families and friends have made Sweden into what it has become—an economically powerful, politically important country far in excess of its small size and population in the world. We manufacture and export cars, telephones, military airplanes, food products, financial services. And we thought we could also provide a safe haven for political refugees. Our intentions were honorable."

"Mr. Olsson," Carter answered, changing tactics to one of appeasement, "why don't you sit down and join us. Insulting Linda, and threatening me are definitely counterproductive. I think that you have to have a little faith that we are trying to bridge a very wide chasm."

Carter was actually surprised by the vituperative nature

of Olsson's invectives. This was a man who was more than simply frightened. This was a man acting as if he were desperate to save the *ancien régime*. Carter suddenly realized that any deal he would make would have to "save face" for the old Sweden by maintaining the national myths. *How ironic,* he thought. *My mission has changed from assassinating one evil man to trying to transform a myth into a reality. And the only way I can do it is to elicit the help of the very people I came here to stop.* He had to transform from a warrior in battle to a warrior in peace. And that meant he now had to fight in the political arena, which he always abhorred and distrusted.

As Carter argued the case for concessions, he, like Olsson, began to realize what he, personally, had to give up. First, his own narcissism; and, second, the myth that he could function in the international arena as a loner, dependent only on his own resources. For him, to relinquish the myth of the loner, and the grandiosity inherent in the notion of the physician-warrior or assassin, was as painful as Olsson and Johannes's letting an outsider shape the image of a perfect Sweden.

"What value is there in my sitting with three conspirators?" Olsson asked sarcastically, looking for a face-saving opening that would allow him to join the threesome with a modicum of self-respect.

"Your simple presence constitutes a major value to all of us here," Carter answered, hoping Olsson would calm down and stop pacing back and forth in the small shop.

Olsson suddenly stopped by the old record albums and started to laugh. "Can you believe that a few pop songs sung by a group that no longer exists brought us all here?" He chuckled at his next thought. "Maybe we should create a new governmental position called 'Minister of Rock 'n Roll' and bring music into a crisis situation on an 'as needed' basis."

"I think that we all can agree on that, so why don't you come over and help us reach some consensus?" Carter persisted.

"Carter is right," Johannes agreed. "Come over here and be part of the new 'Swedish tea party.' It's not a bad idea to scheme together to create a new society. Reminds me of our days at the university, when you and I spent half our nights plotting out our futures and that of Sweden."

"He's brainwashing you," Olsson responded, but with less fervor, "as he did those immigrants. But he doesn't even need an ABBA record."

"What difference does it make?" Johannes asked. "The time has come to make some changes. As of last week I wouldn't have predicted that we would be making those changes from stools in a looted music store in Gamla Stan. But we knew that changes would have to be made relatively soon. And here we are. If our interests are compatible, why do we have to continue to fight reality?"

"Perhaps our interests are not compatible," Olsson responded, but only halfheartedly.

"Then we will make history without you," Carter interjected. "There's no point wasting valuable time on someone who doesn't know when the hand of history is touching him on the shoulder." He waited to see if Olsson took the bait of envy and competition. "There are giants of national security who never make a mark on their country or their time because they are too invested with a strong sense of self to admit that they may not know everything."

"The issue of amnesty will be important to us," Johannes said, trying to ignore his friend's remark and put the conversation back on track.

"I'm sure that can be handled by a panel of highly respected judges, lawyers, and prominent citizens from your own country," Carter responded.

"We must have an agreement in principle that limits the prosecution of people directly responsible for past and present... immigrant conditions," Olsson demanded, looking to Johannes for support. There was no way that Olsson was going to be tried as a war criminal of any sort.

"In principle," Johannes argued, "I don't disagree. But in

reality this will be a very sensitive subject over which Parliament will have to have extensive discussion."

"I don't disagree," Carter replied.

"For example, I can see where my political enemies may try to force me to go on trial for alleged offenses against humanity and other infractions of the law." Johannes voiced Olsson's concerns.

"That's correct, but perhaps we can figure out how to make it more symbolic than real," Carter said, realizing that in politics, everyone had to win something.

"There's nothing symbolic about spending your life in prison," Olsson said finally pulling up a wobbly three-legged chair into the circle.

"Your police and security units must remain apolitical," Carter said. "A respected organization, like the United States Institute of Peace, could train them to manage the ongoing immigration crisis until the larger world community can assist with the problem."

"I suddenly feel optimistic," Johannes said, ever the statesman. "If South Africa could heal its wounds with truth and reconciliation councils, and those wounds were deeper and longer than the ones we are talking about . . ." He turned toward his friend, who had placed his head in his hands. "What do you think, old friend?"

Olsson nodded in agreement, although he didn't look up.

49

STOCKHOLM, SWEDEN

"I think that we've discussed all the relevant issues," Carter said, with a sense of relief.

"We're clear that this will be simply a memorandum of understanding?" Johannes asked, glancing at his scribbles on the backs and corners of stained sheet music. "I will have my notes typed up in the appropriate format and sent to your hotel tomorrow for your review." He stood up to leave; they had been in the music store for over four hours.

"Mr. Prime Minister," Linda said, trying to be supportive, "I congratulate you for turning a disastrous situation into a breath of new life for Sweden in the twenty-first century."

"You Americans are really quite something," Olsson commented. "Everything you do is like a McDonald's fast-food meal. Pre-cooked food, eaten in a few minutes, dishes bussed before you leave. This should be called the 'Ronald McDonald Memorandum of Understanding.'"

"Ah, my dear friend," Johannes interjected, placing his arms around Olsson's shoulders, "you're too cynical. You are beginning to sound like a Swede, complaining about one of our typical dark winters."

"There's no question," Carter added, pleased with the outcome of the talks, "that we have all helped to create a momentum for change. And I think that the Swedish people will be better candidates for atoning for past sins than were the Swiss. In my book, that's impressive. It certainly bespeaks for the courage and wisdom of you, Prime Minister . . . and you, as well, Olsson."

"Please," Johannes responded, shaking hands with both Carter and Linda, "you give me too much credit." He paused and looked at Carter as if he was still taking the measure of the man. "I expect that all documents pertaining to Sweden in the file will be turned over to me, personally, when the memorandum is signed off by both of us."

Thank God, Johannes thought, *that Carter had not insisted that the memorandum be voted upon by the Swedish parliament.* He was too knowledgeable for that. Carter knew that Johannes would never be able to obtain a consensus vote. Instead, he had promised Carter that he would implement the agreed-upon terms using the discretionary powers granted to the Office of the Prime Minister.

The successful outcome of the negotiations was really the result of the trust that Carter and Johannes had each developed in the integrity of the other as the hours passed. Carter knew that Johannes was taking the biggest political risk of his career. He was agreeing to initiate a plan that might transform the face of Sweden from a homogeneous to a heterogeneous nation. The demographics of Sweden could change drastically over the coming decades with the admission of thousands of refugees as permanent residents.

Carter also knew how difficult it would be for Johannes to be the first prime minister to publicly recognize and apologize for past and present atrocities committed against various nationalities and countries, within the guise of Swedish neutrality. Yet Carter trusted Johannes to do his best in implementing the spirit, if not the exact terms, of the memorandum.

Like any good politician, Johannes knew that the memorandum was, in reality, only an outline. Since Carter and Linda officially represented no nation or recognized international organization, the memorandum was only as good as the intentions of its signators. It was unlikely that the memorandum had any legal standing, whatsoever.

But Johannes knew that the entire crisis was a blessing in disguise. Good intentions—to provide a temporary haven for refugees—had produced a disastrous mess in which he had been a willing participant. He was certain he could arise again like a political phoenix. Unlike his playwright ancestor, who wrote dismal truths and disturbing insights about man's fate, Johannes preferred the more uplifting spiritual writings of Count Leo Tolstoy, who in his book *Resurrection* could redeem a fallen man through the good graces and Christian virtues of a prostitute. Perhaps this was both his, and Sweden's, time of redemption. It might not come again. History was a jealous mistress who would tolerate no distractions. Unlike Tolstoy, he felt that individuals determined the course of history. And he, Johannes Strindberg, Prime Minister of Sweden, would not allow history to escape from his grasp.

Wasn't the United States populated with various ethnic groups? The mix of peoples, cultures and ideas was exactly what had given America its vitality, creativity, and strength. Sweden could use a little of that, Johannes mused. Perhaps not an overwhelming amount, all at once, but a new dynamic beginning.

Olsson had said nothing for the last twenty minutes. He had only telephoned for security officers to be available once the meeting disbanded. The march, he found out, had caused a great deal of property damage along its path, but few deaths.

"I think that before we leave here," Carter suggested, "we should all be comfortable with what we've agreed to. If there are any misgivings, let's discuss them right now. Otherwise . . ."

"Otherwise, what?" Olsson asked, fearful that Carter would threaten to withhold the documents in the file.

"You make it sound so ominous, Olsson," Linda interjected. "Carter is simply trying to make sure that when we walk outside we're all singing the same song, to make a poor pun."

"What a quaint American expression," Olsson responded, with his usual sarcasm. "Does it matter that the sheet music is composed of a lot of diminished cords and flat notes?"

"Enough, Nils!" Johannes said. "We all understand that you have some serious misgivings concerning the memorandum. My intention is to present this to the public and Carter's intention is to turn over information on our sordid history. No one considers what we've done here perfect. And everyone has to trust the other to do his part. But this is the best we can do at this moment in time." He walked over to Olsson and placed his hands on Olsson's shoulders. "Nils, as my oldest, dearest friend, I ask that you, above everyone else, understand that this is the beginning of great changes to come in Sweden. Have a little bit of faith in me."

"Quite frankly," Olsson replied, "I'm worried that a lot of Swedes will think you a traitor to your heritage."

"I don't think Olsson is entirely wrong," Carter interjected. "But if you don't 'push the envelope,' to use another American expression, then the chance for Sweden to make needed internal changes will pass you by."

Johannes looked through the broken display window and saw the press waiting for him. His attractive, red-headed press secretary waved to him; her other body language indicated that the journalists were becoming restless. "I think it's time for us to walk outside and for me to make a major announcement."

"How much police protection is out there?" Carter asked, as Johannes went to the door.

"That's a strange question," Johannes said, "considering the fact that you've spent half your time in Sweden running away from the police."

"A simple, judicious precautionary question," Carter responded. "Just call me paranoid."

"Even paranoids have enemies," Linda reminded him. "Now it's your turn to be on the hot seat, Carter. What are you concerned about?"

I don't know," Carter responded, hesitantly. "I guess I distrust crowds."

"Lady and gentlemen, you may want to stay in here until the crowds thin out, but I must be leaving. 'My public awaits,' as they say in Hollywood."

Johannes shook hands with Carter again, opened the door of the store, and walked to a makeshift podium his press office had ordered constructed. Journalists swarmed the area. Disheveled and bruised refugees pushed journalists and cameramen out of the way in order to get a closer look at the prime minister. Everyone wanted to hear what the prime minister was going to say.

"Ladies and gentlemen of the press," Johannes began, "fellow citizens and non-citizens of Sweden, as your prime minister I would like to make a very simple statement." He paused, feeling the electricity in the audience. "I am here, on behalf of both myself and my party, to ask for your patience and forgiveness. Sweden—with good intentions—has committed many mistakes in the past and under my leadership, mistakes that have been covered up, ignored, and wished away. I apologize to our non-Swedish friends and neighbors for acts which have disguised the true, generous nature of the Swedish people. And I apologize to my Swedish compatriots for not encouraging the best of our tradition and character to rise to the surface in difficult times. Perhaps it has taken all of us more time than it should have to come to grips with our place in the twenty-first century, and what that might mean in terms of changes that all of us have to make in our lives. But history has taught us that it is never too late for a fresh start." He stopped for a moment, emotionally exhausted.

Carter listened closely and was impressed. Johannes would uphold his end of the bargain. He'd use the political rhetoric and muscle he would need to, but he'd stick with the spirit of their understanding.

"In the next few days," Johannes continued, "I will be outlining some principles and plans for Sweden's leading international role in the twenty-first century. I look forward to public reaction. Thank you."

The crowd broke into loud cheers and applause.

No one even recognized the sound of a gunshot pierce the air until Johannes fell onto the podium, face forward, covered in blood.

50

STOCKHOLM, SWEDEN

"He's dead," Carter pronounced, after a cursory examination. "One bullet straight through the forehead. This was a professional job." Considering the small size of the hole the bullet left, Carter calculated that someone had been shooting from about five hundred feet away. And, considering the downward angle of the shot, probably from one of the rooftops across the street. Since all rooftops were strategically occupied by the police, only someone with a proper security clearance could have gained access to the roof. It had to be one of the Pönis, Carter concluded.

"Who do you suspect might have done this?" Carter asked an ashen-gray faced Olsson.

"How should I know?" Olsson was clearly emotionally drained by the death of his best friend.

The crowd in front of the store was stunned. Some of the marchers spontaneously lit matches and raised them above their heads as a sign of respect. Others expressed their grief by chanting his name in a whining, almost plaintive, voice. Others merely cried.

Carter watched the crowd and realized that while they were responding to ugliness, the truth of the assassination was that they were also creating a martyr—the most dangerous outcome an assassin could want. Thankfully, it hadn't been Eriksson. It was Johannes who had suddenly been transformed from an oppressor to a hero. Someone who by giving his life to Sweden had empowered its inhabitants. Whoever had planned his death had made a very big mistake, Carter concluded. A legend was being born in front of Carter's eyes.

"What is there to say?" Linda asked Carter, not expecting or really looking for an answer. "In some ways, he was at the beginning of a memorable career . . ."

"That's very touching, Ms. Watson," Olsson interjected sarcastically, "but I'm certain that he would have preferred to be a living prime minister than a dead legend."

"I'm sorry if I offended you," she responded defensively, "but I only meant that . . ."

"I appreciate your sentiments," Olsson said, "but I'm afraid that they will not bring him back to us."

"Who might have wanted to have him killed?" Carter asked again.

"Why do I have this disturbing feeling that you think that I am involved with his murder?" Olsson asked, watching the police and paramedics place Johannes's lifeless body on a stretcher.

Perhaps, Carter thought, *I've misread Olsson's character.* He was clearly disturbed by his friend's death, trying to hide the tears in his eyes. Yet, Carter had no doubts that Olsson and the industrialists he represented would benefit the most from the murder. It was now highly unlikely that the economic and political reform Johannes had committed himself and his party to in the music store would be implemented. According to the memorandum, Johannes had agreed to seek reparation payments, fair minimum wages, admission of past injustices, and prosecution of responsible officials. Throughout the meeting, Olsson had been on his cellular telephone, ostensibly arranging for security and monitoring the progress of the march. Olsson had objected to paying reparations with the argument that it could destroy foreign currency reserves the Swedish government owned and throw the government into the same bankrupt condition that had occurred in Asia in 1998–1999. The industrialists could not afford to compensate their workers at dramatically higher levels without debilitating corporate losses and stock declines. Carter understood that while the industrialists needed cheap labor, they had supported Dr. Eriksson's plan in order to maintain a homogeneous Sweden and a viable welfare system.

Why was Carter having such a hard time trying to reconcile the sight of the weeping friend in front of him with the ruthless capitalist he knew him to be? Was he capable of having his best friend killed because it was going to interfere with business? If anything, experience had taught Carter that the rules of business superseded the rules of friendship in any competition. So why was he having such a hard time believing that Olsson could have ordered the assassination of his closest friend? All they had to do was to agree when to disagree. After he, Carter, had transferred the documents over to Johannes, then Olsson and Johannes could fight about which to release to the media and which policies they would push in parliament. The timing was off, thought Carter.

Once the stretcher was lifted into the ambulance, Carter went back into the store for the file. He once again placed it beneath his shirt.

"Carter," Linda grabbed his arm as he walked out of the shop, "let's get out of here before we become the next targets." Even in her former job as an intelligence operative, she had never been comfortable with the concept of assassination as a method of dealing with a head of state. "Please, Carter," she whispered in his ear, "I'm afraid . . ."

"Don't be afraid," Carter responded, patting his chest. "As long as I have these and they don't, no one is going to kill me. And furthermore," he added jokingly, "I'm too ugly to kill. And you're too pretty to die."

She looked at him quizzically.

"Just stay close to me," he reassured her, "and I guarantee you that nothing, but nothing will happen to either one of us."

"How can you be so certain?" she asked.

"Don't you have faith in your good doctor anymore?" Carter asked with a hint of sarcasm.

"As a matter of fact," she whispered in his ear seductively, "I'm afraid that I have too much faith in you."

"Good," Carter responded. He patted his chest one more time, obsessively making sure that the file was resting comfortably.

51

STOCKHOLM, SWEDEN

As Carter and Linda elbowed their way through the crowd, it was again becoming unruly. Profanities were being muttered, as well as fears of what would happen now that a champion was dead. In response, the Swedish police began to tighten its security ring around the shifting bodies.

"Stay close," Carter repeated.

"Can we go back to the hotel?" Linda asked. "I'd like to take a plane back to the States as soon as we can." She paused in thought. "Whoever ordered Johannes's death is certainly going to be looking for us."

"How do you know?" Carter asked, curious about her reasoning.

"If they killed Johannes for the file, then why wouldn't they want to kill us?" she asked, indignantly.

"But why do you think they killed him for the file?" Carter asked, pushing through the crowd.

"Because he's the one who could take down the whole Swedish government with the incriminating evidence in those documents," Linda replied, sounding a little flustered.

"Then why wasn't I shot?" Carter demanded. "I was the one who had them. Not Johannes."

"How do you know that someone is not waiting to kill you right now?" Linda asked, irritated by Carter's accusatory tone. "Why are you trying to make me feel defensive? Especially now, when we've come through so much together."

"You're right," Carter replied, realizing that the time for confrontation was not yet right.

"Where are you going?" Olsson shouted, running up to them.

"Please get rid of him!" Linda whispered in Carter's ear. "I don't like him or trust him."

"We're on our way to the Grand Hotel," Carter responded.

"May I join you?" Olsson asked. "I'm particularly fond of the view from their restaurant and I could use a stiff drink right now."

"I thought you couldn't stand our guts, to use a well-worn but apt expression," Linda responded. "If I played back some of the things you said to us over the last four hours, it did not sound like someone who now wants to share a drink."

"I apologize for anything that I said that may have offended either one of you," he said contritely, looking extremely tired. "I said what I thought needed to be said. Obviously, I lost my case. Now I've lost my friend..."

"I'd like to talk to Linda for a moment, if you don't mind?" Carter said, pulling her into the crowd. "Let's just go with it, okay? Assume the best, not the worst. He looks like he's hurting badly. He lost his best friend. He sees that his financial empire is going to be in decline pretty soon. What do we lose?"

"You sound like a social worker," she responded curtly. "Do you remember how mistrustful you were of him just a few hours ago? What has happened since then? Nothing has changed." She glanced back at Olsson. "I still think that he's the one who ordered Johannes's death. You're the one who almost made the accusation."

"Maybe you're right," Carter replied, reflecting on all the events that had transpired and Linda's emotional state at the moment.

"Olsson," Carter said, returning to him, "Linda and I are really exhausted. We need to make some telephone calls. We need to shower. If you don't mind, we'll take a rain check on that drink."

"Of course," Olsson said. "I understand." He looked around at the menacing crowd. "The least I can do is help you get out of Gamla Stan."

"That's all right," Linda responded, "we'll do just fine. I think if we head down Lilla Nygatan to Riddar-Holmen, across the Centralbron, make a right, we'll practically walk straight into the hotel."

"I'm impressed with your knowledge of the city, Ms. Watson," Olsson said, realizing that he would not be able to end their relationship on a positive note. "But the quickest way to the hotel is to go three streets over..."

"And go down Stora Nygatan?" Linda interrupted him. "That's the long route out of here. It doesn't make any sense to make such a large detour just to get to the bridge."

"Again," Olsson responded undaunted, "you're right. But given the route of the marchers, that street is significantly less congested than this one. So it may be a longer way around, but it will take much less time to navigate."

"Carter," Linda whispered sotto voce, "I don't trust him. Let's just go my way. At least there will be crowds around us. And I'd feel safer with people around than on a more isolated street."

"Olsson," Carter said, feeling caught in the middle of two highly distrustful people, "I think we'll take the route Linda feels most comfortable with." He was astounded by the fact that in the midst of all of this turmoil, these two people were ready to fight over which was the easiest route to the hotel. "I think we'll take our chances walking through the huddled masses."

"Then do you mind if I accompany you a little further down Lilla Nygatan?" Olsson asked. "I just want to make sure of your safety." He accepted their nods as agreement. "And I would enjoy a few more minutes of your companionship."

Why this sudden change in character? Carter wondered. A few hours ago, Olsson couldn't get rid of them fast enough.

Now he couldn't stick more closely to them than if they were covered with honey. Maybe Linda was right, and Olsson was leading them into an ambush. But maybe it was time to let the paranoia subside on all sides. And finally go home.

As they pushed their way through the crowd on Lilla Nygatan, Carter tucked his shirt in more tightly to keep the file pressed closely against his body.

"Can we stop here in this little alley?" Linda asked, appearing exhausted from having to push through the crowd. "Maybe you were right, Olsson. We should have taken the other street."

"Too late to change route, I'm afraid," Olsson responded, appreciative of her backhanded compliment.

The alley they stopped in was six feet wide; no more than a place for trash receptacles or as a walk-thru to the next street. The wall on the right was part of a small bakery. The wall on the left was the end of a souvenir shop.

At some level, Olsson understood that he was hanging on to these two relative strangers, people he didn't even like, because these were the two people who had spent the last hours of Johannes's life together with him. And that would always have a special meaning. Perhaps, by being with them, he was keeping some part of Johannes alive. Whether or not it was magical thinking, the pain of the loss of his childhood friend was so profound that he was ready to grab on to anything that gave him sustenance. Even the companionship of two Americans who were about to destroy everything that he and Johannes used to believe in.

"Dr. Carter," a male voice yelled out from behind him in the alley, "I have an L9A1 Browning 9mm automatic pistol pointed at the back of your head. As you know, it has thirteen rounds of ammunition. Enough to take you and your friends out without any effort."

"What do you want?" Carter asked, not entirely surprised. He knew precisely what the man wanted. It was exactly what Linda had warned him against—an ambush set up by Olsson. But there was only one problem. It was on the wrong street.

"Please hand over the file," the voice continued, "and no one will get hurt."

"Why not just shoot me," Carter asked, "and take the file? This way, you don't have to exert yourself to even be polite." He saw the startled looks on both Olsson's and Linda's faces.

"Just give it to him," Olsson said. "The file isn't worth another life."

"Please don't resist him," Linda pleaded, her eyes filling with tears.

"You're probably right," Carter responded calmly. "But before I hand over anything to anyone, I want to see my thief's face."

"Then turn around slowly," the gunman said. "Everyone, put your hands up in the air. Carter, just unbutton your shirt and lay the file on the ground. Then our transaction will be complete."

"What guarantee do I have that you won't take the file and then kill me and my friends?" Carter asked, turning slowly toward the voice.

"I think you already know the answer to that question," the gunman said. "You've been in the business."

"You mean this is a no-win situation," Carter said, knowing that none of them would be left alive by the gunman.

The man Carter saw when he turned around had a stocky muscular build. The kind of physique that requires a two-hour workout each day. His eyes were focused, cold, and unflinching. This man was a killer.

"Did you shoot the prime minister?" Olsson demanded.

"Do you really expect me to answer that?" the gunman asked.

"Please," Linda repeated, "hand him the file."

"Why make it easy for him, Linda? He's going to kill us all anyway," Carter repeated. "You heard him, this is a no-win situation. Anyone who would kill Johannes the way he did, and then a few minutes later creep up on us in the middle of a riot smells Special Ops to me. Only someone trained by an elite military unit could do that."

There was no response from the gunman, other than holding out his hand to indicate that the file be turned over to him.

Carter did nothing except stare at the man. Suddenly, there was a spark of recognition. He was one of the young men who had beaten up the immigrant youths when Linda and he were walking in Gamla Stan a week before; one of the young Swedish nationalists Captain Hansson had refused to arrest. Was there a connection to Olsson as well?

Without any warning, Carter threw the file at the gunman. The documents inside flew everywhere. During the first moments of the distraction, Carter charged the gunman.

A single shot rang out, followed by a scream.

52

STOCKHOLM, SWEDEN

Carter and the gunman struggled on the ground for control of the gun. A second shot went off into the air. But the position gave Carter the ability to take both hands and twist the gunman's head until he heard the crack of his neck breaking and the sensation of his head dropping like a floppy doll onto his chest. Carter lay on the ground, exhausted and reached for the gun.

"Don't move! Or I will shoot," Linda stated, without any trace of the former exhaustion in her voice.

Ignoring her demand, Carter grabbed the gunman's gun and pointed it at her.

"It looks like we have a Mexican standoff!" Carter said. "Funny, I was waiting for this moment," he said, "but I was hoping it would never come. We could have had some good times together."

Linda stood before him, holding the gun she had taken from the guard as they escaped from the prison cells under City Hall. "Aren't you tired of always being right? It must be a hell of a burden to carry around."

"Thank you for the backhanded compliment," Carter said, holding the Browning 9mm firmly in his right hand while gathering some of the scattered documents with his left. "I hate to disappoint you, but I wasn't that smart. I saw you pocket the gun. And when you insisted that we walk down Lilla Hygatan instead of Stora Nygatan, I knew something was very wrong. Up until today, I admit, you had me fooled. Well, if not fooled, at least confused. That was some good work."

"Thank you," Linda responded coldly, bending down to pick up the documents that had settled near her feet. "But flattery doesn't go a long way with me." Her face was stern. Her eyes focused on Carter. Her gun steady.

"That's something worth looking into someday," Carter responded, sarcastically. "Any halfway good shrink could help solve that one for you."

"When did you figure out how deeply I was involved?"

"Looking back on the week," Carter responded, "probably from the first day we met. Only I didn't know it. The first day we met at the hotel, I saw Londsdale walk past. But, to be honest, as much as I suspected that you weren't quite what you claimed to be, it wasn't until yesterday, when LaGreca showed us the material on the automobile companies and their activities during World War Two that I realized you were sent to keep track of what, if anything, I learned while I was in Sweden. And you even had me fooled there; you seemed just as earnest as LaGreca really was, to fill me in on America's sordid past."

"I'm sorry you learned so much," Linda responded, in a chilling tone. "Is it necessary for me to go through the ritual of asking for the documents in your hand? Or are we going to play games?"

"Why don't you just try and ask me nicely?" he responded calmly.

"Please, give me the papers," she said, in a falsely endearing way.

That depends on what you want to do with them," he responded, with his most seductive, boyish smile.

"I said that I didn't want to play any games. And what do you do . . . ?"

"Start playing games," he responded, repositioning his

gun so that the barrel pointed straight at her forehead. I have to admit, you're really a pro."

"Why are you so sure?" she asked, cocking her gun. They both heard the 9mm bullet fall into the chamber.

"Your stance, the way you hold the gun, the way you played everyone off. All that speaks highly for those who trained you. I guess the car companies knew what they were getting when they hired you."

Carter noticed some passersby glance into the alley as they walked by. He couldn't tell how much they saw, since Linda's back blocked most of the view. But if they understood what was going on, somebody probably would get the police. And if that was the case, this matter needed to be resolved quickly. Once the police arrived, they would confiscate the documents and incarcerate both of them. And this time there would be no LaGreca, Johannes or even Olsson to help him out.

"Hand me those documents," Linda ordered, her voice peremptory. "Don't force me to kill you."

"Linda, it's not worth it," Carter said, dropping his gun to the ground. "Here, take them. I don't want any more lives spilled over this. Especially my own."

"Thank you," Linda said, never really believing he would hand them to her without her having to pull the trigger. "I wonder why we had to get to this point." She relaxed her gun arm as she stuffed the documents into the file.

"You tell me!" Carter replied. If he weren't very careful right now in the way he handled Linda, he would soon be laying alongside Olsson.

"Would you mind kicking the gun over this way," Linda asked, her gun still pointed at Carter. "Make sure that it doesn't go off accidentally! That would be most disruptive to our new relationship."

"Is this what your clients wanted all the time?" Carter asked, pointing to the file she held in her hand.

"They knew it existed," Linda answered matter-of-factly, "but they weren't certain where it was. They found out that the Swedish government was also aware of it because they were implicated as well. And the Swedes started getting suspicious that someone in our embassy was playing a role in amassing the documents."

"Did Ambassador LaGreca work for your clients?"

"Indirectly, I guess," she answered. "They had funded his political campaign when he was a congressman. Typical democracy-in-action kind of stuff. We give you money and, in turn, you help to pass favorable legislation. Then, when he was appointed Ambassador, my clients pressed the State Department and the Senators involved in the Senate confirmation hearing to post him to Sweden. Carl didn't seem to mind doing double-duty. Being the ambassador, and taking more money to find and destroy any documents that were negative about my clients."

"But instead of sticking to the original deal, LaGreca got greedy. He wanted more for himself. Or he got patriotic. I guess we'll never know which it was," Carter interjected. "And you, you also had double-duty. You were originally sent over just to track me, so that your clients would find out how much I got to know. But once I discovered what I shouldn't have," he paused, assessing her reaction, "they wanted to make sure that I could never leak the information about their history of Nazi collaboration. Which, of course, meant only one thing."

"And what might that one thing be?" she asked.

"That you have no other choice but to kill me," Carter answered calmly.

"You tell me. What other choice do I have?" she asked. "If I kill you now, my employers won't have any future worries about being exposed in the media. Or whether to hire another assassin to kill you. If I don't, my life might be on the line."

"I really can't think of too many other alternatives," Carter said, certain that he had to act now. "However, the alternative I'm going to take is to turn my back on you, walk down this alley to the next street, and hail a cab to take me to the hotel. I will then proceed to pack my bags, take a shower, and board a return flight to Washington, D.C."

"And after that?" she asked, not sure how she was going to respond.

"I haven't thought it through any further," he answered. "Once in the States..."

"...you become a walking time bomb for my employers," she said, coldly.

"That's one interpretation," he said, starting to turn around.

"Where are you going?" she yelled. "You can't just walk away."

"Why not?" he answered.

"Do you really want me to shoot you in the back?" she asked, bewildered.

"I guess I'll have to take the chance."

"Cat with nine lives?"

"Something like that!" he responded, pointing to heaven. "When the old man or lady upstairs wants me," he responded cockily, "then my number is up, and I'm all packed and ready to go."

"So, you're not afraid of death?" she asked, her finger tightening around the trigger.

"Good-bye, Linda," Carter replied, "nice knowing you. Take care of yourself!"

A gunshot resonated throughout the alley.

53

WASHINGTON, D.C.

The Holocaust Museum in Washington, D.C., is a darkly imposing structure of gray granite, a grim reminder of what it represents. Its vestibule is chiseled with statements and sayings that are intended to elicit a somber silence. Remembrance of past atrocities is the central motif, with the unspoken and unwritten understanding that the heinous acts committed against six million Jews, and millions of gypsies, political prisoners, homosexuals, priests, and others caught up in the Nazi war machinery would never be forgotten.

Inside are exhibits that allow the visitor to experience what it felt like to be a concentration camp victim. There are also exhibits of man's inhumanity to man, pictures of physicians using living prisoners in ungodly medical experiments. Injecting live typhoid bacteria into a prisoner to induce a lethal infection so that its course could be monitored and a potential vaccine discovered. Removing a live fetus from a pregnant mother by doing an incomplete cesarean operation without anesthesia. Performing an autopsy on living twins to see what their organ systems were like *in vivo*. This building was a testimony to man's infinite capacity for sadism, barbaric behavior, creative violence, and hatred for life.

James Atherton stood restlessly on the corner of Raoul

Wallenberg Place, scanning each visitor approaching the museum. Usually unforgiving if someone was late for an appointment, in this case he would make an exception because Carter was bringing him something very special. To stave off boredom he was counting the number of visitors who entered and left the museum. He had reached 120 when Carter tapped him on the shoulder from behind.

"Christ, Almighty!" Atherton exclaimed. "You scared the bejesuzz out of me."

"That may be the first and only time I may have gotten a chance to do that," Carter said, shaking Atherton's hand vigorously.

"How are you?" Atherton asked, looking him up and down. "I have a calendar in my office that is completely dedicated to the 'Dr. Alison Carter Scandinavian Tour Package.'"

"Per your request, sir," Carter answered in a more formal tone, "the mission is accomplished," and handed Atherton a thick manila envelope.

"What in God's name is in here?" Atherton asked, feigning surprise. "Did you bring me naughty pictures and magazines from the land of beautiful women, handsome men, and bucolic tranquility?" Atherton opened the envelope and quickly flipped through some of its contents.

"I must compliment you, sir," Carter responded, "on your acting skills."

"But I am surprised, old boy," Atherton replied disingenuously. "I'm astonished by the information that you have presented to me. And, I might add, this is the icing on the cake. You have accomplished your mission, and then some." His thick lips spread into a broad smile, revealing yellow stained teeth, the result of an incurable habit of chewing tobacco.

"Or perhaps," Carter interjected, "it's the very cake itself." He paused while Atherton rechecked some of the documents in the envelope.

"I have a matter to ask you about, General," Carter added,

outwardly calm, but determined not to let the general see how important it was to him.

"Now, let me guess what that could be," Atherton responded sardonically. He let at least 30 seconds pass by. "Linda?"

"You hit it right on the head, General," Carter responded. "Linda!"

"I imagine you want to know who she was, and why I sent her to follow you," Atherton said, matter-of-factly.

"That would be a good start," Carter responded, suddenly wanting to choke this man.

"Linda worked for me several years ago," Atherton began, "when she was a Navy Intelligence Officer at the White House, on the NSC staff."

"How did she get involved in this whole mess?" Carter interrupted. "And how could you let an operative die for nothing."

"Are you taking her death personally?" Atherton asked, truly surprised this time. "Never let your emotions run rampant. At best, they'll give you a false positive reading, which certainly would not give you an accurate reflection of who she was and why she was sent to Sweden."

"Sorry, sir. I'm all ears," Carter responded. "Please continue."

"Linda left the military, with my blessings, to make herself the kind of money that would allow her the lifestyle that would give her 'fuck you' money."

"But where does automotive industry come into this? And whose idea was it to tail me?" Carter asked, impatient despite himself.

"She took my advice," Atherton continued, "and I helped her attain a prestigious job in the most influential automotive association."

"Now let me guess," Carter interrupted, "as *quid pro quo* for obtaining her job and creating a new lifestyle for herself, she was highly indebted to one General James Atherton."

"One gold star, Dr. Carter."

"But you also had a dream. Not to make money, although I'm sure it came anyway, but to set up a private company which was a bit unique—an assassination group made up of men and women who already had government clearances, and whom you could trust because you had personally worked with them. And as we are both well aware, you were in a position to predict DOD's outsourcing capabilities."

"Two gold stars," Atherton assured him. "I'll stop you only when I think that you are going astray."

"So you helped Linda find a job in the automotive industry. First, I'd guess because there's a lot of loose money rolling around there that would support the lifestyle Linda wanted. Oh, but you already said that. And second, because you suspected early on in your military career that our automotive companies had never been brought to justice and paid for their earlier sins," Carter said. "You are, first and foremost, a military man."

"Three gold stars." Atherton always enjoyed Carter. Straightforward and to the point.

"She worked double-duty for both the car companies and you, on an 'as needed' basis," Carter continued. "But at some point you suspected that she was becoming more loyal to industry than to her original mentor."

"No arguments, there!"

"So you sent her over to keep tabs on me, wondering whether I would uncover any information about the car companies as I set about my more immediate task of assassinating Eriksson, but also as your little test of her loyalty to you." Carter continued. "If there were indicting documents against the Big Three, who would she give them to?"

"Four gold stars, my boy! One more and you'll be a five-star general! "

"You didn't quite trust her," Carter added, "and you did not quite trust me."

"Excellent analysis of the psychological dialectic," Atherton approved with a beaming smile.

"So you sent two people over to do the same thing," Carter said, "in true intelligence operative style, making certain that each watched the other, and then waiting to see who, in fact, was most loyal."

"Bingo!" Atherton responded. "You won. She lost. That's why she's not here with us today."

"But why did you need me? You could have sent her alone to accomplish the original assignment," Carter asked.

"What's that old expression, the one that's politically incorrect," Atherton responded, " 'never send over a boy, or in this case a woman, to do a man's job'! The long and short of it is that she was not qualified to take out Eriksson. You were. Furthermore, there was a certain symmetry in sending one doctor to eliminate another doctor. Even you would have to admit that there was an elegance, panache, perhaps even poetry, to that. Linda was just not in the same league as you or Eriksson. She was what you would call in baseball a relief pitcher, who also happened to have a very strong personal relationship with Carl LaGreca. I predicted that, in time, you would use her as mercilessly as you needed to."

"So killing Eriksson was never the primary objective, was it?"

"That, my dear Dr. Carter," Atherton responded, quizzically, I leave up to you to determine." He paused and smiled. "Eriksson certainly was a man who needed killing. But did it really matter, in the long run, as long as both objectives were accomplished, as I suspected they would be?"

"I think it would be fair to say that I was used by you," Carter interjected, with more than a hint of anger.

"Why get so upset?" Atherton asked. "For the right purpose, you are, whatever else you like to call it, a gun for hire. Aren't you?"

"I imagine so," Carter responded, quietly. "However, the term 'physician-warrior' would sound more noble."

"Mere pretense," Atherton answered dismissively, "that's all. Be you a baker, shoemaker, or physician, the outcome is all the same. The very core of what you do is assassinations. The rest is pretense and, worse yet, rationalization."

"I'm deeply indebted to you for that moral lesson," Carter said, ruefully.

"But now tell me, what did happen in that alley? I really was hoping that both you and Linda would be meeting me on this corner, today. My usual sources were not enlightening, so all I had to go on were the newspaper clippings of the march that talked about a new refugee to Sweden killing an American female tourist in an alley in an attempted robbery."

Carter was tempted to tell Atherton to go fuck himself, but thought better of it. "I guess you were too successful in your manipulations. Linda's loyalty did lay with the men who paid her salary, and was ready to kill me to provide them with the information you are holding in your hand." Carter paused for at least fifteen seconds, sadistically knowing that Atherton was hooked, and needed closure. "She was ready to shoot me in the back when Nils Olsson, who was lying on the ground, wounded by a Swedish Nationalist, picked up the Nationalist's gun from the ground and shot her."

Even Atherton showed surprise.

"I ran from the alley before the police arrived. Who said what to whom, after I left Stockholm, is your guess as well as mine. But I gather that Olsson will be fine and is thinking of running for parliament."

"So your mission was quite successful."

"That's true," Carter added, like a responsive schoolboy, "but . . ."

"But, nothing, Carter," Atherton interrupted. At this point, the less said the better. "Your assignment was successfully completed. Your final payment will be wired to your bank account in the Cayman Islands. The charities will be taken care of. That's all there is to the story! Do you understand me, Dr. Carter?"

Atherton became very serious. "There is to be no written or verbal record of the assignment or our transaction. In fact, as of this moment, 'we' do not exist. When 'we' do exist again, 'we' will contact you. And that's the way it has to be, Dr. Carter. Any further discussions about hidden motives, accidental findings, or national myths will be strictly taboo."

"And what will you do with those documents?" Carter asked, assuming that Atherton would not respond.

"I will hand this envelope over to the Justice Department and trust they will find some prosecutable offenses," Atherton smiled. "I suspect that some of this information will find its way into the hands of financially motivated lawyers who will seek damages and reparations from our sterling automobile companies for collaborating with our enemy, possibly extending the war, itself, and causing the death of many of our country's finest. I think they call it a 'class action suit'." Atherton realized that he had surprised Carter by actually informing him of the consequences of his assignment. But he was excited about his game plan for the documents, and proud of Carter. Carter needed to know that.

"Thank you," Carter said, grateful for the compliment of an explanation.

"Well," Atherton said, looking at his watch, "our time is up. I assume you must be heading back to State to make certain that our FSO's don't weasel out of their overseas assignments by claiming some esoteric medical disability."

"Good-bye, General," Carter said, shaking his hand. "Thank you for the opportunity."

"Don't thank me," Atherton replied, smiling. "Only the insane and the romantic would ever undertake the assignments you do." He tucked the manila envelope under his arm and disappeared around the corner.

Carter stood for a minute more, watching the visitors enter and exit the Holocaust Museum. How many wars and how many people had died since the last Great War—World War II? In Latin America there was Guatemala, 1960–1996: 200,000; Colombia, 1960's–1999: 35,000. In Asia there was Afghanistan, 1979–1992: 2 million; Sri Lanka, 1983–1999: 57,000. In the Middle East there was Algeria, 1991–1995: 250,000; Iraq, 1991: 45,000; Turkey, 1984–1999: 37,000. In Africa there was Sudan, 1983–1999: 1.5 million; Rwanda, 1994–1999: 800,000; Angola, 1975–1999: 500,000; Burundi,

1993–1999: 250,000; Liberia, 1989–1997: 150,000; Ethiopia/Eritrea, 1998–1999: 30,000; Sierra Leone, 1992–1999: 14,000; Congo, 1996–1998: 10,000. In Europe there was Bosnia, 1992–1995: 250,000; Kosovo, Yugoslavia, 1998–1999: 30,000; Chechnya, Russia, 1994–1996: 100,000; Northern Ireland: 1968–1998: 3,250.

As a physician, Carter could treat man's addiction to drugs, alcohol, gambling, sex, work, chocolate, and many other legal and illegal habits. But there was one addiction for which he could find no cure whatsoever—man's addiction to killing man.

About the Author

Alexander Court is a world-recognized "operational expert" who works on contract in a variety of overseas assignments. He has been a primary target for assassination by: Italy's notorious Red Brigade terrorist group for over twenty years; the former Soviet Unions' KGB; the Cubans' Directorate General of Intelligence; the Cambodians' terrifying Khmer Rouge; and the infamous General Noriega, who accused Court of "assassinating over two hundred people in Panama." Court's expertise includes the ability to destabilize governments and conduct psychological warfare, using a panoply of methods to neutralize adversaries, be they individuals, groups, or countries. He has no known place of residence other than the location of his next assignment. This is his first novel.

THE #1 *NEW YORK TIMES* BESTSELLER!

Tom Clancy's Op-Center

Created by Tom Clancy and Steve Pieczenik
written by Jeff Rovin

__TOM CLANCY'S OP-CENTER
0-425-14736-3/$7.99

__TOM CLANCY'S OP-CENTER:
MIRROR IMAGE
0-425-15014-3/$7.99

__TOM CLANCY'S OP-CENTER:
GAMES OF STATE
0-425-15187-5/$7.99

__TOM CLANCY'S OP-CENTER:
ACTS OF WAR
0-425-15601-X/$7.99

__TOM CLANCY'S OP-CENTER:
BALANCE OF POWER
0-425-16556-6/$7.99

__TOM CLANCY'S OP-CENTER:
STATE OF SIEGE
0-425-16822-0/$7.99

Prices slightly higher in Canada

Payable by Visa, MC or AMEX only ($10.00 min.), No cash, checks or COD. Shipping & handling: US/Can. $2.75 for one book, $1.00 for each add'l book; Int'l $5.00 for one book, $1.00 for each add'l. Call (800) 788-6262 or (201) 933-9292, fax (201) 896-8569 or mail your orders to:

Penguin Putnam Inc.
P.O. Box 12289, Dept. B
Newark, NJ 07101-5289
Please allow 4-6 weeks for delivery.
Foreign and Canadian delivery 6-8 weeks.

Bill my: ☐ Visa ☐ MasterCard ☐ Amex _____(expires)
Card#_____
Signature _____

Bill to:
Name _____
Address _____City_____
State/ZIP _____Daytime Phone #_____

Ship to:
Name _____Book Total $ _____
Address _____Applicable Sales Tax $ _____
City _____Postage & Handling $ _____
State/ZIP _____Total Amount Due $ _____

This offer subject to change without notice.   Ad # 559 (7/00)